PRINCE IVAN

PRINCE IVAN

Peter Morwood

First published 1990

2 4 6 8 10 9 7 5 3

Copyright © Peter Morwood 1990

Peter Morwood has asserted his
right under the Copyright, Designs, and Patents Act, 1988
to be identified as the author of this work

First published in Great Britain in 1990 by Century

This Legend Edition 1991
Random House, 20 Vauxhall Bridge Road, London SW1V 2SA

Random House Australia (Pty) Limited
20 Alfred Street, Milsons Point, Sydney,
New South Wales 2061, Australia

Random House New Zealand Limited
18 Poland Road, Glenfield
Auckland 10, New Zealand

Random House South Africa (Pty) Limited
PO Box 337, Bergvlei, South Africa

Random House UK Limited Reg. No. 954009

A CIP catalogue record for this book
is available from the British Library

ISBN 0 09 967820 9

Printed and bound in Great Britain by
Cox & Wyman Ltd, Reading, Berkshire

This one's for Mum!
and for Diane, as always (without comment on her comic-book version of this story.)

Acknowledgements

With thanks:

To the good people in the Slavonic Department at Colletts Bookshop, London.

To Diane Davis and her laser printer.

And finally, most especially to Tym Rondomanski, for his cheerful help in correcting all the dreadful things I tried to do to Russian!
Spasibo, Timofeychik, prevoskhodniyy perevodchik!

(NOTE: I have not attempted to reproduce the sounds of spoken Russian, but have represented the Cyrillic alphabet in Roman letters using one of the standard transliteration tables. Any mistakes in 'pronunciation' that have slipped through are therefore mine.)

Dramatis Personae

KHORLOVTSY – the people of Khorlov:

Aleksandr Andreyevich Khorlov – Tsar of Khorlov.

Ludmyla Ivanovna – the Tsaritsa, his wife.

Yekaterina Aleksandrovna – the Tsarevna, his eldest daughter. (Katya, Katyusha, Katyushka, Katyushechka)

Yelizaveta Aleksandrovna – the Tsarevna, his second daughter. (Liza, Lizok, Lizochka)

Yelena Aleksandrovna – the Tsarevna, his third daughter. (Lena, Lenyushka, Lenochka)

Ivan Aleksandrovich – the Tsarevich, his son and youngest child. (Vanya, Vanyushka, Vanyushechka)

Dmitriy Vasil'yevich Strel'tsin – High Steward and First Minister of the Tsars of Khorlov, also court wizard.

Captain Akimov – Captain of Guards of Khorlov.

Levon Popovich Volkhv – Patriarch and Metropolitan Archbishop of Khorlov.

VOLSHEBNIKI – the sorcerers:

Fenist Charodeyevich Sokolov, the Falcon, *Knyaz' vysokikh gor* – Prince of the High Mountains. (Fenik)

Vasiliy Charodeyevich Orlov, the Eagle, *Knyaz' shirokoy stepi* – Prince of the Wide Steppes. (Vasya)

Mikhail Charodeyevich Voronov, the Raven, *Knyaz' tyomnogo lesa* – Prince of the Dark Forests. (Mischa)

Mar'ya Koldunovna Morevna, *Krasivaya Tsarevna, prekrasneyshaya iz tsarits vseya Rusi* – the beautiful Tsarevna, fairest Princess in all the Russias.

Baba Yaga – Grandmother Hag, the witch with the iron teeth.

Koshchey *Bessmertnyy Chernoknizhnik* – the Undying necromancer.

CHAPTER ONE

Concerning Tsar Aleksandr and his children

The walled town of Khorlov was no city, and the mansion at the centre of it was no palace: but the citadel at the heart of the mansion was a kremlin just as much as the great palace – strongholds in the great cities of the greatest princes in the land. The best that could be said about it was that at least it looked as though it had been placed there to protect Khorlov, rather than to dominate and threaten it as so many of the larger fortresses seemed to do to the cities cowering around the hems of their grim stone garments.

That it looked reassuring instead of sinister did not mean that this particular kremlin was an unimpressive place. Its lofty outer wall was still high enough to repel all but the most determined foe, its Hall of Audience was known to be among the largest in all the Russias, and its gardens were among the fairest. While those gardens might not be known for size, certainly there was enough room within their carefully-trimmed hedges for ladies and gentlemen to take the air, to walk and talk.

And often enough, to argue.

*

'You've heard me say *no* so many times, Vanya. And sometimes you've prompted the *no* when what I truly might have said was *yes*. So tell me, who else is there to blame except the two of us?'

Tsarevna Yekaterina Aleksandrovna looked at her brother, but she was not expecting any sort of answer. As inheriting son and eldest daughter, after their father they held most responsibility in the Tsardom: the one to marry and bring the realm to a favourable alliance; the other simply to marry and, by fathering children, secure the succession. It was not an appealing prospect, especially for Yekaterina, the eldest of three sisters.

Tsarevich Ivan did much as she had expected and said nothing. He had already said enough, and every word had been a waste of breath. It had been one of those annoying conversations which go round and round without ever coming to an end, or even reaching an agreement just to differ. At one stage of the proceedings, there had been a very real risk that one or other of his own drinking-companions might be considered as possible members of the family. In making himself secure against that most unpleasant possibility, he had stepped a little too far and successfully soured his sisters' opinion of any young man who might put himself forward as a worthy would-be husband.

Yekaterina herself had expressed such opinions of most of them as to put marriage, or indeed their remaining long in Khorlov, out of the question. Ivan had long been guiltily aware that he had performed his self-appointed task too well, because now any attempts to alter or retract his views were seen as false – the result of outside pressure rather than a change of mind – and duly ignored.

What made matters worse was that it had become obvious that the feasts at which he and his three sisters were intended to find husbands and a wife would have to stop, or quite soon there would not be enough silver in the treasury to provide even one dowry for one husband. And yet, despite that, there was a feast going on in the Hall of Audience at this very minute.

Which was why Yekaterina Tsarevna had retreated out of doors.

Ivan looked around the gardens of the kremlin where he had walked and talked and argued with Katya for something close to an hour. Spring was gradually changing to an early summer, and the air was warm and pleasant, heavy with the sound of bees at work amongst the flowers. The ornamental trees were in full leaf and loud with bird-song. All of the warmth and greenness and beauty meant only one thing to

2

Tsarevich Ivan: that two seasons had slipped by since his father the Tsar had summoned him urgently from the frozen ramparts of the kremlin, and for all that urgency of five months ago not a thing of note had happened yet. Except, of course, for impending bankruptcy. . . .

A dry, distant crack of thunder cut through the *toska* gloominess of his thoughts and he looked up, beyond the walls of the garden. Bankruptcy was not the only thing impending, it seemed. There was a bank of dark clouds piling up in the east; the kind of clouds that were laden with rain and indiscriminate in their dropping of it. As he watched, a flicker of lightning ran along the edges of their contours, making them for an instant as sharp and clear as outlines cut from blackened copper. The tearing thunder-crash repeated itself a few seconds later, and just a little louder than before.

'Damn!' said Katya. 'Looks like there's a storm coming in.'

'I know,' agreed Ivan sombrely. 'But the storm I'm thinking about has nothing to do with the weather.'

'You shouldn't have been so convincing in your dismissals of our suitors, dear brother.' The tone of Yekaterina's voice was neither grim nor melancholy; instead she sounded waspish, impatient with her brother and his moods. Katya too was feeling guilty, knowing that as first-born child and senior among her sisters she should have done something more than simply follow a spiteful lead. It had made her spiteful in her turn. 'Although I notice that our Metropolitan Archbishop has yet to publish any banns of marriage in your name, either.'

'That was uncalled-for.'

'Was it? At least when you marry, you'll have taken some sort of step towards securing the succession – and brought a little money into the treasury besides.'

'If Levon Popovich wasn't such a stiff-necked old—'

'—Archbishop! Remember it.'

'He always does, so why should I? But "priest", I was going to say, and nothing worse.'

'Indeed?'

'Indeed.' Ivan held his breath, and with it whatever else he might have said that would have done only harm. Then he shook his head, annoyed with himself more than with Katya. 'Forget about it. All that's past.'

His sister gazed at him sidelong, without staring, and her own volatile temper swung at once from irritation to good-humoured sympathy. 'Past, but not done with entirely,' she said. 'Not when the thought of it still vexes you so.'

'Not vexes. Irritates. Annoys. I *am* the Tsar's son, after all.'

'Sometimes the trouble with old men is that they don't know when they've lived long enough,' said Katya.

'No. It's more that sometimes they forget what it was like to be young. Father never did. But then he had no objections to my learning how to read, either.'

Ivan had been five years old when the Metropolitan Levon made it known that he could not accept a Tsarevich who studied magic. It was widely considered that he would have banned anyone from practising even the smallest spells, had he not been assured that his congregation would dwindle to almost nothing. Everyone in Khorlov, from the Tsar down, had formed a solid, silent wall of disapproval. The Rus had used magic – the kind of small, useful, everyday spells which for instance allowed them to light a fire without rummaging for flint, steel, tinder and dry wood or, if they were skilled and strong enough, any wood at all – since before the Christians came to Kiev.

After momentary dismay, those same Christian bishops and abbots made sure that what they were seeing was not a manifestation of the Evil One by such a waving of crosses and incense as had never been seen before. The demand for holy water alone had been such that the Metropolitan Patriarch of Novgorod had actually blessed a cross-section of the River Volkhov and sent his Archpriests wading out with buckets. After that first fine frenzy had died away, cooler heads prevailed; particularly amongst the Archpriests of Novgorod, who found that river-wading in November cooled almost anything. The following Easter, under carefully controlled conditions – surrounded with ikons, thoroughly doused in holy water and censed until he sneezed – the Archbishop personally lit a sacred candle with fire summoned by magic. After such a feat, he allowed that there was indeed nothing

4

reprehensible about sorcery, especially since the effort of channelling a spell through his relatively untutored mind had brought him out in a sweat equivalent to that of honest toil, but without the skinned knuckles that a tinderbox would leave behind.

The Archbishop of Khorlov was another matter. Like every other child of noble birth across the Tsardom, Ivan had learned his magic and his letters, but only at the cost of frowning disapproval from Metropolitan Levon. It had been an unsettling few years for a small boy, until he grew tall enough and bold enough not to care . . . . or to appear not to care. And then, a little after his sixteenth birthday, he learnt what was wrong. In the same way that some people were unable to read because their eyes saw only nonsense instead of words, Metropolitan Levon Popovich was unable to learn spells. He could read the words, or have them read aloud to him, he could – and had – even have them sung in six-part harmony by the cathedral choir. But the connection, the spark that lit the fire, the string that made the bow more than just a piece of wood, never took place. It was as simple as that, and a simplicity that Ivan could understand. This was not the first time he had encountered jealousy. . . .

'If I hadn't been so worried about what the Archbishop would tell God,' said Ivan wistfully, 'I might actually have learnt something.' He grinned briefly, and let the subject go as a vivid glare of lightning painted his shadow across the grass. This time there was nothing coy or distant about the thunder; it was a long, rolling bellow of sound that seemed to come from almost above their heads, the echoes and the remnants of it rumbling and muttering away off towards the western horizon.

Prince Ivan leaned back and gazed straight up at a summer sky which had been blue but was now swiftly turning to the colour of lead. 'That sounded like some sort of comment,' he said as the first heavy drops of rain spattered his crimson tunic with purple spots and silvered the fur of its collar.

'I know you don't much like the feast, Vanya,' said Katya in the tone of voice which suggested that whatever comment he might make, her mind was already made up. 'So you can stay out here if you like. I, however, am going to find some shelter.' She reached out and tugged with finger and thumb at the fabric covering his right shoulder; it was already damp. 'And you would come too, if you knew how long it takes brocaded velvet to dry out – or what a wolf-pelt trimming smells like when it's wet.'

Ivan laughed. 'I do know, on both counts. Let's go. But there's no need to get any wetter.' He muttered under his breath, then raised one hand in the air above their heads, making a little grunt of effort as though he were lifting something much larger than his empty hand. The rain didn't stop – that would have been too much of a strain, and would have knocked him flat on his back had he attempted it – but at least the falling drops now bounced away from Ivan's outstretched fingers as though he carried a large circular table made of the clearest glass. With the other hand, he took Katya's arm and helped her scurry through the grass as quickly as dignity and long skirts would allow. 'We can continue this argument in comfort, if you like.'

Katya shook her head and pearls of water flew from the pearls of her lofty headdress; it was too tall, and Ivan too short, for his charm to cover it over. 'I don't like. We've already said everything that we can say twice ten times over, and I'm sick of the sound of the words.'

'All right.' Ivan put his hand to the door and opened it, then ushered Katya back inside the palace before cancelling the spell and leaping through himself to avoid the splash of suddenly-released raindrops. 'One day,' he muttered, 'there'll be a means of doing that which won't leave puddles on the floor.' He shook water out of his sleeve and glanced at his sister. 'Answer me one question, just for the sake of curiosity.'

'Ask – though you won't get the answer if I don't like the question.'

'Forthcoming as ever, Katyushka. Just tell me this: what sort of a man *would* you marry?' Just as he finished speaking, the clouds opened and released what seemed almost a solid wall of water onto Khorlov. Katya stared out of the open door, listening to the hiss of rain and the gurgling of more water in

6

the gutters than they could cope with, and watching the rebounding dance of drops against the ground. Lightning flashed until the world was all white light and black shadows, and thunder rolled until the ground trembled and the palace of the kremlin vibrated like a drum.

'What sort of a man?' she echoed him, in a soft and dreamy voice so that she seemed to be speaking to herself, yet so clearly that Ivan could hear her words above the sound of the storm and even above the sound of the thunder. 'Vanya, my brother, if I was sure that I could love him with my heart as my mother loves my father, I would marry the first man who asked for my hand.' As she said it the lightning flashed again, from the garden and through the open door at Katya's back so that she was outlined in the jewels of rain and a great flaring of white fire, and Ivan blinked to drive the dazzle from his eyes. Hard on its heels, the thunder roared.

And the kremlin roof and ceiling split asunder.

Ivan threw himself forward to protect his sister from the falling debris – but there was none. The stones and timbers had not been destroyed; instead, they had parted like a door, or like a curtain, or like the opening of a tent, and through that opening, with the lightning flaming at its back, came a bright falcon. Its stoop struck it against the floor of the kremlin palace, hard enough to shatter the tiles on which it smote, hard enough to shatter bones and tiles together. But instead of broken tiles and a broken, dying bird, there was another flash of light, less bright than the lightning but more blue, a brilliant sapphire blue, as blue as the sunlit sky above from which all the storm-clouds had now fled.

The light coiled about the falcon, wreathing it in tongues of flame until the eyes of those who watched saw a bird whose wings and plumage were all made of that blue fire. A second time it struck against the ground, and then a third – and at the third, the fire and the falcon faded clean away and became a fine young man. He was dressed all in blue and grey, embroidered with silver, and where another man would trim his coat with fur, his was trimmed with a falcon's blue-grey feathers.

He stood quietly, his bright, sharp, blue gaze fixed on

7

Yekaterina Tsarevna as though there were no one else in the palace, and he continued to stand and gaze so while the room filled with guards who had come at the double when they heard the commotion. For their part, Ivan and Katya stared at him, unwilling to trust the evidence of their own eyes – except that the young man was there, and the great rent in the ceiling was there, with the sky plain to see beyond it, and as a consequence they had little choice in the matter except to believe exactly what they saw.

Ivan stood in front of his sister, to defend her if it became necessary, even though the only weapon he carried was the small knife that lived hilt-downwards at the back of his belt. He had drawn it in the instant of the falcon's transformation. Now it was poised at the length of his arm and the level of his shoulder as though it were a long sword; but Ivan was grateful that it was no such thing, for only the shortness of the blade concealed just how much his hands were trembling. 'You!' he snapped at the nearest guardsman. 'Go summon our father the Tsar – and *run!*'

Only a few minutes passed before the room beyond the garden had filled with every worthy or notable personage who had been anywhere within the kremlin palace. Tsar Aleksandr and Ludmyla Tsaritsa, summoned by a breathless soldier all but steaming inside his heavy harness, had hurried down from the small tower where they took refuge from such cares of the world as watching yet another swarm of would-be suitors devour the contents of the treasury. High Steward Dmitriy Vasil'yevich Strel'tsin had been summoned either by the uproar, or the storm, or by some orderly Court Sorcerer's premonition, for he came in from the library at a run – which sight was almost as astonishing as the strange young man's appearance through the roof; and Guard-Captain Akimov, though unsummoned by anything at all, had arrived just as quickly as the rest and yet still found time to put on a helmet and coat of mail to supplement the heavy sword he wore in all his waking hours. It left very little room for the suitors – at least, those of them who set curiosity above the finest table in Khorlov – but as many as could fit had squeezed their way through the doors and now filled every scrap of space. All of them looked at the young man and then at the riven ceiling, with just one exception. High Steward Strel'tsin looked first at the roof and his soft oath – either of one sorceror recognizing another's handiwork, or of a High Steward reckoning up the cost of repairs – was clearly heard even above the babble of many voices.

It was Ivan who finally stepped forward. In token of peace, he lowered and sheathed his knife, then bowed, warily but with good grace and courtesy.

The stranger bowed in turn, lower than Ivan had done to give him that much more respect. The he smiled. 'Health to you, Tsarevich Ivan,' he said. 'Before, I came as a guest. Now I come as a suitor, and I would wed with your sister Yekaterina Tsarevna.'

Ivan gathered himself together at a good speed, considering the shocks of the past few minutes. 'As to that, sir, it is a matter between you and she, and then between you and my father the Tsar.' He looked more closely at the young man's face and frowned a little. 'And I confess your face is familiar, from some feast or other of the many this year. Although—' he glanced pointedly up at the hole in the kremlin roof and the blue sky beyond, '—your previous visit to Khorlov was somewhat less obvious than this one, or I would not have forgotten the day you arrived.'

'As for that, I was here. Now I am here again.'

'And who are you, for that matter?' Ivan's head shifted slightly sideways at the tone of Tsar Aleksandr's voice, and he felt the little hairs lift on the nape of his neck. From the sound of it his father had recovered from his surprise, and was torn between anger that yet again he should be put to expense over his daughter's would-be husbands, and curiosity about just what had happened to the roof of his palace. 'Your name, young sir,' he requested, all freezing dignity, 'and your rank.'

The young man smiled again, more broadly this time than before. His eyes were very bright and sharp indeed, missing nothing. It was certain he had observed what had roused the Tsar to be so brusque with his first words, for all that Aleksandr Andreyevich had not demanded whether he carried sufficient wealth to pay for repairs. Ivan had seen that much, from long acquaintance with his father's moods and ways of carrying himself.

'Majesty,' said the stranger, and bowed the lowest that he had yet done, 'I am Fenist Charodeyevich Sokolov, *Knyaz' vysokikh gor*, and my bride-price is already in your coffers. If she will have me, I wish to marry your daughter.'

'Send a servant to the treasury,' said the Tsar. 'You will forgive our rude haste, Fenist the Falcon, sorcerer's son and Prince of the High Mountains, but we are eager to learn if your silver exists. For surely your title does not. Dmitriy Vasil'yevich, have you heard of any such rank or style?'

'Without consulting my books . . .' the High Steward began, then fell silent as Tsar Aleksandr raised his hand.

'You've spent long enough with those books to just guess,' he said. 'So guess.'

'Then I would say no, Majesty. Otherwise it seems certain that this young gentleman,' he managed to make the words sound faintly insulting, 'would indeed have been here as a guest. Yet the Tsarevich has already said that he has no memory of having seen him in Khorlov before.'

'And what,' said the Tsar to Prince Fenist the Falcon, 'would you say about that?'

'I would say, Majesty, wait for the servant you sent to the treasury. And there's more to the world than you read in a book.'

'So and indeed. Then we wait.' Silence hung heavy as the seconds crawled by, for no one dared speak when the Tsar had so plainly not finished. But his wife, the Tsaritsa Ludmyla Ivanovna, touched her husband lightly on the arm and without saying a word, showed him that there was another matter to bear in mind.

It was the look in the eyes of his daughter as she gazed at Prince Fenist the Falcon. Tsar Aleksandr's breath caught in his chest, and a smile moved beneath his moustaches before he hid it behind his hand. He had seen such a look in a young woman's eyes before: in the eyes of her mother, when he first met her and knew that they had both fallen in love.

That same look was in the Tsaritsa's eyes now as she took his hand between hers. It had never left them, not since that

10

first time, but had only changed and softened and gentled during the passing of years. He smiled again and this time did not trouble to hide it, as he decided not to wait for any report on what was or was not in the treasury chests.

At that moment the servant returned, breathless and panting. 'Majesty,' he gasped, 'and my Lord Steward, I returned at once, without waiting for the Exchequer clerks to weigh or to count, so that I might tell you the treasury contains twenty poods that they say was not there this morning!'

'Prince Fenist,' said the Tsar, and inclined his head for a courtesy, 'twenty poods of silver is most generous. More generous, I fear, than any dowry I might have offered, had you not preferred the old ways. I am—'

'No, Majesty,' said the servant, interrupting despite a warning glare from High Steward Strel'tsin, 'I didn't say poods of silver. They were gold!'

Overhead, in perfect punctuation, the hole in the ceiling slammed shut like the lid of a box. For the first time in his life, Prince Ivan saw his father completely nonplussed. The Tsar opened his mouth like a fish, then closed it again without any sound coming out. Even Dmitriy Vasil'yevich Strel'tsin could find nothing to say appropriate to the circumstances, for though all of Khorlov was familiar with magic to one degree or another, such lavish squandering of power left each and every one of them staring in wonder as to the source of it.

Only Ivan had begun to suspect something of the sort, thanks in large part to the *skazki* tales which he had been told were a waste of his time. Thus only he was in sufficient command of himself to bow, very slightly – and then grin like a loon. He burst out in a peal of laughter that was not because of the much-needed gold in the treasury, but at the perfect timing of the joke. Fenist the Falcon laughed with him, until everyone present was wiping tears of delight from their cheeks.

Only Katya was not laughing aloud. Instead she was gazing at Fenist with a small smile on her lips, and all of her soul in her eyes.

*

The Metropolitan Archbishop Levon Popovich was summoned to perform the wedding ceremony, at once and without the publishing of banns – for as Prince Ivan was heard to observe, the town and the people of Khorlov had been awaiting such an event for quite long enough. The comment displeased the Archbishop – as Ivan had hoped it might – so that he said several things about the bridegroom's dubious arrival and still more dubious repair of the damage he had caused, things which were not quite in the best Christian traditions of forgiveness and tolerance.

They were things that provoked Tsar Aleksandr to say a few words of his own, with such force that Metropolitan Levon completed the marriage service and then took to his bed. Thus he missed the fine sight of Yekaterina Tsarevna and her new husband driving away, very fine and splendid in a smart carriage that was all blue and silver, drawn by grey horses. That was just as well, for the arrival of the carriage, its horses and its driver, was quite as dubious as the arrival of Prince Fenist the Falcon, and a great deal more obvious than the arrival of his gold. . . .

*

It had all begun almost half a year past, when the midwinter snow lay unsettlingly deep and broken-glass crisp and treacherously uneven round about the walls of Khorlov. This was a season of the year to be indoors, or at least under the eaves, for the wolves were howling hungrily in the distant birch-woods and Ivan Aleksandrovich, *Tsarevich Khorlovskiy*, was amusing himself by dropping snowballs from the ice-encrusted ramparts on to the helmet-spikes of the unfortunate sentries far below.

It had been political culture that morning; social history and the theory of government for three hours, with questions at the end. One Thousand and One Things Every Tsar's Son Should Know. Ivan had survived without actually yawning full in Dmitriy Vasil'yevich's face, even though – when he was Royal Tutor rather than High Steward or First Minister or Court Sorcerer – Strel'tsin taught politics in much the same way as a drip of water wears away a stone. Constant repetition and no variance in his theme was the standard approach to every subject, from Low Magic to the Reading and Writing of the Court Hand, and in almost fifty years he had seen little reason to vary it. Sooner or later his pupils made sure to remember what they had been told, if only in the hope that by getting it right they could make Strel'tsin move on to some other subject.

Ivan had also received what he had come to recognize as the standard homily on how it was incumbent on every Tsar's Son to Consider the Wellbeing of the Tsardom and how Marrying and Providing it with an Heir – Strel'tsin always contrived to get full value from his Capital Letters; there was Greek Byzantine blood in there somewhere among the piss and ice-water – was the best demonstration of faith that any Son and Ruler-to-Be could give to his Father and People. Hearing the same lecture for the third time in a week had been what had raised Ivan's suspicions that his free-and-easy life about the kremlin was about to end.

The arrival of a servant summoning him to the Hall of Audience confirmed them.

*

Khorlov's Hall of Audience had been built a hundred years before, and the principal intention of the Great Prince who had it built was that it should impress those who stepped inside. That meant size, and it meant grandeur, and in providing both, his architects and artists had surpassed themselves. It was large enough to contain two thousand people without making them feel cramped, and patterned mosaic-work on the floor where they would stand was bright with colour and the deeds of heroes. Their gaze was then led aloft by vaulted pillars inlaid with marble and semi-precious stones, towards a ceiling whose arches were intricately painted with scenes of hunting and war. But all of that stony echoing space led inevitably to the one commodity – if such it was – that Khorlov and all the Russias possessed in abundance. *Cold*. Only when the Hall was full of people did it seem truly warm, and even then its walls leaked a slow, soft, steady chill that not even the hottest summer could abate. In winter, it could cut like a knife.

It was cutting right now and Ivan made his bow from the doorway as quickly as he could, then moved with unseemly haste up the hall and closer to the great fires banked up on either side of his father's throne. Tsar Aleksandr was wearing his crown, the winter one with fur inside it, and a long crimson kaftan embroidered with gold and lined with lustrous sable. High Steward Strel'tsin was standing to one side, dressed all in grey as usual. They both looked uncomfortably formal.

'Son of mine,' said the Tsar in that tone of infinite patience possessed only by saints and the parents of several children. 'Soon you will be twenty years old, and soon I will be sixty-five. What steps are you taking to secure the succession?'

It was a direct question, unpadded even with a royal plural, and it took Ivan off his guard. He had been expecting a lengthy preamble such as those beloved of Strel'tsin, wordy enough that he could prepare his defence, or his excuse, or whatever the situation might require, long before his father had finished speaking. This caught him in much the same way as a rake left in the garden's long grass had once done, right between the eyes. 'I, uh,' said Prince Ivan, and stopped. Though what he had said wasn't much, it was more than enough.

'As I thought,' said the Tsar wearily. 'Nothing has changed. Vanya, I have no desire to arrange my children's marriages, not after promising them a freedom of choice. But if I must, then I will.' He sat back and glanced sidelong at the High Steward with a glitter of sardonic amusement in his blue eyes. Ivan saw that glitter, and saw too the shadow of a smile that hid within his father's silver beard as a fox hides in a thicket.

'Dmitriy Vasil'yevich assures me you have been advised that our own little kingdom lacks enough importance for any of the great Princes to need an alliance with us.' Ivan nodded. 'However, there have been recent developments which have caused something of a change in matters.'

'Prince Yuriy,' put in Ivan softly, before High Steward Strel'tsin could speak.

Tsar Aleksandr struck his hands together, applauding.

'Well done!' he said. 'And well done to you also, Dmitriy Vasil'yevich. You still teach facts well enough for at least some of them to stick in the memory of my dear son.'

Ivan grimaced slightly, but changed it to a smile in time. Yet another groove had been worn in the surface of his brain to produce that prompt answer. He had often wondered whether it would not be easier to find some small spell which would lock such education into his head, but the High Steward – as Court Wizard this time – had warned against it. Since magic itself was a part of memory, using it to memorize other matters would (he claimed) set up such cross-currents in the brain that one might have to sort through the contents of an entire library before remembering what day it was. Ivan had found vodka to have much the same effect, but didn't mention it. Strel'tsin was not known for his sense of humour.

'As you so rightly say, Ivan,' said Tsar Aleksandr, 'Prince Yuriy Vladimirovich of Kiev. And why would you say this name rather than, perhaps, Boris Mikhaylovich of Novgorod, or his brother Pavel?'

'Because these two Princes will not move against any foe, not even Manguyu Temir of the Sky-Blue Wolves, for fear that when one brother moves, whichever of the other who remains in Novgorod will lay sole claim to the sceptre and take all for himself.' Ivan paused, gathered his thoughts and smiled a thin smile that, though he remained unaware of it, was the most adult expression to cross his face since he entered the audience chamber. 'The encouragement of which belief, and all the others to augment it, currently costs us seven poods of silver every year. Whereas Prince Yuriy is responsible to none but himself. All three of them desire our land, but only Yuriy of Kiev will dare leave his own kremlin in an attempt to get it.'

It was uncomfortably true. Ivan, and the desired male child resulting from a marriage that he had not yet even considered, were the only things that would prevent Khorlov from being swallowed up by the ambitions of such princes as Yuriy, who was already taking an interest in the Tsardom; though with an eye less towards alliance by marrying one of three eligible daughters than simple annexation by main force. Even so high and mighty a ruler as Yuriy Vladimirovich was not so high and mighty that he would miss an opportunity to acquire yet more land for his own burgeoning domain, and if the acquisition required no financial outlay on his part so much the better.

Only a legitimate heir to the Tsardom of Khorlov would give Prince Yuriy pause for thought: Kiev was not yet so powerful that he could move with impunity against a realm where the succession had been assured, for such an action would be seen as what it was, a threat against the independence of all the other little kingdoms of the Rus. It would not be tolerated, it would be opposed – and the combined opposition would outnumber Prince Yuriy's armies ten to one.

'It seems,' said Ivan, 'that I must start looking for an appropriate bride.'

He smiled wryly at the prospect, for he had already gained something of a reputation amongst the ladies of the court. Having to restrict his attentions to only one of them was less than appealing – for once the more immediate delights of their company had been set aside, there was not a lady among the lot with whom he would care to spend the rest of his life. Which meant – and the thought when it ran through his head provoked a little smile – that he had no need to restrict his choice to the ladies of Khorlov at all. A deal of entertainment could probably be squeezed from the round of banquets and ceremonials that would of necessity precede his choice.

Except that such things were expensive, and unnecessary expense was the province of the First Minister rather than the High Steward. Fortunately, or otherwise in Ivan's view, there was no need to summon him.

'Majesty,' said Dmitriy Vasil'yevich Strel'tsin, bowing to the Tsar, 'it would be better on the grounds of economy if not only a wife for the noble Tsarevich were sought, but also husbands for the Tsarevnas. Catching, as it were, four birds with but a single strew of grain.'

Ivan stared at Strel'tsin and slowly raised one eyebrow. The man spoke sense and logic, of course – Khorlov was not rich, and paying for maintenance of confusion between the Novgorodskiy princes had not helped that situation – but he spoke it with a relish that Ivan didn't like. It was almost as if the High Steward had caught Ivan's smile and the thought that had prompted it, and was trying to be deliberately annoying.

'Your words are as always, First Minister,' he said, 'full of wisdom and the dry consideration of dry years. We thank you.'

Dmitriy Vasil'yevich knew a dismissal when he heard one. No Steward and minister who had served two Tsars and hoped one day to serve a third ever needed to be told twice when to leave the Presence. He leaned on his staff and bowed more deeply than ever – so that this time his long grey beard came close to sweeping like a besom across the floor – looked once and most thoughtfully at Prince Ivan through dark eyes that betrayed none of whatever thoughts swam deep within them, and took his leave in silence. The click of the door-latch sounded very loud indeed.

Tsar Aleksandr leaned forward and raised a disapproving eyebrow – then smiled a little as he realized he had seen Ivan do the same thing only minutes earlier. There were portraits in the palace of the kremlin that were almost fifty years old, portraits of when he too had been a young Tsarevich, Tsar Andrey's eldest son. They might have been a mirror, reflecting then the face which looked up now at Aleksandr Andreyevich: the same blue eyes, the same hair so flaxen-pale as to be almost white, which showed how strongly the blood of Rurik the Norseman still flowed in the veins of the Tsars of Khorlov.

'Like father, like son,' said Tsar Aleksandr to the mirror image of himself, and to Ivan's astonishment he grinned. 'I have a confession to make, Vanyushka.' The Tsar looked about the empty audience chamber like a conspirator, or like a father playing games with his children, then concealed his mouth behind one shielding hand. 'When I was your age, I didn't like Strel'tsin either. I used to think that he was born old. That he was always so wise, and so thin, and so grey. Do you know, Vanya, that I've never once seen him laugh?'

'Batyushka moy, he'd crack in two if he tried it.' With a shrug, Ivan dismissed the High Steward from his mind and instead went to the small table close by the steps to the throne, where he poured wine into a goblet of figured Persian crystal that was as heavy and cool as carven ice. It was red wine, the favoured drink of the Romans of old, and as far-travelled as the soldiers of that ancient empire: brought at great price from the warm Tuscan hills to be drunk here in Khorlov, a city built on the edge of forests of birch and pine so vast that they could swallow all the land of Italy and leave not a trace behind. Tsarevich Ivan looked into its darkness and thought, *It can travel, why not I? Before duty and politics nail me to this one piece of ground.*

'Father?'

'I said, are you going to give your poor thirsty old father some of that – or would you rather stare at it all day?'

Ivan felt the warmth of the mild reproof in his face and ears. His fair skin showed it like a beacon across his cheeks, as red as the wine, and he made so much haste in filling and delivering a second cup that he came close to spilling it.

Tsar Aleksandr accepted the goblet of wine, pointed the tip of his finger at a drip running down the outside and concentrated a moment so that it turned about and ran back into the cup, then glanced at his son. 'If you want to travel so much, Vanya,' he said, 'then why not do it?'

Ivan turned to look at him, wondering when his father had begun lessons in the reading of thoughts. He met the steady gaze of eyes as coldly blue as his own, and would not look away for all that it was an uncomfortable scrutiny, disturbingly close to the yes-no-maybe consideration of a lazy cat watching a mouse go by. Ivan wondered why, but in common with many others in such a situation was reluctant to ask in case he found out.

Aleksandr Andreyevich, Tsar of Khorlov, sat quite still and silent, and though his eyes had not left those of his son, neither they nor his mouth nor the expression of his face said anything of the thoughts that passed within. It was as if a shutter had been locked, and the lights within put out. That closing of his face was another necessary skill in political debate, for if one art was that of the reading of expression, then it followed that another would be the concealment of

18

such betraying looks. Tsar Aleksandr was a master of them both, and many more besides. It was said of him that in negotiation he could out-bluster a Kievan Rus, outwit a Khan of Krim Tatary and outstare a cat, and that only the last was false.

Ivan was no cat, and to be subjected to that cool gaze was not how he had planned to spend his day. He sipped casually at the wine in his goblet until there was no wine left and then, not wanting to be the first to move by rising to refill it, was reduced to fidgeting with the empty cup. And still his father gazed at him, and gave no hint of what went on within his mind.

'Put down the cup before you break it.' It was not what Ivan had expected to hear, but he did as he was bidden and afterwards sat as still as he was able. 'When you were a child,' Tsar Aleksandr continued in that same soft voice, 'you loved *skazki* tales and the *byliny* epics of the old heroes.'

'I wanted to be a *bogatyr*',' said Ivan. 'I wanted to ride my horse across the white world, and find adventures, and be brave, and be known so.'

'But instead you find yourself the son of a small Tsar, being trained in the dull duties of ruling a small Tsardom.' If there was irony or bitterness in Aleksandr's voice he hid it well. 'You *will* travel, Ivan. And for all your eagerness, that travel will be farther and harder than you would wish. Perhaps the dull duties might be better after all.' He shook his head, and something seemed to vanish from around it like mist in the morning. 'There were other things, but they were clouded, so that I could not see them. Perhaps it's just as well.'

Ivan said nothing until he had refilled and emptied his goblet, not once but twice. Whether the Tsar was speculating, or whether he had truly seen something of the future, was not something that Prince Ivan wanted to know. Though not so impressive as some forms of magic, he had always found True Sight to be among the most eerie. It could be little comfort to any man to know the time and manner of his own death.

Tsar Aleksandr tasted his wine. 'You've had your youth and your freedom, Vanya. If you want to see the world, then best you do it soon. That's why I called you here, because at last I agreed with Dmitriy Vasil'yevich that the matter of your marriage was something other than a subject for discussion next week, or next month, or next year. Now it's the time for your life's duties to begin. Not the worst, and not the least; only the first, and perhaps the best.'

'That sounds like one of Strel'tsin's little homilies,' said Ivan.

'Probably it is, now,' agreed his father absently. 'But the words are older even than the High Steward. Much older. They're true enough for all that.' Aleksandr took another, longer draught of wine and then set the goblet aside. 'I love my daughters, but I would as soon Khorlov went to my son and to his sons after him.'

For the first and only time, Ivan heard weariness in his father's voice. There had been a time when there were only daughters, and the end of his name and his line had seemed a very real possibility. Aleksandr and Ludmyla had been married more than five years before having a child which survived infancy. The first to do so had been Yekaterina, and it was Ivan's unkind view that Death had been too wary to go anywhere near her.

With Yelizaveta and Yelena following after, it must have seemed to Tsar Aleksandr that he would never have a son to carry on his name, and Khorlov would be inherited by whichever husband finally succeeded in winning the hand of Yekaterina Tsarevna. The Tsar did not envy the young princes of surrounding realms their task in the years to come, for even at three years old, Katya was already displaying the beginnings of such qualities of bravery, strong will and intelligence as any Tsar would have been glad to see. . . .

At least, in a son. . . . In a daughter, never mind in *three* daughters – for as time passed Liza and Lena soon showed that they were indeed Katya's sisters in more than just parentage – theirs were qualities which made suitors choose to fight the Tatars on the steppes of Central Asia rather than risk incurring the wrath of such an intended bride.

To hear it told about the kremlin palace, Prince Ivan's birth had been greeted not so much with a fanfare of trumpets as by a general sigh of relief. . . .

Now the Tsar leaned against the high back of his throne and drummed his fingers on the carved eagle-heads that capped its arms. 'You may speak.'

'There is little for me to say, *batyushka*.'

'Quite so. If you're as wise as I believe, my son, you'll not look for trouble. With the Princes of Kiev and Novgorod, and the Tatars, and the Teutonic Knights with their fine black crosses, life is hard enough.'

'Especially now that I have to find myself a wife.'

Tsar Aleksandr clapped his hands and laughed with ironic amusement. 'No, Tsarevich Ivan,' he said, smiling thinly behind his beard. 'Finding is easy. You have to *keep* her!'

CHAPTER TWO

Concerning a choice of husbands, and what the Tsarevnas thought of them

Days followed days, and hours followed hours, until at last the summer was gone and the leaves fell from the trees, rustling to and fro in drifts of red and gold all across the gardens of the kremlin.

The Tsarevnas Yelizaveta and Yelena had walked there on each and every day since the marriage of their sister, at first in hopes of yet another princely suitor making his appearance as Fenist the Falcon had done. As time slipped by, never slowing, never stopping, until it was gone beyond recall, they realized at last that all of the lost time was time that they had wasted, time which might have been better spent in a search for a more ordinary husband, a Lord's son or a *boyar*'s, rather than the son of a sorcerer. At least by doing so Archbishop Levon would speak kindly to them again, instead of making the sign of the cross at them whenever they chanced to meet.

The good Archbishop had – at last – ceased to object to good Christian magic, by which he meant those small and simple sorceries which had as much cost in physical and mental effort as any honest toil. However, he had formed his own opinions as to the source of Fenist the Falcon's seemingly limitless power, and that source was not one of which he or Holy Mother Church could approve.

As the sun slipped down the sky the air grew chilly, until at last Yelena went indoors. Yelizaveta walked alone for a while, kicking at the fallen leaves, then looked up quickly at the sound of other footsteps. Her face fell almost at once.

'You know how to make someone feel welcome,' said Prince Ivan. He fell into step beside her, taking turns to jab his red-heeled boots into the heaps of windblown leaves, so that they slithered across each other with a sound like parchment, and they walked so in a companionable silence for several minutes. Then he said, 'It was cool when I came out. Now it's downright cold. Look, I can see my breath. Come inside, Lizochka, and have something warm to drink.'

Ivan had never taken the trouble to speak to a stone wall and now he had no need, for he had formed a reasonable idea of what the conversation would be like. He breathed out again, this time not for any kind of demonstration but to make a small noise that was in part a grunt of irritation but mostly a sympathetic sigh. It sounded like some sort of sneeze.

'Liza, look up. The sky's clear. No storm-clouds. No clouds at all, right to the horizon. Not a potential prince in sight anywhere. Just a star or two, and it's going to get too cold even to watch them once the sun sets.'

'I wish,' said Yelizaveta, then hesitated and changed what she had been about to say, 'that you'd go away and let me walk in peace.'

'I said that I'd bring you indoors, and I will.'

'Wouldn't you like to walk a little closer to that ornamental pond?' There was only the faintest suggestion of a twinkle in the way she glanced at him – a poor, watered-down version of the mischievous glint that normally would have accompanied such a threat. It was as if she had been sick and, though recovering, was still far from well.

The glance unfocused and looked past Ivan in a way that made him wonder if there was an insect on his ear; but then Liza spoke.

'I thought you told me that there were no clouds in the sky. . . ?' Her voice was so strangely changed that Ivan asked no questions but swung right around, very fast, as if he was still at the fencing class which he had left barely half an hour before. Liza didn't need to tell him anything else, because he could see quite well enough for himself.

It was as if a ragged patch of sunset had managed to detach itself from the golden glow on the western horizon, but it came flitting across the sky more like a bat at dusk than any kind of cloud which Ivan had seen before. Its colours

23

darkened as it left the light behind, shifting from gold to copper, and at last to the dark shades of bronze.

And it was then that they heard the first faint growl of thunder. 'It looks, sister of mine, as though you've got whatever wish you *didn't* speak aloud.'

Lisa smiled a tight, uncertain smile. 'That's what the old tales say that you should do.' Lightning flickered in the twilight, sending a hot rose-gold light running through the approaching cloud, and the thunder sound that followed in its wake had risen from a growling to a snarl. Yelizaveta looked still more uncertain, and her smile wavered out of true for two whole seconds before straightening up again. As accurately as if he had heard her thoughts, that told Ivan what other wise old saying she had remembered from the stories: 'Be careful what you ask for – you may get it'.

He wondered just exactly what it was she *had* asked for, and what they would do if it was other than expected. Then he realized with a sudden, nasty shiver of apprehension that he hadn't an answer to either question, but plenty of uncomfortable possibilities for both. Since the arrival and departure of Prince Fenist the Falcon had torn down the established barriers of his world, Ivan had taken time to look again at all the old stories he thought that he knew so well – and had been reminded, to his unease, that there were more things living in the new and wider world beyond those barriers than merely young men who could change their shape. . . .

At least – and the realization came to him in a comforting rush like the warmth of a fire on a winter's day – he was rather better armed than he had been the last time something untoward began to happen. Having walked to the garden more or less directly from receiving tuition in swordplay from Captain Akimov, Ivan still had a sword at his hip. It was a *shashka*, a light, curved sabre of the sort that Akimov's people preferred, and though it had none of the heft of a broad, straight Rus *shpaga*, the weapon was still a reassuring weight in his hand.

Yelizaveta started a little as the edge of the blade made a long, harsh scraping sound as it slid from its scabbard. It suggested to her, more than any words could have done, that there might be more to this mysterious cloud and more to mysterious strangers than had seemed at first likely. Certainly there was more to her little brother, who seemed suddenly much older and more serious with a drawn sword in his hand. *Almost dangerous* was her thought until he turned to face her, and for the first time she saw a glint in his eyes which was more than a mere reflection from the sunset and the steel. There was no *almost* about it.

'Go inside,' he said, and it sounded as if the words had been clipped short by the sword-blade. Ivan spoke in a voice of command, a voice which would not disgrace the Tsar that he would some day become. Liza did not hesitate; she went inside at once and then summoned the guards.

Ivan looked at the sweep of the *shashka*'s razor-sharp edge, and then at the swiftly-approaching cloud. He shook his head, more nervous than he would ever have admitted to Lizochka. Having seen what the powers of the Falcon Prince had done to stone and timber, steel was unlikely to be much protection against something malevolent. Ivan swallowed, and crossed himself three times in case that would do some good. He could hear the clatter of Captain Akimov's soldiers as they marched from the kremlin and drew up in battle array, but he didn't turn. He didn't want to take his eyes off the cloud, not for the duration of a single heartbeat – even though, at the rate his own heart was beating, that interval would have been brief indeed.

There was another flash of lightning at the heart of the cloud, not blue-white like the other natural and unnatural lightnings which Ivan had seen, but a golden light, strangely ruddy, like that of heated copper. As if borne on the wings of the thunder that rumbled across the garden, a wind began to rise. At first it merely sifted among the drifts of leaves, disturbing them no more than Ivan and Liza had done when kicking with their boots. Then suddenly, and without any warning, it rose to a whistling gale which flung the piled leaves high so that the air was filled with bronze and russet fragments lit by the glare of that strange lightning. Tsarevich Ivan put both hands to his sabre's hilt, braced his feet against the storm and waited for the worst.

A ragged spear of lightning thrust out of the very heart of the dark cloud and rode the thunder through the splitting air right over Ivan's head before stabbing in a great splash of blinding golden sparks against the kremlin roof. Vivid light spilled out through the open doorway where the guardsmen stood, flinging their shadows straight and stark across the windblown garden until it seemed as though there had been silhouettes of armed men painted black upon the farther wall. It was nothing that a sword could have protected him against – so it was just as well that neither he nor Liza needed that protection. Ivan grinned with pure relief as he slammed the sabre back into its scabbard, and by then he was already running for the kremlin's garden door.

There was a hole in the roof and in the ceiling, but no debris across the floor except the leaves blown inside by the wind. In the midst of it all was a roiling column of fire, a rich bronze-coloured fire that gave no heat and did no harm: and in the midst of the fire, its wings spread wide, there was an eagle with feathers as bright as gold, as red as copper.

As Ivan watched, the eagle struck itself against the floor, and instinctively he knew that was the second time. Again it struck, and the fire surrounding it swirled once and went away. With the fire went the eagle, for it became a fine young man dressed all in red and russet. His coat was brocaded with pure gold, and instead of fur its trimming was all of bronze-gold eagle's feathers.

The young man, broad-shouldered and strong, looked at Yelizaveta Tsarevna with his light brown eyes, and they smiled at one another like lovers who have long been parted. Standing in the doorway with the guardsmen crowding at his back, Ivan uttered a single swift order: that his father and the dignitaries of the court should be brought here without delay. Then he cleared his throat with the small, significant cough of someone who would rather not be ignored for a moment longer. The Eagle Prince – for though he had not yet spoken, it was certain he would call himself by such a title – nodded slightly to Liza, the nod of one who breaks a conversation which will surely be resumed as soon as possible, and bowed deeply to Ivan.

'Wealth to you, Tsarevich Ivan,' he said. 'When I was in Khorlov before, I came as but a guest. Now I return as a suitor, and I would ask that you give me the hand of your sister, Yelizaveta Tsarevna.'

Ivan bowed in his turn and when he straightened he was smiling. 'Sir,' he said, 'a wise man does not give commands to his sisters. First, you must speak to the Tsar my father, and ask his permission to wed.'

'And you may do so on the instant,' said Tsar Aleksandr from the doorway of the palace behind them, his voice filled with the satisfaction of one who, by his own effort, has arrived right on cue. He was flanked by two guards and they were all three out of breath, though that did not detract in the slightest from his dignity as he stared at this latest uninvited guest within his walls. 'But before that, you should tell us your name.'

Still smiling, the young man bowed again, more deeply than before. 'Tsar's Majesty,' he said, 'I am Vasiliy Charodeyevich Orlov, *Knyaz' shirokoy stepi*, and I have come here to marry your daughter.'

'Then, Prince of the Wide Steppes, sorcerer's son, you must know of the promise we gave to our children. Bear this in mind when I tell you I will not give permission to wed, but only permission to woo. I say only this: if Lizochka will have you, she may.'

There were no words spoken between them, for there were no words required. Yelizaveta stretched out her hand to the Prince and he took it, and put a ring on it from his own finger. 'Tsar's Majesty,' he said, 'the bride-price is in your treasury already, and I trust you will find it sufficient.'

Only a few seconds passed before a servant came running in. He was the same servant as they had seen on a similar errand when Fenist the Falcon came courting – just as breathless, just as startled and just as delighted as before. 'Majesty,' he said, dropping down on one knee, 'another new and additional quantity of gold has just this moment been discovered in the Tsardom's coffers! It is estimated by the clerks to be a weight of twenty poods in bullion ingots!' And as he spoke, the ceiling above closed quickly and quietly until it was as complete as ever.

'Will it suffice?' asked Prince Vasiliy the Eagle.

Ivan Tsarevich hastily covered his mouth with his hand, and coughed sharply to explain it. A grin of the kind which had just spread all over his face might well have been understandable, but that would not have made it any the more seemly. Though *Knyaz'* Vasiliy Orlov had spoken in the most innocent tones of enquiry, there had been an amused glint in his tawny eagle's eyes that Ivan had caught straight away. Besides which, he'd used that same tone of voice himself in the past and would doubtless do so in the future.

Tsar Aleksandr took only a second to answer, and in that second prevented the stammer which had tried to slip into his words. 'Oh, most surely it will,' he said; then he looked sharply at the Eagle Prince and laughed at the humour he saw there. 'As your brother Prince Fenist has told you. . . .'

*

Metropolitan Levon was asked to officiate at this marriage as he had at the first. He listened and was not equally displeased, but much more so, saying aloud that from what he could see of their suitors the Tsarevnas had no need of a Christian priest and a Christian ceremony in a Christian church. For some hours before the service he went about muttering in his beard about pagan recidivists and sorcerous gold, but at last was persuaded to put on his archbishop's crown and his vestments, and come into Khorlov's cathedral.

There, as had happened before with Prince Fenist the Falcon, he was comforted to see that Prince Vasiliy the Eagle did not flinch away from the holy words and the holy water, or from being signed three times with the life-giving cross. Indeed, it seemed to the Archbishop that this Prince, and any other who might come along – since he knew as well as anyone else that such sorcerous happenings normally took place in threes – might not be so bad a match after all. This time he did not take to his bed, but watched with the rest of the people as Yelizaveta Tsarevna drove off with her husband, looking splendid and fine in a handsome coach which was all red and gold, drawn by strong chestnut horses. It said much for his new peace of mind that he showed no curiosity as to how that coach came to be outside the cathedral after the wedding, when there had been no such coach anywhere in the city before it; though some said it was simply a sign of his wisdom when he knew not to ask any questions.

Prince Ivan watched them go, and at the same time watched Dmitriy Vasil'yevich Strel'tsin. The beginnings of a small, amused suspicion were taking shape in his mind, and he determined that once he was convinced he would have a long talk with the Court Wizard. Provided, of course, that he could catch him as such rather than as the High Steward or the First Minister, neither of which incarnations held the slightest interest. . . .

*

Before any choice could be made by Tsarevich or Tsarevnas, a decision had first to be taken as to those members of the nobility and gentry from whom they might choose. The decision did not take one day, and it did not take two, but when ten days had gone by there were at last names to be seen and selected. And that was when the problems began.

Tsar Aleksandr had known that the search for three husbands and a wife for his children was not going to be an easy task; but not even his High Steward had foreseen just how difficult it would be. Somewhere in the back of the Tsar's mind had been an optimistic half-formed notion that everything would resolve itself once banquet invitations had filled the palace with suitably eligible young men and women.

However that had been before Dmitriy Vasil'yevich Strel'tsin consulted his books, then put pen to paper and drew up a list which defined just exactly what 'eligible' could be assumed to mean in terms of alliance, allegiance, ancestry, precedence, protocol and rank. It was not an encouraging list, and much shorter than anyone had expected, since for this reason or for that it had omitted most of the young people whom the Tsar had seen in company with his son and daughters.

Ivan, when first he saw it, poured himself a cup of spiced-honey *sbiten'* and sipped at it in silence, saying nothing at all. It occurred to him that Dmitriy Vasil'yevich might have done himself more good by wearing his Court Wizard's hat. That way, at least he might have shown a little imagination.

His eldest sister the Tsarevna Yekaterina felt herself bound by no such constraint. 'Dmitriy Vasil'yevich,' she said coldly, 'I have always been under the impression that the words of my father's promise contained no unvoiced restrictions as to the birth and lineage of prospective husbands.'

She picked up the sheets of fine parchment and leafed through them, counting off the names and accomplishments of worthy *boyaryy* and their doubtless equally worthy sons. 'Twenty names, and no more than twenty, is not what I had in mind.' Her voice was, and remained, as deceptively gentle as the thin-lipped smile that she bestowed on him, inviting a reply.

Ivan heard and saw both of the warning signals. *Better if she had shouted*, he thought, and picked up his cup prior to what Captain Akimov would have called a strategic withdrawal from an untenable position. Instead, he found himself pierced by Yekaterina's glittering blue stare as though by a pin.

'Where do you think you're going?' she asked icily, not bothering to say more. The three Tsarevnas had spent a lifetime keeping their brother in what they considered to be his proper place – Ivan, being the youngest child, had never been consulted as to what that proper place might be – and by now a single short sentence was more than sufficient.

'I was just making myself more comfortable, Katyushka.' Ivan's bland smile fooled nobody – himself included, since the heated stoneware of the cup was starting to burn his fingers – and his sister least of all. Looking and feeling as if he was taking shelter behind a kremlin rampart, he managed to sit lower in his chair than was really possible. His cup he kept below the level of the table, well clear of the paperwork. Ivan knew what sort of storm was gathering.

The High Steward, however, did not. His rank and position had been so much concerned with matters of state that he had never really troubled to acquaint himself with the Tsar's three daughters, any more than to realize that some day they would have to be married off as advantageously as possible. More, he neither knew nor probably cared . . . . which was unfortunate.

Defending himself with reasoned and long-winded argument was still more unfortunate, for Yekaterina was in no mood for reason. She wanted apologies – grovelling and abject for preference, or at the very least excuses with a spark of originality about them – and Strel'tsin's words had more the effect of sparks near a Chinese firework. Katya's fuse took a time in burning, but her ultimate detonation was well worth the wait.

'Court Sorcerer, High Steward and First Minister of the Tsars of Khorlov,' she said, her voice laced with the deceptive acid sweetness of unripe fruit, and studied Strel'tsin as if not entirely sure he was worthy of a single one of his several positions, styles and titles.

Ivan could have described that look more accurately. Her expression suggested that she had just met a louse with a hat on, and it had made an improper suggestion. He managed to work his way a little lower into the wooden embrace of the chair, and wished that Strel'tsin had enough sense to do the same. The only time that she had ever called *him* by his full title – 'Tsar's son and Prince of Khorlov' – he had finished up in the lake, and it had taken hours to get the frogspawn, the weeds and at least two small dead fish out of his hair.

Also, it had been damnably cold.

They had been children then, and flinging people into lakes had been the extent of her fury. Now that she was a Princess of twenty-two years, and therefore a grown woman of marriageable age, her displays of irritation had also grown until they had achieved the status of near-legend.

'It were as well for you to remember, Dmitriy Vasil'yevich, the we are the eldest daughter of your master and liege Lord. We are not to be addressed as common folk, nor are we to be patronized. . . .' She drew a long breath, and Ivan held his.

'And we will not be spoken to as though we were an assembly of thick-minded *muzhikiy*! You may speak to your own peasants as you desire, master High Steward, but you will not use that same tone to me! To us! Any of us! And as for

31

this heap of useless scribblings' – Yekaterina seized the pile of documents in both hands and shook them as though they had a neck and it was between her fingers – 'you can take them *away*!'

Strel'tsin's carefully prepared list spun across the table in a flat, solid blade of parchment that looked capable of taking his head off his shoulders. An instant before it hit – and whether Strel'tsin or Katya was responsible, Ivan couldn't tell – it exploded into separate sheets which flared up with a sweet scent and a coruscation of dazzling multicoloured lights. The ashes, smelling like scorched roses, swirled about his shoulders, rustling softly as they fluttered to the ground with a sound like autumn.

Yekaterina turned her back on him and stalked from the room, leaving the High Steward looking distinctly foolish. 'One must be more careful of passionate young women,' he remarked, speaking to himself as he sometimes did, without seeming to move his mouth. The words appeared, and were audible, but their source was never certain. Perhaps that was Strel'tsin's intention, or perhaps there was no hidden motive at all – just a long grey beard, and drooping grey moustaches.

Ivan grinned crookedly and straightened his shoulders as Strel'tsin came around the table and sat down facing him. For want of anything better to do, he took a long swallow of the fast-cooling *sbiten'* remaining in his cup. He found himself wishing that it had been wine, or *kvas*, or vodka, or had at least some trace of alcohol hiding in it. He had a feeling that he would need something, and certainly more than lukewarm spiced honey, to bolster up his small reserve of courage against whatever the High Steward might want to say. Strel'tsin had that businesslike look which Ivan had come to know and avoid.

'Scarcely passionate,' Ivan said, then paused, choosing his words carefully. One never knew in what form they would be reported back to any number of ears which would be better off not hearing them at all. 'Indignant, certainly. Annoyed. Outraged. Even when we were much younger, one or other of my beloved sisters was always being annoyed or outraged about something or other. They were moods I learned to

32

recognize if I wanted to survive childhood outnumbered three to one. But never passionate. It seems an improper word for a brother to use when describing his sisters.'

Strel'tsin looked at him and Ivan could see both curiosity and a certain amused satisfaction. 'Improper perhaps, highness,' said the High Steward smoothly, 'but in this instance, accurate.'

There was little for Ivan to do but raise his eyebrows at that, so he did. At least he raised the right one, in an elegant, understated gesture of interrogation which he had envied from the first time he had seen Guard-Captain Akimov use it when listening to the inadequate excuses of an erring sentry. Ivan had practised in his mirror every morning and evening after that, and at one stage had come close to setting up a permanent nervous tic in one side of his face before he mastered the trick; but it had come right at last and now looked just as coolly impressive as he had always hoped it might. *'Ob'yasnyat','* he said, putting all that he could gather of his father's quiet power into the single word. 'Explain.'

This time, when Strel'tsin looked at him, there was a new respect in the High Steward's eyes. If a Prince could sound like a Tsar, there was every possibility that he might also act like one – and there were such Tsar's in Ivan's ancestry that a braver man than Dmitriy Vasil'yevich might flinch from the encounter. Instead of flinching he bowed low, from the waist, not rising from his seat.

'The explanation, Highness, is money. Or more precisely, bride-price. You will remember from our last lesson how when the daughter of one of the old kings or chieftains was to be married, her prospective husband would show how he could support his new wife by listing his wealth and what expectation of profit, plunder or inheritance he might have, and prove these claims by a rich gift of bride-money to the maiden's father and family.'

'I remember, Dmitriy Vasil'yevich, I *remember*!' Ivan interrupted before the gates of the scholarly flood could open any further. 'Do *you* remember that you lectured me on just this subject no more than ten, no, nine days ago?'

'So recently, Highness?'

'Yes. So there's no need to repeat it all again. Please?'

'As you command, Highness.'

Investigating the jug on the table which had mercifully remained unspilled despite Katya's efforts, Ivan had found more *sbiten'* in it. Barely warm, though, since the flurrying of paperwork had extinguished the little spirit lamp built into its stand. Ivan thought about re-lighting it, then dismissed the idea. There were too many things already in his mind for it to contain a properly constructed focus pattern, and without it . . . . well, last time the blisters on his fingertips had taken more than a week to heal. Nonetheless, the discovery cheered him up considerably. 'No, no, no,' he said, 'not command. Request. That should be enough.'

'Of course, Highness.'

'And have some of this *sbiten'*, man. There's plenty for two, and if . . . .' Ivan grinned crookedly, his father's grin, '. . . . you're planning to talk as much as I think you are, you'll need refreshment.'

'Thank you, Highness. Most amusing.'

Ivan eyed him over the rim of his cup as he took a small mouthful of the spiced honey drink, and decided abruptly that it was late enough in the afternoon to justify something stronger. He emptied the cup in a single swallow, smacked its hot stoneware against the surface of the table and clapped his hands for attention.

A servant and two mailed guards were through the door before the room had returned to silence. Ivan glanced at the servant, nodded acknowledgement of the man's presence and said, '*Prisluzhnik! Myod, nemedlenno!*'

The mead arrived in less than a minute; *Sbiten'* for adults was how Ivan thought of it. He poured a cup of mead for himself and then one for Strel'tsin, filling both with the fine, brimming abandon of one who didn't really care about the quantity of alcohol being offered. Ivan was quietly curious as to what truths might emerge after the High Steward had emptied his third or fourth cup. For his own part, he had learnt – practised? experienced? – drinking under the tuition of Guard-Captain Akimov.

That worthy and martial gentleman held certain opinions;

one was, that any Tsar who could drink both his own courtiers and the ambassadors from other realms under the table had a considerable advantage over all of them. In Akimov's view, it was a political weapon just as much as swords, arrows and armies. He had introduced Ivan Aleksandrovich to hard liquor with the same cool precision (and the same Tsar's permission) as he had employed the first time he drew sharp steel in the Tsarevich's presence. One was as dangerous as the other; or as safe, depending on how it was treated.

Ivan had learnt that for every glass of vodka, he should drink five times that quantity of water, and three cups of water for every one of wine. He had been advised that every trusted servant worthy of his hire would know how to serve water in a vessel which looked just the same as those containing wine or vodka, and to deliver those harmless jugs only to the Tsar and his ministers. Even without such precautions, Ivan was young and fit enough to drink all of his companions under whatever table they might have sat around. He looked at the gold transparence of the mead and smelt its scent of fermented honey wafting around his nostrils, and suddenly the world was not quite such an annoying place.

'*Davay glaz nal'yom!*' said Ivan, and drank down the cup of mead in a single long draught. He was deliberately daring the High Steward to match him, and was surprised when Strel'tsin did just that.

It was clear that Dmitriy Vasil'yevich was ready and willing – and God alone knew, perhaps even able – to go cup for cup with someone forty years his junior. If anyone had suggested that so dry and shrivelled an individual was capable of such a thing, Ivan would have laughed aloud in their face. Confronted with the reality, he did nothing of the sort. He dismissed at once the notion of drinking Strel'tsin into foolishness, and instead watched the grey-haired, grey-bearded face with something close to respect.

'All right, then,' he said. 'So the payment of bride-price by the would-be husband was the custom in the old days. That much I remember. But nowadays the payment goes out of the coffers, instead of in. Yes?'

'Yes, Highness. As a dowry payment by the family of the bride to the family of her husband. Yekaterina Tsarevna was aware that your noble father the Tsar must find such a dowry not once, but three times.'

Ivan blinked; it was one of the many facts that he already knew and, because they were unpleasant, had carefully forgotten until that dry, emotionless voice reminded him. He did not like the reminder. 'Damn,' he said, and knew it was an inadequate response.

'Just so, Highness. Khorlov is not wealthy, and three daughters . . . .'

'. . . . Are three daughters, and scarcely the fault either of my father or my mother. Unless you would like to discuss the matter with them personally. . . ?' Quite suddenly there was a malevolence beyond his years in Ivan's face and voice, the sound of a young man ready and eager for the kind of quarrel kept bottled up for far too long.

The kind of quarrel which could only be disarmed by an admission of guilt.

'Highness,' said Strel'tsin, 'the matter has already been discussed, and they have honoured me with their opinions many times. No matter how we may approach it, this affair always means the same thing: three dowries leaving the treasury and only one coming in. A matter of simple arithmetic and simpler economics. The Tsardom loses gold and land that it can ill afford, three times over.'

'Then why your wretched list, Dmitriy Vasil'yevich? Why was it restricted only to the high and the mighty?'

'Highness?' There was a tone in the High Steward's voice that suggested he simply didn't understand what Ivan was saying. 'The Tsarevnas are Princesses of royal blood. It would be unseemly if any—'

'Peasant?'

'—Person of unsuitable rank,' Strel'tsin continued without missing a beat, 'should make proposals of marriage to any of them. Yekaterina Tsarevna is a young woman of such high passions that she might accept the hand of an improper suitor, and live to regret her choice.'

Ivan shook his head and drank a little more mead, then

topped up the cup with plain cold water. 'I don't think Katya would do any such thing,' he said. 'But I'm forced to agree with what you say on one count at least: in the present circumstance, passionate is the right word for her. Because it seems to me, High Steward Strel'tsin, that displays of high passion are the only way to make you notice anything.'

'As it pleases you, Highness.'

'You see? that was an insult, if you like – but all you say is "Yes, sir" and "No, sir". Have you no passions of your own?'

'Yes, Highness, I have. A passion for order, for propriety, for the fitness of things. A passion for ensuring that if a thing is done, it should be done correctly and in a seemly fashion.'

'Such as the arrangement of "suitable" marriages, despite the promise which our father the Tsar made to each of us?'

Strel'tsin drew breath as if to reply; then he hesitated, as if editing that same reply into something which would sound more acceptable to the ears of a Tsarevich. Ivan snapped his fingers – a small, sharp sound that seemed excessively loud in the stillness of the High Steward's considerations.

'Just say it,' he said, impatient and growing just a little weary. 'I'll forget whatever I hear.'

'Very well, Highness.'

'Then you may speak.'

'Thank you, Highness.' Again he paused, but Ivan waved him on. 'Firstly, there are, ah, certain personages of my acquaintance who might well appreciate an invitation to any courting-feast that might be arranged.'

'Relatives of yours?' asked Ivan innocently.

Strel'tsin didn't even blush. 'Fellows in the Art,' he said with dignity. 'And powerful, in more ways than the mere filling of coffers.'

Either Tatars or sorcerers, thought Ivan, but was too well-mannered to say so aloud. 'Very well, then. Put their names down on the next list, by my authority.'

'Thank you, Highness.'

'Don't thank me until you're finished. Carry on.'

'Then you should realize, Highness, that I have long believed your father's promise, though kindly meant, was impolitic. Such good fortune as befell the Tsar in his own marriage is – forgive me, Highness – unlikely to occur again. Most certainly it cannot occur four times in a row. One would need to travel far for such good fortune.'

Ivan looked at Strel'tsin very sharply, wondering what lay beneath that simple statement, knowing from long experience of the High Steward's pedantic speech that he was not given to making obscure references without good reason. And yet there was nothing to suggest he had made more than a comment. Certainly he hadn't stopped talking for an instant.

'Also, your father had no need to consider the ambitions of the Great Prince of Kiev. You have. All of his children must marry so as to bind strong allies to Khorlov; otherwise one day Yuriy Vladimirovich will simply reach out and close his fist, and there will be no more Khorlov. Only another vassal.'

'*Velikiy knyaz'Kiyevskiy* will reach too far one of these fine days, and he'll pull back a bloody stump,' said Ivan quietly. He had been expecting Strel'tsin's lecture to bore or anger him, the way all the other litanies of policy and duty had done in the past. Instead – and to his private surprise – he had found Dmitriy Vasil'yevich to be as passionate on this one subject – in his own dry and inimitable fashion – as his sister Katya had become on more personal matters.

'Very well, First Minister.' Ivan used the High Steward's second title deliberately, to emphasize that he understood the political significance of what had been said. 'I understand your reasoning; but now you should understand mine.' He reached out to refill Strel'tsin's cup, for during the course of the discussion the grey man had emptied it not once but three times. 'Lords of lesser rank might make lesser allies; but at the same time they would also command lesser dowries.' Ivan shrugged wryly, knowing that he was beginning to sound like a merchant at the barter table. 'More to the point, the sons and daughters of the lower nobility live in and around Khorlov, much closer than the estates of the great Lords. They have been the friends of our youth and childhood. Including their names in your list might enable both the needs of the Tsardom and the words of the Tsar to his children to be honoured.'

Strel'tsin bowed again, getting to his feet this time. He

raised the replenished mead-cup in a salute, then drained it and began gathering his papers together. 'You reason well, Highness. *Zdorovo, mudrets!* I shall put this proposal to the Tsar's Majesty at once.'

Ivan watched him leave the room in a curious gait which fell somewhere between his usual controlled, reptilian elegance and the bustle of a man eager to restore himself to something like good grace. The door closed behind him, leaving Ivan Aleksandrovich alone with the empty table and the half-empty mead jug. It occurred to him that he should have asked the names of Strel'tsin's mysterious acquaintances. . . .

And then, without the High Steward's beady eye on him, Ivan realized just what he had done. It had nothing to do with Fellows in the Art, or anything so outlandish. He groaned softly, closing his eyes for several seconds like a man with a headache.

Several headaches – and he knew them all by name.

Not that he had given any specific names to High Steward Strel'tsin, oh no. But Ivan knew – the instant it was too late to recall the words of his so-wise advice – that when he suggested the inclusion of those sprigs of the lesser nobility who were his friends, he hadn't given enough thought to all the implications. They were good fellows all, amused and amusing; fine companions for a day spent hunting in the great dark forests of birch and pine, or an evening spent drinking in the little taverns beneath the shadow of the kremlin. . . .

But he certainly wouldn't want his sisters to marry any one of them.

*

The new list was drawn up, and it was just as Ivan feared: Sergey Stepanovich, Pavel Zhukovskiy, Nikolai Feodorov, all of them. Familiarity had not really bred contempt for the young lordlings whose names were there; they were his friends, after all. But that same familiarity had given him an intimate acquaintance with the way high-spirited young men could behave in the company of their peers and a sufficient quantity of alcohol.

None of their various drunken vices was very dreadful, and

most would receive no more from the Metropolitan Levon than an admonishment and a wrinkling of his long, patrician nose. However, Ivan was discovering a fact that many brothers before him had learned about their gang of closest cronies. The sort of ribald antics which among a group of bachelors provoke only roars of laughter and deeper drinking, become rapidly less and less endearing when those same jesters are among the men who might be courting one's sisters.

Worst of all was to see the half-dozen *boyar*'s sons that he knew only as a bunch of drunken reprobates, acting with all the studied manners and gallantry of characters from an old – and badly written – romantic tale. Certainly courtly speeches and perfume in his beard seemed out of place on Sasha Levonovich; Ivan's most recent memory of that dignified and sweet-smelling gentleman was of horrible oaths and a still more horrible stench. For some reason, probably to do with the half-bottle of vodka he had consumed, Sasha had laid a wager that the ice on the cesspit behind the tavern was thick enough to support his weight. . . .

Ivan had but one advantage, and that was thanks to the season. There would be time for only one banquet during *Maslenitsa*, Butter Week, before Shrovetide came to an end and the Long Fast began. Khorlov's Metropolitan Archbishop, Levon Popovich Volkhv, had spent many years of ministry in the hard lands where as a matter of simple caution the old gods were still given respect. After much wasted effort in his zealous youth, he had discarded proselytizing in favour of pragmatism – but no matter how worthy its cause, he would never be persuaded to countenance feasting during Lent.

Tsarevich Ivan knew that the Archbishop's intransigence would give him forty uninterrupted days in which to make sure that certain facts were made known about certain names on the High Steward's new list. In ordinary circumstances, he knew that he would really need no more than forty minutes . . . . but he also knew, from wet and bitter-cold experience, that there was no such thing as an ordinary circumstance when a brother tries to influence his three sisters in their views of love and marriage.

Ivan wondered more than once, when the gloom and melancholy of the Rus stole over him, just how they would break the five-foot-thick layer of ice which covered the lake in winter, so as to throw him in. . . .

CHAPTER THREE

How the Tsarevnas found suitors who pleased them

Invitations to this first and only banquet before Lent were sent out by rider where the roads permitted it, or by swift *troyki* up and down the frozen rivers. Tsar Aleksandr sent his messengers mostly along the Dneipr, but also as far north and south as the Dvina and Dneistr and as far east and west as the reaches of the Pripyat' and the Upper Volga. More than anything else, it was those great distances across the face of Moist-Mother-Earth which meant there would be no more than the one feast before Lent.

For all that, he made certain to invite the powerful as well as the eligible. Manguyu Temir of the Tatar Golden Horde was to be a guest, as were the Princes Oleg Vladislav and Aleksandr Yaroslavich – although arrangements were already being made to seat those worthies and their supporters well away from one another. After consultation with Archbishop Levon, it was decided that the banquet should begin on the Monday morning before Ash Wednesday, so that Friday for the Moslem guests, Saturday for the Jews and Sunday for the Christians could all be soberly observed without complaint from whichever God happened to be watching at the time, and though the old prelate made slight noises of dissent where the unbelievers were concerned, he finally agreed.

*

As the banquet began, Ivan wasn't so concerned with the daintiness of the political machinations as with the presence of a mob of his very good friends, all of them scrubbed and scented and dressed in their finest garments. It was fairly certain that neither the visiting Princes nor any of the Tatar delegation were at any risk of being chosen as husbands by any of his sisters – though if Manguyu Temir found himself married to Yekaterina, it would assure peace in all the Russias for years to come. Not even an Ilkhan of the Sky-Blue Wolves could survive that experience for long without being thoroughly domesticated. Those who *were* at risk – and the risk was entirely his own, thanks to too much mead and not enough thought – were the sort of people whom Tsarevich Ivan wouldn't let near his horses, never mind his sisters.

The feast was held in the great Hall of Audience and began in its usual fashion, with the principal guests being guided to the places deemed proper to their greater or lesser dignity. From those places they could be amused by the scufflings as everyone else endeavoured to find seating that might suggest a higher rank than they actually possessed. Only Ivan didn't laugh; he merely smiled thinly and watched with narrowed eyes, because most of those doing the scuffling were his own splendidly attired companions. For all their fine clothing, and for all that every one of them was plainly hoping to catch the eye of one or other of the Tsarevnas, he could see that whenever their concentration slipped they still behaved at table as they had always done. That much was a relief: it would make what he intended to say about them all the more easily believed.

Except for its function, this banquet was like all others during *Maslenitsa*, a celebration of the end of winter and a preparation for the Great Fast that followed. In his younger day, Archbishop Levon had tried to insist that no meat should be served and no alcohol drunk. But he had finally given up the task, saying that he might as well keep winter at bay by picking up each snowflake with tweezers. Old Tsar Andrey had been a man who enjoyed all the pleasures that God sent, and hadn't been about to give up a single one of them. He had agreed to the Lent fast only on the grounds that it would give larders depleted by Butter Week a chance to be restocked – just in time for another feast at Easter. Tsar Aleksandr was his father's son in that respect as well as in so many others, and the quality of his table was famous.

Before the eating began, the Archbishop read a grace and

choristers from the cathedral sang an anthem. Then a figure was brought into the hall and set upright in the only hearth which had no fire in it. Though the figure was made of straw, it had been left out of doors sufficiently long to be crusted now with snow, and it seemed as though it wore a long beard and hair of icicles. The Tsar rose to his feet, took a copper cup from the table in front of him and gave it to one of the servants who had brought the straw figure into the hall.

The cup was filled with a mixture of lamp-oil and distilled spirit, and everyone present watched as it was emptied over the straw man, then set alight – not by sorcery, for this one ritual, but with a burning brand. Despite its covering of snow, the figure's straw was dry and it burned fast and fiercely until nothing remained in the hearth but a mound of black and grey ash with small flames dancing around it. The smell of the burning was sweet, since scent and incense had been mixed with both the straw and the oil. Tsar Aleksandr lifted another cup, this one filled with vodka, and held it high in salute to the fire. 'Winter is dead!' he said, then drank the vodka down in one gulp and flung the glass into the fireplace, where it shattered and the remains of the vodka burned blue.

'Winter is dead!' echoed everyone, even the foreigners – at least, once the ceremony had been explained to them. Certainly it was as good an excuse as any to lay hands on the first drink of the evening. A shower of glasses crashed into whichever of the great hearths was closest, and then the serious business of the feast began with the arrival of the first tureens of soup.

There was *shchi* and *borshch*, fish *rassol'nik* and *solyanka* with mushrooms, great platters of black bread hot from the ovens, and for those who thought soup was too thin without something floating in it, dishes of dumplings and buckwheat noodles. Ivan drank his own soup thoughtfully, not really appreciating its splendid flavour, for once again his attention was elsewhere. He was watching the doings at the farthest table, where Pavel and Nikolai had already started flicking little pellets of bread at one another, and he wasn't alone.

'Was this why you wanted them invited, Vanya?' asked his mother in her soft voice. Ludmyla Ivanovna was known for

44

her wisdom as well as for her beauty, and if she had gone to the trouble of making a comment, Ivan dared not even think of making an excuse.

'No, *matushka*,' he replied, just as quietly. 'They were invited because I wasn't thinking.'

The Tsaritsa smiled and glanced at the unruly guests again. 'I suspected as much, when Dmitriy Vasil'yevich arrived with his idea for a new list of suitors. He gave you full credit, of course. Another of his little jokes: I'm sure he's fully aware of the way your friends behave. It's his business to know such things.'

Ivan stared at his soup-bowl, tapping it with his spoon while he debated whether to laugh or be angry. Anger would be justified, of course – he disliked being made fun of – but at the same time there was a certain elegance about the way the High Steward had sprung his trap. Even while disliking the man just as much as ever, Ivan could appreciate the neatness of the trick. Strel'tsin knew perfectly well that Ivan's friends would never make good suitors on the best day of their lives, but at the same time their behaviour would reflect badly on the Tsarevich and so pay him out nicely for a great many sharp words and barely-veiled insults. All of which he had achieved without once leaving himself in a position to be blamed for anything. Ivan shook his head slowly, shrugged, laughed, finished up his soup . . . then noticed just how very good it was and called for a second helping.

The Hall was a sea of colour, for it was not merely Ivan's friends who had dressed in their best. All of the Rus wore long kaftans, brocaded, jewelled or richly embroidered, and the tall furred hats that were the fashion in the deeps of winter – although many had taken off their hats to prevent them from falling in the soup. The Jews and the Moslems wore those robes that were traditional at holidays, and even Manguyu Temir had made an effort, which was a high compliment indeed.

The stocky, deep-chested Tatar wore his hair in the usual four-tailed tonsure of his people, but had gone to the trouble of washing both it and himself in the recent past. There was still a faint aroma of grease and horses hanging around him,

45

but at least the most recent layer of grease had been one containing some kind of perfume. The robe that covered his two coats was of rare and beautiful watered silk, in a Persian style and pattern, and it seemed improbable that he had acquired it by honest trading. Only good manners – also widely separated tables and the presence of Tsar Aleksandr's guards – prevented various of the princely guests and their attendant *boyaryy* from making the sort of observation which might have provoked a regrettable scene.

The soup was cleared away and the feasting progressed to more solid fare: poultry, fish and game of all sorts, *kolbasy* sausages and blood-sausage with thyme in it, buckwheat *kasha*, pickled cucumbers, cabbage and *golubtsy*, great joints of beef with sour cream and horseradish, and succulent pieces of pork for those whose religions did not forbid it.

As usual, there was a brisk discussion amongst the Moslems; not about their meat, which had all been carved from cleanly animals, but about the drink that came with it. Tsar Aleksandr had provided everything that anyone might wish to drink, from ale, *kvas*, wine, birch-beer, mead and vodka –and even *kumys* for the Tatars – to innocent beverages like buttermilk, *sbiten'* and the new *chaiy* from the East. Their discussion arose not from a lack of choice, but from interpreting a point of doctrine in a religion that of all present was the only one still young enough to permit such erudite wrangling over rules which as yet had not been inflexibly cut in stone. Some were saying that the Prophet Mohammed's instruction to the Faithful forbade all alcohol, while others held that his words referred only to that which came from the juice of grapes.

Ivan listened to all of this with the curiosity and fascination of one who had travelled only through the pages of books. Since the Moslems came from several parts of the Caliphate, they spoke Russian as a common tongue and, despite their heavy accents, Prince Ivan understood all of it. At least, all that he could hear, for with the first edge of their appetites blunted by the good soups that began the meal everyone else in the hall had found the time to talk as well. Finishing with the food on his plate, he wiped his fork and spoon and eating-knife, put them back in their case on his belt, then made his excuses and pushed back from the table.

Many others had already done the same, moving from their own places the more easily to hold conversations with friends or acquaintances elsewhere, but so far none of the suitors had screwed up enough courage to approach any of the Tsarevnas. Ivan filled his glass with wine and sauntered over to where they sat, gossiping with one another and making observations about this young man or that.

'Now *that* one I like,' Yelena was saying, pointing with her spoon in a tipsy and suggestive manner that was completely deceptive, since Ivan had never seen her tipsy in his life. He glanced down the line indicated by the spoon and frowned slightly, for though the young man in question was seated amongst his own noisy friends, that particular pale face above black clothing was unfamiliar. For just a moment their eyes met across the length and width of the crowded hall and the young man, recognizing Ivan as the Tsar's son, rose from his seat and bowed low.

Ivan matched the bow, but with slightly less than good manners since he was staring all the time. Yelena made a tsk-tsk noise and rapped him sharply on the elbow with her spoon. 'Vanya!' she said, 'I thought you were supposed to be watching the young *ladies*!'

'Only when I see one worth watching,' he said, and grinned. 'That one, in the black – who is he?'

'Oh.' Yelena looked flustered and had the expression of someone about to rummage for a piece of paper with names written on it, except that the piece of paper was already gripped in Katya's fingers.

'Mikhail Voronov,' Katya read, and managed to sound disapproving. 'He and two brothers. They all claim to be Princes, but . . . .' she waved the paper under Ivan's nose, '. . . . though they've claimed the style and title, they haven't bothered providing the names of their domains.' Yekaterina Tsarevna hiccupped in a manner that was most restrained and ladylike, but was a hiccup nonetheless. 'Otherwise it would be too easy for Strel'tsin to track down where they aren't, in his damned books.' She dropped the piece of paper

47

on to the table, where Yelena scooped it up and blinked at Ivan through the eyes of someone who has started their party an hour or so before the other guests. Katya, oldest of the family and still a spinster with a reputed savage temper, had her own reasons for disliking celebrations like this one, and her own way of either surviving or of leaving early. 'Are you having a good time?' she asked, speaking very, very carefully so that all the letters fell – or staggered – into their proper place.

'Very good,' said Ivan. 'Try the hazel-hen with jam,' he said. 'It's excellent.' Directly he tried to change the subject, they all looked at him at once, with expressions that varied from amusement to the kind of steely glint that had him thinking about freezing lake-water.

'I've tried it,' said Yekaterina Tsarevna, 'and it's not as good as it might be. The cooks need livening up.'

'You'd do it with a knout, I suppose?'

'If necessary. This is an important occasion, and—'

'—And I haven't heard complaints from anyone else.' Oh yes, it would definitely be the lake for him, if he wasn't more careful. 'So we'll leave the food aside. What about the, er, other selection?'

Yelizaveta Tsarevna looked down the hall at Ivan's cronies and hid a most un-Princess-like giggle behind her hand. '*Matushka* said that you were responsible for them being here. True?'

Ivan grinned wryly. 'In a manner of speaking. But when Katya saw the first list, she said—'

'—Nothing like what you must have thought you heard! There was one – he was wearing blue and grey – but I can't see him any more.'

'Still, these are the sort of people you meant, aren't they? Good lads, all of them. Even bandy-legs Temir.'

'You really must like the notion of swimming in winter, Vanyushka,' said Yelena Tsarevna, smiling at him. It was a sweet smile, as sweet as jam – but jam that had broken glass stirred well into it. Ivan sat down on the corner of the table and drank some wine, knowing that he had just been given his final warning.

Lena didn't usually even bother with threats – she preferred to leave them to Katya, who being taller made them sound much more impressive – but when she did trouble to issue one the person threatened knew it was their last chance. There was a bowl of *tvorog* cream-cheese on the table in front of his sisters. They studied it, and then him, until Ivan moved the bowl a diplomatic distance away. 'Oh, don't do that,' said Liza. 'I think you'd look very fetching with it poured over your hat.'

'And ornamented with some of these almonds,' added Katya, pouring a dozen of them from one hand to the other. Never mind the ornamentation, she could do more damage just by throwing them.

'Then I can take it that there's no chance of Sergey Stepanovich becoming a part of the family?' he said, sounding relieved.

'*Izbavi Bog!*' exclaimed Liza. 'God forbid! Unless you know something about him that we don't?'

'Probably I do. And probably you don't want to hear about it.'

'Whatever in the world makes you think that, little brother Vanyushechka?' Katya had set the almonds aside and was propping her chin on her hands, smiling the demure smile of a lady just in the mood for a bit of really juicy, salacious gossip. 'Tell us all about dear Sergey. Or perhaps you really *do* feel like a dip in the lake later today. . . ?'

'He boasts,' said Ivan hastily. His sisters blinked, looked at one another and then stared hard at him.

'Is that all?' asked Katya.

'What about?' enquired Liza.

'Keep talking, or go swimming,' ordered Lena.

'About drinking. About how much he can drink.'

'Not much of a boast,' said Katya. '*We* could probably drink as much.'

'And about other skills.' Ivan turned a little and watched as Sergey, Feliks and Pavel started on yet another bottle of wine.

'Do tell,' said Liza. 'I presume it has to do with how well he can hold his liquor.'

'Not quite. When he's really overstepped the mark, we

have to do that for him.' The three Tsarevnas stared even harder, and he could see the beginnings of a horrible suspicion begin to grow in their eyes.

'No,' said Lena.

'Yes,' said Ivan. 'In his hat.'

'Ugh,' said his sisters in chorus, and lost any interest they might have had in the *tvorog* cream-cheese.

'From the distance of two *arshiniy*,' Ivan persisted, without mercy. 'And twice – to prove that the first time had been skill and not an accident.' A huge grin spread across his face at their expressions, and he bowed low before making his escape. 'If you're interested, I'll tell you about Nikolai and Pavel some other time. . . .'

*

'Ivan, my son . . . . just exactly *what* are you trying to do? Besides make certain that your sisters never marry at all?' Tsar Aleksandr turned from the window and came back towards his throne, stalking stiff-backed with anger along the same route which he had paced more than a hundred times since summoning Ivan to his private chambers on that cold Ash Wednesday morning. The Tsarevich said nothing; he felt fairly certain that despite the questions he wasn't expected to give an answer. He was right.

'Have you any idea, young man, of the cost to Khorlov's exchequer of that little party during the last two days? Have you? I think not! Five poods of silver! Your own weight, sir! An acceptable dowry to accompany any one of your sisters to her husband's home – if it hadn't just been spent on a total waste of time. Thank you, Ivan Aleksandrovich. Thank you very much indeed, for nothing.'

'My Lord father. . . .' The Tsar had resumed his pacing, and either didn't hear or didn't want to hear. Ivan tried again. '*Batyushka*. . . .' The pacing stopped abruptly and Tsar Aleksandr's silver lion's head rose from staring at the floor to glare at his son.

'Until this matter has been settled, Ivan Tsarevich, you will not address me in that familiar fashion. You have made all of us look foolish in many several ways, and do not presume that this will soon be forgotten.'

'I. . . .' Ivan's tongue had gone abruptly dry inside his mouth, so that the words refused to leave it. He was remembering how Tsars in the past had lost their tempers in a violent and fatal way with sons who had annoyed them, and though the chronicles had always said they had been sorry afterwards, it hadn't done the sons very much good. 'They may have been my friends, Majesty, but you would not have cared for any of them as a son-in-law.'

'It was not your friends who concerned me, *bolvan*, though why they should have been invited to a formal banquet in the first place is presently beyond my comprehension. It was the other guests, and it was the way in which your stupid comments set my daughters to think critically of every Prince, every *boyar*, every potential husband in the entire palace.' Tsar Aleksandr paused beside the throne, drumming his fingers on its high back, then sat down hard and noisily on its velvet cushions, toying with his long, spike-tipped sceptre in a way that made Ivan careful to keep his distance.

' "Prince Oleg Vladislav?" I asked them. "Too fat," they said. "Prince Aleksandr Yaroslavich?" "Too thin," they said. Konstantin *bogatyr'* was too tall, and Mstislav Mikhailovich was too short. They thought that Boris Rostislavl' should have had a smooth face instead of that fine red beard of his, though everyone knows that he'd sooner die than suffer the shame of shaving it – but they also thought Ryurik Gyorg'yevich, the *boyar*'s son, would have looked better with whiskers, even though he's two years younger than you are and that much less able to grow more than fluff on his chin.'

Ivan felt himself blushing redder and redder throughout his father's recitation, until he felt certain that his ears were glowing enough to light the room. He felt just as certain that if he said the wrong thing he would live to regret it, though perhaps not long enough to set it right. 'Then you must make the choice for them,' he said carefully, one eye constantly on the four-inch spike which capped his father's sceptre. 'And for me, too.'

'So your only advice is that I break my sworn word to my own children?'

' "If the need requires it, do what is needed". ' Ivan was hoping that surely, surely, the Tsar wouldn't take exception to hearing his own words quoted back at him, but even so, when the sceptre's spike grated on the tiles of the floor he was already tensed to duck or dodge or run.

'*Tak*,' said Aleksandr Andreyevich. 'So.' From the look on his face, he had reached and passed the peak of his anger and now it was tapering down to mere annoyance – though a Tsar's annoyance was still something tht the wise preferred to avoid, by the width of a steppe or two. 'It may well come to that.' He sat back and stroked his moustaches between finger and thumb for a few minutes, until they had ceased to droop and had returned to their customary handsome sweep of silver across his upper lip. 'Besides criticizing some of our guests, Prince Ivan, did you happen to notice any of the others? Those here through politeness or invitation, rather than those hoping to get the daughter of a Tsar for their wife?'

'Rich Jewish merchants,' said Ivan after a moment's thought, 'and Moslem traders from the Caliph's country. Also certain crook-legged Tatars wearing dead men's finery. Two, no, three men claiming to be Lords or Princes, even though nobody – not even Strel'tsin – could find where they were supposed to rule. Besides, of course, the powerful genuine Princes who were too much of this and not enough of that. . . .'

'Carefully, my son.' The Tsar glowered at him from beneath heavy brows and Ivan subsided at once. 'Carefully. You'll know when you've been forgiven enough to make idiotic jokes in safety, and by Saint Basil, that time hasn't come yet.' Aleksandr Andreyevich rattled another brief tattoo with his fingers on one arm of the throne. 'But you saw enough. Merchants and traders indeed – even though they weren't from the Caliphate or from Khazar.'

'Then where. . . ?'

'You said it yourself, before, Kiev and Novgorod. Or Novgorod and Kiev. They'd come to see how we were doing in the search for heirs, alliances and dowries. And thanks to you, they saw nothing especially impressive!'

'Then if they're still within the walls,' said Ivan coldly, 'we should find them, learn where they came from and send their heads back to whoever sent them. Smoked and salted, of course,' he added as an afterthought. 'Making the point that we won't be spied on is one thing, but we don't want to cause needless offence.'

'Of course not,' agreed Tsar Aleksandr weakly. He had listened to this outrageous suggestion, and looked at his son, and realized with a very small shiver that Ivan meant every word. Whether it was just that the boy felt out of sorts after being chastised, or was an indication of something that went deeper, the Tsar didn't know; but he made a mental note to keep an eye open from now on. Even the best sons sometimes grew impatient. . . .

'The notion has already been considered,' he said, 'and it's not without a certain appeal. Unfortunately, it would be no more than one of the actions that the Great Princes hope I might take. They have long had too much of an interest in Khorlov, with an eye less to marriage and alliance than to annexation. Yuriy and the Mikhaylovichi may be high and mighty rulers, but they're not so high or mighty that they'll miss whatever chance they find to acquire yet more land. Such a provocation as sending people's pickled heads about the country would justify their sending an army against me – and anyway, my son, this Tsardom has never been large enough to back up such grandiose gestures with the level of force they need. Not even with the support of the Golden Horde.'

'You surely don't want an alliance with *them*?'

'Of course not!' The Tsar sounded faintly disgusted at the very thought. 'But Yuriy of Kiev and Boris Mikhaylovich won't know that. One more reason for leaving their spies alive: to report back what they saw here. And one of the things they'll have to report is the sight of Manguyu Temir, eating his meal in my hall like a Christian and well enough dressed that he must have done it to honour a new ally.'

'This is one of Strel'tsin's plots,' said Ivan softly.

'It is. Why?'

'No reason. I was simply curious to know if I'd guessed

right. It has the High Steward's touch about it.' Ivan wondered to himself about the brief, broken conversation he had had with Dmitriy Vasil'yevich. There had been the 'personages of importance' who had, so far as he knew, failed to appear at the feast. And he began to wonder what advantages might be gained by such a highly placed minister, if his pretence of friendship with the Ilkhan of the Horde was rather more than just pretence. . . .

*

Velikiy Post of Lent came, was endured as a holy festival must be and at last became *Paskha*, the joyful time of Easter. The Great Fast became the Great Feast and special foods were prepared: tall *kulich* cakes full of dried fruit and nuts, *paskha tvorog* enriched with cream and formed in a mould that left the sign of the cross impressed in its sides, and lambs modelled in fresh butter.

Of course there were more banquets, attended by more suitors. None of the banquets was as large or impressive as the very first one, which was just as well: if anything, they were even less successful than that had been. Tsar Aleksandr Andreyevich was spending considerable quantities of silver, only to find himself and his realm exactly where they had been before all of this began, with one vital and unpleasant difference: not only did he still have his unmarried children to wed, but also by now the Tsardom was in debt.

It no longer required spies from Novgorod and Kiev; the Great Princes of those cities had come in person to Khorlov, self-invited guests to one of the banquets, and had seen matters for themselves. It was only too clear that support for Khorlov and for Tsar Aleksandr was lukewarm at best among his neighbours, that his rumoured alliance with the Khan of the Golden Horde was indeed no more than a rumour, and that any territorial ambitions they might entertain were unlikely to be opposed – except, perhaps, by one another. It became plain to the people of Khorlov, and even at last to the children of its Tsar, that there was a storm coming in, and the only question remaining was: from which direction would it strike first. . . ?

But the storm held off, except for those two strange storms which since that time had taken away the Tsar's eldest daughters. Hours became days, the days became weeks and the snows of winter began to fall, covering the grass and the flowers and the dead leaves of autumn, until all was still and silent and a shroud of white lay across the gardens of the kremlin.

It had been a long time since Yelena Tsarevna had walked there with her sisters, and almost as long since she had first begun to hope that she too would find a suitor as they had done. But for all the hours and days and weeks which had gone by, and for all the cold and darkness of the Russian winter that lay beyond the firelit warmth of the kremlin palace, she had never given up that hope. Her hair was always arranged correctly, her garments always rich and fine, her face always painted with that small amount of paint permitted to a maiden daughter of the Tsar.

For his own part, Prince Ivan was relieved that all the interest in marrying had settled on his sisters and not so much on himself. He knew well enough that after Lena was wed and gone that interest – and the pressure that went with it – would be transferred to him; so he spent each day in merriment, when he was not learning the lessons that a Tsar's son must know if he is to be a wise Tsar when his own time comes. Ivan lived each of those days as though it were the last day of his freedom, aware that soon or late it would be the truth.

When at last it came, it was not a day but a night, and one when the snow-laden wind of Svarog's storm was moaning under the eaves and around the kremlin's onion-shaped domes. All were gathered in the warmth of the lesser hall, where its walls were panelled with wood and then hung with tapestries so that the heat from the great log fire could not escape. Musicians were playing, and while the Tsaritsa and Yelena Tsarevna worked at their embroidery and listened to a storyteller recite the *bylina* called 'The Tale of Dobrynya Nikit'ych', Ivan played his father at chess and lost as gracefully as he could. He had just begun to set the pieces up for another and, he hoped, more successful game . . . . when snow began falling on to the board.

Tsar Aleksandr stared at the snowflakes for a second or two before sweeping them away with the back of his hand, then looked at Ivan and grinned in his beard as fathers will grin at their sons – especially fathers who have just beaten those same sons three times in a row at chess. 'Lenochka,' he said, 'do you look pretty tonight?' He was rewarded by the sound of an embroidery tambour falling over, and the swiftly stifled beginnings of the kind of oath that Princesses have to learn when they have a brother.

Above their heads, as silently as snow falling, the ceiling had split open as wide as a door, and descending through it on wings muffled by winter came a raven, black as the night beyond the candle-light. It struck once against the floor and immediately a fire sprang up, enveloping its outspread wings in leaping flames of black and silver so darkly bright that they dazzled the eyes of those who watched. The raven struck twice and then again, so that the flames leapt high and higher still. Then they winked out in the drawing of a breath and the raven became a fine young man dressed all in deepest black, embroidered and brocaded in black silk so cunningly figured with hair-fine silver thread that its brightness only served to make the darkness darker yet, and its trimming was not fur but of raven's feathers.

If the Falcon had seemed sharp-eyed, and the Eagle had seemed strong, then this young man seemed very wise indeed; and yet for all the difference in dress and in looks, he was without a doubt their brother. He looked around him with dark eyes in a pale face, and when that dark gaze fell on Yelena Tsarevna the young man smiled and nodded, seeming much content. Then he bowed low to all present, and saluted Ivan as one young man of noble blood salutes another. 'Long life to you, Tsarevich Ivan,' he said. 'I used to come here as a guest; now I have come as a suitor, to marry your sister Yelena Tsarevna.'

With a bow and a nod Ivan returned the salute. 'Prince Mikhail Voronov,' he said, 'of three brothers who have claimed my acquaintance, you at least I remember.' He made a courtly gesture to show where the Tsar sat beside him.

'Where your request is concerned, you must speak to my father on that; but so far as my sister is concerned she may have her own views on the matter.'

The Raven Prince nodded to show that he understood, but the look he exchanged with Yelena Tsarevna said plainly as words that her mind was already made up. 'Most High Majesty,' he said, 'I am Mikhail Charodeyevich Voronov, *Knyaz' tyomnogo lesa*, and if your daughter loves me I would have her to wife.'

Tsar Aleksandr saw the look which had passed between them, and he smiled. 'Prince of the Dark Forests,' he said, putting out one of his hands to Prince Mikhail the Raven and the other to his youngest daughter, 'I give you her hand, for your gladness and hers.'

'As both of your brothers and both of my sisters enjoy already, O sorcerer's son,' said Ivan. 'Which leaves, of course, me.' He thought that it would sound better coming first from him than from someone like the High Steward, who would surely now raise the subject at the first opportunity.

Knyaz' Mikhail Voronov glanced at him with good humour in his eyes, and was about to say something when the doorward admitted a servant. Ivan looked first at the servant, then at his father and finally back at the servant again. Out of breath and warm despite the winter weather, the man looked distinctly familiar. 'Twenty, in gold?' he enquired just before the servant opened his mouth.

'Yes, Majesty,' the man said and bowed low. 'Just as before.' And just as before, the great opening in the ceiling of the kremlin closed as if it had never been there. Ivan smiled and wiped snow from the chessboard again. . . .

*

This time there were no objections, either voiced or silent, from Metropolitan Archbishop Levon Popovich Volkhv. He agreed to the wedding at once, and his voice had the tone of a man growing used to all manner of strangenesses should they but be repeated often enough. He merely looked long and hard at the Tsar, stroked his beard and finally said: 'Once is strange, twice is coincidence, but three times is becoming a habit – so, Majesty, why should I differ from you?'

When once they were married, Yelena Tsarevna drove away across the snow with her husband the Raven, very splendid and fine in a *troika* sleigh that was all glossy black except for the small silver bells on the harness of its three black horses.

*

And that, indeed, left Ivan. His guess had been right, for it was on the very next day that High Steward Strel'tsin approached with the first draft of a list of young ladies suitable for Tsars' sons to marry. Ivan was more even-tempered than his eldest sister, but as he read the list of names he came to understand more and more why Katya had flung paper in the High Steward's face.

That winter proved to be one of the longest in his memory. It was filled not with snow but with a seemingly endless succession of young women, blonde-haired and red-haired and mousey and black, all keen to be married – and each of them had one thing in common. They looked at him, and saw not a husband, a lover and a man but a Tsar's son, a title and a crown.

Anastasya Fedorovna Solov'ev was the worst of them. It was evident that her family reckoned femininity by weight, or height, or volume, because she qualified on all three counts. Ivan had long ago admitted to himself that he would never be particularly tall; in fact, he had grown to a comfortably average height of about two *arshiniy*, or a little less than six feet. To encounter a hopeful would-be bride who towered over him by that 'little less' and a little more besides, and who by dint of the pleasures of the table matched his height with her circumference, was something of an experience.

Certainly it was a challenge; despite his personal opinions, Ivan Aleksandrovich was still the son of the Tsar and a gentleman. Extricating himself from Countess Anastasya's optimistically enthusiastic embraces had been as much an exercise in diplomacy as in escapology, for despite her size, her weight and the fact that she seemed to have more than the usual allocation of hands, her father was one of his father's more important nobles. Hurting the lady's feelings would have been worse that tactless, it would have been downright impolitic. And dangerous: Anastasya Fedorovna may have appeared no more than fat but Ivan – through no fault of his own – had gained a somewhat more intimate knowledge of her body. Presumably by dint of carrying her own excessive weight about, she was disturbingly muscular, so that any vigorous display of romantic attachment, or grief at parting, was likely to fracture his ribs.

That was the week when Ivan discovered a hitherto unknown talent: the writing of fiction. His letters to Anastasya, sent by hand from the kremlin to the Solov'ev town mansion, passed from originality through inventiveness to a soaring understated exaggeration. It was her father who put an end to the one-side romance when one of the letters was mistakenly handed to him instead of to his daughter. Count Fedor Solov'ev was a man with a better sense of humour than Ivan had given him credit for, and he recognized not only that the Tsar's son was growing increasingly harried by Anastasya's attentions but also that she was using the potential liaison simply as a means to pass the dull winter days. That a man's daughter should risk offending the Tsar's son, and hence the Tsar, simply to relieve her boredom, was not something the Count wished to tolerate – not when the potential for repercussions was increasing with the shrillness of Ivan's letters. There was a certain amount of well-feigned regret on both sides when Count Fedor decided it was high time he and his family went visiting their estates near the city of Suzdal', but not so much that mock sincerity might have been mistaken for the real thing. Tsarevich Ivan, gentleman to the last, waved the Solov'ev *troyki* out of sight from the ramparts of the kremlin.

Then he went and got very, very drunk.

*

Finally the winter was over, the snow was gone and so, for a blessed respite, were the swarms of high-born maidens with hungry eyes. That was when he was summoned once more to the Tsar's Chamber of Audience to give an account of himself.

'We had this discussion last year, Vanya,' began Tsar Aleksandr. 'Indeed, more than a year ago, because I remember the snow was still deep when I first brought the subject before you. So, son of mine: your sisters are married. What about you, and the succession, and the security of the Tsardom?'

'I thought it was secure again, *batyushka*. You said so yourself.'

'Temporarily, because of the bride-gifts your brothers-in-law left in the treasury. It gave Yuriy of Kiev and the others some pause for thought; but they've seen none of the armies which so rich an ally might have, and no sign of a wife for you – much less a son to follow you.'

'There was once a time when I thought you were putting a deal of pressure on me,' said Ivan, smiling a bit wearily at his father. 'I was wrong, wasn't I?'

'You were, my son. Because now that the pressure isn't divided four ways, you've got it all to yourself.'

'Being the focus of attention isn't as entertaining as it might be.'

'It's perceptive of you to notice that, Vanya. Now, answer the question: what are you going to do?'

Ivan thought desperately for an excuse that wouldn't sound like one. 'I had thought,' he said, 'that before I settle down, I should travel. Go to visit Katya and Liza and Lena. Find out for myself what married life is like for people of my own age.'

Tsar Aleksandr Andreyevich nodded his head in agreement, trying not to laugh as he heard something he had been expecting ever since the business with Anastasya Fedorovna. 'That would be wise,' he agreed. 'Many is the time that I've seen you staring towards the horizon, when you think that nobody is watching you.' The Tsar smiled. 'Even when you pour wine, my son, your face shows how you wonder what lands the wine came from; and how you wonder if a simple barrel can journey across the face of Moist-Mother-Earth, why can a Tsar's son not do the same and better. Go visit them: see how happy they are. And then,' the Tsar leaned forward in his throne, 'come back and start behaving like an adult and the heir to my sceptre. Do you understand me, Ivan?'

'Clearly, father. Quite clearly.' Then he hesitated, not sure how his next suggestion would be received.

'Come along, boy, speak. I won't bite you—' Tsar Aleksandr grinned, and laughed the kind of laugh that turned the humour in it sour, '—unless I don't like what you say!'

'I want to travel alone.'

'What? You can't travel alone! You'll need a guard of honour and a retinue! Dammit, Ivan, you're a Tsarevich! You're my son!'

'So you keep reminding me, father. But I'm also supposed to behave like an adult. Then just this once, let me behave like a *bogatyr'* and make my own way through the white world.'

'It doesn't seem right, somehow,' grumbled the Tsar. 'You shouldn't be riding about on a solitary horse as if it was all that you owned.'

The argument swayed this way and that for many minutes, but secretly Ivan was smiling. From long experience, he knew that when his father reached the stage of grumbling to himself in his beard, then willing or not he would grant whatever foolish request his children had troubled him with, and not grudge it to them till the next time.

Assuming there was ever a next time at all. . . .

CHAPTER FOUR

How Prince Ivan went journeying across Moist-Mother-Earth, and how he learned something to his advantage

Such a journey as was planned by Ivan Tsarevich was not something to be embarked upon lightly, carelessly or without thought. Many preparations were required before the first step could be taken. The first of these was when he brought the best of his horses, grey Burka, to a smith so that its hooves could be trimmed and all the animal's shoes replaced, both for the horse's comfort and for his own. Ivan didn't need to have experienced it to know that being lost on the empty desolation of the steppes with a horse which has thrown a shoe was one of the best places in all the Russias not to be.

Then he took his bow to be re-strung and his arrows to be re-fletched, straightened and given sharp new points. He took several spare bowstrings and a lump of fresh beeswax from the kremlin armouries, and while there he had both of his swords newly sharpened. The heavy, straight *shpaga* went on one side of his saddle, under his knee; but the sabre he hung on his belt, to balance his bow-case and quiver.

Ivan took no armour, except that his mother the Tsaritsa Ludmyla prevailed upon him to sling a round shield across his back. When all that was done, he put fresh clothing and several clean shirts into one of his saddle-sacks. Dried meat and smoked sausage, black bread and cheese, leather bottles of *kvas* and ale all went into the other, and then he was ready to take his leave.

High Steward Strel'tsin, astoundingly smug and pleased with himself since Prince Fenist's first appearance, gave him several letters of introduction to the abbots of monasteries which he might pass along his way. That familiarity with the route had caused Ivan to look at Strel'tsin very hard; but the old grey man had merely smiled and said nothing. His mother wept over him, for it was the first time that all her children had been gone from Khorlov; but his father the Tsar gave him silver for his belt and then hugged him hard before letting him ride out on his first adventure.

Ivan had no map of where his sisters lived with their husbands, nor had anyone told him which way to ride: but he knew it all the same. There were spells enough for that, small charms whose price was little more than a nagging headache between the brows and a lassitude little different from that which occasionally kept him sleeping late of a morning. It was a strange sensation, as if there was an invisible guide riding on his shoulder, steering him this way and that. He heard no words, not even the small voice of thought or of conscience that everyone hears at the back of their mind sooner or later. Instead, he had no more than a sense of this road being right or that track being wrong. It was a sense that served him well as he rode out across the face of Moist-Mother-Earth, keeping him from swamps or from brambles, leading him to the easier route up a hill or through a stand of trees.

There were few enough of those as he rode onward, for within a matter of days he had left the birch forest and the hills around Khorlov far behind, and had come to the wide steppe of the white world. Prince Ivan Aleksandrovich stood by his horse's side on the last hill before the Great Steppe began, a low mound dignified with the title of hill for no other reason than that it was the only place for *vyorsty* all around him that was higher than the rest, and looked out across the land to the east. It was a flat and featureless plain of swaying, whispering grass that stretched out on all sides to the uttermost edge of the world for as far as his eyes could see. Ivan had good eyes, if not quite so sharp as those of Prince Fenist the Falcon, but they saw nothing in every direction because there was nothing to see. The steppe was empty of trees, empty of animals, empty of houses, empty of everything. There was not even a horizon for a man to ride towards, for though the sky arched overhead clear and blue, where it swept down to join with the world there was no sharp-edged junction of earth and sky, but only a soft, blurring greyness where one haze dissolved into the other. Ivan patted Burka's neck and swung into his saddle, then rode down from the hill and away east, into the grey and the haze of the endless, eternal steppe.

*

He rode one day, and two days, and three, and before long learned that appearances were not everything. The steppe was less desolate than he had thought, although its inhabitants were not for the most part those with whom he could carry on a conversation and so relieve the boredom. The occasional scuffling of feet in the grass was more often followed by the brief sight of a hare sprinting for cover, or a quick flutter of apprehensive wings, than by the sound of a voice upraised in greeting.

There were a few of those, all the same. Hunters for the most part: rangy, weatherbeaten men who watched Ivan – and his two swords and his bow and his shield – with the wariness of the wild animals they hunted, until absolutely convinced that he meant them no harm. He shared more than one meal with the steppe hunters, if sharing was the proper word when, as often as not, the man he shared it with took pains to keep the fire between them at all times. Polite conversation, when the hunters gathered enough courage to reply, tended to involve traps and tracking, variations in the value of pelts and, every now and again, a muttered complaint about how difficult it was to find an honest fur-merchant nowadays.

As the days passed, even those contacts grew farther and farther apart. Ivan saw more wolves than he had ever encountered before in his life, and was grateful that he had chosen to make his journey during a time of the year when they had more to eat than passing Princes. He wondered when he would begin to see the monasteries that Strel'tsin had mentioned, or perhaps a village owing allegiance to one or another of his brothers-in-law.

Instead of which, he saw nothing but the steppe. At least there were no brigands to worry about. Brigands, Ivan decided, would not be so foolish as to come out here. There was little profit in robbing wolves and rabbits, and from the look of them not much more in robbing the hunters. He began to grow suspicious of the few birds flapping lazily across the sky, wondering which of them might be looking down at him and laughing; and then even the wolves and the birds went away.

*

For some days more Ivan rode without even a wolf to look at, until at noon on one of those long, depressing, monotonous days he saw more in the distance than greyness and haze. He reined in and stood up in his stirrups, the better to look at what it might be. There, far away – yet not so far as it might be – stood a palace and a kremlin, built of grey stone, roofed with blue tiles and set square in the midst of the steppe.

Tsarevich Ivan set heels to his horse and rode closer, watching narrowly all the while. There was no town surrounding the kremlin, nor any roads leading into it or out again. It just sat there, huge and handsome, as if it had dropped from the sky overnight – and Ivan, already suspecting who owned it, wondered smiling to himself if he was meant to ride in at the gate or drop through the roof and the ceiling. How he was supposed to do that with Burka beneath him, he hadn't a notion.

To his relief there was a gate in the wall of the kremlin, its wood painted blue as the sky and its nails of polished silver, and standing alongside the gateway was a tall birch tree. The kremlin and its palace was the first building Ivan had seen since leaving Khorlov, and the birch tree was the first growing thing which stood taller than the grass, so he paused to rest his eyes on them both. That was when he saw he was being watched from a branch at the top of the tree, where a bright Falcon perched and gazed down with sharp eyes.

Prince Ivan laughed as he saluted the bird, because he was glad to have reached the right place. There was a look about this Falcon, a brightness of the eye and a brilliance of the plumage that told him plainly it was more than just another of the hawks he had seen quartering the grassland in search of some unsuspecting mouse. The Falcon took wing, and when it had flown down it struck three times on the ground before

65

him and became a fine young man. 'Health to you, brother-in-law Ivan,' said Prince Fenist Sokolov. 'How does God favour you?'

'Well enough,' replied Ivan, dismounting. 'But the rest of the world wants me married.'

Fenist laughed and clapped him on the shoulders, and when servants had come to take care of Ivan's horse they went together into the kremlin and up to the palace. Yekaterina was there, waiting as though warned by her husband's voice that they were about to have company – and Ivan was the one to say that it was less than the truth. She ran down the great stairs and threw her arms around Ivan to welcome him, then immediately began asking questions about his life, and his health, and her sisters, and their parents.

Married life, thought Prince Ivan later, *agrees with her*. There had been no mention of lakes or cold water in the course of an entire conversation, and that was something of note; of course the conversation had been rather one-sided, since Katya had asked question after question without once giving him the opportunity to answer any of them. At length, Fenist the Falcon extracted him from Katya's grasp and showed him to the rooms in the tower which had been made ready for his visit.

After that, and rather pointedly, Fenist took him to where the bath-house was. Ivan wasn't surprised. After so many days in the saddle, his clothes were so dusty, muddy and sweaty that they would probably be able to walk back to Khorlov all by themselves, and despite his attempts at washing them and himself in rivers so cold they made the teeth ache in his head, the body inside the garments wasn't much better. The thought of hot water and steam, and soap and razors, was a pleasant one and worthy of his attention, because besides feeling dirtier than any Tsar's son should, the beard that was too light to be worth cultivating had grown back with a vengeance, and even though it was still all but invisible it was making him itch.

'Dry heat first, to start a good sweat,' said Fenist a few minutes later, waving a wooden water-dipper. 'Then thin steam, very hot.' He was sitting with Ivan in the steam-bath –

no longer two Princes, but just two young men wrapped in towels on either side of an iron basket of red-hot stones, flicking each other with water and amiably discussing the strength of the steam.

'Not too hot,' said Ivan, scrubbing the back of his hand across a jaw lined with pale blond bristles, 'and make it dense. These damned whiskers need wetting down and softening before I put a razor anywhere near them.' He laughed. 'None of the *bogatyri* in the tales ever have this trouble. They always get from one place to another in fine robes and bright armour, with never a hair out of place to upset their grandeur.'

'When you're a *bogatyr*', you pay your chroniclers well enough that they don't mention the dirt or discomfort,' said Fenist the Falcon, carefully pouring water from the dipper on to the stones so that the air in the bath-house was transformed at once into a thick fog.

Ivan sighed with pleasure and lay back on the slatted bench, feeling the moist heat soak into his bones and drain the ache out of his tired muscles. For the next half-hour, he decided, he would forget about the needs of the Tsardom and the requirements of the succession, about Strel'tsin and his lists, and about all the eager young women who wanted to be the Tsar's wife once his father died. It was unfortunate that he failed to warn Fenist the Falcon of his decision, for the Prince of the High Mountains had been asked for advice and before God he was going to give it.

'Have you ever asked yourself,' enquired Fenist, 'the same question that you asked your sister?'

Ivan opened one eye, saw nothing but a wall of white steam and closed it again. 'What question was that?' he mumbled drowsily.

'The one about "Who would you marry if left to yourself?" She told me you asked it that day in the garden, just before I arrived.'

'Never given it a thought.'

'Don't you think that you should? Or are you riding across the white world just for the good of your health?'

Though the fog was too dense to see the look on his brother-in-law's face, Ivan could imagine it well enough. The

67

tone of Fenist's voice had already told him that the Falcon Prince was learning certain tricks of speech from Yekaterina, and there was no reason to doubt that he had learnt the expressions to go with them. And maybe other things as well. . . .

Suddenly quite awake, Ivan sat up straight and stared into the blank whiteness where he was certain he could hear stealthy movement and the dripping of cold water. '*Skoro budet!*' he said. 'Stop right there! And put that dipper down at once!'

There was a pause in which nothing happened, and then a clatter of wood and a splash, and a laugh that came from out of the heart of the stream – well removed from where Prince Fenist had been sitting. 'And they tell me that *my* eyes are sharp!' he said. 'All right, Ivan my brother. *Ostavaysya.* Stay there. We'll continue this discussion over dinner and a glass of something good.' Ivan relaxed a little, but not completely until he had heard Fenist return to his own bench and sit down. 'Besides which,' the Falcon continued, laughing again, 'if we came to any conclusions without letting Katyushechka interfere with the process, she'd have us both in the moat.'

*

Prince Ivan was once more clean, and shaved, and dressed as a Tsarevich should be, and much refreshed after a few hours' nap on a bed far softer than the steppe with a blanket laid on it. He sat at the banqueting table in the Falcon's great hall, with meat and drink in front of him and more spread handsomely to either side, and drank wine while his sister and brother-in-law watched him indulgently. When he had pronounced it good, they fell to together.

After the first edge of their hunger had been blunted, and there was time for talk, Ivan pointed with his eating-knife at the great vaulted ceiling, at the rich rugs from Bokhara and from Isfahan and most particularly at the many servants and the great variety of dishes that they carried to and fro. Besides those he had tasted already, he could see *tsyplyata tabaka* from Georgia, and *kopchyonaya keta* from Siberia, and a great many others from equally disparate places.

'Maybe I'm tired, or maybe I'm slow, or maybe I'm just missing something,' he said at last. 'But I didn't see a single road as I came here across the steppe, and neither, *Knyaz' vysokikh gor*, did I see anything higher than tussocks of grass. So where have you hidden these high mountains of which you're supposed to be Prince?'

Fenist sat back in his chair and smiled at Katya his wife in a conspiratorial way. 'We have ways. We have means. The wealth of this realm is in building-stone rather than farmland, so of course we have ways and means of getting it to those who will pay well for good granite.'

'And that's all?' asked Ivan, quite rightly not satisfied with the reply. 'There has to be more to all this than just ways and means, even if . . . .' He pulled himself up short and grinned crookedly, feeling no end of a fool. 'Even if you can change yourself into a Falcon.' Shaking his head at himself, he drank some more wine to take the taste of short-sightedness out of his mouth. 'And more than that, I should think.'

'But something like that, *golubchik*,' said Yekaterina. 'We all go where we please, when we please. My Fenik isn't called the sorcerer's son without reason. Though,' and she smiled briefly, 'I could wish he might conjure up some way of keeping the estate ledgers in order without my needing to touch them. Now, while we're talking about reason: what are you doing? Hunting a wife, or avoiding a wife, or just staying far from home?'

Ivan played with his wine and toyed with his food, for a while reluctant to speak. Then he shrugged, one-shouldered just like the Tsar his father, and began to speak. All of it came out, about Strel'tsin and his lists, and the ambitious ladies who wanted to marry a rank rather than a man, and the constant quiet, nagging pressure both from inside and from out to make a choice, any choice, and settle down to carry on the Khorlov dynasty and ensure the safety of the realm.

They regarded him with sympathy, and listened without comment until he was done. Then Katya looked at her husband and nodded. 'We had guessed most of it already,' she said. 'What I had to live with, but worse. Four times worse, and more. So while you slept, Fenik and I had a long talk together and decided that we should send you to look for a bride of *our* choosing, and not one selected by that dry stick Dmitriy Vasil'yevich. Not immediately, of course: Vasiliy and Liza, and Mikhail and Lena, would have hard words with us if we kept you all to ourselves. You should visit them and stay a while before you go to find your wife.'

Ivan smiled, hearing the faintly bossy sound of the sister he remembered from his younger days. Sorcerer's son or no, Prince Fenist the Falcon hadn't smoothed off all her sharp edges, not by a very long way. 'You use "bride" and "wife" as if the wedding was already certain,' he said, then raised his eyebrows a touch when both of them chuckled. 'Just who is this paragon of all the virtues, and how am I going to know when I've found her?'

'You'll know when you meet her,' said the Falcon, and grinned at him. 'Believe me, you'll know.'

'How could anyone not know Mar'ya Morevna, *krasivaya Tsarevna*,' said Yekaterina.

'*Prekrasneyshaya iz tsarits vseya Rusi*,' Prince Fenist said helpfully.

Ivan's eyebrows went even higher up his forehead. He had heard the lady's name before, but from Guard-Captain Akimov rather than someone who was waving potential wives at him. The Captain had mentioned her casually, as a curiosity – a Princess who commanded her own army rather than letting her captains do it. It was a situation he disapproved of, and not because she was a woman acting like a man; Akimov was too pragmatic for that. What concerned him was an employer doing an employee's work; if enough Lords across the wide white world took such a notion into their heads, then a professional Captain-of-Guards like Petr Mikhailovich Akimov could find himself out of a job.

There had been no mention of great beauty, but then Akimov had been thinking financially rather than romantically. Ivan would certainly have remembered Mar'ya Morevna's style and titles had they been mentioned. He was accustomed to such things, titles which said something about those who carried them, but usually such titles were governed by some degree of accuracy. 'So she calls herself "the fairest

Princess in all the Russias", ' he said, unable to help the sceptical edge that had crept into his voice. 'I could always call myself "the wisest Prince". And who'd believe that?'

Katya looked at him, and her lips trembled as she valiantly restrained only the good God knew what sort of remark. Then she controlled herself, smiled like a sister and said, 'Everyone else calls her by that title. She doesn't. She calls herself by her name, and by nothing else: Mar'ya Koldunovna Morevna. That's all.'

'That's enough,' said Fenist, and his voice was not one inviting questions or quibbles. 'Her father, to whom God grant rest,' he crossed himself, as did they all, 'was an enchanter as skilled as my own father the sorcerer. Both of them did only good, and both of them taught the Art to their children. Mar'ya Morevna needs no titles than those she was born with; but she grew into the others.'

'Ah,' said Ivan, as carefully non-committal as he could manage, and let the matter drop as he began to talk of other things.

*

He stayed with his sister Katya and her husband Fenist the Falcon for three cheerful days and three comfortable nights, then judged it right and proper to take his leave of them, they having told him that he was expected further on. No rider had entered or left the kremlin in those three days, but Ivan knew well enough that his brothers-in-law had no need of horses when they had need of haste, so let his questions all go by unasked and unanswered. For his own part, he needed a horse and so saddled up grey Burka, secured all his weapons and gear and made his farewells.

'God guard you, my brother,' they both said, and all the many other words exchanged at such a leave-taking. But then Prince Fenist the Falcon came closer and laid his hand on Burka's reins. 'Ivan,' he said, strangely formal, 'I ask a gift from you, and give a warning in return.'

Prince Ivan glanced towards his sister Katya, and noticed that Fenist had taken care to leave her out of earshot when he spoke. 'Ask, and give,' he said.

71

The Falcon set aside his formality at once, leaning close in against the horse's neck so that he would have no need to raise his voice. 'We haven't seen you for almost a year, Vanya, and who knows what the next year will bring before you ride to our door again? Leave us your silver eating-knife as a keepsake, to remember you by.' Ivan, puzzled, but reluctant as ever to ask the questions which received only smiles or oblique and evasive replies, took the knife out of its case on his belt and handed it over. Fenist gave him another, a gold one, to take its place, then looked again at his wife to ensure that she still couldn't hear him. 'And beware,' he said, 'of Koshchey the Undying. Now ride on.' He stepped back, slapped Burka on the rump, and then he and Katya stood by the gate of their palace, waving, until Ivan could see them no more.

*

He rode onward and eastward, until as evening approached he came to a village. It was the first he had seen since leaving Khorlov, and though the people who came out to watch his approach were definitely peasants, even to their cross-gartered trousers and woven *bast* shoes, their houses were built of cut grey stone, as impressively sturdy as the town-mansions of his father's lesser lords. Carved into each wall and painted in blue and silver, bright against the grey, was the outline of a falcon.

Ivan spent that night in the headman's house, gossiping with strangers as he had not been able to do before. These people were not timid, nervous hunters but well-fed and well-protected peasants as sturdy as their houses. They told him of their lord, Prince Fenist the Falcon, and of the beautiful bride he had brought from a far country. Ivan smiled; he had not told them more than his name and that he was a traveller. After telling them the news and gossip from distant lands – which though not exactly current was much enjoyed simply for its novelty – he sat quietly, listened carefully and let them talk. He felt comfortably certain from their appearance and evident prosperity that the peasants were telling him the truth, rather than what they might want

72

to have reported back. Even so, being peasants, they told him little more than he already knew.

'Prince Fenist is a fine Lord,' said one. 'Have you admired the houses that he builds for us?'

'Your Prince builds them himself? With his own hands?'

The peasant laughed. 'God be good to you, sir! Yes, indeed: as I light this candle.' He furrowed his brow in concentration, and after a moment the candle-wick sputtered, sparked and put forth a tall yellow flame – whereupon the peasant muttered something under his breath and sucked on blistered fingers. 'Of course, Prince Fenist does it better than that,' he said, grinning, and poured everyone another cup of *kvas* . . . .

*

Ivan rode onward and eastward for thrice three days, and now the peasant villages were dotted here and there all across the steppe. Where once he might have ridden from dawn until dusk without seeing a single hut, now he could not ride for more than two hours together without at least one village, and perhaps two, becoming visible out in the distance. He stopped in one or another every night, paying for hospitality in the same currency as before – news, gossip, old tales and new songs. What in Khorlov had been impossibly outdated was fresh and exciting here.

Then the signs painted on the houses began to change, so that he saw fewer falcons and more eagles, and the peasants talked less of trade in stone from the high mountains and more of trade in leather, furs and cattle, until a day came when he no longer saw the falcon any more. At noon on that day, he saw another palace and its kremlin in the dim distance. This one was built of red stone and roofed with golden-yellow tiles, so that he knew at once who lived there. The gate of the kremlin was painted deep red, the nails driven into its wood were capped with solid gold, and growing tall beside the gate was a sturdy oak tree with an Eagle perched in its topmost branches. Ivan reined in his grey horse and saluted the Eagle, so that it flew down, struck three times on the ground and became Prince Vasiliy Orlov.

73

'Wealth to you, Tsarevich Ivan!' he said, embracing Ivan with his great arms until all the joints squeaked, 'and may God give you grace!'

'Stronger ribs would suffice,' answered Ivan, gasping somewhat, his face near the colour of Prince Vasiliy's coat. The Eagle Prince roared his great laugh and clapped Ivan between the shoulders in good fellowship that knocked out what breath was remaining. Once his brother-in-law had stopped coughing, and his horse had been taken to the stables, Vasiliy brought him into the palace where Yelizaveta waited to greet them both. She too threw her arms about him, and if Katya had learnt some gentle speech from her husband the Falcon, it was instantly plain that Liza had learnt how to hug from the Eagle. At least she had the patience to restrain all but her most immediate questions till later, so that it was no more than ten minutes before Ivan escaped to his rooms in the tower, and thence to the steam-bath to wash before dinner – and despite the creaking in all of his joints and his ribs, he grinned all the way there.

*

'Mar'ya Morevna is a fine woman,' said Vasiliy, paying her the highest compliment he knew, 'not only strong of will and mind but strong of body too.' Prince Ivan lifted an eyebrow at that. He had little patience with strength in any form just at this minute, for after Vasya's greeting he had taken strong steam for an hour and his ribs were still aching regardless.

'And beautiful as the sun in the morning,' said Yelizaveta Tsarevna. 'The fairest Princess in all the Russias.'

'Excepting, of course, present company – and her sisters,' said Ivan, speaking gallantly, but well aware of the moat.

'*Nikak nyet!*' The vehemence of Lizochka's denial was surprising: he had known his sisters far longer than their husbands and it was rare indeed that they – or in his experience, any other man, woman or child – would refuse a compliment that was honestly meant. Hearing all this was unusual indeed, and as she said more – about Mar'ya Morevna's beauty, and how much superior it was to that of other women – he found himself growing increasingly

74

intrigued with this mysterious Tsarevna. Ivan did not make such good company at dinner as he might otherwise have done, for he was lost in thought from that moment until he laid his head on the pillow and slept. But Liza and her husband Vasiliy the Eagle did not mind; instead they looked at his dreamy face, and then at one another, and they smiled.

The next day he was better company, and for the days after that while he remained a guest with them. On the third day, while he prepared his horse for departure, Prince Vasiliy came to him in the stable and asked for his silver eating-fork as a keepsake until the time he might return. Ivan gave it willingly and received a gold one in exchange, but once he had replaced it where the silver fork had been, he looked long and hard at the Eagle.

'Well, Vasya,' he said quietly, buckling a girth-strap as though the matter did not interest him at all, 'I suppose that now you'll warn me to beware of Koshchey the Undying. Just the way Fenik did: a warning without any explanation. Yes?'

'Almost,' said Vasiliy. The big man spoke without his usual bluff heartiness, which in itself was enough to make Ivan pay closer attention than usual. 'Consider the warning given, at least. As for the explanation, it's not much of a one. Fenist the Falcon might have given it, but your sister Katya was close by. Had she heard, she would fret without need. And anyway, you might have forgotten.'

Of course, Vasya would already know about that, thought Ivan. His skill at forgetting things had been a byword in the kremlin of Khorlov since he was a small boy, and an intermittent source of teasing by his sisters when they were unable to think of any more original torments. *The sorcerer's sons have their own ways of keeping in touch*. He abandoned his pretence of disinterest completely; given what he was hearing, it had been getting harder to maintain, and consequently thinner and more ridiculous, for the past few minutes. He gave the girth one final tug, really meaning it this time, and came out of Burka's stall. 'What would she have to fret about, needless or otherwise?'

'Koshchey,' said Vasya simply. 'What Fenik should have told you is that he's a wizard.'

'And you're a wizard, or at least the child of one. So's Fenist, and Mikhail – and if what I've been hearing is true, the beautiful Mar'ya Morevna is another! Thank you, Vasya, but if I'm related by marriage to three sorcerers' sons, and recommended by all three to marry an enchanter's daughter, then I doubt I should worry too much about Koshchey the Undying. For all I know, he's another relative.'

Vasiliy curled his lip in disgust. 'I hope not. He is *chernoknizhnik.* A necromancer. A dabbler with corpses and with worse than corpses. Nobody in their right mind would want to be related to that, either by marriage – or by any other means.'

Ivan said nothing, but he stepped past his brother-in-law and out into the sunlight with rather more haste than he intended. A small shiver had trickled down his spine like a drop of ice-water, and for the merest instant the stable had seemed somehow darker than it had any reason to be. All of it utterly foolish, of course, and just to be laughed at later, with a glass of good wine in one hand. And yet. . . .

And yet, Ivan could not put from his mind how he felt when the roof of Khorlov's kremlin tore open and sorcerous fire came stabbing through a rip in solid stone to blaze across the floor. A year ago, he would have dismissed the shiver as a reaction to some movement of air and the darkness to a shadow crossing the low sun. A year ago *volkhvovaniy,* the High Magic, was just another word written in a book. But then so were the words *krov'* and *bol'* and *smert',* and it didn't make blood or pain or death any less real for that.

The comforting weight of Prince Vasiliy's big hand settled briefly on his shoulder, and Ivan shook his head. It wasn't a rejection of the Eagle's reassuring gesture, but more the way a man will jerk his head sideways after swimming so as to get rid of water in his ears. Ivan had done it without thinking, but it was almost as if he was trying to shake the sombre thoughts out of his mind. The warmth of the clear blue day was doing something to warm his mood as well, so that when he turned back towards his brother-in-law and the stable, there was an expression very like a smile on his face.

'I don't plan to be related to him at all,' he said, 'or even meet him, if it comes to that. From what you and Liza tell me of Mar'ya Morevna, when I encounter her there'll be plenty to think about.' Ivan looked at Vasiliy, then grinned cheekily and cocked his head to one side. 'Assuming, of course, that this isn't all a joke. . . ?'

'Why not wait, and see for yourself?' countered Vasiliy. 'Now come, say goodbye to Lizochka and be on your way. Prince Mikhail the Raven and your sister Yelena are already waiting for you.'

Though he made no comment about them either then or later, Prince Vasiliy's words struck Ivan as slightly amusing: that with yet another journey of several days' duration ahead of him, he should hurry to get started because he was expected at the other end of it. It seemed that urgency took on a whole new meaning when one was able to fly the distance involved. Ivan grinned again and leaned forward to pat his mount on the neck. Burka was a good horse, but while his talents were many, flying wasn't one of them. . . .

*

He rode eastward, always eastward, for many days, constantly keeping his eyes open for the villages that dotted the steppe, so small in that vast emptiness that it was easy to believe they were not there at all. And then he found one of the monasteries that High Steward Strel'tsin had spoken of. Dmitriy Vasil'yevich had scarcely done it justice when he described it as a wooden building. The walls and Holy Gates were handsomely plastered and painted, though ordinary enough, but the church inside was not ordinary in the slightest. It was a wooden confection, a *kulich* feast-cake of softly weathered timber and gilded shingles, capped and capped and capped again with an extraordinary assembly of onion-shaped domes and cupolas, covered in gold leaf which caught the low sun and reflected it back as a rich glow. Tsarevich Ivan sat astride his horse in the monastery gateway, staring like a peasant and not caring who might see him. Then he made the sign of the life-giving cross, slipped from Burka's back and went looking for the abbot.

Ivan was reluctant to leave the monastery. The brothers

were if anything more eager for news than the most inquisitive peasant, due in part to the fact that they were supposed to distance themselves from the world beyond their walls. However, that distancing did not extend to ignoring that world when a part of it was living in their guest annex.

They had nothing but good to say about Ivan's brothers-in-law, and no criticisms of their sorcery. He found out why when the abbot gave him a guided tour of the remarkable church, whose interior was as richly carved and gilded as the outside was equipped with domes. Everywhere, inside and out, he saw the signs of falcon, eagle and raven; in one place they were painted on the surrounding frames of ikons, in another they were carved into the wood of pillars, sheathed in gold leaf and crusted with jewels. This was their church, and that of their family for generations back, and though the abbot professed not to know anyone by the name of Strel'tsin, Ivan's suspicions were finally confirmed as to the opportune first visit of three successful suitors.

He wondered what the High Steward had gained from it. . . .

*

'. . . . And these letters, Majesty.'

Tsar Aleksandr leafed through them. Simple sheets of paper and elaborate rolls of parchment with pendant seals, but all having one thing in common – they had come from far away at a speed that mocked the distance. He tapped one and looked at his High Steward. 'How have you managed this, Dmitriy Vasil'yevich?'

Strel'tsin lowered his eyes and made a sound indicative of modesty, but did not offer any explanation.

'Very well, forget that question. But answer me another one: why?'

This time the High Steward, First Minister, Court Sorcerer did not look away. Instead he gazed at his Tsar and said simply, 'To know things, and to keep the realm safe. Knowledge is power, power is safety. So.'

Tsar Aleksandr nodded. 'And my son? Will it keep him safe?'

Strel'tsin considered. 'Perhaps, Majesty. At least it will keep us informed . . .'

*

Ivan rode eastward, always eastward, for three days and three days and four, and at noon after ten days of riding he saw the kremlin and the palace he had hoped to see. It was all of deepest black, from the tiles of its roof to the stones of its walls, and its great gate with nails of burnished iron was painted in the bright and glinting black of freshly shattered coal. Beside that gate stood a pine tree, dark and tall, and in its highest branches perched the Raven, watching him.

Ivan reined Burka to a halt, but he neither laughed nor saluted, for in the shadows of that kremlin – where not even the wind made any sound – none of those things seemed right or proper. Instead, he slipped from his high saddle and bowed with all the courtesy that he would give to any wise and noble Prince. Above him, the Raven spread black wings and glided to the ground as silently as snow. It smote three times against the ground and became a fine young man clad all in black, who regarded Ivan with dark, wise eyes before bowing in his turn. 'Long life to you, brother-in-law,' said Prince Mikhail Voronov. 'God be between you and all harm.'

Ivan crossed himself piously, then laughed. 'Excepting flies and mosquitoes, He has been so far,' he said.

Mikhail eyed him quizzically. 'Then I must presume that big brother Vasya has moderated the enthusiasm of his greeting since I last went visiting,' he observed drily, 'and that little brother Fenya's idea of fun no longer includes waiting until people taking steam drift off to sleep before dousing them with cold water.'

'*Tak, tak,*' said Ivan, laughing again. 'I survived them both. It's always been said that the wise man knows his brothers.'

'Quite.' The Raven allowed himself a small smile, though he sounded drier than ever. 'And the wiser man, his sisters. We had best go in at once to make your introductions, before Lenyushka grows tired of waiting and does something we'll both regret. The moat,' he flipped a disparaging hand towards the still, dark water that reflected the sky from around the base of the kremlin ramparts, 'was cleaned out recently by my vassals, and restocked with fish – but I for one have no desire to check their work too closely.'

If Yekaterina Tsarevna had learned the use of soft words from her husband, and Yelizaveta Tsarevna had learnt boisterousness from hers, it was plain to Ivan from the first moment they met that Yelena Tsarevna had learnt a deal of cool dignity from Prince Mikhail the Raven. She was awaiting both of them in a great dark chamber that was larger than Tsar Aleksandr's Hall of Audience in Khorlov, seated in a high-backed chair which was not a throne and yet became so from the manner of her sitting in it.

Of carven ebony, the chair was figured with antique Chinese silver and inlaid with patterns of white ivory. That had been cut from the curling tusks of ancient elephants which now and again were discovered in the frozen lands far to the east of the great steppes. Scholars believed that they had roamed the world in a time long gone, when Moist-Mother-Earth was warmer and had more time for her stranger children. The elephants were gone now, so that only their prized tusks remained as a memory of their passing . . . . but Ivan knew better than any scholar that strangeness and wonder remained on the face of the white world.

'Travelling becomes you,' remarked Yelena, not moving from where she sat in her tall chair as Ivan and Mikhail walked towards her. 'My memory is of a beardless boy, who wanted to become a man; and now the man stands before me.' She stood up, with a rustle of the silver-shot black silk that she was wearing, and paused a moment looking at her brother. Then all her dignity was put aside as she flung her arms around Ivan's neck and hugged him tight. Only when she let him go did a little touch of that coolness return, and even then it was fighting with the smile which came as she put one hand up to a cheek reddened by contact with the bristles of a nine-day beard. 'And not *quite* beardless any more.'

She returned to her seat and appraised him with her head tilted thoughtfully to one side. 'Yes, indeed,' she said at last. 'My little brother has grown up. The others said as much – but I wanted to be sure. They were right. As am I,

Vanyushechka. Travelling certainly becomes you.' Yelena patted again at the scrubbed patch on her face, and grinned in the way Ivan remembered best. 'The beard doesn't. Get rid of it. And Vanya. . . ?'

'Lena?'

'Try our steam-house while you're at it. You smell most frightfully of hot horse—'

'—And unbathed brother. *Da!* I've heard it before.'

Ivan gave her his deepest and most elegant bow of salutation, although the general effect was distinctly diluted by his biggest and most sloppy-looking grin – the kind which had annoyed all his sisters since they were children together because they claimed it made him look like one of Tsar Aleksandr's less intelligent hunting-dogs.

'Ah yes,' said Yelena, resting her chin on interwoven fingers and smiling benevolently down at him, 'the world may turn and snow may fall, but it's good to know that some things stay the same.'

And thus put crushingly in his place, Prince Ivan went off for a bath.

*

Ivan might have thought that the kremlins of the other Princes had been sumptuous, but they were nothing beside the luxury and state in which Prince Mikhail Voronov and his wife Yelena kept themselves. There was no question that this was being done merely to impress a brother-in-law, so that he would say favourable things about the way in which the Tsar's daughters were being kept by their husbands. Mikhail the Raven lived in such splendour for no other reason than that it was the way he wanted it. His life was still more magnificent when set against the sombre majesty of the black and silver kremlin, so that Ivan Aleksandrovich – a Tsar's son and no stranger to rich surroundings – found it hard to believe his own blue eyes. Every once in a while he caught himself gaping at one or another rare object like a *kulak* just up from the country. When that happened he would smile weakly at himself, occasionally catching a glimpse of it in some finely polished surface or another, and pretend that nothing was out

81

of the ordinary. This fooled no one, neither his sister, nor the Raven, nor the servants, nor himself – but the effort, having been made, was respected.

Yelena and her husband paid him the courtesy of discussing only inconsequential family matters at that first night's dinner. It was plain that they both knew there was nowhere else for him to go after visiting with them except to seek his bride, and it seemed they wanted to give him a little ease before continuing with the instruction that the Falcon and the Eagle had begun. Knowing that, without needing to be told, it seemed to Ivan as though dinner on the second night came all too swiftly.

And with it came the lecture.

There was just one advantage about being given this particular lecture by this particular sister: Yelena, the youngest of the three, lacked Yekaterina's and Yelizaveta's practice in lecturing and badgering and generally ordering Ivan about. Her words were without much of the bite which either of her elder sisters would have put into them, and Ivan was grateful for it. Even so, what Lena lacked in cutting edge she more than made up with measured rhythmic phrasing and with wise maxims so oblique that there were times when Ivan wasn't entirely sure just what she was talking about. It was like being back in the tutorial room with High Steward Strel'tsin, only worse – because he couldn't find it in his heart to work up a good dislike of Yelena as he could do with Dmitriy Vasil'yevich, and without that refuge he had no choice except to sit quietly and look as if it all made sense.

There was a certain back-handed comfort about the carefully expressionless expression that Prince Mikhail Voronov wore like a mask throughout. It suggested that the Raven Prince was occasionally just as overwhelmed by his dear wife's powers of rhetoric, and that this once he was simply grateful that he could sit back and let it all wash over him without the need to make intelligent remarks. He and Ivan blinked back to full awareness in the same instant, both of them prompted by the same words.

'So then, what do *you* think?'

They were the sort of deadly words that might refer to

almost anything which Lena had said in the past quarter of an hour, and both Ivan and Mikhail were equally aware that neither of them would be able to make anything like the right kind of response. They looked at one another, and both of them could see the same thing: a moat newly refilled with deep, dark and extremely cold water.

It was Prince Ivan who finally chose to grasp the nettle, in a way that would cause least offence – unless of course Yelena was in a mood to take offence, in which case he knew from past experience that she could be very offensive indeed. He raised his glass and stared through the wine within it at one of the candles burning down the centre of the dinner-table. 'I think it's quite excellent,' he said. 'A good colour, a fine flavour, and evidently as well-travelled as you say I am.'

There was an ominous little silence as Yelena looked first at her brother, then at her husband, and finally back at her brother as being the most likely source of any joke being indulged at her expense. Both of the Princes looked as innocent as Archpriests, but Yelena Tsarevna knew her brother and her husband far too well for that to fool her. 'You two,' she said, 'bear watching.'

Ivan intensified his innocent expression until he felt as though he was going cross-eyed with the effort, and took great care not to say anything that might be subject to misinterpretation. Which meant that he said nothing at all until Lena's suspicion had abated. It took a few minutes, and several sips of wine, but at last she smiled. 'All right,' she said, 'so I sound like our own dear tutor and High Steward. That's enough to put anyone to sleep. At least you both did me the courtesy of staying awake – even if you *weren't* listening.'

Now that it was safe to do so, there was a quick round of throat-clearing and shuffling amongst the wine-glasses, before Ivan looked his sister in the eye and said, 'Liza told me all you've just said in half a dozen sentences.' He shrugged. 'Though I'm always glad to see people get good value from their words . . . .'

It took a few minutes for Yelena to tell him just what she thought of people in general and younger brothers in particular who thought that they could make that sort of remark and get away with it; a few minutes more while Prince Mikhail the Raven soothed her ruffled feathers, although there was an amused tone in his voice which suggested he knew perfectly well how much she was enjoying this little family fight; and several minutes after that while the remains of the present supply of wine was drunk so that the servants could clear the table and bring in fresh flagons.

Once that important piece of business had been taken care of, it was – inevitably – time for still more important and somewhat serious business. It began innocently enough, with Yelena Tsarevna and her husband the Raven gazing across the table with narrowed, thoughtful eyes which looked as though they had never, ever blinked. Ivan had been subjected to such scrutiny before, most often by his father the Tsar, but that did not necessarily mean he had to enjoy it, either then or now. Nonetheless he gave a good account of himself by sitting quite still and returning the examination through his own eyes – which could become cold and fathomless as blue mid-winter ice and like his father's could outstare a cat.

Except that while Yelena eventually found more interesting things to look at on the table, it became increasingly and eye-wateringly apparent that though Ivan could outstare the average palace feline eight times out of ten, Prince Mikhail Voronov was able to outstare a tiger cast in bronze. Finally Ivan pulled away his gaze with an audible little grunt of effort like someone who has been supporting a heavy weight for far too long, and only then did Mikhail the Raven sit back in his seat and pour more wine for his wife and for himself. 'I am impressed,' he said.

As the Raven leaned forward to push the wine-flagon across the table, Ivan saw with a little start that beads of sweat were catching the candle-light from high up on Prince Mikhail's brows. Evidently the effort had not been all on one side, and though no one paid him any compliments on that subject Ivan felt strangely pleased that he had acquitted himself so well.

'You have already heard,' said Mikhail Voronov, 'of Mar'ya Morevna, *krasivaya Tsarevna.*'

Ivan grinned: he had indeed, and if it wasn't quite enough

to whet his appetite – that being an unseemly attitude for a Prince to have towards ladies of rank – then it was certainly sufficient to bring him beyond curiosity and well into fascination. ' "Beautiful as the sun in the morning" was how Lizochka described her. Also strong, both of mind and of body.'

'And powerful,' said the Raven. 'Both as your father the Tsar would reckon it, in command of wide lands and brave armies, and – and as I and my brothers would reckon it – in command of bright magic.'

'*Koldunovna*,' said Prince Ivan thoughtfully. 'The enchanter's daughter. Vasiliy told me about that, a little.'

'He told you enough.'

Ivan stared again, as he had stared before; but this time there was a certain amount of feeling behind it. Impatience mixed with annoyance simmered behind that stare; the look of a man who had grown tired of subtle, mysterious replies that answered nothing; a man who was on the brink of asking hard questions and wanting solid answers, and be damned to manners and courtesy. 'And are you going to tell me more?' he asked, and though he kept the abrupt snap from his voice the echo of it was very plain. 'Or must I demand the information from you right out here before the good God and your wife, my sister?'

That same sister tut-tutted disapprovingly at him. '*Okh, Vanyushka!*' she said. '*Nakhal'no. Ochen' nakhal'no.*'

'No, my love, not rude,' said Mikhail the Raven, and he was a Raven without one feather out of place despite Ivan's outburst. 'Understandable, if nothing else. He has heard nothing but surmise and hint and vagueness ever since Mar'ya Morevna's name was ever mentioned. That would try the patience of a saint – and from what your sisters tell me of his exploits, Ivan Tsarevich is no saint.'

'More sinned against than sinning, all the same,' retorted Ivan tartly. 'You're becoming evasive again, Mikhail Charodeyevich. Are you going to give me an honest answer – even if it's only to tell me to mind my own damned business?'

'*Khorosho*,' said the Raven. 'All right. Then mind your own damned business.'

All the same, there was a twinkle in his eye as he said it – or was it the dangerous glint of a man and a Prince unaccustomed to being addressed so in his own hall and at his own table. . . ? Feeling a little knot of tension forming in the pit of his stomach Ivan wondered if, as he had done before on far too many occasions, he had overstepped the bounds of what anyone was willing to accept as a fair comment. He picked up his wine-cup, pledged Mikhail and Yelena as he drank its contents with an air, then sat back and waited for events to develop further.

'Of course,' said Prince Mikhail Voronov in a voice as smooth and suave as silk, 'you should realize by now that Mar'ya Morevna *is* your business. . . .'

'What makes you think that?'

'Because I know her. And I think I also know you – enough at least to make a guess at the way things might develop.'

Ivan glanced back and forth between the two of them, unsure whether to be amused or annoyed by all this. The reason for the annoyance was obvious enough, at least. 'I decided to go travelling,' he said, 'in the hope that it would get me away from the arrangers of marriages who fill Khorlov's kremlin at the moment. It looks rather as though they've been keeping pace with me all along.'

'We're not arranging your marriage, Vanya,' said Yelena. 'Just arranging a meeting between you and a prospective bride. After that, the decision rests very much with you.'

'So that once I meet the woman, if I don't like her. . . ?'

'You can leave again.'

'What does Mar'ya Morevna know about all this?'

Yelena glanced at her husband, who shrugged expressively and shook his head. 'Nothing, it seems. I'm glad of it. All of our arrangements have been one-sided, because anything more would leave us no better than Dmitriy Vasil'yevich Strel'tsin and his lists of ranks and titles.'

'I'm glad to hear it.' Ivan swirled wine around the inside of his glass and watched the garnet spirals smooth and settle. 'One last question on this subject: where am I to meet her?' Of all the responses he had been expecting, the most unlikely was a repeat of Mikhail's shrug.

'Somewhere,' said the Raven, and this time he no longer sounded like someone being deliberately vague for dramatic effect.

'You really don't know?'

'None of us is so well acquainted with the beautiful Tsarevna that we keep a track of all her movements across the white world,' said Mikhail Voronov. He smiled again, a little smile with little humour. 'She is a person who would resent such following, and her resentment is not something the wise would wish to attract.'

Ivan wasn't quite sure what to make of that, though he puzzled over its implications for several minutes while a fresh wine-flagon was opened, the cups were refilled and dishes of *medovye pryaniki* were set out on the table. Still puzzling, he took one of the sticky little honey-cakes and absently pulled it into pieces too small to eat but too large to ignore – especially when the crumbs adhered to his fingers and made taking an inspirational swallow of wine something of an adventure.

'Quite finished thinking it through?' asked Yelena, who had been watching the performance with the honey-cake and hiding a smile behind her hand.

'Yes, so far as thinking makes any difference.' Ivan wiped his crumb-and-honey-coated fingers rather ineffectually on a linen napkin, then set dignity to one side and licked them clean while his sister watched and rolled her eyes despairingly and giggled.

Ivan muttered something under his breath about that, but didn't bother saying anything aloud. There was another matter on his mind than honeyed crumbs, and it wasn't Mar'ya Morevna. He saved it until he was properly unsticky, then rinsed the sweetness from his mouth with a long draught of snow-chilled white wine and gave both Yelena and the Raven another of those long stares. There had been a lot of staring and gazing and considering during this dinner, one way and another, but this time he had another motive than simply proving how steady he might be under pressure. Ivan wanted to fix their expressions in his mind's eye, so that he could more easily see how they might change. He wiped his silver eating-spoon with the napkin and spun it on the table, around and around, before halting its rotation with one finger and sliding the spoon out towards Prince Mikhail and his sister. They looked at it and then at him, as he took one of the gold spoons from the table setting and dropped it into the case at his belt.

'Have mine as a keepsake,' he said softly, 'to help you remember me. And now I suppose I should beware of Koshchey the Undying. . . ?'

Ivan had been expecting some small change, so subtle that it would need all the sharpness of his eyes to see. Instead Yelena's face went white, a shocking pallor against the rich black of her garments and surroundings, and she crossed herself three times so vehemently that he wondered if he shouldn't have kept that subject private between himself and Mikhail Voronov. For his own part, Prince Mikhail the Raven shifted not a finger, not a muscle, not an eyelash: but the involuntary dilation of his pupils turned his eyes into pits of darkness that reflected only the flames of the candles, and those small as though very far away. The flames did not gutter, or dance in an unfelt wind, or burn low and blue. It might have been better if they had, for the very unchanging ordinariness of his surroundings was beginning to send chills down Ivan's spine.

'You are too easy with what you know nothing about, Vanya my brother,' said the Raven, in a voice such as a dead man might use. ' "Speak the name, summon the named." True or not true, be more careful.'

By now Ivan felt foolish and guilty and scared all at once. 'I spoke that same name to Vasiliy,' he began, reluctant as always to take refuge behind an excuse, and at the same time wanting to vindicate himself. 'Though he told me things about it, he wasn't shocked.'

'Perhaps because at his closest, he lives nine days' hard ride away.' Yelena had regained some of that terrible loss of colour, and some of the chilly majesty that Ivan had first seen around her but which had been put to one side once she became his sister again as well as the wife of a sorcerer Prince. It was very obvious that she was using that controlled grandeur as a prop, and as a shield so that Ivan could not see how she truly felt behind it. To find that his own sister felt such need to hide her real feelings from him was as unpleasant as any of the other abrupt revelations of the past few minutes, and left Ivan Tsarevich with no desire to upset her any further. 'Koshchey *Bessmertnyy* was said to live much closer to where we are now. We would as soon not have our kremlin here, but since you were travelling in this direction. . . .'

Already recovering from his initial embarrassed discomfort, Ivan noted two important things in what Yelena said: firstly – and as he had suspected ever since setting eyes on the palace of Fenist the Falcon – the kremlins of the three brothers were no more fixed in one place than a Falcon or an Eagle or a Raven would choose to be. Secondly, and right now much more to the point, Koshchey the Deathless was for one reason or another no longer a near neighbour.

'He was said to live? Then where is he now?'

'Only the good God knows that,' said Mikhail. 'There has been no mention of the old rattlebones for half a lifetime now; but just because you don't hear the wolf howl it doesn't mean he's not in the forest. That's why I would as soon you guarded your tongue when speaking his name, at least until you become aware of what it is you might be summoning.'

'A necromancer,' said Ivan flatly, not wanting the conversation to go spiralling off into aphorisms again. 'So Vasiliy the Eagle told me – unless he was wrong about that as well.'

'He was right, but less than complete.' Prince Mikhail Voronov leaned his elbows on the table and made a steeple of his fingers, gazing for a long time at their interwoven tips before he began to speak. 'Koshchey cannot die. He is Evil. Do you understand what I mean? Not merely evil in the way that someone may be wicked, but as a source of that wickedness. Koshchey *Bessmertnyy* is as evil as you are human, and,' the Raven unlinked his fingers and stroked one open hand self-consciously across the lustrous blue-black feathers that trimmed his robe, 'rather less likely to change. Remember it, Vanya. Lenyushka tells me that your memory was never of the best, but I would advise you not to forget the words you spoke yourself: beware of Koshchey the Undying. . . .'

Even the remark about his memory was not enough to provoke a reaction from Ivan, for it seemed to him that the fires in the hall were not as warm as they had been when dinner began, nor the candles as bright. He shivered, and even when the conversation shifted to more pleasant things, he drank rather more than was good for him and forgot Guard-Captain Akimov's advice on drinking enough water to keep the wine and vodka balanced.

*

That was why he had no memory at all of being helped to bed. Not that there was any room for memory inside his skull next morning, or even space for a coherent thought, because a pounding headache had filled it from nape to crown to temples so that even his brain was reduced to a hot cinder pressed against the backs of his closed eyes. After Ivan had been spectacularly sick he felt somewhat better; and when he had vomited twice more and drunk the long-delayed water he felt better still, even beginning to concede that there might indeed be a life before death, if he could survive long enough to live it – but it was only when he had taken strong steam with a determination worthy of a better cause that he was finally able to dismiss the notion of being measured for a coffin.

'Never mind my wife, your sister, getting good value from her words, Ivan Aleksandrovich,' said Prince Mikhail the Raven as he watched his brother-in-law reach for the water-jug in the gloom of his heavily-curtained bedchamber. 'You evidently get still better value from your food and drink. Whichever direction it's travelling.'

Ivan's mouth quirked at unpleasant memories and he swirled the water around his backmost teeth as if still trying to get rid of equally unpleasant tastes.

'*Nu, p'yanitsa,*' said Mikhail, rather more kindly. He poured clear liquid from a silver flask into the small silver cup that was its lid, and held it out. '*Opokhmelyaysya.* A hair of the dog that bit you.'

Ivan looked at the vodka-brimming cup with a bleary, jaundiced eye and made a sound like a cat with a fur-ball. But he took his medicine in a single wincing gulp – if not quite like a man, then certainly like something which ought to become a man once its hangover has gone away. 'Never again,' he said in a voice which despite an hour in the warmth and moisture of the steam was still ragged at the edges.

'Until the next time.'

Ivan would have glared at such inappropriate cheerfulness if his facial muscles hadn't still been hurting him. Instead he contented himself with another cat-strangling noise, drank another cupful of the vodka and lay back very gently on the wonderful coolness of the pillows. 'If I'm dead, bury me,' he mumbled as he composed himself for another attempt at sleep. 'And if there's a next time, I don't want to know.'

Mikhail smiled a small smile that crossed his face like the beat of a bird's wing, but bleary or not, that glint of humour was not so swiftly stifled that Ivan failed to see it. His dear brother-in-law was plainly wondering to himself just what the fairest Princess in all the Russias would think of this pessimistic would-be corpse as a candidate for her prospective husband, and the answer evidently amused him – although to Ivan's relief, for kindness' sake Mikhail didn't laugh out loud. Instead he put the flask of vodka and its cup where it could be found without Ivan having to move his head too much, and left the room to tell Yelena Tsarevna that despite his own insistence, her little brother was in fact not dead after all.

Prince Ivan watched him go, then closed his eyes and tried to convince himself of that as well.

CHAPTER FIVE

How Prince Ivan met an old drinking-companion, and what happened afterwards

By the time he was ready to ride away from the kremlin palace of Prince Mikhail the Raven, Ivan was feeling rather better; indeed, had he not been feeling so, his sister Yelena would never have permitted him to leave. Both of them fussed around him on the morning of his departure: Mikhail Voronov in a cool and understated way which would never have been called fussing by one who did not know him better than most, and Lenyushka in that charming fashion in which sisters have always taken care of their younger brothers' health and welfare. Ivan tolerated it with a good grace, but found a certain significance in the way that Prince Mikhail insisted on inspecting both his swords. 'Anticipation of trouble?' he asked.

'Nothing more than caution,' replied Prince Mikhail. He put one hand to the guardless silvered hilt of his *shashka* sabre and drew the weapon from its scabbard, turning the sabre this way and that, admiring the play of light and shade along its subtle curve of ridged and polished steel as he braced the back of the blade against his sleeve. The *shashka* made a thin metallic whispering as Mikhail re-sheathed it with a quick, economic movement, then clashed and rattled within its silver-mounted scabbard as he tossed it towards Ivan. 'And nothing wrong with this. Just mind your fingers.'

Ivan gave him a crooked grin as he hooked the sabre back on to his belt, arranging the hangers as he had been taught, so that it hung properly with the edge uppermost rather than curving downward like the scimitars of the Moslems. 'I haven't cut my fingers yet,' he said, 'mainly because I pay attention to warnings.'

'Just make sure you keep doing that,' said Mikhail, 'and you'll stay healthy.' He lifted the broad, heavy *shpaga* from where it lived under the flap at the left side of Ivan's saddle, and studied its hilt and pommel for several long, thoughtful moments before drawing out two handspans of the blade and no more. That was when he whistled, long and low between his teeth, and said, 'Old, and very pretty.'

Ivan wondered about the Raven's reaction. He had always thought the broadsword a cumbersome, outdated antique, and carried it for no other reason than that it had been in the Khorlov family since the time of Rurik the Northman. 'That thing?' His tone said more than any number of words.

Mikhail looked at him with something of a shocked expression. 'Yes, this thing! Look, it has "Ingelrii" written on the blade.'

'Is that what it says? I sometimes wondered.' Ivan sounded anything but interested, and managed to suggest that those times of wondering had been few and far between. 'I never learned to read the Roman letters – so many of them seem to be the wrong way round.'

Prince Mikhail the Raven shook his head, perhaps in despair, or regret, or even as a dismissal of some mild annoyance at Ivan's lack of concern over his own family's heirloom. 'This sword is far older than that. The letters aren't Roman, but the old rune alphabet.'

Ivan Tsarevich continued packing a saddle-sack with tightly folded clothes and merely raised an eyebrow. 'Does that mean something important?'

'It means this sword was made by the North people, before there were any Rus in the white world.'

There was a smile glinting in Ivan's eyes, even though he had managed to keep it from his mouth: the smile of someone who, though not sharing the enthusiasms of another person's pastime, has still shared – and suffered – their enthusiastic chatter too many times to waste any more breath on objections. Mikhail and Captain Akimov plainly shared a fascination for sharpened steel in all its manifestations, whereas Ivan could not really see the beauty and the interest but only the ultimate function of cutting flesh and causing pain. Swords he found particularly disturbing. Bows and spears at least had the excuse that they might be employed in hunting; axes could cut down trees, to build a house or a fire; knives could carve meat for food, or wood for use or ornament. Only the sword, of all weapons, was designed specifically for the killing of other human beings, and even the blunt, harmless, over-jewelled swords of state held their authority only as a reminder of what their plainer brethren could do if and when that authority required enforcement. For all his hopes of proving himself a worthy *bogatyr'*, Ivan was secretly glad that so far – though he had more than once drawn a blade in anger or in fright – he had never yet used one.

'I hope they both stay sheathed,' said the Raven as he returned the broadsword to its place, so that Ivan wondered how many of his own private thoughts had been visible on his face. 'With luck you'll not need weapons on this adventure.'

'Except for his own pretty smile,' put in Yelena Tsarevna, stepping out of the kremlin's tall double doorway on the tag-end of her husband's words. When she came down the black basalt steps and put her hands on his shoulders, Lena looked at his face as Mikhail Voronov had looked at the swords. Whatever she saw there pleased her, for she hugged her brother tightly, kissing him on the forehead and on both cheeks before releasing him. 'Go with care,' she said. 'Go with God. And remember us, as we remember you.'

Ivan grinned at her, as his sister; then bowed to her as the noble lady she became when she sat on the black throne in the black hall of her husband's black kremlin palace. He bowed also to the Raven, for though he was brother-in-law Misha – friend, drinking-companion and most recently adviser – he was also Mikhail Charodeyevich Voronov, *Knyaz' tyomnogo lesa* and a very great Prince indeed.

They stood by the great gate to watch him ride away, dwindling smaller and smaller each time he looked back until at last their small dark shapes were lost against the great black bulk of the kremlin at their backs. A little after that, when the kremlin itself had become dimmed in the grey haze of distance across the steppe, Ivan glanced back one final time –

and wrenched on the reins so that Burka came from a canter to a skidding stop.

There was a cloud on the far horizon where the kremlin had been, a cloud like the smoke of a great burning. Except that instead of rising in a column towards the sky, it was spreading out from side to side across the meagre horizon of the steppe. Spreading like the wings of some vast bird . . . . the black wings of a raven. Ivan watched, unwilling to believe his own eyes despite what those eyes had already seen within the past year, as the cloud rose up out of the horizon-haze and swept with ever-increasing speed off and away to the south-west. And when the cloud was gone, so was Prince Mikhail's kremlin. . . .

*

Ivan rode as he had done before, towards the east. There had been a few minutes on that first day when he had said very elaborate and anatomically complicated things in a very loud voice about his brother-in-law the Raven, most of which had to do with his failure to offer journeying relatives a lift towards their destination. But after he had cooled down a little, Ivan was able to laugh at his own outrage. Regardless of the doings of the *bogatyri* in the old tales, there was little to be said for an adventure conducted from a seat beside the fire of a magic castle which wafted its occupants wherever they desired in ease and comfort. Besides, the Raven's kremlin palace hadn't been going Ivan's way.

He stopped laughing and began to swear again shortly afterwards, when it started to rain. Fortunately it was not yet *rasputitsa*, the season of bad roads. Instead of settling into a solid drenching downpour, the rain merely sprinkled Ivan with enough water to leave him damp, uncomfortable and out of sorts, and then cleared away to let the sun make him start to steam instead.

As if the good God was having a joke, or *mat'-syraya-zemlya* was trying to prove the accuracy of her title, it rained on Ivan the next day as well. And the day after. By that time not only Moist-Mother-Earth but also he, and his horse, and his gear, and his food, and his clothes, were all as moist as they were likely to become without having spent a week submerged in the Dneipr – or perhaps the Volga, since that was much closer but equally wet.

Ivan Aleksandrovich had run out of sufficient energy to keep the rain at bay quite some time before, and had run out of original oaths within a very few minutes after that. He was reduced to repeating himself with as many elaborations as his somewhat damp mind could create until even those ran short of inventiveness. 'This weather stinks,' he muttered at last, stating the obvious as the last raindrop from the last shower dribbled miserably and ticklishly down his nose. Burka, just as wet, snorted his approval of the sentiment.

Then Ivan reined in and sniffed hard, coughed twice and sneezed that last raindrop from where it had no right to be, and realized that more than the damned weather was stinking. Literally stinking, too. He knew well enough that it was neither Burka not himself; his noble steed smelt very much like all noble steeds left out in the rain, and he had bathed in a small stream only that morning. Neither the weather nor the stream had seemed too cold until he had undressed beyond the point where it made any difference, and then the rain had started again. His shower-bath, as it had become, had been another tooth-chattering affair, but it had still left him a lot fresher than whatever he was smelling now.

And then he heard the hoofbeats. . . .

They came out of the drizzle like Perun's storm, ten of them, an *arban* of Tatars, too close to evade and too many for a fight to be more than a protracted form of suicide. Ivan's sabre was lost somewhere inside the clinging, sodden folds of his supposedly weatherproof cloak, and it was only when he reached for the heavy broadsword by his saddle that he learned just how far it had slipped down its rain-greased straps. By the time he had found the weapon's hilt and straightened with the wide blade half-way from its scabbard, Ivan Tsarevich discovered that he was looking at six Tatar arrows already on the strings of six Tatar bows, three hooked Tatar spearheads that looked set fair to follow the erring raindrop up his nose, and a drawn Tatar scimitar that might once have been Turkish and now rested on its owner's shoulder simply because pointing it at him under present circumstances would have been superfluous even for a Tatar.

The ten grinning, droopy-moustached Tatar faces would perhaps have been worst of all – except for the miasma of stench that hung around them like a cloud. Despite the stillness of the rain-washed, misty air, the Tatars and their scruffy horses were upwind of him and Ivan was getting the full aromatic benefit of their well-known lack of cleanliness. Even so, he considered it impolitic just now to do anything so provocative as hold his nose. The raiders looked at him, and when he let go of the hilt of his broadsword so that it dropped with a clank back into its scabbard they grinned even wider. The one with the sword grinned widest of all and uttered a laugh like the barking of a dog. He sniffed – a noisy, wet and thoroughly unpleasant sound – and said in clumsy but quite understandable Rus, 'Huu! Before, the steppes were clean, but now I smell a Russian smell!'

Then all ten of them leaned forward in their saddles, weapons poised, and watched Ivan closely to see how he would react.

For all that he was deadly scared, Ivan's first thought was of doubt that any of the Tatars could smell anything except for their own filthy selves; his second thought was that such a response was exactly what they were expecting, a good insult so that they could kill him. And his third thought was to wonder why, after all he had heard of these ruthless horsemen, they needed any kind of reason to start chopping him up. If they had been part of an invading army, he would have been dead long before he even reached for his sword, knocked out of his saddle by a swarm of arrows he would most likely not have seen released.

So what was going on. . . ?

His brain was racing faster than it had ever done when playing chess against the Tsar his father, for this time there was a higher forfeit to be paid than simply toppling a king of carven ivory. The arrows and the spears told him as much with tongues of rain-misted steel. He had to say something, make some reply so that they would not simply kill him on the grounds of insult by dumb insolence, and at the same time the very idea of some cringing acceptance of what had been said stuck in his throat more painfully than any blade. Quite probably they would kill him for agreeing with them anyway, for what man of the Golden Horde would ever respect a coward? Ivan could feel the beat of his own racing pulse, so loud and fast that it was a wonder the Tatars had not already noticed and done something that would still it. Only the soft dripping of spent raindrops from the furred rim of his hat concealed the beads of icy sweat which had sprung up all along his forehead.

Finally he bowed, deeply but not so suddenly as to startle the Tatars into starting something which only they would finish, and when he straightened up again he grinned at them as openly and honestly as he could manage. Confused, the Tatars glanced at one another and then at their captain-of-ten – who, so far as Ivan could see, was as confused as his *arban* troop but covering it rather better.

'Greetings to you, *bagatur*,' said Ivan, taking care to give the captain's rank its proper pronunciation and not the Rus one, which might have put that wickedly curved sword through his neck before he could correct the mistake. 'I salute the Sky-Blue Wolves, whose nostrils must be keen indeed to scent a Rus across so many *vyorsty*.' He took a quick, shallow breath, for what he said next would determine how long he was likely to live, and he had to appear bold rather than craven – but not so bold that the Tatars would think him better dead. 'Especially since, if your coats and hats are made from the hides and fleece of Russian sheep, you all must smell as bad as I. . . .'

There was a protracted and horrible silence while the *bagatur* captain digested this piece of information, and then translated it into the Tatar language for the benefit of his men. Ivan made sure that he could reach a weapon quickly enough to make his death so expensive that – if worst came to worst – those of this band of Tatars who survived would regret meeting him at all; but the making sure was only with his eyes, and he took care not to move until there was no other choice.

The sudden chorus of barking Tatar laughter was almost too much for his stretched and jangling nerves. He recognized it for what it was a bare instant before ripping the old Northern broadsword out from under his knee and doing as much damage as he could before they cut him down; and afterwards, there was no need.

'Who are you, bold Rus?' asked the captain, and directly he began to speak the laughter of his men cut off as abruptly as a snuffed candle so that their leader could make himself heard without need to shout.

Ivan thought fast, then faster still. Having avoided the risk of death, he was suddenly facing the risk of ransom – yet if he lied, he was heading rapidly towards the risk of death again, this time as a deceitful and untrustworthy person. It had always seemed peculiar that the Tatars, who lied and cheated as a form of military art, should place such value on the truth of those they dealt with. Finally he shrugged. It wasn't simply that he should be killed, but that it should happen because he spoke a lie. Ivan was a Tsar's son, and though that Tsar's realm was small when set against some others, yet the honour and integrity of that same Tsar's children should be something all could consider of more value than the purest gold.

'Ivan Aleksandrovich, *Tsarevich Khorlovskiy*,' he said, and this time his bow was a mere inclination of the head which would have done credit to the Khakhan himself.

'Huu,' grunted the Tatar captain approvingly, and proceeded to translate what had been said. As its meaning became clear, Ivan could see the glint of anticipated gold and silver growing in their slitted eyes. The captain's next words came as no surprise. '*Khorosho, Knyaz' Rusi*,' he said, 'you are now a guest. What else, we decide later.'

His next short phrases were in the Tatar language, and though the men with arrows took them from their bows and then put both bows and arrows back in the cases hanging from their belts, two of the other riders, those with spears, kneed their horses forward, turned them around at Burka's flanks and braced their spears so that the hooked steel points nudged into either armpit. Even through the heavy coat, they stung.

'You ride along with us—' the Tatar said and then, with an elaboration that Ivan thought completely unnecessary, continued, '—or be carried in a way you will not like.'

Ivan looked over each shoulder, at the long spears and at the flat, implacable faces of the men who carried them, shrugged as much as the upward pressure of sharp metal would permit and did just as he was bidden.

*

The Tatar camp, *bok* as it was called in their guttural language, was not so vast as Ivan had been told camps of the Tatars might be; but it was vast enough. The great horse-herds that milled about its edges, guarded by stocky riders astride equally stocky ponies, comprised three and perhaps more remounts for every fighting-man in the host, and each of those men had a *yurtu* – a hunched, dome-topped tent made of black felt – for himself and whichever concubines or captives he had decided should accompany him on campaign. The tents extended for a long way in all directions, even though they did not stretch to the horizon as the old tales said they should.

Certainly they went far enough to impress Prince Ivan, for he could see more of them than his companions. The two Tatars with the spears had decided that not only would it keep his hands in plain view and away from his weapons, but it would prove amusing to see how far they could lift their prisoner out of his saddle on their spear-points without doing permanent and devaluing damage – so that Ivan rode into the camp standing on tip-toe in his stirrups, with arms outstretched like the wings of a bird.

And a thin but constant trickling of blood running down inside his sleeves to dribble from his fingertips. . . .

That he had not complained or cried out when the spear-blades went through first his clothes and then his skin had most likely saved him from worse harm. A long time before, Guard-Captain Akimov had warned the pupils of his weapon-class that if a prisoner should chance to yelp at what a Tatar did, then the Tatar's casual response would be to see how much more loudly that yelp could be repeated. Ivan had forgotten Akimov's warning, as he tended to forget so much which had no direct influence on his own life, but it had returned forcefully when he had been praised for fortitude over a wrist fractured when he was thrown by an unruly, barely-broken horse. That he had thought the wrist no more than twisted, and therefore not enough to make a fuss about, had been something he had kept to himself. . . .

Thanks to the doubled thicknesses of coat and cloak, he had suffered little actual harm and less discomfort than seemed likely from the injuries. Though neither garment was as waterproof as had been claimed when he had bought them, when wadded together by the pressure in his armpits they served to keep all but the extreme tips of the eight-inch spear blades out of his flesh. The wounds themselves were probably less serious than some things he had done to his own chin when first let loose with a razor at the age of sixteen, and only Burka's jogging gait was keeping them open and producing that dramatic rain of ruby drops on to the horse-cropped grass. Except for the nagging, itching sting of broken skin, they hardly even hurt.

Although given his own choice in the matter, and the way his captors were chortling to each other at a volume that was increasing with the pressure of the spears, Ivan would as soon they stopped laughing and lifting – and quite soon, please.

Just as his brain formed the thought they did stop, and let him down; abruptly enough for the impact of his tail-bone on his own saddle to make him say the kind of word which a wise Rus keeps in check while within the confines of a Tatar camp.

'Hah! Good spirit, this one!' said another of the harsh Tatar voices, not one that he had heard before. Spirited or not, Ivan didn't repeat himself. Directly the numbing upward pressure was released, feeling came flooding back, so that now both of his arms were wrapped around himself, cuddling away a sensation that suggested he had tried to shave off his armpit hair with a blunted battle-axe while on horseback at full gallop. The cuts from the spear-points were of small account, but his own weight against them was going to produce the kind of bruised and outraged muscles that would leave him walking about like an animated scarecrow for several days to come.

He blinked several times before he could see more than little dancing red-hot sparks, and then focused on someone who – though as high-cheekboned, slitty-eyed and droopy-moustached as every other Tatar face he had seen so far on this increasingly unpleasant day – was still somehow familiar. And then, having recognized the face, his wretched memory obliged as it so rarely did – Ivan was a master at that sort of conversation which went on and on most amiably, but never addressed the other person because he could *not* remember the appropriate name – and recalled where and when that same face had been seen before. It gave him a name to work with, too.

Sub-khan Manguyu Temir, of the Golden Horde.

That warlord had been one of the high-ranking guests at the first, most expensive and least successful husband-finding feast in Khorlov. His presence had been more a diplomatic move by Tsar Aleksandr, since nobody – and certainly not the Ilkhan, since Tatars were not lacking in intelligence – thought that any of the Tsar's daughters would choose him above the round-eyed, white-faced and nominally Orthodox Christian youths who made up the bulk of the suitors. He had been there simply to imply to other, equally round-eyed, white-faced Christian Princes that the Tsardom of Khorlov might just have friends that no one could challenge with impunity. Ilkhan Manguyu had certainly recognized the deception for what it was, just as well as he knew sunrise meant morning and that rain was wet – and even so, to make it more impressive, he had bathed before the feast and worn clean garments during his attendance.

He was still wearing them now, something which suggested to Ivan that they hadn't been changed since. There was a certain unwashed tang in the air which might have been his captors, or simply confirmation of the thought. Manguyu Temir was clad in the robe of Persian silk that Ivan remembered from the feast, but this time it covered a long coat of lamellar armour, and the robe itself had been sadly re-worked and re-patterned with numerous long slits corresponding with shiny scratches on the armour, and with the stiff, rusty-purple blotches of old and recent blood. Though

Manguyu Temir might have been responsible for them, Ivan doubted that any of the stains belonged to the Ilkhan in their most proper sense.

Certainly not in the way that the stiff darkness of his own sleeves belonged to him. Ivan could hear his garments crackle as he bowed to Manguyu Temir over the pommel of his horse's saddle – high-peaked, and fortunately so, since that was the only thing keeping him on Burka's back right now – and wondered whether that sound implied that he had lost a lot of blood or just a little bit, spread thin. He was rather surprised, in a muzzy sort of way that suggested he had indeed dripped away more blood than was healthy, when the Tatar khan rattled out several orders which produced stalwart warriors seemingly out of nowhere to help him from his saddle.

There was a brisk chattering in the Tatar speech as the soldiers began to lead him away; presumably his captors protesting their loss of a valuable ransom. Certainly it was interesting enough that the two men who were supporting Ivan – what with one thing and another, his legs had refused to carry his weight – paused to hear what was being said.

As a result Ivan heard some of it himself, for the voice which he had identified as that of Manguyu Temir was speaking Rus. 'Idiots!' it said. 'Who gave you leave to make so free with any prisoner?'

The reply was in Tatar, but delivered in such a tone that the speaker had to be making some sort of weak excuse.

'So you wanted to test his courage, did you?' came the reply, more irritable than ever. 'And if you had tested it so that there was nothing left alive to sell back to his people, what then? Would you have paid the ransom? *Vakh!* Get out of my sight, before I deprive the Great Khan of ten soldiers!'

There was a damp thudding of hoofbeats followed by a long silence in which Ivan felt relief, curiosity, apprehension and a vast uncaring lassitude. Fingers gripped his chin and raised his drooping head, turned it from one side to the other and then – very gently – let it sag forward again. 'I know you, Rus, do I not, uu?' said Ilkhan Manguyu's voice. 'From Khorlov. The Tsar's son. Huu, I remember. It was just a year, and maybe less than that, since you poured drink into my cup, from courtesy to a guest and not through asking. And now look at you.'

From Manguyu Temir's choice of words alone, Ivan was glad there were no mirrors of German glass in the encampment. If a Tatar lord thought he looked ill-used, then prbably he looked like something dead warmed up, and badly, come to that. Certainly he felt that way. The throbbing in his armpits had diluted, but that dilution had caused the pain to spread, so that instead of two small points of wavering anguish on which he could focus some control his entire body was pounding with a low ache that refused to go away.

'I would rather not, just now,' he said with as much dignity as he could summon up. 'I probably don't look my best.'

The khan laughed harshly at such bold words and clapped his hands. Both noises hurt Ivan's head, though he didn't bother mentioning the fact. There was another string of commands, and in the intervals of trying to suppress his own reaction to the various aches and bumps and cuts and bruises, he saw that he was being helped towards the black *yurtu* tents.

Though normally the inside of a Tatar tent was the last place where Ivan would have wanted to be, just now he was feeling much too sore and weary to make any objections. However, the *yurtu* into which he was brought was most probably the Ilkhan's own, much larger than any other in the camp. Indeed, it was so large that it rested on the bed of its own wagon so that there would be no need to take it to pieces when the time came for the Tatars to move onward, and as a consequence the interior had not the sparseness of a transient dwelling but was comfortable to the point of luxury.

His escort made Prince Ivan comfortable on a cushioned couch, then made way for a much more elderly Tatar who carried a leather bag like the sort of satchel Ivan had come to associate with physicians. His half-formed guess was confirmed when the newcomer nodded his head casually and said, 'Juchi, *vrach*,' before proceeding first to inspect and then to dress the spear-wounds in Ivan's arms and chest with a speed and adroitness which suggested vast experience with the damage that a weapon left behind.

It was apparent from his skill that the old man Juchi was either the senior surgeon of this small army or, just as possibly, Manguyu Temir's personal physician. What made the latter supposition far more likely was the way in which he grumbled and muttered to himself during his work. *Vrach*, 'Doctor', was evidently the only word of Russian that he knew, because none of what Ivan said to him produced a reply, but the stream of Tatar that he uttered under his breath sounded so much like irritable criticisms of the soldiers who had done the damage that it seemed he shared his Ilkhan's view on the matter. No matter where a doctor might be found, and no matter how eager he might be to keep himself employed, it seemed that there was never one practising his art without at some stage needing to complain about those who forced him to its use.

Since there was no way he could begin, or once started continue a conversation with old Doctor Juchi, Ivan simply sat quietly and without complaint while the physician went about his business with bandages and pads of soft white cotton. Certainly he felt better at the end of the treatment than he had done at the beginning, well enough to protest at the cupful of *kumys* mixed with bitter-smelling herbs that was held out to him. However Juchi was like all those of his calling in that a patient saying 'No' became an immediate and personal challenge to his authority. Besides even that, the old man was a Tatar, a race not well accustomed to the refusal of their commands. Despite their lack of a mutual language, it was made clear to Ivan that either he could take his medicine willingly, or Doctor Juchi had it in his power to summon a sufficient number of guards and a large enough pouring-funnel that matters could become distinctly undignified.

Ivan considered his options for a few seconds – then with a feeble smile he took the cup and drained it in a single wincing gulp.

*

Whatever had been in the cup besides fermented mares'-milk, if its purpose had been to induce sleep then it was remarkably effective. When Ivan's eyes opened again – even though he knew that he had only closed them for an instant – the light outside the *yurtu*'s half-closed door curtain had that unmistakable rose colour of late evening. He blinked once or twice, just to make sure it didn't change to the more ordinary light of the wet afternoon he had just left, then ran his tongue over lips which had gone too dry for mere minutes to have passed. There was still a faint aftertaste of *kumys* in his mouth, and while he had never been especially fond of the thin, sour stuff there were always times, and now was one of them, when it could be most wonderfully refreshing.

Except that there was nothing to drink anywhere in the whole great space of Manguyu Temir's tent. Ivan verified that to his own satisfaction, because like anyone left entirely alone in a strange place filled with unusual and interesting things he spent a number of minutes in careful, surreptitious rummaging. When he had finished – and not because he had seen everything, but because it was becoming increasingly likely that someone might step through the *yurtu*'s flapped doorway and catch him in the act – he sat down on the couch again and wondered what to do.

He had learned something at least in his perfunctory search through Manguyu Temir's belongings. This khan, and by extension his small horde of some three thousand men, were not executing some decision handed down from the *kuriltai* of the Great Khakhan; they were simply raiding on their own account, like common bandits.

Ivan knew little more about the Tatars than what Captain Akimov had told him, augmented by the untrustworthy chroniclers who preferred their horror stories of atrocity and massacre to anything which might be of some use to a traveller. However, he was well aware that Tatars on a full-scale campaign of invasion brought their womenfolk and families along – though well to the rear of the army, the more easily to settle conquered territory after all the bloody work of conquering was done. But not, it seemed, this time. There had been no flimsy women's clothes in this *yurtu*, and no feminine fripperies except those which had been seized for their value rather than their appearance.

It was evident from these few scraps of evidence that Ilkhan

Manguyu Temir thought himself far, far away from the usual regions of Tatar influence, otherwise he would never have dared use three *minghanan* of the Great Khan's warriors as a means of personal enrichment. The Khakhan would take as dim a view of that behaviour as would any Tsar who discovered his Captain-of-Guards had been employing the soldiers under him as a personal band of brigands – although from what those unreliable chroniclers had to say about Tatar displays of irritation the punishment, though just as severe and terminal, would almost certainly be much more original . . . . and far more painfully protracted.

Someone outside flung the *yurtu's* door-flap up and back, flooding the tent's interior with that warm sunset light. It was no longer rose but darkening towards peach, and was further diffused by the doorway facing in an auspicious southerly direction, like those of all the other black tents Ivan had seen. The man outside was sufficiently tall that he had to duck his head to enter, but he straightened once he was inside and glanced from side to side as though expecting to find Ivan elsewhere than on the couch. If he was surprised, the big Tatar gave no sign of it. He merely saluted, by raising both hands level with his face and punching one hand into the other cupped palm as he inclined his head, and then spoke in heavily accented Rus. From the manner of its delivery the speech had only recently been learned by heart, so that it was unlikely the man knew just what he was saying. However, the meaning was quite clear enough to Ivan.

'Arise, Rus Ivan of Khorlov, for the Ilkhan Manguyu Temir, representative of the Great Khakhan Ogedei, commands your attendance at his table!'

Thanks to the ministrations of the good Doctor Juchi, Ivan was feeling sufficiently restored to resent being commanded anywhere by anyone who smelt the way the soldier did, and he noticed that neither the punch-salute nor the inclination were more than sketches of what they should have been. However – and since the Tatar was considerably taller, heavier and better armed – he speedily concluded that he should be grateful to get any sign of respect whatsoever. At least an invitation to dinner counted for something; following on the heels of Juchi's doctoring, that seemed a comforting assurance of good treatment towards hostages.

Of course, it was likely to stop abruptly if Tsar Aleksandr proved reluctant to pay ransom for his captive son. Manguyu Temir would be just the sort of Tatar lord who would maintain his people's reputation for casually vicious behaviour, if he thought the gift of a trimmed-off ear or finger would encourage the Tsar to make up his mind. Ivan thought about it for a few shuddersome seconds, and then spent several more wishing he had not and trying to forget the entire subject. He was not helped in that endeavour by the two burly Tatars beside the cart-*yurtu* that was his destination, for both of them were busily engaged in lopping off the heads of a dozen or so sheep. It mattered not one whit that they were butchering animals instead of men: in Ivan's present mood, neither the sight nor the sound nor the smell of fresh blood did anything to make him feel more cheerful, even though no matter what else would be presented on the Ilkhan's table, he knew the meat was fresh enough.

This *yurtu* was almost as big as Manguyu Temir's own and actually seemed larger, since all the impedimenta of living had been pushed to one side or stacked along the walls and the centre of its felt-rugged floor was now an open eating-space. The furniture was simple enough, cushions for sitting on and low tables that were no more than wooden planks trestled across boxes: but it was their covering which made them splendid. Each table was draped with a mismatched but extraordinarily beautiful variety of cloths and fabrics, from the intricate woven rugs and carpets of the Moslem countries to the delicate translucent silks of distant China. Threads of precious metal glistened softly in the light of many lamps, and no two of those lamps was of the same design. Every one of the rare valuable things under the dome of that black tent was different in some way from the next, whether by form, or age, or place of origin.

Ivan Tsarevich could feel the fine hairs on the nape of his neck lift a little, for he knew that he was looking at the cream of a plundering that had engulfed empires, kingdoms, towns and farmsteads. The price of all that jumbled beauty could not be measured in the gold or silver that might normally have purchased it – but only in the rivers of blood which had been spilled to bring it here.

'Huu! Our guest the Rus! Sit with us! Eat and drink!'

Ilkhan Manguyu Temir waved a drinking-cup in Ivan's direction. To his vast relief it was an ordinary cup of plain turned wood and not the silver-mounted skull he had been half-expecting. In fact there were no skulls on the table at all, nor any prisoners under it, supporting the planks with their bodies as the Tatars were sometimes said to make them do. All in all, it would have seemed a tranquil enough dinner, had it not been for the thought of what had surely happened to all the original owners of the finery strewn so carelessly around – and had it not been for the other diners.

Seated around the tables were thirty-three Tatar officers: the captains of thousands and the captains of hundreds, all of them armoured in coats of lamellar scales polished so brightly that each scale reflected back the lamplight like a mirror. Many, like their khan, wore decorative robes over the metal, but those who did not were clad from neck to knees in a shifting coruscation of small lights. They were slit-eyed professional warriors, as cruel as cats, as emotionless as an abacus, and they would have been both terrifying and magnificent . . . .

. . . . Except for the way they smelled. And that left them simply terrifying. Prince Ivan constantly reminded himself that he was here as an invited guest, but to be the invited guest of a lash of the Scourge of God meant only that he was in the presence of that Scourge by sufferance instead of suffering. There was uncomfortably little difference in the long run.

As he took his seat at Manguyu Temir's right hand and facing the fortunate south, Ivan Tsarevich discovered yet another truth in the many useful things which Captain Akimov had told him. A man can only be scared of nothing for so long; after that, either something happens to justify his fear or gradually he ceases to be frightened. That was happening now. For all his apprehension of the company and his surroundings, these Tatars had so far offered him no violence: indeed, quite the reverse. His wounds had been cared for, he had been given a place to sleep in their khan's own tent and now he had been invited to share a meal. The payment of the piper had not yet been demanded, and until then Ivan Aleksandrovich determined that he would enjoy the tune.

He knew the rules about speaking to Tatars encountered unexpectedly: never to ask them 'From where?' or 'Where to?'; never to ask them 'How many?' or 'For how long?'; and most of all, never *ever* to ask them 'When?' It made for stilted conversation at best, and there was less talk at dinner than he had expected, even between one Tatar and the next. It seemed to him that the words which were spoken had been given thought and scrutiny before their utterance. The reason was simple to understand: none of the Tatar officers, except perhaps their khan, were certain how much or little of their language Ivan really understood. It was easy for a man to claim ignorance of a certain subject, but to such masters of dissimulation as Tatar captains-of-thousands, the claim and the actuality might be as far apart as sun and moon.

Only Manguyu Temir said much to his guest and that was on insignificant matters such as the quality of Ivan's horse, the care given by Doctor Juchi or, strangely like a Rus, complaints about the past inclement weather. They spoke also about the food, when not engaged in eating it, and Ivan was glad that he could give it honest praise.

Inwardly he was glad that he liked the taste of mutton, for each and every one of the dozen sheep he had seen killed was on the table in some form or another, whether roasted, fried or boiled. The most curious dish, and thus the most entertaining to a stranger, was served in its separate parts of a bowl of sharp hot sauce and a platter of thinly-sliced raw meat for each diner, and a curious deep pot filled with savoury stock. This pot had a chimney rising from its centre so that the stock formed a moat around it – and a fiercely bubbling moat at that, since the chimney allowed the slow burning of hot coals in the thick base of the pot, thus keeping the stock at a boil. The principle was straightforward enough: that each man should spike his chosen slice of meat on a skewer and cook it as he preferred it, then dip it in the bowl of sauce and eat it with whatever vegetable or rice took his fancy.

Being Tatars, of course, Ivan's companions could not leave a good thing alone without augmenting it. In this instance the augmentation was a forfeit: that if a man should have his slice of meat come adrift from the skewer while it was cooking in the stock, then he would drink a cup of *kumys* for every person sharing that pot with him. It meant however that at some tables, the loser was swilling down eight cupfuls hard on the heels of one another.

Ivan watched all of this, and the increasing rowdiness it caused, and made certain that – since he shared his table and the bubbling stock-pot with Manguyu Temir and eight of his captains – any piece of meat he put on his skewer was impaled there to stay until he pulled it off again. Finally, when he judged he had survived long enough for manners, he pleaded pain and weariness as reasons to take his leave. Ivan took care to ignore the looks of contempt from those officers who understood his words and would not have let so trifling a matter interrupt their feast. But then he was just a weak and half-grown Rus, while they were Tatars and the accredited Scourge of God.

The Ilkhan Manguyu looked up from his contemplation of nine brimming cups of *kumys*, the consequence of misplacing his last slice of mutton somewhere in the seething depths of the stock-pot. 'I have made my choice, Tsarevich Ivan,' he said tipsily – that lost slice of meat had not been the first – 'and from this moment you are no longer a hostage. I know the Rus of old; they are a ridiculous people who never know when they have been properly defeated. Unless I surrounded you with soldiers, you would only escape or be killed in the attempt. Either way I would still lose your ransom, or lose the use of whatever number of my soldiers were needed to guard you. All that is too much trouble just now. Instead you are free to go. *Urrrp!*' The khan's slit eyes widened momentarily as a truly monumental belch erupted from his gullet, then closed down again. 'The instruction has gone out. You are to be neither halted nor hindered by any in this *bok*, once you choose to leave. Now stay a while. There is plenty left of food and drink!'

Ivan bowed low, thoroughly relieved and genuinely

grateful, even though slightly insulted that the khan was setting him free because his nuisance value outweighed any other. The thought of trying to escape from the midst of this horde of enemies had hung from his shoulders like a lead weight, and now he felt poods lighter – but not so much lighter that he wanted to freight his stomach with yet more *kumys* and mutton. 'Thank you, Lord, but no,' he said. 'I bid you and all your officers a pleasant night, and a clear-headed morning.'

Manguyu quaffed the contents of his sixth cup and grinned at Ivan over its rim. 'And you, Tsar's son Ivan. Be safe. After all, we'll want to capture you again when we finally decide to conquer Khorlov. . . .'

The burst of coarse laughter which accompanied his words – first from the khan himself and then from all his officers – made Ivan sure that he had heard no threat or policy but just a nasty jest. With that in mind, so that his face would help to give the lie some basis in mock truth, he joined them in their laughter.

Then he left and went back to the tent assigned to him, where he lay open-eyed on the couch until some degree of control had come back to his body.

*

Ivan woke next morning with only the back-taste of very sour milk to remind him of the Ilkan's dinner-party. It was yellowish grey outside, that muddy colour preceding dawn, but the Tatars were already up and about. Indeed they were taking down their camp even as he watched. *Yurtu* tents were disappearing into improbably small packages; first the felt coverings, rolled and tied into tight cylinders, and then the cane or wicker frames. Ivan had passed the night in Manguyu Temir's own *yurtu*, that very first one where he had been brought with spear-wounds underneath each arm, and he had been untroubled by anything – either the tent's owner, or other Tatars, or even dreams – except for a vague memory of rapid hoofbeats in the early morning which had roused him just enough to see that it was far too early to be getting up.

Those hoofbeats had probably marked the arrival of a courier, and what Ivan was now watching was a result of the courier's message. Already groups of horsemen were moving eastward, ten by ten by ten in the Tatar way. Others were bringing up two-score yokes of oxen that were needed to pull the great cart-*yurtu*. When he saw that, Ivan began to dress as quickly as stiff joints and a delicate head would let him. His own coat had been rendered useless but either Ilkhan Manguyu himself, or someone acting on his orders, had added a new coat to the pile of Ivan's clothes. This was rich scarlet, furred with black fox and embroidered with thread that was solid gold sufficiently soft to take the indentation of a fingernail.

Dressed, but unsure where either his horse or the rest of his gear had gone, Ivan emerged from the cart-*yurtu* just as the oxen began to swing it around and on to the line of march. He watched that delicate manoeuvre with interest – the thing turned clumsily, and too much haste would have flattened every lesser *yurtu* around it, something that it seemed not even the Ilkhan could do without recrimination. And he was so busy watching that he was almost trampled by the arrival of his missing property.

The Tatar who led Burka was none other than the *bagatur* captain-of-ten who had captured him only the day before, and though the man had the flat and impassive features of his race he still managed to convey what he thought of Ivan going free without resorting to anything so crude as a snarl or oath. Ivan simply smiled, and caught Burka's reins when they were flung at – not to – him.

'When at last we come to Khorlov,' said the Tatar, 'it will please me to sit you on a spear.' He said no more, but wheeled his horse about and galloped away.

That captain was the only one among the three thousand strong host who gave Prince Ivan more than an incurious glance. The rest were more concerned with riding or driving as swiftly as they could in the wake of the early-departing vanguard. Manguyu Temir was nowhere to be seen. Probably, thought Ivan, he was leading from the front, holding his head and wishing that the good God had created a breed of horse that walked more smoothly than the rest for mornings just like these.

Prince Ivan watched until the last *yurtu* had been

dismantled, and until the last squad of riders had gone thudding away into the brightness of the sunrise. Then he crossed himself three times and muttered a small prayer of thanks for deliverance. After that, he hobbled Burka so that the horse could graze but not wander far, rummaged in his gear until he found his own bed-roll and blanket, lay down on the ground and quite deliberately went back to sleep.

*

Ivan woke up again in full daylight, somewhat more refreshed by three hours of sleep in the fresh air than he had been by an entire night within the confines of the *yurtu*. He had no intention of going any further east until tomorrow, since that would give the Tatars a full day in which to draw ahead of him. Whatever warning, command or instruction the pre-dawn courier had brought, Ivan Aleksandrovich wanted no part of it. Even so, a day spent doing nothing was a day wasted from the few he had to spare. He grinned sourly at nothing. A year ago he had given hardly any thought to what might be involved when at last he began to search for a suitable bride to secure the succession and the Tsardom. Certainly he had never dreamt that time – or the lack of it – would play a part in his considerations. But every day of idleness, every day in which Khorlov remained a realm without an heir, was one more day in which the Great Princes of Novgorod and Kiev might decide their patience was at an end.

His day of idleness, uneasy though it was, went by more quickly than he would otherwise have thought. Ivan hadn't really been idle, he had crisscrossed the Tatar encampment on horseback just to get a feel of its sheer size, but it had felt strange to ride about without continuing in one direction for hours on end, and stranger still to finish more or less where he had started. There had been little else to do, or look at. When the Tatars moved out they had thriftily packed up every last pin, or comb or broken knife and taken them for re-use or repair.

When at last Ivan set off in the wake of the small Tatar army, he moved at a slow and cautious pace. He had no intention of overhauling them, and no desire to be caught unawares a second time by their outriders – and if that meant moving with the timidity of a virgin at a spring fair, then so be it. One afternoon of spear-points jabbing underneath his arms was quite enough for any single lifetime. And yet, despite his care, Ivan did indeed come up on Manguyu Temir's host more suddenly than he had intended.

He saw the smoke from a long distance away, dark streaks rising above the wearisome flatness of the steppe to climb straight up into a clear sky. It was strange smoke, too dense for the traces of cook-fires and yet – his mind hesitated over the conclusion – not thick nor heavy enough to signal the sacking of a town. But a village or a monastery, was another matter. Ivan found himself regretting that he had not taken his mother's advice. The Tsaritsa Ludmyla had warned him that if he took a shirt of mail he would never need it – although she had been very much mistaken when she said the same about his rainproof cloak.

Reining Burka to a halt, he sat very still himself before accepting that this time he should be prepared for whatever bold adventure the good God might send his way. Ivan loosened both his swords in their scabbards, and unslung the shield which had been jarring his shoulder-blades all the way from Khorlov. He exchanged his riding-whip for the mace that hung from his saddle, and made sure that his cased bow and arrows were close to hand. Then he considered what to do. The choices were limited: go on, go back, go around or stay just where he was. None of them was appealing, but playing the craven appealed least of all. Tsarevich Ivan took a long, deep breath that shuddered only slightly in his throat, and rode on.

Without the constant breeze which on every other day had sighed across the steppe, it seemed as though Moist-Mother-Earth had held her breath. The beating of Ivan's heart and the hoofbeats of his horse were an intrusion on the silence of the white world. The weight of the mace dragged downwards from its strap around his wrist, a constant reminder that he might have to raise that weight and bring it down upon another living being. He sighed; in the old tales, even though they were meant to behave with forbearance to all the world, no *bogatyr'* was ever so reluctant to fight his enemies. Ivan had not realized that it would be so hard to play the hero of his childhood dreams.

Then all the dreams were shattered by the hammer of approaching hoofs. Prince Ivan ducked behind his shield, and without thought the iron mace was already poised to strike. He looked just once at the wicked flanges of its striking surfaces, shivered deep within himself . . . .

. . . . And exchanged no more than two clanging strokes with the five wild-eyed Tatars who galloped frenziedly towards him, before they were past and gone.

Burka reared and danced, squealing, pawing the air, as eager for combat as his master was reluctant. Ivan fought his mount down again and stared in utter confusion at the five distant riders. He had never heard of such a thing – that five Tatars should meet a single Rus and not attempt to capture or kill him. There was more: in the brief glimpse as they thunderd by – and the nearest had cut at him more to clear him from the path than for any other reason – he had seen blind terror on each slit-eyed face. Prince Ivan was not at all sure that he wanted to meet whatever could put such fear into a Tatar, for it was widely known that they were wary of their Great Khan, and of thunder, and of nothing else in the wide white world.

Ivan's lips skinned back from his teeth in a death's-head grin that contained no humour at all. He had already faced the question, and made his own choice in the matter: to ride on and come face to face with the adventure. At the very least, he could be as the Tatars: he could see what it was they saw – and then if necessary he could run away.

The land stretched out beneath the towering columns of dark smoke was not so flat and featureless as in all other places. It was dotted everywhere with lumps and bumps and tussocks, as if low bushes had been seeded broadcast all across it, and it had a fuzzed look as though barley had grown between the bushes. Between stark emptiness and this low vegetation, it was the perfect place for an ambuscade. Ivan felt the old familiar tension gathering in his stomach, a fluttering like the wings of trapped sparrows. There was no sign of the other Tatars, and though he had slowed Burka to a walk he knew he might be moving deeper into someone's trap. Then the horse jolted to a stop, snorting, and refused to take another step. Tsarevich Ivan could not blame his noble steed for that, because he was looking at the remainder of Manguyu Temir's horde – three thousand Tatar horsemen – and every one of them was dead.

There were no tussocks or bushes, and never had been. Only corpses. They lay where they had fallen, like peasants taking their ease in a field of standing barley. Ivan turned his head from side to side, staring, struck shock-still in the saddle of his stock-still horse. The barley-stalks were the shafts of innumerable arrows and the barley-heads were brightly painted fletchings. The field had been well ploughed by the slashing downward strike of sharp steel heads, and by the scrabbling fingers of dying men, and it was richly watered with their blood. The smoke – that strange smoke which had been neither one thing nor another – trickled upward from the blackened skeletons of burning cart-*yurtuy*. It hung over the plain, freighted with the heavy smell of scorching horsehair felt, a fitting monument for many, many murdered towns.

Ivan looked at the devastation, and he felt. . . .

Nothing.

Ivan had never seen death, either in family or friends. He had not even witnessed one of the judicial executions that happened so rarely in his father's Tsardom. These Tatars were the ancestral enemies of the Rus but, even so, Manguyu Temir killed in falling from a horse he might have regretted: the khan had been kind to him when there was no reason to act so. Doctor Juchi dead of the extreme age he wore like a badge of office would have made him sad. But this . . . . this could not be grasped, either by the mind or the imagination. It was too vast.

If you must do murder, he thought, *do it on a scale like this. Or even bigger. Then no one will believe it really happened.*

This, however, was not murder but the aftermath of battle. It was described in *byliniy*, epics made in the courts of Lords and noblemen whose warriors had seen the reality of war, and smelt it, and wiped it from their swords and armour. Peasant *skazki* ignored it, pretending that such things never happened, that all battles were a glitter of steel and a sheen of gold. As he closed his eyes and muffled his nose in his kerchief, Ivan wondered why. Everyone bled when they were cut, peasants and Lords alike – though the great Princes chose not to accept that view any more .... not since they had begun to use their peasants as foot-soldiers. He swallowed and was grateful to whichever god – old or new or White Christ – had made sure that he followed the Tatar horde so soon. Ivan had been told what battlefields could be like in summer, when the freshness had gone from them and the crows and wolves and blowflies had become intimate with the unburied dead.

Who did this? The unvoiced thought rattled through his head like dice in a cup. Whichever general had bested so redoubtable a foe in open battle was either a friend, or someone to avoid – and until he knew which action was appropriate, Ivan was at a loss for what to do next. 'Who did this?' he repeated. Burka flicked his ears, but did not venture any further information. At last Prince Ivan stood up in his stirrups and shouted the question at the top of his lungs, the only sound to be heard all across the desolate field. 'If there is any man here still alive, tell me: who defeated Manguyu Temir, and vanquished this Tatar horde?'

No one spoke that he could hear, and nothing moved that he could see – until a spearhead reached out and tapped him on the shoulder, so that for an instant the blood froze in his veins. Ivan held out his hands, open and empty, and only then he turned. Ten warriors stood behind him, with swords drawn, or spears poised, or arrows on the string.

Their captain saluted with the spear that had touched Ivan's shoulder, then looked from side to side across the field and stared at Ivan long and hard. 'Your question has a simple answer,' he said. 'These were vanquished by our liege lady, Mar'ya Morevna, *krasivaya Tsarevna.*' The captain paused, and his spear dropped from the salute to rest its point beneath Prince Ivan's chin. 'And now you will come with us to meet her.'

Ivan looked down at the braced spear and then at all the

other weapons. 'Then bring me to her presence,' he said, brushing the spear's point aside as coldly as a Tsar's son should; but inwardly he smiled. *Falcon, Eagle, Raven*, he said to men who were not there, *you told me I would meet this lady, oh, my brothers! But I wish that you had told me when and where and how. . . !*

CHAPTER SIX

How Prince Ivan met Mar'ya Morevna, and what he later learned concerning ears and mirrors

Leading his horse by the bridle, they escorted Ivan around the edges of the battlefield instead of straight across. It was something for which he was grateful, since he had seen more than enough of it already. Soldiers were working their way through the bodies, recovering spent arrows, discarded swords and all the other things for which the Tatars had no further use. Ivan shuddered slightly, thinking that they were also killing the wounded: but when he summoned up the nerve to look more closely, he realized that there were no wounded left to kill. After such a storm of arrows as had fallen here, there could only be the dead.

'Your liege lady fights fierce battles,' he said to the leader of the escort.

The captain, a grizzled man with a beard that was the silver-shot grey of a badger's pelt, glanced at him and smiled slightly. It was the weary expression of someone who had also fought fiercely today, but in it was the tolerant amusement of a long-serving soldier who had probably heard every prisoner's attempt at inconsequential chatter several times over. 'These were fierce enemies,' he replied, 'and their intentions for her people and her land were not such as any ruler would permit.'

'But they were Tatars!' said Ivan. 'Three thousand of them!'

'*Tak*,' agreed the captain, 'that they were.' He managed to suggest his surprise that anyone could think it made the slightest difference where Mar'ya Morevna was concerned. 'And now they're dead Tatars. Best kind.'

Ivan gave up, with the feeling that if he was the only person still alive around here who was impressed by the Tatars' reputation, then he was heavily outnumbered and might as well forget it. Certainly he felt much more at ease with this escort than with the Tatars who had captured him; these soldiers at least had the courtesy to keep intrusive spear-points from his person. He looked around some more, ignoring the corpse-strewn battlefield as best he could, although it took considerable effort not to stare in horror at what some of the archers had to do to get their arrows back.

Far more pleasant was the war-camp of white tents towards which he was being guided, even though its location was rather a surprise. Guard-Captain Akimov had managed – after much perseverance – to teach him something of the other side of war, about forage, about rations and about the disposition of an army and its baggage train, both while on the march and on the field of battle. It was the boring part, the one which came before descriptions of the *boyaryy* in their shining armour, riding noble steeds which neighed and pranced and shook their manes, but never needed to be groomed, re-shod or mucked out, and never kicked or bit anyone except their master's enemies. Very little of that teaching had stuck in Ivan's head; his fondness had always been for the sparkle in the story, never for the elbow-grease from which the sparkle came. But one of the few things he did remember was that the camp and the battlefield were kept apart, for fear that an enemy raiding party might break free of the main engagement and leave their opponents without food, fresh horses or a place to sleep. It was an enticement and something to avoid, so the white tents with their gold tassels and banners set up along the far edge of this field indicated either stupidity and an ignorance of the rules of war – which was nonsense, since proof to the contrary was scattered all round – or haughty arrogance in the face of superior odds – which was unlikely, since the camp was more than twice the size the Tatar *bok* had been – or a suggestion that Mar'ya Morevna planned her battles so completely that the risk of raiding enemies did not arise.

Which, given what had happened to the Tatars, seemed absolutely certain.

They stopped in front of a pavilion that was larger and finer than all the others, and the captain went inside while Ivan sat quietly in Burka's saddle, awaited developments and admired the pavilion's richness. Its tasselling and fringes had the deep lustre which comes only when such things are spun from solid gold, and though there was no wind, and only the barest movement of the air, the banners overhead were made of silks so delicate that they still rippled with slow waves like the deep Ocean-sea, their colours shining wonderfully in the bright sunshine.

A servant carrying a golden cup came out of the pavilion and offered it to Prince Ivan. The cup was filled not with *kumys* or *kvas*, but with such a good golden ale as might have been drunk in celebration by the old North people, his ancestors. It was the drink that Ivan would have chosen above all others, to slake his thirst and ease his weariness, and finding it here was the granting of an unasked wish. He took the cup and turned to face the unseen eyes which he suspected might be watching him from within the shadows of the pavilion, and said, '*Mar'ya Morevna, krasivaya Tsarevna, prekrasneyshaya iz tsarits vseya Rusi, za vashe zdorov'ye!*' He raised the cup high to pledge that health, then put it to his mouth and drank with such a will that when he returned it to the servant it was empty. He heard laughter, and hands clapping in approval of his feat, and Mar'ya Morevna came out of her tent to greet him face to face.

It was as if a fist of fire and ice had clenched around Prince Ivan's chest, for it squeezed the air out of his lungs so that he could not breathe, and it squeezed the blood out of his heart so that it surged instead up to his brain, drowning the buzzing of the ale with a thunder like the beating of a demon drummer. It felt, indeed, as though he was falling under a spell – and if so, Ivan had no wish to resist it. He could see Mar'ya Morevna smiling at him, and he could see the looks her guards exchanged with one another, but Ivan could really, truly see only one thing that mattered.

All that had been said concerning Mar'ya Morevna fell far short of the truth.

Although she was without doubt the fairest Princess in all

the Russias, the words of her title did not describe more than that and could not begin to do her justice. The beautiful Tsarevna was like a precious ikon, made all of burnished gold and silver, jewelled with sapphires and with steel so that she was like the sky and snow of Mother Russia. Her hair had been braided and caught up beneath her helm, but now it was released and hanging free along her armoured shoulders and her spine, as pale and gilt against the silvery polished iron as the noon sun striking snow. All her wars and her campaigning had left no more mark upon her than a soft golden tanning of skin which had the pale blush of a setting sun on snow. Her eyes had the bright blue of sapphire gems and the dark blue of the Ocean-sea, all blended with the cool grey of the clouds that bear the winter snows to Russia, and though she was as tall and stately as a queen, and forbidding in her armour, when she smiled she was as warm and sweet and gentle as any woman that a man could love.

Prince Ivan looked on her, and loved her, and was lost.

Mar'ya Morevna glanced at the half-dozen guards who still surrounded Ivan, though they had been most courteous about it and not once prodded him with spears, and dismissed them with a wave of her hand. 'This man,' she said, 'is not my prisoner.'

'I am your prisoner, Tsarevna,' Ivan replied, and bowed gracefully low in his saddle. 'Your beauty has made me so, as swords and spears could not.'

'Health, wealth and long life to you, Tsarevich,' she said, smiling gently at his courtly speech. 'Where does the good God lead you? Is it a journey travelled by your will, or against it?'

Ivan grinned and shook his head, still dazed with Mar'ya Morevna's beauty, but with that question and its reply he was on familiar ground again at last. 'Brave men, my lady, do not journey anywhere against their will!'

'I'm very glad to hear it.' Her blue-grey eyes rested on him again, the eyes of a sorcerer's daughter, seeing more than most. 'Well then,' she said, in the tones of one reaching a decision not entirely unpleasant, 'If your purpose is your own, and you are without need to hurry anywhere, stay to eat bread

123

and salt with me.' The beautiful Tsarevna studied Ivan once more, liking what she saw; it was plain enough even to those who had not sorcerers' eyes that Ivan also liked what he was seeing. 'And it would please me,' said Mar'ya Morevna, softly as falling silk, 'if it pleased you, to pay me a visit, and perhaps even to rest a while in my tent . . . .'

*

Prince Ivan Aleksandrovich paid a visit to her tent later in that same afternoon. He went in, and for a long time neither he nor Mar'ya Morevna came out again, since it was evident to every man and woman in the Tsarevna's host that she had matters of importance to discuss with this young man. His visit lasted two nights, and two days, and the most part of a third, and how much Ivan might have rested – if at all – was no concern of anyone except himself and Mar'ya Morevna.

Whatever else had or had not happened in the passing of those two nights, Mar'ya Morevna's army could see plainly when their liege lady emerged from her tent that she loved Ivan Tsarevich just as much as he loved her. If that assumption needed any confirmation, then it was confirmed without a doubt when the beautiful Tsarevna sent at once for her personal chaplain, and commanded him to prepare a wedding ceremony of appropriate magnificence which would be performed as soon as they had all returned to her own lands and to her kremlin palace. Thereupon she summoned all her captains and commanders, and let it be known that here present campaign against the Tatars was now at an end – though many were of the opinion that it was less because Manguyu Temir's horde had been defeated than because Mar'ya Morevna now had something much more entertaining to occupy her time.

Kanonarch Protodeacon Sergey Strigunov had been chaplain to Mar'ya Morevna since first she inherited her father's lands and sceptre. He had consoled himself for remaining in the religious service of a known enchantress with the knowledge that neither the lady nor her father had done anything but good with the powers and wisdoms at their command, and now he made haste to be about her latest bidding. Protodeacon Sergey was a wise priest, with a proper respect for his lady, for her temper and for the placement of his head, which he preferred to keep securely on his neck. For these reasons he had never lectured her on the advantages of marriage or the disadvantages of leading her armies into battle, but it made his heart glad to see that at last she had made up her mind to settle down. He was, however, more reluctant to assume that this would mean she would behave like a proper wife and mother, and in that Kanonarch Protodeacon Sergey Strigunov showed his wisdom yet again.

Letters of invitation were sent out by messengers mounted on the swiftest horses in Mar'ya Morevna's stables; courteous letters for the most part, to Ivan's family in Khorlov and – after several days spent in trying to find where their kremlins might be – to his three sisters and their husbands. Less courteous and more sharply worded letters were also sent to the Princes of Kiev and Novgorod, inviting them to the wedding while at the same time advising them to curb their ambitions.

The wedding was as magnificent as was proper, when the bride was known to be the fairest Princess in all the Russias. And all the Russias were there. The great Princes of Novgorod, Boris and Pavel Mikhaylovich, arrived together, riding side by side on white horses. Neither one had trusted the other to be left behind, and neither trusted what the other might say if permitted to travel alone in such company as was coming to this wedding.

With them, and watching them, was Yuriy Vladimirovich, who had ridden all the way from Kiev to see with his own eyes what manner of woman Khorlov's heir was taking as his wife. All of them had heard Mar'ya Morevna's name before as a commander of armies, but only as something to be heard, commented lewdly upon or smiled at, and then dismissed as the quaint indulgence of some elderly spinster past marriageable age who had given herself flattering titles and commanded the captains of her army to claim that their orders came from her.

The reality, as they discovered, was somewhat different. Tsar Aleksandr arrived with Ludmyla Tsaritsa and High Steward Strel'tsin on the same day as his daughters and their husbands, and for some hours afterwards there was a deal of talking, laughing and even some tears. The Tsar's eyes were torn between the beauty of his son's bride and the strength of her armed host as it drew up in battle array on the meadows beyond her kremlin. When Mar'ya Morevna was not there to distract him, he watched the soldiers with Dmitriy Vasil'yevich by his side, and both old men gained a deal of innocent pleasure from the expressions of frustrated rage that blackened Yuriy Vladimirovich's face.

In Ivan's memory, the wedding ceremony itself blurred into a rich, confused tapestry of sounds and scents and colours. Some parts were more clearly recalled than others: the many blessings and signings with the twin and triple candles; the smoke and heavy perfume as censers of solid gold swung back and forth, back and forth; the soaring sweetness of the singing, and the voices of Archpriest Vladimir and hieromonk Nafanail as they led the anthems in their glorious deep bass that seemed almost to thunder in the very bones of those who heard it. But most of all Ivan remembered Mar'ya Morevna's hand in his, and the warmth and softness of it, and the unaccustomed tremor in the voice of a warrior lady as she spoke her responses. He remembered the stinging in his eyes which came from more than just the incense smoke, and the cool weight of the golden wedding ring which had been his great-grandfather's, brought from Khorlov by his own father now that at last he had found some use for it. That use had been found indeed, for now it gleamed on Mar'ya Morevna's hand as her ring gleamed on his.

The rest had been like any of the other three weddings he had attended recently, excepting only that it was he and not someone else who slipped away as the festivities reached their height, and it was he who was the butt and not the source of all the old rude jokes which surface at such times.

The jokes, the food and the drinking had all reached their end at last, but Ivan had not seen them end. For him there had been candle-light, and soft warmth, and a shared cup; there had been darkness, and silence, and the gentle sound of breathing not his own; and at the end of all there had been content, and an end to loneliness, and sleep with his own dear wife cradled in his arms.

*

Mar'ya Morevna came up the steps of her kremlin two at a time, paused at the top to take off her armoured gloves and helmet, then strode through the great doors, acknowledging the salutes of her guards with a wave of one hand as she went looking for her husband.

Prince Ivan was in the library, consulting maps in an attempt to chart his journey from Khorlov and finding that either all of the cartographers had been so wrong that drunkeness was their only excuse – or that he had travelled a much longer distance than could be justified by the number of days he had spent on horseback. Given that he had been keeping company with his sorcerous in-laws, whose kremlins were never in the same place two days running, it was possible that the cartographers had been right all along. He glanced up as the door was opened, then smiled and put the maps aside the better to embrace his wife.

Ivan had long since stopped wondering how he fell in love so fast, and long since given up suspecting that some kind of spell had been involved, for the more he thought about the matter the more he realized that he was simply following what seemed to have become the custom of his family. Katya, and Liza, and Lena – and even their father the Tsar, if truth be known – had all recognized their wife or husband in the first moments of meeting and had needed no questions after that. After almost three months of marriage, Ivan knew that he was following yet another family custom in that he had never been happier.

He kissed Mar'ya Morevna and hugged her tight, but when they had released one another Ivan looked at her with his head quirked on one side, eyeing her armour and her sword. He reached out one hand and tapped his fingertips over her breasts. It made a small metallic click, as his nails struck the rings of a mail-mesh so fine it represented almost a year of someone's life, making the rings and then weaving them into a clinging, lustrous fabric of steel. 'Pretty enough,' he said,

'But scarcely the most feminine of garments. Why,' Ivan continued, putting a question he had often pondered but only just now thought to ask, 'do you, *krasivaya Tsarevna*, lead your armies in person instead of paying a professional? There must be any number released from the Emperor's service in Byzantium.'

'Probably – but they would see my realm as the source of their pay and nothing else, whereas I – I see it as the responsibility and the duty handed down to me by my father, God give him rest'—she crossed herself, as did Ivan—'and the people are *my* people, mine to rule, but by that token, mine to protect to the utmost.' She smiled, knowing that her reply sounded exactly what it was, something carefully considered and rehearsed against the day it would be needed. 'Is your question answered?'

'Half-way.'

Mar'ya Morevna groaned and rolled her eyes, but continued to stroke her fingers through and through Ivan's fair hair as he poured her a cup of *beryozovitsa*, only stopping – with a small, friendly tug – when he held the birch-beer up to her. She took the cup and drank from it, slowly and thoughtfully, gazing at him all the time from above the rim. At last she put the cup aside, went to the door of the library, turned its key and smiled. 'Then help me out of these unladylike iron garments,' she said, 'and after that, if you still want to, ask me the other half.'

A little time went by, and then a little more, before Prince Ivan went back to the library door and unlocked it again. He turned, folded his arms, leaned back against the door and said, 'Now answer me the other half.'

Mar'ya Morevna finished lacing up the doeskin shirt she wore beneath her armour, then looked at her husband and raised both her eyebrows. 'I suppose,' she said, 'that I should really have expected you would be persistent in this matter as well.' She sat down and swung her booted feet up on to a convenient table. 'So ask me the other half – or how can I answer?'

'Simple enough. Wherever did you learn to lead an army?'

'Simple indeed. My father taught me, and paid

professional soldiers to teach me what little he didn't know. He brought them from Byzantium, of course, and from the Moslem Caliphate, and even from the Tatar Khanates in the east.'

Ivan laughed softly, shaking his head in disbelief. 'I had to ask, hadn't I?' he said. 'Very well, beloved, you win the match.'

'But . . .?' said Mar'ya Morevna, and drank her birch-beer with a bold air. 'I know you: you're not finished with the questions yet. There has to be a "but" hiding somewhere in that handsome head.'

This time Prince Ivan laughed out loud and struck his hands together. 'All right, you win the match and gain an extra point!' He pushed himself upright and came over to the table before his wife could drink all the *beryozovitsa* and rescued the remaining cupful for himself. 'But – there, are you happy now? – but why would a father train his daughter to lead an army in the first place?'

'My mother died bringing me into the world,' said Mar'ya Morevna, making the sign of the life-giving cross, 'and my father was not such a man as would marry again. He said he had been as happy with my mother as he had any right to be, and it would do no honour to her memory, or that lost happiness, to take another wife. So there were no other children. No sons. I was his only child, so I grew up to be both a daughter and a son. By the time I became the ruler of this realm, I knew better than most men of my age how to command its armies in the field. So there seemed no reason why I should not.' She emptied her cup and set it down. 'It seems I have a certain talent for it.'

'So I saw,' said Ivan, remembering a Tatar horde served as they had served so many others. 'And who will you be fighting next – unless I'm mistaken about the reason for all the training that I've seen this past few days?'

'Observant one,' said Mar'ya Morevna. 'I go to finish what was started on the day we met.'

'More Tatars?'

'The rest of them, the balance of Manguyu Temir's horde. Remember what you suspected – that they were raiding for profit rather than preparing the ground for an invasion?' Ivan nodded his head. 'You were entirely right. The khan had half a *tuman* under his command, five thousand men in all. We know now where the remaining two thousand are and, more importantly, where they'll be in three days' time. And then,' Mar'ya Morevna closed her fist, 'I'll return the favours they bestowed on the towns and people in my care.'

'Kill them all?'

'*Yest', tak tochno,*' she said ironically. 'Of course! How else does one deal with that sort of people?'

'Five thousand dead in . . . how many weeks?' If Ivan's voice was a little faint, it mirrored exactly how he felt. The love for his wife never diminished and never would, no matter what she might do; but a respect for her ferocity was increasing by leaps and bounds. And of course she was right. Manguyu Temir's actions had been no more than those of a common brigand – but given chance, or opportunity, or perhaps so small a thing as the Great Khan's indigestion making him pugnacious, and the Tatars would roll over all the Russias and stamp them flat. If wariness over how many would survive to do the stamping made them hesitate and think again, and send their hordes another way, then it would do nothing but good.

So long as he thought like that, Ivan had no time to think of all the blood and corpses it involved. . . .

*

'I want to come with you!' said Prince Ivan between his teeth. 'I *ask* this.'

Her mind made up, Mar'ya Morevna shook her head. Ivan breathed out through his nose and swore great inward oaths, although outwardly he was silent, seeing clearly just how ironic was the present situation. If asked questions on the subject of the coming battle, he would have conceded that he was no warrior and so would have preferred not to be involved in such butchery as he had seen before, but now that his wife had left her household and her kremlin and all her wide realm in his charge, he felt like a child denied a treat and left at home. Ivan did his best to curb his temper, knowing that it threatened to make him sound just as petulant as the way he felt.

'Vanyushechka, my love,' said Mar'ya Morevna, 'I know what angers you, perhaps better than you think: but I met you when I began this war and I have a strange fear that I might lose you when I end it.' She touched his hand, and felt the tremor that neither fear nor cold but the angry pride of one who would die sooner than be called a coward. 'My father always warned me that I should be wary of such fears. He and I, we knew more than most about such things.'

The trembling in Ivan's hand eased somewhat and Mar'ya Morevna watched him with her beautiful eyes until she saw what might become a smile. 'Let me make a bargain,' she suggested 'This time you stay here, away from whatever loose horse or stray arrow casts its shadow in my mind. And next time, *I* shall stay behind and let you lead the army. I might even practise my embroidery.'

This time Ivan did smile, though it was still somewhat thin. 'All right,' he said. 'I agree. But I hold you to that bargain. Just don't'—his smile grew warmer—'expect *me* to embroider while you're gone.'

Mar'ya Morevna laughed and kissed him. 'No, indeed!' she said. 'I expect you to guard and rule. Go everywhere, watch over everything. But Vanya, I expect something else as well.'

'Name it, *golubushka*.'

'Remember what I told you: these are my people, not yours. Not yet. As you guard and as you rule, remember that and treat them kindly so that they will come to treat you so. I would have you loved as I am loved, and as I love you, but that love is earned and not gained by marriage. Do you understand me?'

'Have I been so arrogant, these past months?' asked Ivan, surprised.

'No, never,' answered Mar'ya Morevna. Then she smiled at him, and there was a glitter of wicked humour hiding in its depths. 'But then, you've never had a realm to rule alone, have you?'

Ivan stared, almost on the edge of anger as he guessed at the original source of his wife's lecture. 'Just what has Fedor Konstantinovich been telling you?'

'That, more or less.' She reached out to touch the anger as it began to glow red beneath his fair skin, and with her fingertips and her next words stroked it away. 'But then, he was talking to your father's man Dmitriy Vasil'yevich during the wedding. It looks as though High Stewards are much the same in any Tsardom, eh?'

'So it seems.' Ivan's mouth shaped a crooked grin. 'So it seems.'

Mar'ya Morevna reached down to her belt and unhooked the great ring of keys that opened every door and window, every chest and closet, in the whole of their great kremlin palace. 'Here,' she said. 'You get to carry these for now.'

Ivan took them in both hands, treating them carefully as they shifted and rang together. The weight of the laden ring was such that it was not so much a bunch of keys as a mass of metal with a myriad ragged edges, any one of which could open up his fingers with as much ease as any individual key could open up a lock. '*Bozhe moy!* Surely I don't lug this lot everywhere I go?' He glanced at Mar'ya Morevna just in time to see the unheard chuckle vanish from her face. 'I notice that *you* don't!'

'Of course not, that's what servants are for. Among all your other duties, it is your function to keep them busy without demeaning them by your choice of tasks. You simply take whichever keys you think are needed for the day's work, and leave the rest with the High Steward.'

'And how do I know which are needed?'

'The High Steward will give them to you.'

'Uh. Yes. I understand. I think. And if I want any other keys?'

'You won't need them.' Mar'ya Morevna chuckled again at Ivan's expression, and this time made no attempt to hide it.

'Why not?' he started to say, then hesitated, hefted the keys and grinned. 'Oh, I see. Because that's what servants are for!'

'You see?' Mar'ya Morevna laughed and clapped her hands. 'You're learning how to be a good ruler already.'

For all her power and riches, Mar'ya Morevna was a woman who found delight in the smallest things and Ivan loved her all the more for that. He lifted the keys and hung them from his belt, sagging comically to one side as he did so just to make her laugh, and then escorted his wife from her kremlin to the courtyard where the captains of her army waited to salute their Princess and commander.

Those stern, bearded warriors raised a great cheer when Prince Ivan kissed Mar'ya Morevna in the plain sight of them all and set a helmet on her head, and cheered again when he helped her to her saddle in a stirrup made of his own two hands. '*Vsego khoroshego,*' he said softly. That simple wishing of luck was the only thing they said to one another; all else between them had long since passed beyond words. Then Mar'ya Morevna, fairest Princess in all the Russias, set heels to her tall horse and led her army out to war . . . .

*

There were many and enough things that needed doing in the running of a princely state for Ivan Tsarevich to realize at last why his education under High Steward Strel'tsin had been so wide-ranging and severe. In his youthful days, his knowledge of what it meant to rule had been gleaned from *byliny* epics and from *skazki* folk-tales, which told him all about the noble cities where free-handed lords reigned in splendour, but nothing of what was needed to maintain that splendour, that nobility, that free-handedness.

He learned . . . .

That first night after Mar'ya Morevna had gone, Ivan thought he might have found sleep hard to achieve, alone in their great bed for the first time in many weeks. Instead he slept like someone stunned with a cudgel, exhausted with papers and discussions and inspections as he had not been tired by endless days of riding out across the endless steppe, and next morning the Groom of the Bed-chamber had to shake him awake. That was a surprise, and not a pleasant one; Ivan Aleksandrovich had woken with the sunrise for as long as he could remember, except on those occasions when wine or ale or vodka had taken the place of that judiciously-applied cudgel. He began to realize why it was that his father and Dmitriy Vasil'yevich Strel'stin could seem so weary and short of temper despite having done nothing more strenuous than sit around a desk all day; and he began to appreciate that Mar'ya Morevna had paid him a considerable compliment in trusting him with such a burthen of responsibility.

For several minutes he lay in the dream-time between sleep and wakefulness, watching the play of sunlight across the elaborate mouldings of the ceiling, half-way glad to be awake on so fine a morning and half-way annoyed that he had not been left alone till nearer noon. Much nearer; perhaps even the early part of the afternoon. Then he made a small sound that might, less early in the day, have been a laugh, and made his way to the bath-house in the hope that enough hot steam and cold water might make him feel less dead.

That day's workload was as severe as the one which had preceded it, but to his surprise and hidden pleasure Prince Ivan found that it was easier. Not much, but enough to transform what he had to do from drudgery to no more than extremely hard work. The Tsarevna's secretaries were certainly pleased at not having to repeat themselves so many times, and the clerks of the treasury were able to concentrate more on their columns of figures and somewhat less on explaining matters to their Prince. That small improvement was as much as Ivan achieved in the next few days. It was of course the forced and rapid recollection of things taught him by Strel'tsin, which he had put aside as being of no immediate use but which – *Slava Bogu!* – came back into his mind the second or third time he needed them, and rather faster than he really deserved. Any further easing of his duties would take longer and require more effort, as he worked to grow accustomed to the various idiosyncrasies of each kremlin official. For the present, he remained in the position of the person crossing a deep river who, unable yet to swim, is reduced to crossing slowly and carefully with both feet shuffling firmly along the bottom. At least he had been able to find where the shingle began . . . .

*

Ivan Tsarevich awoke with a start in the lonely acreage of his bed, knowing even as he opened his eyes that once again he had stretched out in sleep to touch someone who was not there. Then a little thrill of pleasure flickered through him, a pleasure that had two sources: first, that he had woken at dawn – without, that is, Bedchamber-Groom Oleg Pavlovich shaking at his shoulder and shouting politely in his ear – for the first time in almost a week. And second, that if the couriers who had galloped to the kremlin every noon had timed their reports correctly, then Mar'ya Morevna would return victorious some time in the early afternoon.

Though Ivan was pleased by the return of his more normal sleep and waking patterns, it was plain by the lightness of his step and the cheerfulness of his demeanour that the return of his beloved pleased him still more. Though work proceeded as it had on all the preceding mornings, Mar'ya Morevna's own High Steward could see that his Lord's mind was on other things than the administration of *obrok* and *barshchina* taxes. Indeed after correcting his Lord's writing with sharp knife and silver sand for the seventh time, High Steward Fedor Konstantinovich suggested in his best and most courteous tones that perhaps it would be best if the Prince might care to walk in the fresh air, and thus blow the fumes of ink and parchment from his doubtless-busy mind.

Ivan looked at the Steward in that hooded, heavy-lidded way he had honed to perfection on Dmitriy Vasil'yevich. The look recognized a high servant's apparent solicitude for the delicate impudence it so often was and, having recognized, did not punish other than by dismissing both as unimportant. Thus with honours equal, and feeling as he had felt years earlier when his tuitions ended earlier than expected, Prince Ivan made his escape from the treasury counting-house.

He walked for a time as High Steward Fedor had suggested, on the walk-ways of the kremlin ramparts, where the cool wind smelt faintly of birch-wood and the distant promise of rain before nightfall, and the dry aroma of ledgers was no more than an unpleasant memory. Ivan felt a little guilty at thus evading his duties; but not so guilty that he was in any hurry to go back. He suspected, and his morning's performance gave him ample reason, that right now Fedor Konstantinovich and his clerks were better off without him.

There were doubtless other things to do before Mar'ya Morevna returned home, but Ivan was feeling sufficiently lazy that just now none of them seemed important. True, there were his tentative plans to deal with the Prince of Kiev, or the Princes of Novgorod – or perhaps even the Tatars, and thus secure peace not only for Khorlov but also for all of Mother Russia. But those plans involved maps, and charts, and logistical tables for the disposition of troops and the raising of levies. For something little more than a daydream, it seemed too much like hard work. On the other hand, there was his self-imposed study of the many magic books in the library, if something so fascinating could be called an imposition. But there again, matters were progressing slowly without Mar'ya Morevna's tuition, and again were more like work than play. If work had been what he wanted, Ivan knew quite well that he would have stayed in the counting-house. No. What Ivan Aleksandrovich wanted first and foremost was his own wife back in his arms. After that, and after having been married a full quarter of a year, it was about time that they visited their relatives and in-laws. Ivan's mother and father were easy to find, since the town and palace of Khorlov was good enough to stay in one place. It was another matter where his sisters and their sorcerer husbands were concerned, however. Most of the effort in sending their wedding invitations had been expended in making sure where their kremlins might be on any given day. And perhaps – Ivan grinned at the thought – while they were travelling to one place or another, he and Mar'ya could have an adventure. Nothing impressive, or expensive, or elaborate. Just something small and comfortable. Without Tatars in it.

He rested his elbows on one of the high merlons and gazed towards the north-west, hoping – though it was at least four hours too soon – that he might see the banners of the returning army. There was nothing to see but the steppe grasses rippling as the wind stroked across them, nothing to hear but noises from the town beneath the kremlin walls and, off on the edge of hearing, the hiss and rustle of the birch forest that grew to the north. That soft wind carried more than sounds and scents down from the north; it carried the chill of distant snow that had fallen many *vyorsty* beyond the birches, and its touch made Ivan shiver – suddenly, and with a startling violence which rattled one row of his teeth against the other. In a belted tunic-shirt he was dressed adequately for a Lord's duties indoors, behind a desk, but those same garments were less appropriate for the upper ramparts of a kremlin with a north-east wind sighing across the steppe. Prince Ivan was as much a bread and salt man as the lowest, toughest peasant, and as ready to go about in the deepest winter with his collar open and the life-giving cross at his throat on show; but he preferred a warmer coat when he was doing it. He shivered again, more sharply still, and turned down the nearest stairway that would get him off the battlements and back to somewhere sensibly warm.

Even though he didn't recognize it as somewhere he had been before, the passage at the foot of the stair was warm enough, and Ivan spent several minutes leaning against its wood-panelled wall just to let himself thaw out. He smiled to himself that he, a married man of almost four months now, should be so lost in moon-calf yearnings that he didn't notice even when he began to freeze. All of that thought was exaggeration, of course, but it would make Mar'ya Morevna smile when he told her about it. And then, right then, at once, he would give her back the keys that he had carried with him so assiduously ever since she left. This morning, the day of his liege lady's return, High Steward Fedor had ceremoniously returned each and every key to its proper place and then, with equal ceremony and a certain degree of relief, had handed over the ponderous ring to Prince Ivan.

He patted them, where they hung from their ring and chain at his belt, and found each and every one just as cold as he had thought they would be. The feel of the icy metal made him grimace, especially when he thought of what it must be like to be encased in linked steel when a wind like that was blowing. Ivan had not spent so long in armour that he knew from personal experience, and would as soon not find out until the weather turned a little warmer. He glanced from side to side along the corridor, decided which would be the shortest route to take him back to those parts of the kremlin that he knew, and with a mental note to explore the sprawl of his own home sometime he walked off in more or less the right direction.

Some fifteen minutes later Ivan stopped and looked around him, feeling puzzled and faintly foolish. With the direction that he walked, and the speed at which he walked, he felt sure that he should have run out of corridor – and kremlin, town and all, and be on the edges of the birch forest by now. Instead there was only more corridor – both behind him, which was entirely right and proper, and stretching ahead of him . . . .

. . . . Which was ridiculous.

He was more than half inclined to turn round and retrace his steps, right up to the ramparts, before going back into the kremlin by one of the entrances he knew. Only the thought of the distance he had already walked influenced him against the idea. There were several doors along the right-hand wall ahead of him, and unless he had lost all sense of direction Ivan knew that one of them would open on to either the rear-most part of the kremlin palace or the whispering expanse of birch to the north of it. And it couldn't do *that*, since he knew perfectly well that there was no stone-walled covered corridor running from the kremlin out into the woods, for otherwise he would have seen it plainly on any one of the many occasions when he had strolled around the ramparts to enjoy the view. He walked towards the nearest door, ignoring the dreary sound of water dripping from a spigot in the wall and thence to a wooden bucket underneath, and reached out to tug it open.

It was locked.

'*Chyort voz'mi!*' swore Ivan, flapping his hand to work the wrench out of his wrist. Expecting the door to open straight away, he had put too much pressure on the handle, too fast and at an awkward angle. He stared at the door, and then at the keyhole of its lock, crusted with months – no, years – of dirt and rust, and began uneasily to wonder.

Mar'ya Morevna had not yet guided him all through her kremlin, and the more he thought about that and about the way she had gently instructed him in the use and non-use of her keys, the more Ivan began to suspect that opening locked doors was not something that she wanted him to do. Of course, if the door was *not* locked that was another matter entirely – but to find one meant trying all the handles that he could see, rather more carefully than the first, and then if necessary following his first inclination to go back to the ramparts. He looked back along the torch-lit passageway and muttered another oath under his breath. It was a long walk, and now that he had stopped moving he was becoming uncomfortably aware that this place was only warm by comparison with outside. He could see his breath as mist hanging in the air, and like any other sensible person, Rus or not, Ivan merely tolerated cold. He preferred warmth and comfort, and one way or another he intended to experience them just as soon as possible.

Except that the next door was locked as well, and the one after that. Another shiver racked through him and his teeth began to chatter. Whether that was a reaction to the increasingly clammy chill of the stone-walled corridor – its wooden panelling had given way to damp-streaked raw stone long before he stopped to wonder where he was – or a manifestation of annoyance building up inside him, Prince Ivan didn't care. What he wanted most of all right now was to be out of here and sitting in front of a well-stoked fire, waiting for his dear wife to return from her war.

And getting his wish was going to involve a walk, for the last door was locked as well. Ivan looked at it with loathing, wondering why he had even wasted the effort to try its handle, since with chains and bars and padlocks forming a mesh of metal all across its surface it was more thoroughly secured than all the others put together. He kicked it, hard enough to relieve his feelings but not so hard as to put his toes at risk, then stalked angrily away.

An instant later he stopped, frozen in his tracks by a tiny sound where none should be . . . . in the empty corridor, right behind his back. Ivan turned around very, very slowly, with his heart hammering as far up the inside of his throat as when Manguyu Temir's Tatars captured him. There was nothing; even the dripping water-pipe had stopped.

Ivan stared, his eyes narrowed. He *had* heard something,

and it wasn't a drip landing in the overflowing bucket. Anyway, the bucket had been in front of him and in plain sight when he had heard . . . whatever it was. He was no longer wishing for a chair by the fire but for several guards, or a sword, or even a knife. He had nothing.

Nothing – except for a bunch of keys that were almost as heavy as the mace hung from the pommel of his horse's saddle. Ivan fumbled with the key-ring and its chain, unhooked them at long last from his belt and hefted the satisfying weight in his right hand. Keys and chain rang together with a soft metallic clangour that was as ominous as any weapon. It was a more encouraging noise than the one which had caught him so unawares, not least because he could see the source of the small chiming. Not so with the other sound, although now he could hear it again and identify it for what it was.

Sobbing . . . .

The hackles lose on the back of Ivan's neck, and a flurry of conflicting images went flooding through his mind. He found himself wondering about Mar'ya Morevna's father, a sorcerer and a man who had trained his only daughter to be a skilled and deadly commander of armies. He thought about that daughter, now his wife, a lady so soft, so gentle, so loving – and so ruthless in encounters with her enemies. He thought of the sight of thousands of corpses strewn like mown grass across the steppe, and the firm, decisive sound of Mar'ya Morevna's own voice, asking him a question that he dared not answer: *How else does one deal with that sort of people. . . ?*

And the desolate sound of someone weeping behind one of those locked doors.

Ivan Tsarevich stared at the chains and padlocks for a dragging, silent minute while honour and conscience, sympathy and horror and overwhelming morbid curiosity all fought for precedence within his mind. Though he hadn't exactly promised not to open locked doors – and even if he had, everyone knew that some promises were more honourably breached than observed – Ivan felt certain that Mar'ya Morevna would not see matters quite that way. The alternative was to ignore a sound that he would never have ignored at any other time or place than this. Ivan closed his eyes and muttered viciously for several seconds, using all the filthy language he knew in the hope that it would make him feel better. It did not, and finally he began to fumble for the proper keys.

They were more easily found than he had expected; it seemed as though, once his mind has made up, his fingers moved more nimbly to make a reality of that decision. The dark iron of the locks clinked as the wards of each key engaged with tumblers that were better oiled and much more easily opened than Ivan had expected, then went scraping across the floor as each one was pulled free and flung aside with all the disgust that his righteous anger had created. Before long there was only the lock of the door itself, and that was when Prince Ivan hesitated. The other locks, the bars and the chains now strewn across the paving could all be replaced – but open this, and open the door, and the last step would have been taken from which there would be no retreat.

Despite the thickness of the oaken timbers Ivan heard a tiny, feeble moan, and there were no more second thoughts. He turned the key and pulled the handle, and after an instant's resistance the door groaned open. A breath of chill rolled out of it and, holding one of the torches pulled from the wall of the corridor, he looked inside. At first there was only darkness, the long black sweep of his own shadow and the dance of light and shade cast by the guttering torch-flame. And then something turned over in the pit of Prince Ivan's stomach, and there was a buzzing like a swarm of bees inside his head which drove out every other thought but shock and pity, for he could see the prisoner who stood against the wall.

He was little, and shrivelled by privation so that his nose was like a blade, his eyes were sunk into his head and there was not flesh enough on his bones to feed a louse, and he was very, very old. His hair was white and hung down past his shoulders; his moustache was white and hung down past his chin; and his white beard hung down past his knees and almost to the floor, for he was fettered upright, shackled to a beam and to the wall of his cell with twelve iron chains. Two were at each wrist and two at each ankle; two were at his waist and two at his neck; and all of them ran to a hook in the beam and through a padlock that was bigger than his head.

Ivan stared while the buzzing in his head grew louder, not wanting to believe the evidence of his own eyes. That Mar'ya Morevna was like his brothers-in-law in being more than she seemed was something he accepted willingly, and that she was a Tsarevna who ruled her own realm and fought her own wars was something he had grown accustomed to. But learning that she had such a secret as this, whether it was her own fault or that of the sorcerer father of whom Ivan knew next to nothing, was more than he could bear. Any claim that she knew nothing, that her father had locked doors before he died and she had honoured his memory by keeping them that way, was no more than an excuse, and a weak one easily disproved. Leaving aside all the other locked doors in this same corridor, if only this door had remained shut and undisturbed for such a length of time, then the prisoner inside would have died from thirst or starvation long ago. It was not a discovery that would encourage any husband, and especially the husband of such a wife.

Then the old man raised his drooping head and opened his eyes, blinking them as they began to water in the torch-light. He looked towards the doorway, even though Prince Ivan felt sure that just now he could see no more than a great brightness invading his dark cell. 'Pity me,' said the old man into this bright darkness, and his voice was weak and quavering. 'Give me the mercy of a drink, for I have been given neither drink nor mercy these ten years past, and I am parched!'

Ivan cringed to think that the old man's gaolers were so cruel that such desperate exaggeration was needed to arouse their pity. More and more he was determined that there would be words between Mar'ya Morevna and himself when she came home, and the bee-buzzing in his head took on the sharper sound of rage. He looked around and his eye fell on the brimming bucket. Wine would be better to restore the old man's spirits, but the water was closer and at least it was cold and clean, the better to quench thirst. There was only one remaining problem: Ivan could see no drinking-vessel other than the bucket, either in the cell or out of it. Need prevailed over nicety, and after tipping water from it, so that it wouldn't spill too much, he hefted the bucket and held it to the mouth of the prisoner . . . .

. . . . Who drank its contents all down in a single draught. Ivan stared for a moment, his head so filled with buzzing that he felt no more than a brief, dull surprise that the old man should have been so thirsty. Then he set the bucket down, but the ancient prisoner looked at it as he might on the life-giving cross and said, 'My thirst is such that one is not enough to quench it. Good sir, of your charity, give me another.'

There was no harm in it so Ivan took the bucket, filled it full and brought it back to where the old man hung helpless in his chains. Again it was drunk to the dregs, this time not in one gulp but more slowly as the first fierce edge of that cruel thirst abated.

'One more, and only one,' the old man said, 'so that I might feel restored.'

In truth, Ivan could see that although there was water in his beard he looked better already, and was pleased that so small an act of kindness could do so much good. Bringing the bucket for a third time, he took care to hold it with more care and watched contentedly as the old prisoner savoured every drop.

'Ah,' he said, sighing deeply, 'Now I am myself again. Many thanks to you, Prince Ivan.'

The bucket dropped with a crash from Ivan's hand at the sound of his name, and his mouth shaped questions that were never voiced, for at that self-same same instant the buzzing vanished from his mind, his memory gave him the answers – and he realized just what he had done.

' "Who am I when I am myself, and how do I know your name?" ' said the old man, uttering Ivan's own unspoken questions in a voice no longer frail and tremulous but become as harsh and bleak as winter. 'I know because of who I am – and who I am is Koshchey the Undying!'

He stood up straight, as though the twelve chains no longer weighed him down, and a moment later they did not indeed – for he drew a deep breath and moved his limbs, bursting all the forged and welded links that were his fetters so that they fell away like rotten rope. When the harsh clangour of iron chains falling to the stone floor died away, he combed his fingers through his beard and smiled a smile that never reached his cold, cold eyes.

Ivan met that smile with a stare of horror – then he plunged out through the door, slammed it shut and shot every lock and bolt that he could reach, before leaning back against the wall and panting like a man who has just run a race. His breath caught in his chest when the passage filled with the smoke and smell of burning timber, and with the blacksmith stench of heated metal. Before Ivan's eyes the bars and bolts glowed red, then pink, then white, then ran like wax; the parts of the door's lock oozed in searing streams out of the keyhole, leaving tracks of scorch all down its wood; and when the hinges melted from their sockets, the useless door fell down.

Koshchey walked out across it as though it was a bridge between his cell and the white world outside, and as he passed the heavy oak turned black and crumbled into dust and ashes. 'Again I give you thanks, Ivan Tsarevich,' said Koshchey *Bessmertnyy*, though he glowered beneath his brows, 'and your kindness brings you safety. Three times you gave me water when I was a prisoner, and three times I will forgive a wrong. You tried to put me back in prison, and that was one. Guard the second and third, for they contain your life. If you are wise, you will not see me again.' Koshchey laughed like the grinding of ice on a frozen river. 'Nor will you see Mar'ya Morevna. She owes me thrice three years of liberty for every one her father stole from me, and you could not live so long. Farewell.'

The old man turned from Ivan and began to walk away, along the corridor that led to Mar'ya Morevna's kremlin palace. Despite the threats which had been uttered, Ivan knew he could not stand helplessly while such a necromancer was released into the world, to steal his wife and do only the good God knew what other harm. If only he had thought to wear a sword. . . . But there were other things.

Ignored by Koshchey as beneath his notice, Ivan stepped softly, lightly, back into the cell. When he came out, the wooden bucket hung by its handle from his right hand. He swung it once, and twice, and three times as he ran towards Koshchey the Undying, and on the third he brought it down with all his strength across the wizard's skull. The bucket flew to shards and staves and Koshchey was hurled to the floor, slack-limbed and sprawling like a dead man.

Then he rolled over, rose and seized Prince Ivan by the shirt. 'That was two,' he said, and lifted Ivan until the Prince's feet had left the ground. 'Understand my name, young fool. You waste your time and mine with such foolishness as this. It has taken many years and many lives for me to become what I have become, and now I cannot be slain. Not by such as you, nor by any man. Remember that – but be advised, forget Mar'ya Morevna. I need but hold her in my kremlin until the dark of the moon, and she will be mine until I decide to let her go. By then, Prince Ivan, you will be long dead. Find another woman, make yourself another life. You will sooner see your ears without a mirror than set eyes on your wife!' He flung Ivan aside as a man might hurl an apple – straight at the wall.

Ivan was upside-down when he hit it, and when the floor came up to meet him, very fast. There was a great roaring in his ears as Koshchey the Undying vanished from sight on a storm of his own making, but the roaring went on for a long time after that, until it faded into warmth and darkness as the torches in the passage all went out.

*

When Prince Ivan recovered his senses, there was no way for him to tell if he had been without them for a long or a short time. The stones of the floor, where his face was pressed against them, were as cold as he remembered, and the torches were still burning – but they had been burning when he came from the ramparts of the kremlin to this passageway, so that was of no help in telling how much time had passed. For a few seconds he closed his eyes again, hoping against all hope that when he opened them once more he would be in his own bed after no more than a foul and vivid dream.

It was no dream. The charred door with its twisted, melted metalwork was still on the floor beside him, and when he made the painful effort of raising his head he could see the cell beyond, littered with the links of broken chains. Ivan squeezed his eyes tight shut in an attempt to block out the evidence of his own stupidity, and in an effort to quell the spasm of nausea that the movement of his head had caused. Both attempts were unsuccessful.

He knew of old, after many falls from horses, that the old lie of 'bring it up, you'll feel much better afterwards,' was just that: a lie. He had been sick twice before he risked standing up, and that had simply made him sick again. With the water-bucket broken, he was reduced to collecting handfuls from the spigot and splashing them onto his face. Despite what was said about the effectiveness of that, it was probably another lie. The only difference that it made was to leave him feeling wet *and* wretched instead of simply wretched.

After an eternity of minutes, Ivan Tsarevich felt strong enough to start the long walk back towards the kremlin and the way out which had been his way into this mess. He was afraid to stay in this gloomy corridor which ran through some underground of the palace that seemed to have no existence on the surface, but he was even more afraid to find out what had happened in the world.

The worst had happened.

Two couriers from Mar'ya Morevna's army were awaiting his return in the Lesser Hall of Audience, and though Ivan knew he would look as much out of place there as he would anywhere else he went to meet them straight away. Or as straight as still-wobbly legs allowed. Palace servants had been searching for him since the riders arrived – a matter of some quarter of an hour, from which he guessed that he had not been senseless very long. Their fussing concern over the state of his clothing and the state of his health followed him the whole way to the audience room, where just a little later it was overtaken by concern for the state of the realm.

The couriers' report, though garbled and confused by their not knowing what it was they saw, told Ivan far more than they knew. Mar'ya Morevna's host had been victorious again, trapping the remaining Tatars in yet another ambush of her devising. Very few of the brigands were left to return to their home khanate, and none of the survivors would have anything to brag about except, perhaps, their luck and the speed of their horses. Thus successful, the army had turned for home and had been an easy two hours' march away when *something* descended out of a clear sky. One man described it as a great gust of wind that was somehow dark enough to see; the other likened it to a black storm-cloud. Regardless of their conflicting descriptions, both agreed on what it did: which was to snatch Mar'ya Morevna from the saddle of her horse and bear her away, even though she rode in the midst of all her captains and her personal guards. It had been one of those captains who had thought to send them at a gallop to the kremlin, though what the poor man expected would be gained from that Ivan did not know.

The only thing of which he was completely certain was that all of this was his own fault, and he could shift the blame to no one else. He thanked each soldier in turn for his information, dismissed them and then sat staring at the wall for more than an hour. Servants and officials came walking in, saw his expression and promptly tiptoed out, but Prince Ivan saw none of them. He did not even see the wall; only the image, repeated over and over again, of his hands turning keys, of his hands pouring water, of his hands loosing Koshchey *Bessmertnyy* on the world again. And finally he saw nothing but the blur beyond his tears.

*

Ivan stood on the battlements of the kremlin as he had stood earlier that day. Then he had been waiting for the return of his wife but now, cheated of that, he waited for his first sight of the moon. It was cold despite the illusory warmth of a glowing sunset, and Ivan was wrapped in a grey coat made of the pelts of Siberian wolves. That coat, and the deadly look in his eyes, had been enough to send the more superstitious of his guards to the farthest end of the rampart. Any man who looked so and dressed so and awaited the moon with such intensity was not a man they intended staying close by, be he Prince or not. Only those who knew the moon was not yet full remained near him. Ivan would have found it amusing, had his mind been able to grasp such a concept as humour with his wife newly stolen away.

He waited, staring at the horizon through the grey drifts of his own breath, and tried without success to remember what phase the moon had shown last night. Except that last night, he had not noticed. Last night, it had not been important. If it had already reached moon-dark, did that mean he had already lost? Or was it Koshchey's sport to give his victims a month of useless hope before letting the jaws of his trap close on the remnant of their lives? Ivan closed his eyes as a shudder of despair racked through his body, but opened them again with a snap as one of the guards on the uppermost tower cried something that was lost on the cold wind. His words were unimportant; it was what had prompted them that mattered.

The moon was visible at last. A pale crescent like the curve of a Turki scimitar unsheathed itself from a bank of cloud still gilt-edged by the sunset, and gleamed briefly before it too dipped beneath the horizon. Ivan felt his heart lift out of absolute despair, heard the renewed thunder of blood in his ears and knew by the great smoky cloud hanging before him that he had been holding his breath. That crescent told him he had three weeks, perhaps a little more, in which to find Mar'ya Morevna. Less than he had hoped, yet more than he had feared. Ivan squared his shoulders and hurried down to the kremlin library.

Within an hour he had virtually torn the library apart in his search for maps and charts. Besides not knowing his way around the kremlin, he was discovering to his chagrin that he barely knew his way around its library either. In all his rummaging and learning of small spells, he had barely skimmed its surface. Mar'ya Morevna and her father before her had acquired enough reading matter – whether as books, rolled parchments, cased scrolls or any other form by which the written word could be preserved – to fill every shelf three volumes deep. It made finding any single thing a task of near-impossible magnitude. At last, almost knee-deep in paper, Ivan lost his temper. Dropping the armful of ribbon-tied loose manuscript that he carried, so that its ribbon broke and the leaves scattered across the floor like those of some literary autumn, he hunted out one of the few volumes whose location he knew well.

It was the first of all Mar'ya Morevna's grimoires that he had ever read. The first, the simplest, and thus the easiest to understand and use for a man unskilled in sorcery who was also in a hurry. Ivan found the spell – 'To Reveal That Which Would Be Discovered' – a small spell appropriate to his purposes in that it was only good for lost keys, misplaced wallets and other relatively unimportant items. Books, for instance, in an overcrowded library. He took less than a minute to arrange the spell's geometric construction in his mind's eye and then, with only the most token focusing of concentration on the map, chart, note or whatever it was he needed, read it aloud. Perhaps that was why there was a sudden, almost random explosion of activity on half-a-dozen shelves at once. Ivan didn't care.

For one thing, a ragged spike of agony had lanced through his skull as if someone had hammered a stylus up his nose, leaving a throbbing headache in its wake, and for another that nose – as if in protest – had begun to bleed all over the grimoire. Magic was never without cost, and careless magic was more costly than most. Occasionally its cost was life. As the tears of pain faded from his eyes and left his vision more or less clear, Ivan realized with a shiver just how close he had come to pulping the inside of his own head with the pressure of the spell. If, through his own inadequate preparation, the magic had been unable to find the subject or item he sought in the outside world of the library shelves, it would have inverted, snapped back into his mind like a breaking bowstave and presented him with his own recollection of the item in the shape of the relevant piece of his own brain. It was a mistake few sorcerers made more than once.

Ivan snuffled uncomfortably and glanced around for something with which to wipe the spattered grimoire before his bloodstains became a permanent feature of its text. Then he realized that there was no need. The blood was gone. Prince Ivan looked at the small, simple book with a new respect that bordered on wariness, then closed its covers and set it carefully aside.

Besides his nosebleed, the spell had caused a series of extrusions among the still-shelved books. It looked distinctly unmagical, as though someone with more knowledge than he of what the library contained had gone along the shelves, pulling volumes slightly out of line to make finding them again that much easier. Ivan moved hurriedly through the room, gathering books and charts, then took them back to the table and cleared it by the simple expedient of an open-handed sweep. The place could be tidied later.

That was what servants were for.

It took another hour of leafing through maps before at last he found what sense told him he had been looking for: a tattered sheet of parchment whose outlines lacked the precision of other cartographers' work. This looked clumsy, amateurish – it looked, in short, like the sort of chart a man might draw himself if he wished to keep a secret. There would be no buried teasure here, Ivan felt sure of that, and there were so few lines and features scribbled in that the bulk of the information must have been stored in that safest of all repositories, the map-maker's memory. A memory which had been dead and gone these ten years past, for the writing on the map was in the same crabbed hand that Ivan had seen on old official documents – that of Mar'ya Morevna's father.

Prince Ivan had not been so optimistic that he had expected a dotted line marked 'Follow this to Koshchey's kremlin', but when he started to compare this sketch against the better maps that was exactly what he found. It did not say 'Koshchey the Undying lives here' in so many words, since for his own reasons Mar'ya's father had preferred writing in Norse runes, but on the sketch-map there was a great deal of the scratchy, angular lettering in places where larger charts showed nothing worthy of remark.

Ivan Aleksandrovich, *Tsarevich Khorlovskiy*, had already ridden farther on less evidence than this, for no more than a social call on three married sisters. And there was no longer time for such niceties as sitting still and sending to his brothers-in-law for help. Before God, finding where they were so that Mar'ya Morevna's messengers could deliver wedding invitations had taken the best part of a week, and hoping that those three kremlins were in the same place as they had been even at sunset was as vain as hoping that Koshchey the Undying would have a change of heart and release Mar'ya Morevna himself. He rolled up the relevant maps and strode from the library towards the stables.

*

The kremlin of Koshchey the Undying looked exactly as Prince Ivan had thought it might. It was no palace but a grim, jag-crested citadel that squatted atop a low hill in the midst of an unpleasant-looking forest, and spread its lowering presence over all the lands that came beneath its shadow. Those lands were bleak and desolate, as if tainted by the presence of the necromancer, though Ivan surmised that it was likely Koshchey lived here because he enjoyed such grim surroundings. Certainly they and he were much in accord.

Finding the place had proved easier than Ivan dared to hope. The old maps and the new had each guided in their turn, and behind and beyond all else had been the same spell which had guided him before, with its strange inner certainty that told him which direction was the right one to follow. It had led him unerringly to the kremlins of each brother-in-law in turn – although Fenik, Vasya and Misha were evidently quite capable of moving their palaces into his path if the mood moved them – and now it had led him to where his wife was being held. It had taken many days of travel: less than he had expected, but more than he wanted, when every day was followed by a night in which the moon had swollen that little bit rounder. At least getting close to Koshchey's ugly dwelling without being seen had been simplicity itself. Only the forest surrounded it; there was no town and no outlying villages, because nobody sane would want to go anywhere near the place.

That had caused Ivan to wonder about himself more than once.

He leaned back against a tree and wondered whether or not it might not be better to lie flat on the ground and creep closer that way, since every one of the many windows of Koshchey's kremlin looked like a malevolent eye, and right now it seemed to Ivan that every one of those eyes was looking straight at him. Despite the dense undergrowth of the ugly forest, Ivan Aleksandrovich still felt horribly exposed. At the same time, he was grateful for Koshchey's arrogance. Anyone else would have cleared the ground for two bowshots all around the walls, just to make sure that nobody could do what he was doing right now; but the necromancer had left the woodland to grow unchecked, so certain was he that no one would be brave enough or stupid enough to approach his home. Ivan laid a hand on Burka's nose to keep the horse quiet, and wondered with grim humour into which category he personally fell.

Half an hour dragged by, resin-scented and stiflingly warm in the shadows beneath the dark pine trees. In that half-hour, despite his apparent immobility Ivan had examined Koshchey's kremlin with his mind's eye. The concentration had left him nerve-drawn and tired just as much as if he had been actually creeping around his enemy's fortress, but he had learned what he had hoped. The distant kremlin was empty of all save Mar'ya Morevna. If Koshchey its master was truly as Deathless as his name implied – something which Ivan still doubted – then certainly his home was lifeless to match. There had been none of the jewel-bright glints of light that would normally have reflected from sentries' weapons as they marched around the ramparts; nobody had ridden in or out of the ominous maw of the open gate; nothing had happened at all, not even the flutter of silk or wings, since neither banners nor birds flew above that grim fortress.

Ivan watched, and though he was glad of it, he wondered why.

He was still wondering as the afternoon turned to dusk, because in all those hours he had seen nothing alive near Koshchey's kremlin, neither bird nor beast nor insect, inside nor out, and the only thing which had moved had been the slow sweep of shadows following the sun.

Now that sun was setting, and with the approaching darkness came an idea that – whether the dark kremlin was empty or not – Ivan would never have contemplated during the day. It was a plan of such elegant simplicity that it deserved to succeed. He would swing into Burka's saddle, slip into the fortress under cover of darkness, find Mar'ya Morevna . . . .

. . . . And rescue her.

*

Even with Burka's hoofs muffled by wadding made of the torn-up remnants of three shirts and a fur hat, the sound of echoes ringing round the hollow courtyard was much too loud. Prince Ivan gritted his teeth at each footfall, for it seemed to ears made over-sharp by jangling nerves that he would have made less noise by simply riding up to the kremlin gate and hammering on it with his mace. That mace was in his hand, both swords had been loosened in their scabbards, his bow in its saddle-case was strung, and had there been some way to set an arrow on its string without needing to hold it in the spare hand he did not possess, Ivan would have done that too.

Burka was uneasy, snorting and stamping, his ears laid right back against his skull and eyes rolling so that Ivan could see their whites glistening in the light of the thin moon. He could sympathize with the horse, for he too was shivering with fright, and though he was brave enough to admit it that admission didn't really help.

Certainly the kremlin of Koshchey the Undying was a place to strike fear into heroes more courageous than Ivan Tsarevich had ever claimed to be. It not only looked wrong, it smelt wrong and even *felt* wrong. By their very nature such citadels were strong, stern places, ominous in the way that a fully armed and armoured *bogatyr'* is ominous, with the tacit threat of the function which follows such a form. Yet Ivan had never encountered one which felt actively malevolent.

Until now.

The roofs and domed cupolas that reared above him, black silhouettes cut from the starshot sky, were spired like others he had seen; yet their tapering points were longer, sharper, more vicious, like taloned fingers straining ever upwards to claw the very clouds out of the good God's Heaven and so show their owner's contempt for God and Heaven both. The windows looked as much like eyes as they had done during the day, but now – black slots in stone washed by the pallid moonlight – rather than resemble anything alive they looked more like the empty sockets of a skull. The arches of the many doorways were the tight-stretched lips of a frozen scream, the planked doors themselves were teeth, glistening under the moon like the teeth of the thousands of Tatar corpses Ivan had seen on the battlefield so few months past. The whole kremlin was a vast celebration of triumphal death – and Koshchey the Undying's vast mockery of that which he did not fear.

'At least the place is empty,' Ivan said, and though he would never have admitted talking to himself and claimed that the sound of a human voice in that loathly place was meant to comfort Burka, it was as much for his own comfort as that of his horse. Suspicions had begun to move about inside his mind, causing swirls and ripples of unease like the movements of something large and ominous lurking beneath the surface of deep water. This rescue, if rescue it would be, was so easy as to be ridiculous. Too easy. And yet he *knew* the place was empty.

Wasn't it?

After a moment's hesitation, reluctant for those few seconds to set his feet on smooth, domed cobblestones that looked like skulls sunk to their eyebrows in the earth, Ivan slipped from his saddle. Except for the noises he and Burka made, the place was as quiet as the gra—

Nyet Izbavi Bog, nyet. . . !

Ivan Aleksandrovich stamped on that thought before it had a chance to form. 'Speak the name, summon the named,' – that was what Mikhail the Raven had said. There might also be 'name the thing, create the named'. In this frightful courtyard graves and death were already far too real, and who was to know what might result from one misplaced word too many. . . ? Ivan had seen the consequences of foolishness too many times already to risk being foolish any more.

Until he saw Mar'ya Morevna standing in a doorway with a lantern in her hand, come to investigate a noise where none should be, and all wisdom and restraint was flung away as he ran across the courtyard to take her in his arms and name her with all the charming small endearments such as lovers use, and hear her sweet voice say—

'Before God, Ivan, why could you not keep one simple promise?!'

He recoiled in shock as if she had slapped him in the face, because her voice was not sweet but had all the harsh impatience that she probably honed when keeping unruly soldiers in their ranks. He spread his hands helplessly and opened his mouth to make some sort of excuse, but the words would not come. He knew why. Any honest excuse would be stupid, while any good excuse would be untrue. He had been stupid already – that was as obvious as the sunrise. Mar'ya Morevna's words to him had been as right and proper as anything said in all the wide white world. But no matter how much they had dented his fast-fading pride, the little of it that remained would never allow him to greet her with a lie.

'Forgive me now, Mar'ya Morevna,' he said quietly, formally, 'or condemn me later. But whatever you choose, I shall not abandon you to this foul place and its fouler Lord.'

Mar'ya Morevna, *krasivyy Tsarevna*, stared at her husband with the expression of someone with very few choices left to them, and the most important is simply whether to laugh or to cry. In the end she did neither, taking his hand in silence as he helped her to the saddle of his horse, then leaning back into the comfort of his embrace as he swung up behind her and reached around to take the reins. Only then did she speak aloud, softly, more gently than she had ever spoken to him before.

'Vanyushechka, *vozlyublennyy moy*, you are a very great fool – but you are a very great hero, and you are mine, and I would not exchange you for the wisest Prince in all the Russias. . . .'

CHAPTER SEVEN

How Prince Ivan rescued Mar'ya Morevna from Koshchey the Undying, and how Koshchey expressed his displeasure

Once Mar'ya Morevna was a prisoner in the echoing emptiness of his ten-years-deserted kremlin, Koshchey the Undying rode out across the face of Moist-Mother-Earth to be about whatever evil business was foremost in his mind. He rode, and slew, and brought terror, during all the days that Ivan Tsarevich spent in searching the white world, until at last the Prince came to Koshchey's dark kremlin and carried his wife away from its grim walls. And in that instant, the very instant when Ivan rode out from Koshchey's kremlin, Koshchey's black horse stumbled in its gait.

Koshchey the Undying, thrown from his seat, rolled upright again, seized bridle and reins together and began to lash the black horse savagely with his riding-whip. 'Has it been so long that you have forgotten what it is to carry me across the wide white world?' he snarled as he struck. 'You shall have practice enough at that before all is done!'

The black horse reared up, rolling red eyes and flaring red nostrils as it pawed the air with iron-shod hoofs as sharp and deadly as the mace of any *bogatyr'*. It neighed shrilly, outraged at being given hard blows and hard words without a good reason for either. 'Practice indeed, Koshchey the Undying, Koshchey the Cruel!' it squealed, and though it spoke words like a man its voice was not the voice of any human born. 'Has it been so long since I last carried you that you have forgotten what I am, and what it cost to earn such a horse as I?'

Koshchey the Undying lowered his whip and released the bridle, then coiled away the dripping lash and thrust it through his belt. 'I remember three days of striving to keep you and your kindred under my eye,' he said. 'I remember how I mastered one and all, and I remember how I chose the best.'

'And I remember how I once was free, and now am free no more,' said the black horse, lowering its head as the red fire died from its eyes.

'That was the bargain,' said Koshchey the Undying, showing the points of his teeth in a cruel smile. 'And you lost.' He set hand to pommel and foot to stirrup, and rose to his saddle again with an ease that gave the lie to his long white hair and beard. 'So tell me, why did you stumble? What do you smell that is wrong?'

'I smell a Russian smell where none should be,' the horse replied. 'Prince Ivan has stolen Mar'ya Morevna from the dark kremlin, and even now is riding for the borders of your wide domain.'

'So, and so, and so,' said Koshchey. He drew the riding-whip out of his belt and twisted it between his hands until the plaited leather creaked with the sound of a tree in a storm. 'It is no more than I should have expected from a fool who wants to be a hero.' Then he rapped the butt of the whip against his horse's neck and spoke with the foul sweetness of something gone rotten. 'Is it possible, best and swiftest of all, to catch up with them?'

'It is possible,' replied the black horse, flinching from the blow on its neck. 'You could take the time to sow flax and harvest it, you could make thread and weave the white linen, you could make yourself clothing and wear it to rags and even if you were to wait so long as all of that, still it would be possible.'

'I hope that it is,' said Koshchey the Undying. 'For your sake.' Then he set heels to the horse, and the whip to its flank, and rode off like a storm in pursuit.

*

Prince Ivan and Mar'ya Morevna rode as swiftly as their need for silence, and as silently as their desire for great speed. For a long time no word was spoken, because both were listening for the sounds of pursuit and neither was willing to say so aloud. The reason was simple: *name the thing, call the thing.* Only when he judged it safe did Ivan rein Burka back from his headlong gallop, and slip to the ground so that he could remove the wads of padding from his horse's feet.

After that they rode on, but more slowly, so that Burka should not be tired any sooner than he must. Even then Ivan knew that his noble steed would be wearied soon enough, with the burden of two riders on his back. The best and kindest way was for one or both to dismount and walk alongside, but for the present such a kindness was impossible. They were still too close to Koshchey's kremlin and, even close to exhaustion, the horse could cover ground much faster than two people on foot. Right now, speed was of the essence. Ivan's suspicions about the ease of the rescue were increasing with every minute; suspicions that if rescue was easy then escape after it was bound to be hard.

Only when they had passed beyond the sinister forest that surrounded Koshchey's kremlin did Ivan judge that it was safe to talk at last. Considering how Mar'ya Morevna had spoken to him when they first met on the steps of the kremlin, it might not be so safe to listen, but there were questions and answers to be exchanged – and Ivan wanted to hear her voice again no matter what she might say. At least there were no condemnations of his conduct in releasing Koshchey the Undying; instead, there was an apology.

'I should have told you about him,' said Mar'ya Morevna, 'about his powers, his strengths, his weaknesses – though God knows they are few enough! And above all I should have simply asked if anyone had warned you to beware of Koshchey the Undying.'

Ivan laughed hollowly, a sound that said much more than words, and the slight squeeze of his wife's hand on his wrist was in itself another apology. 'Asked,' she finished in a small voice, 'and then explained how it was that my father came to capture and imprison him.'

'Why was he only imprisoned, and not . . . .' Ivan faltered

slightly, unwilling to speak his meaning too plainly with the memory of Koshchey's deathly kremlin still far too fresh in his mind. 'Not dealt with as you dealt with Manguyu Temir?' He was curious, for despite the mildness of his father's reign Tsar Aleksandr would never have permitted Koshchey the Undying to survive. He would have been hanged, or burnt, or shot with arrows, or whatever was required to kill so dangerous a prisoner. Koshchey would *not* have been imprisoned, for to imprison such a creature meant that always . . . . somewhere, sometime . . . . was the chance that he might escape. Ivan went on to say as much, and was rewarded with the vibration of laughter as his wife turned awkwardly in the high saddle and tried to hold him close, and all the while shook her head regretfully in the silver moonlight.

'Dealt with?' She returned Ivan's own words with a slight ironic twist to them which said more than any lecturing enhancement could have done. 'Beloved, have you not yet grasped the import of Koshchey's name? No one calls him *Bessmertnyy* as a joke – that title is as right and proper as calling you "Tsar's son".'

She looked up at the moon and smiled without humour. 'Why do you think his kremlin has no need of locks or shuttered gates or armoured guards? Why do you think I was permitted the mockery of enough freedom to walk its empty corridors? Koshchey has far more than the lifetime of any thief to hunt down and restore what might be stolen, or to recover any prisoner who might escape. I could not even do *that* for myself. He laid a charm on me, that I could not leave his kremlin except with the aid of someone from outside. The thought of it amused him. He said it would prove whether or not you were brave, or stupid, or really cared for me.'

'Then he knows,' said Ivan in a small voice.

'By now? Almost certainly. This chase will be a game to him, but a game where he makes and breaks the rules to suit himself. A game that he intends to win. He knows I lack my father's powers, and that I cannot return him to his prison cell without my books of magic. More: he knows they are far enough from here for him to be able to recapture me before I reach them. You see? This is a sport to him!'

'Then kill him!' snarled Ivan.

Mar'ya Morevna swore softly. 'You hear, Vanya, but you don't listen! Koshchey is Undying. *Deathless*. He cannot be slain by any man, or by any weapon wielded by the hand of man.' She must have felt the slight tension running through Ivan's body, for she caught her breath and said sharply. 'Nor the hand of woman either! Before the good God, I tried!'

Ivan could believe it. If Koshchey had wisdom to match all his other powers, he would take care to avoid Mar'ya Morevna now that he had dared to steal her from the midst of her own army. The beautiful Tsarevna was not one to forgive such a slight, offered in plain view of all her captains and her personal guard. Deathless or not, she would surely find some way in which to make her portion of his immortality an everlasting torment.

'He offered an alliance to my father, but his price for peace and safety was my hand in marriage,' she continued in the quiet voice of one remembering times long past, so many years gone and so often thought upon that their unpleasant memories provoked no more now than a bitter amusement. 'My father's reply was that he was not accustomed to bartering the happiness of his family against the peace of thrice nine tsardoms, and least of all to a blasphemous old rattlebones with more right to two *arshiniy* of Russian soil and a carven stone than the hand and bed of a girl less than one-hundredth his own age.'

A thin whistle, indrawn through his teeth, was Ivan's only comment on that. Small wonder that the daughter treated Tatar hordes with such disdain, when her father was so casual in his insults of an undying necromancer. 'So what happened afterwards?'

'Koshchey came against us with an army. That was the only time I saw how wise my father had become in all the ways of strategy and tactics – and because I understood what he was doing, I came to realize how completely *I* had been taught as well. He moved each regiment, each squad, each man, as though they were the pieces on a chess-board: in the way, he told me later, that the antique Romans would conduct their battles. Koshchey's host was beaten and scattered and he was taken in chains – but only at the cost of many lives. Since at that time killing was no threat to him, my father locked him in that cell and tried during the remaining years God granted him to learn the source of Koshchey's death. Instead he found his own, from a fever, and from that day onwards the cell door remained shut . . . .'

Ivan halted his horse, dismounted and held Mar'ya Morevna close, stroking her hair and making soft sounds of comfort until her weeping ended. 'You did what you could,' he said, 'and that was enough.'

'I held him in the empty dark like a rat sealed in a hole,' she replied, sobbing, 'and I hoped that he might die. There was no honour in it, and no right. When none of his followers came to rescue or to ransom, I should at least have let him out to see the clean sunshine and to breathe the fresh air.'

'And what would have happened then?' asked Prince Ivan. 'Only what happened when I released him, except much sooner.'

'And my hands would have been clean!'

Ivan raised one of those hands to his lips and kissed it, very lightly. 'They seem clean enough for me. Leave it – don't waste your tears on Koshchey, who neither needs them nor deserves them. What was done has been done; or undone, where I laid meddling fingers to it.'

'So now you blame yourself, to make us both feel better.' Mar'ya Morevna smiled at her husband in the wan moonlight and dashed the tears from her eyes with her sleeve. 'Idiot!' Ivan raised his eyebrows. 'What makes you think that you have any blame in this at all?'

'I was under the impression, from what you said at first, that opening that door and giving the water might have had something to do with it.'

'Idiot,' she said again and cuffed him lightly, lovingly on one cheek with the tips of her fingers. 'Opening the door, yes. That was your fault, and you can be as guilty over it as pleases you – but what was done has been done, or undone. *Da?* As for all the rest, no. You were the only person in my kremlin unaware of the evil locked up in that cell. The only person not familiar, however slightly, with the sensations that come when self-will is being drained away. When you opened the door, was there suddenly a buzzing in your ears, a heavy sound like bees swarming?' With the hackles lifting on his neck, Ivan nodded. 'So, then. You were doing Koshchey's bidding from that moment onward. He released himself: you were only the tool with which he did it.'

Ivan heard that, and as he listened he could feel the blood of anger pulsing up into his face. That he, a Tsar's son, should be so used was almost beyond bearing, and that Koshchey should then thank him – so that the semblance of guilt was left on Ivan's shoulders alone – was too much to be borne. Had it not been for the presence of Mar'ya Morevna, who though a skilful general and leader of rough soldiers was also his beloved wife and a high-born lady worthy of respect, he would have sworn such vicious oaths as he had heard Guard-Captain Akimov employ when all the world was turned against him. Instead he clenched his fists and ground his teeth until that impulse had subsided, and then, before Mar'ya Morevna could guess what was in his mind and do something to prevent him, said, 'I would that he were here right at this moment, to hear just what I think of him!'

There was a sudden shrill roaring of storm winds, and a beating of hoofs that came from nowhere and yet everywhere, and from the midst of all that sound and fury a cold, thin arm snatched Mar'ya Morevna out of the saddle and out of the circle of her husband's arms while a cold, thin voice said, 'I listen eagerly, Prince Ivan. Tell me all about it!'

Koshchey the Undying sat astride his black horse in the meagre moonlight, with Mar'ya Morevna flung helpless across his saddle, and he was laughing. Trickles of blood glistened bright on the horse's heaving sides where Koshchey's whip had split its skin, and more blood gleamed around the places where the long, sharp Turki spurs which adorned his boots had raked and furrowed its sleek flanks. Its darkness was streaked with the white foam of its furious race, there was more foam around its muzzle, drizzling from the lump of jagged iron that Koshchey used as a bit, and its eyes burned red as a blacksmith's forge.

'I warned you once and twice, Prince Ivan Aleksandrovich,' said Koshchey the Undying. 'I had not thought a third warning would be required.' He stared thoughtfully for a few seconds as he ran the dripping lash of his whip through his fingers and wound it around the stock – then in a single swift movement he reversed it, swung it and clubbed Ivan with the butt. 'Consider the warning given!'

Prince Ivan reeled in his saddle, then spilled sideways out of it and crashed on to the ground. The black horse's blood was smeared cold and wet across his face, warming as it mingled with his own where the leather of the whipstock had smashed against his nose. Though he could barely see through the white pain and red rage burning in his eyes, he staggered to his feet and pulled his sabre from its scabbard.

Koshchey watched him. 'Why, little Prince; what would you do with so terrible a sword?' he asked, leaning forward with his elbows on Mar'ya Morevna's back as though resting on a table.

'I would lay it to your scrawny neck, *chernoknizhnik*!' said Ivan in a low voice, so far gone in his rage that he was past the need of shouting to express it. 'Come down off your horse and fight like a man!'

Koshchey the Undying stroked his beard and smiled, wider and wider until his teeth glistened like tombstones in the moonlight. 'Why should I fight like something I am not? You spoke the reason yourself, Prince Ivan. I am Koshchey *Bessmertnyy Chernoknizhnik*. Men die; I do not die; therefore I am not a man. And therefore I pay no heed to your little challenge and your petty posturing.'

Ivan shook the pain-blindness from his eyes for an instant that was just long enough, and leapt through the crimson mist of fury to where the necromancer was. His sabre was already whirring through the air as his feet left the ground, and he felt the jolt of the weapon striking home before he landed again. Its blade had driven so deep that its hilt was wrenched from his fingers, and though the thump of his landing jolted through all his hurt bones and sent tears from his eyes again, he knew that he had struck as well as he was able.

It was not well enough. With one of his thin, long-fingered hands, Koshchey the Undying lifted Mar'ya Morevna by the scruff of the neck and by the hair of the head, and held her so that she could see what her husband had done. The sabre had hit him in the angle between neck and shoulder and cut down almost to the middle of his body, past where his heart should have been. Its silvered hilt stuck from his chest like a brooch. Koschey grasped it with his free hand – hilt and blade together in those long fingers – and drew the sabre from his body as though out of its proper sheath. And all that horrid while, he laughed.

'You have had your last chance, Prince Ivan. Will you try again,' said Koshchey, throwing down the unstained sabre at Ivan's feet, 'or will you be convinced at last?'

Ivan looked at the blade, gleaming bright and clean in the moonlight. Then he looked at Mar'ya Morevna, hanging like a kitten in Koshchey's huge grasp. And he looked at Koshchey's body, at where a dreadful wound had neither bled nor hurt and was outlined now by nothing more than cloth cut through. Convinced at last, he knew that at this moment, if he made a single finger's move towards his sword-hilt he would die. Slowly, slowly, Prince Ivan sank to his knees and bowed his head.

'Good,' said Koshchey the Undying. 'I have grown weary of this game. My patience with it is at an end. Go away, Ivan Tsarevich, and forget Mar'ya Morevna – or say your prayers, make peace with your God and look out for your head. There will be no more warnings.' He flung Mar'ya Morevna back across his horse's withers, then turned and spurred away.

Clods of earth spattered Ivan's face, but only when the sound of hoofbeats had faded to the silence of the lonely steppe did he collapse forward on to his hands. Any who chanced by might have thought that he was weeping, until they looked more closely; and then they would have seen a fair-haired young man with blood on his face, wearing grubby clothing which once had been fine and princely, rending the grass and the soil of *mat'-syraya-zemlya* with both his hands as he might wish to rend the flesh of his dearest enemy. Had they remained, they might have seen that same young man get to his feet with a curved sabre in his earth-stained hand, look at its edge glittering beneath the moon and smile such a smile as had no place on the face of one so young. It was a smile more right and proper for one steeped in evil over long and cruel years, the sort of smile that made the wise and the wary sign themselves with the life-giving cross and hurry away, glad that such a smile had not been directed at them.

*

A soft wind sighed from the north over the wide white world, carrying the chill of Siberia out over Mother Russia, and with it the first breath of the promise of winter. Ivan Aleksandrovich felt its icy touch, even through his furs, and he shivered; but otherwise he did not move. He was hiding where he had hidden before, snuggled into the forest shadows within easy sight of the dark kremlin that was home to Koshchey the Undying – and prison to his wife Mar'ya Morevna. He lay low, and still, and silent, and he watched.

All was as it had been at an earlier time which Ivan remembered as though it were yesterday. Nothing moved except the wind, and the grasses combed by that wind; nothing breathed except Ivan. He had not seen Koshchey ride from his fortress, but then he had seen nothing with the eyes of his mind or the eyes in his head to suggest that the necromancer dwelt within it. And if he did. . . .

Ivan's hand closed tightly on the hilt of his *shashka* sabre. It was the same sword that had proved so useless before – and yet not the same at all. The heavy broadsword strapped across his back was the same sword as had been handed down through generations of the Khorlov family, yet it too was different. There was a deadliness about them now which had not been there before, a deadliness which could be smelt by those whose nostrils could detect such things. A tang of acids and aromatic spirits, a scent of those herbs and plants left well alone by the wise – a faint, faint whiff of rot and of corruption. And a little more even than that. There were spells that left their aura like a snail-track on the surface of the mind, and what had been done to both swords left them psychically criss-crossed with glistening trails like a damp stone wall by moonlight.

Moonlight that was hovering at the full.

It had cost Ivan much of his store of gold to find and then

buy the distillate that coated his blades with a lethal tarry gum, and most of the remainder to lay those fearful charms into the blades. Once bought, it had cost him much more of his dwindling store of honour to uncork the small stoneware jar and smear what it contained on to the enchanted steel. Once it was done, it was done; but those scents hung about him as a mark and a reminder of exactly what had been done, so that he was unable to dismiss or to forget it.

Perhaps it was the touch of that cold Siberian wind that made him shiver. And perhaps it was something else. . . .

The hours had flickered by as he rode Burka across the steppe, hours that neither he nor Mar'ya Morevna could spare. In those hours Ivan heard again and again the words of Koshchey the Undying: *Forget Mar'ya Morevna, or say your prayers, and make peace with your God, and look out for your head!* Ivan Tsarevich was many things – careless, foolish, forgetful and desperately stubborn – but a coward frightened away by words he was not, especially when they were words he could forget no more than he could forget his wife. Had there been more hours, more days before the dark of the moon, then Ivan would have ridden in the other direction, searching for the Princes who were his brothers by marriage, Princes who were sons of a sorcerer, Princes who might have been able to help him. But there was no time. All he had was his own small store of knowledge and a little courage, all bolstered by love for his lady. So Ivan had said what prayers he knew, signing himself many times with the life-giving cross in the hope that this time, unlike all the other times when soldiers had used it, it might protect him against edge and point. After that he had made his confession to a confused priest in a small village, a gentle holy man who would most likely never know the reasons behind what he had heard and absolved.

And then he had found a blacksmith and bought an iron collar to wear around his throat. It chafed him now, as it had chafed him then, for the cold iron was a full finger thick and rested against the back of his neck like a reminder of the blade it was meant to guard against. Perhaps it would, and perhaps it would not; but the blacksmith's mother had guessed its purpose, and she held it in her hands and said softly, 'May this protect you for your mother's sake, as I wish it might protect my own dear son should he need such a thing.' Ivan hoped against hope that such a blessing would be enough.

Afternoon became evening and day became dusk, and Prince Ivan made his decision. If Koshchey was somewhere near his kremlin, then they would fight sooner; if he was far away, then they would fight later; and if Mar'ya Morevna reached her books of magic before Koshchey caught up with them, then perhaps they would not fight at all. Whatever lay written in her father's hand between the covers of those books had kept the Deathless One secured in his chains throughout all these years, and if it had been used once then of a certainty it could be used again. Ivan rose to his feet, released Burka's reins from the branch where he was tethered and rode out again to save his wife.

*

The kremlin was empty, as it had been before, save for the echoes of Burka's unmuffled hoofs ringing from every wall and down every corridor. Ivan had guessed that if he was to be overheard in this bold venture, then he would be overheard regardless of what he might do to prevent it. Thus there were no pads made of cloth or fur, but only shoes of good forged iron on his horse's feet, as he rode into the skull-cobbled courtyard of Koshchey's kremlin. Instead of waiting in the stone-carven gloom for Mar'ya Morevna, he swung down from Burka's saddle, took his mace in one hand and envenomed sword in the other and went searching.

He found her in a room of the high tower, where any village storyteller might have told him that a Princess would be held captive. She was seated by one of the tall windows that resembled the eye-sockets of a skull, watching without despair, waiting without hope, trusting that somewhere close, sometime soon, her own beloved husband Ivan might rescue her – yet praying he would do nothing so perilous, for this time Koshchey the Undying had made a promise not a threat.

Thus she was slow in rising when Ivan stepped through the door, and slower still to put her arms around him, for she had a dreadful fear that she was embracing one already dead. And then, even though the broadsword had not been drawn and the sabre had been sheathed in the instant of his finding her, she smelt the distilled, ensorcelled death riding on his swords. 'Ivan, beloved, my own and only love, what madness is this?' she asked, and held him close.

'I bought the charms and brew from a *babushka* in a village far from here,' he said, reluctant to speak of it, knowing that the telling did him small honour if at all. 'I asked only for her most sovereign remedy against the malady of life. She gave me this.' He tapped the scabbard of his sabre, seeming almost to feel death burning cold within its wood and leather. 'If it kills him, well and good. If it only leaves him stunned long enough for you to reach your books and the spells within them, then still it's good enough.'

'Directly we leave this kremlin, he will know it,' said Mar'ya Morevna.

'And when he follows us, he will find more than he expects.' Ivan touched the hilts of sabre and broadsword, moving each sword slightly in its scabbard so that the air stank of the venom on their blades.

'Is it enough?'

'*Golubok*, ask me afterwards. For now, all I know is this: if we wait, then I fight him and on his own ground. If we ride away, then he may follow. If he does, then I fight him – but no longer on a ground of his own choosing. And if he fails to follow soon enough, then perhaps, perhaps you will find something in your books of magic that will restore him to his cell, and all will be as it once was before.'

'You hope.'

'I pray.' Prince Ivan took his wife by the hand. 'I can do little else.'

They hurried down the narrow, winding stairs, walking quietly. For all that the kremlin was without living sentries, neither could say with any certainty that it was completely without guardians. They took care not to look too closely at the dreadful carvings which adorned its walls, and wasted no time in reaching the courtyard where Burka awaited their return.

Mar'ya Morevna patted the grey horse on his nose and felt him nuzzle at her hand in return. 'Koshchey's horse was never so friendly,' she said, 'for all that it speaks like a Christian.'

'His horse *speaks?*' Ivan looked from Burka to Mar'ya Morevna and then back again, realizing that though he had thought this adventure was both strange and dangerous, he had given no true thought to just how strange it might become.

'It speaks,' she echoed, stroking Burka again while gazing at her husband and daring him to say that she spoke less than the truth. 'It speaks, and it can sense when someone has given wrong or insult to its master.'

'How so? When I come calling unannounced?'

'No, not when you enter his kremlin. But once you leave it, bearing what Koshchey regards as his.'

'*Tak*,' said Ivan, after he had helped Mar'ya Morevna into Burka's saddle and clambered up behind. 'Then let his horse sense this.' He shook grey Burka's reins and they galloped from the dark kremlin. . . .

*

. . . And Koshchey's black horse stumbled.

The plaited lash of his riding-whip whined like a mosquito as he struck the horse across its neck. '*Chyornaya sukin syn!*' he cried as he struck the horse again and again. It screamed and reared, threatening his seat still more, then slammed its forefeet back against the ground and shook its head desperately, as though trying to believe the skin-splitting blows of the whip troubled it no more than raindrops, for all that the drops falling from its neck were drops of blood.

'Tell me,' said Koshchey curiously, after a time in which his arm had grown weary, 'if you stumble to warn me, then since you have the power of speech why do you not tell me this without bringing yourself pain?'

'I stumble,' said the black horse, speaking the words of men in that voice which was not the voice of men, 'because it is laid upon all my kind that they must stumble when they scent aught amiss. It is no choice of mine, Koshchey the Unskilled Rider, that each time I stumble you are like to fall.'

Koshchey considered this; agreed with it; then beat the black horse again for its insolence in calling him unskilled. He wiped the blood and shreds of skin from his whip before hanging it from his saddle, where it could most easily be reached, and said, 'Then from your words, I must presume that the foolish Tsarevich has shown no more wit than I expected.'

'If by that you mean he has returned, Koshchey the Undying,' said the horse, 'then he has indeed. I smell a Russian smell within your kremlin, for once again he has taken Mar'ya Morevna from the high tower and has stolen her away.'

'And can we catch them?' asked Koshchey, letting the promissory wet lash of his whip trail down like a snake's body across his horse's neck.

The black horse tossed its head, caring now no more for the whip than for a fly in the hot days of summer. 'Of course I can catch them,' it said. 'If you were to pause and sow barley, wait for it to grow and bring the harvest in, and if you were to use that barley to brew good beer and drink it down, become well drunk and sleep it off, and only then ride in pursuit, even after all of that I should surely catch them.' The horse lifted its head and stared at Koshchey out of one blazing red eye. 'But you would have to make quite sure that you did not fall off, if you wanted to catch them too.'

Koshchey the Undying laughed at that. 'Granting you the power of speech,' he said, 'seems sometimes a mistake.' And then, because no serf should dare to mock its master, he beat the black horse with his whip until the red blood ran once more from its shoulders. After that, he put the whip aside.

And instead, drew forth his great sword.

*

Prince Ivan knew what it meant when the shriek of a storm-wind rose out of a clear, quiet sky. He wrenched back on Burka's reins, and once the grey horse came to a skidding halt he threw one leg over the high-peaked saddle and dropped to the ground. By the time he had regained his balance, both the straight sword and the curved were clear of their scabbards and gleaming in his hands. Koshchey the Undying would not take him unawares twice in a row.

Mar'ya Morevna turned the grey Burka back, and while one hand unhooked the heavy mace that had hung from the saddle – holding it poised to swing at whatever enemy rode the whirlwind – her other hand patted the horse's neck to gentle him from his fright at being dragged so roughly to a stop.

For many minutes there was nothing save the hammer of the wind, which tugged their clothing and swirled shreds of torn grass into their eyes. Prince Ivan used that respite to slide his round shield down on to his arm, and found himself more than once wishing for the mail-shirt that his mother Ludmyla Tsaritsa had wanted him to carry on his travels. At least the chafing iron collar had become a comforting weight about his neck, wide enough and thick enough to break the blade of any sword. But the weight of a good shirt of mail would have been more comfortable still.

And then Koshchey the Undying rode out of the evening mist.

The curved sword in his hand was no sabre or Cossack *shashka*, but a butcher's cleaver stretched to obscene proportions – yet he wielded it as featly as he might his riding-whip of plaited leather. Ivan met the first stroke with both of his own swords, crossed to block the blow, but the impact of it drove him to his knees and left his arms shaking with the force of a cut that they had barely turned aside.

Koshchey dragged his black horse to a standstill by main force on the brutal bit; and once it stood quivering and snorting at the end of long tracks torn by its hoofs in the soft earth, he stared at his young adversary. The stare was not that honourable gaze which one opponent gives another; rather, it was that of a gardener regarding a wasp which has been no more than a persistent nuisance, whose time has come at last.

'Come down, Koshchey *Bessmertnyy*,' said Prince Ivan, and rang his swords together. 'Come down, come close and let me see how brave you are.'

'Braver than you, at least,' said Koshchey with an unpleasant smile. 'At least I do not tremble.' It was an ugly jest and one uncalled-for, since the flickering along Ivan's sword-blades came not from fear but simply from muscle-tremors born in the shock of the cut he had warded from his head.

'Dead men do not tremble,' said Ivan Tsarevich, and levelled both his swords to guard. 'Come down and be dead, Koshchey the Undying.'

'That is true,' agreed Koshchey. He swung from his saddle and stamped his boot-soles squarely into the face of Mother Earth. 'But neither do those who have no fear of death. Come here, trembling Prince, and find out what it means to be truly dead.'

'I doubt that you could tell me now,' said Ivan softly, poising the broadsword behind his head and the sabre near his hip. 'But perhaps you might tell me after *this*!'

And Ivan sprang like a grey wolf leaping from a thicket, although no grey wolf ever had such fangs.

Thrust and cut came as a single motion, curved blade and straight scissoring together. And Koshchey was in the middle. The shrill ring of poisoned steel was lost in a thick wet sound such as might be heard in any butcher's shop, and Koshchey the Undying toppled backwards to the ground with both swords buried in his body – and this time, with enough poison in his blood to slay perhaps ten thousand of a Tatar horde. He kicked, and squirmed, and clawed at the bright blades.

And then lay still.

'It worked,' said Ivan softly, almost to himself. Whether it was the poison or the spells which killed Koshchey, he did not know. He did not want to know.

Ivan looked down at the long, lean body lying still in death at last, and shook his head. He had never killed anyone before, and hoped within himself never to do so again, either in combat or by legal process. It was something done so quickly and so easily, yet so impossible to reverse. That was why he sank briefly to one knee, signed himself and then dead Koshchey with the life-giving cross and silently commended the necromancer's soul to God, hoping that He would see fit to receive it as the priests said He had received even the black soul of Judas. 'Hell is a constant threat,' Metropolitan

Archbishop Levon Popovich had told him once, 'but since the Mercy of God is without span or limit, then surely Hell is empty.'

Ivan glanced at Mar'ya Morevna, staring at a sight she had never dreamt of seeing, and then looked at Koshchey's black horse. The poor beast was in ribbons, torn so grievously by whip and spur that each movement of its great muscles was as plain to sight as an anatomist's drawing. 'Poor,' he said softly, stroking its nose as it pushed towards his hand. 'Poor, poor.' No matter that this horse could supposedly use the speech of men, there were times when only gentle noises without meaning were the proper thing to utter, and this held true as much for men as beasts. He put one hand to the reins, meaning to bring it with him, but the horse wrenched back from his grasp, rearing up on its hind legs and cutting the air with fore-hoofs shod like axes.

Ivan flinched back from the hammering strokes, knowing them to be just threats – at least for now. If he gave the black horse any further reason to suspect his motives, there was no doubt that it would trample him.

'It wants to stay with its master,' said Mar'ya Morevna. Though her face was pale, her voice was steady. 'Leave it to luck, or to the wolves.'

Ivan turned to look at his wife, hearing once again that edge of ruthlessness which could dismiss the slaying of five thousand Tatars as the only thing to do. But he understood now more than then. Every other time that she had seen Koshchey's black horse, it had been bearing her away to a captivity longer than most mortal lifetimes. Small wonder she had little affection for the beast. 'As you wish,' he said, and shrugged.

'Bring your swords,' she said more quietly.

Ivan glanced at where the weapons nailed Koshchey's corpse to the ground and shook his head. 'I like them better where they are,' he told her. 'At least until you do something with your spell-books.'

'Still doubting?'

'Just careful. If what slew him was the spell on the steel, then I would rather it stayed in place.'

'Understood.' Mar'ya Morevna returned the mace she

held to its place on Burka's saddle and held out her hand. 'Then mount up. I have no desire to linger in this place.' Faint and far away, the melancholy howl of a Russian wolf hung on the air, and both horses put their ears back. 'The dinner-guests are gathering already.'

Ivan's mouth compressed to a tight, bloodless line as he stared at the rolling, terrified eyes of Koshchey's black horse. 'I would as soon not leave the horse,' he said, an edge of stubbornness creeping into his voice. 'Dumb beast or talking, it deserves better than the wolves. Maruchka, beloved,' his hand was already reaching for the reins again and this time the horse was not backing away, 'if the sight of this creature offends you, then I'll take off its harness and set it free. Just let me bring it clear of wolf country.'

'If you want a horse like that one, get your own,' came a thin, cold voice behind him. 'Otherwise, leave mine alone.'

Ivan Aleksandrovich froze on the spot, unwilling to turn round despite Mar'ya Morevna's tiny gasp of fear. Or perhaps because of it. The voice was that of one whose life he had stilled, one he had struck down and commended to God's mercy. Of someone, the only one, that he had killed ever in his life; and it was not a voice he had thought to hear again, except in his darkest nightmares. And then he turned, and all those nightmares yet undreamed came true at once.

Koshchey the Undying stared at him past the sword-blades criss-crossed in his chest, and hatred in that icy gaze would have been easier for Ivan to bear than the emotionless regard that raked across him like a razor. The necromancer sat upright very slowly, very carefully, made clumsy by the weight and length of steel he carried in his body. A good half-*arshin* of it pinned him to the earth until he wrenched free of its poisonous embrace, and then Koshchey *Bessmertnyy* stood upright again.

'These,' he said, wrenching the swords from his cold flesh, 'belong to you.' The two blades clashed together as they were flung casually to the ground, bright and clean in the evening light. Clean of blood and clean of other, less honourable substances. That meant only one thing: the many, many poisons which had coated them had been washed from the swords' edges and were pumping through the necromancer's body – and other than the first massive shock which had laid him on the ground like something dead, they were causing him no discomfort whatsoever.

Ivan looked at the swords, and saw his death in the instant he picked them up.

He looked at Koshchey the Undying, and saw his death in the instant that the necromancer's amusement ran out once and for all.

He looked at Mar'ya Morevna . . . .

. . . . And saw in her eyes and in her memory the only future he could hope for any more.

The iron collar round his neck was now no more than surplus weight, the swords lying criss-cross at his feet no more than a symbol he could carry as he died, so that any who might speak of him in times yet to come could say that Ivan Aleksandrovich had fallen sword in hand. He had read that phrase frequently enough in the old tales, and had thought that it was little comfort to the ones who fell. How very small that comfort truly was, he had not known until now.

During those few, few times when Ivan had stood beside his father on the ramparts as a witness to some judgement or other, he had wondered how those condemned to die could go to it with such ease of mind. On those occasions he had never had sufficient strength of stomach to watch right to the end, but . . . .

But he knew now.

When nothing else remains, no hope of reprieve and no final chance of escape, then dignity becomes the final refuge. And death itself, the end and the beginning, must surely become such an adventure as no one of courage could approach except with boldness.

Give thanks to the good God, said the old story, *that in His wisdom he set death at the end of life, and not at the beginning* . . . .

Ivan stopped as swiftly as he had ever moved, closing his hand on the hilt of his sabre, and as he straightened he swung its razor edge right at the centre of the grin half-hidden in the midst of Koshchey's beard. He felt the cool, ribbed metal of the sabre's grip in his closing fingers, and he felt the weight of its blade tug forward as the weapon left the ground.

And then he heard Mar'ya Morevna scream, a sound that was not one which his brave, beloved wife should make; and he heard a shrill hissing like something heavy moving swiftly through the air, and he heard a ringing sound like iron cut through by steel, and he heard . . . . felt . . . . *blackness*.

*

Koshchey the Deathless waved his hands in the air and blew on his fingers to relieve their sting. His huge, curved sword had sunk for half its length into the ground, still thrumming from buried point to blurring pommel with the force of a cut which had sliced cleanly through an unsuspected iron collar and the neck it was supposed to guard. 'Almost, little Prince,' said Koshchey. 'You were very, very close. But not quite close enough.'

Prince Ivan Aleksandrovich lay in two pieces at his feet, head parted from shoulders by the sharp-edged sword. There was very little blood. Some had soaked into the fabric of a crimson coat trimmed with sable, and a little more had beaded among the strands of the dead Prince's pale blond hair. The rest had drained into the yielding earth, leaving a trace of steam to hang on the cool evening air.

Ivan Tsarevich stared up through the bitter-scented steam. His eyes and mouth were open and his expression was surprised, so that it seemed he might have put more trust in the collar at his neck than had been justified. It had been sheared through, back to front. Only just – but then, even half-way would have been enough.

Koshchey looked down at the head and body, separated not only by the blade of that long, sharp sword but also by an *arshin* of wet, darkened Russian soil and by all the distance between the living and the dead. Then he looked up.

Mar'ya Morevna was still sitting astride the ordinary grey horse which had given him so much trouble, and there was a mace in her hand. The horse was sidling and stamping amidst the heavy smell of blood, and Mar'ya Morevna had let the mace hang slack and useless. Instead she chewed at the knuckles of the fist thrust into her mouth, shocked by the sight of a dead husband as if there had never before been

176

widows in Russia. The good God knew – when the Tatars came from the east and the Germans came from the west – there had been many and more than enough, and there would doubtless be many more again.

Koshchey *Bessmertnyy* stared at both horse and rider for several moments, then wrenched his great cleaver of a sword out of the blood-warmed earth. He wiped it between his fingers, flickered the spatters aside and thrust it back into its manskin scabbard.

'Mar'ya Morevna,' he said, paying no heed to the silent tears that ran slowly down her cheeks, 'you are well aware of where my kremlin is. Go to it, go to the chambers set aside for you and stay there.'

Mar'ya Morevna did not move. 'And if I do not?' she said. 'Will you cut off my head too?'

'Cut off the head of the fairest Princess in all the Russias?' asked Koshchey the Undying, grinning with all his teeth. 'No, I will not. For that would be a waste, Mar'ya Morevna, and besides, if I cut off your head you would scarcely remember so well how much I grow displeased with thieves.'

'So why do you send me away,' she asked, 'knowing that you could catch me at any time you chose?'

He looked at her, then shrugged. 'I would have sent you away, foolish woman, so that you might not witness the full extent of my displeasure. But since you choose to remain, then watching what follows is not my choice but yours.'

Koshchey took an axe from the saddle strapped to his black and bloody horse, then drew his sword once more out of its sheath made of the skins of men. Holding one weapon in each hand, he raised them before Mar'ya Morevna's eyes and said, 'This is your final opportunity. If you fail to leave now, I will not let you leave until I am done.'

Mar'ya Morevna looked at the axe and at the sword, knowing what it was that he intended, and bowed her head. 'Do what you will, Koshchey,' she said. 'But no matter what you do, know this: for all the days of your long life, I shall compare you to my own beloved husband, and always I shall find you wanting.' Then she straightened her back and stared straight before her, her eyes seeing only the Ivan Tsarevich of her memory, smiling and bold, laughing and merry, courageous and stern.

But Koshchey the Undying took both sword and worked for almost an hour, until he was in perspiration with his labour and until all that remained of Prince Ivan Aleksandrovich Khorlov was a heap of scattered fragments that glistened in the light of the newly-risen moon. He took a small barrel from his saddle – such a barrel as holds small-beer for riders who grow thirsty – and drank it dry. Then he opened it and stuffed the bloody shreds and bones inside, without even such prayers as dead Prince Ivan in his kindness had spoken over Koshchey's corpse. After that, with no more shriving than a spit and a curse, he flung the barrel into a swift river leading over many *vyorsty* to the bitter Azov Sea, and dragged Mar'ya Morevna weeping back to his dark kremlin.

*

It was close on a quarter of a year since Prince Ivan's sisters had heard any news of their brother, apart from an occasional letter which told them little more than what they knew already: that except when trying to divert the attention of Anastasya Solov'ev, Ivan had little talent for writing. The sorcerers Fenist and Vasiliy and Mikhail had made many and many comforting excuses concerning that long silence. Chief among these was – with a smile – the reasoning that since Ivan had recently married the fairest Princess in all the Russias, sending letters to his relatives would have a low priority. Besides of course, they said, there was the difficulty of keeping track of constant changes of address.

This was reasoning which Yekaterina and Yelizaveta and Yelena laughed to the proper degree of scorn, and then several degrees beyond. *They*, they pointed out – once or twice using the cold water of the kremlin moat as a source of emphasis – had never failed to stay in contact with their parents the Tsar and Tsaritsa Khorlovskiy, therefore why should their brother the Tsarevich be any different? They said so with sufficient frequency that at last their husbands went to certain well-locked drawers and cabinets, the better to assure their wives . . . .

. . . . And there found items which they, being wise, chose not to mention.

Prince Ivan – on being asked and perhaps, just slightly, persuaded – had left items of silver with his brothers-in-law. At the time of asking they had been keepsakes, mementoes, nothing more. Now they had become something far, far more.

In that part of the wide white world where the heretics lived – the Catholics whose priests spoke Church Latin rather than Orthodox Church Slavonic – the black-tarnished pieces of silver would have been called *memento mori*, memories of death. A reminder of what comes to all, in God's good time. In Holy Mother Russia they were warnings instead of memories. Ivan Aleksandrovich had left a knife, a fork, a spoon, all from the pouch at his belt and all as personal as his own fingers.

And now all of these were black.

Mikhail Voronov, the Raven, Lord of the Dark Forests, looked at the silver spoon left him by Prince Ivan. It had been bright when it was given, polished enough to challenge the stars and the waning moon in the night sky overhead.

Now it was not only black, but it stank of death.

Knyaz' Mikhail sat for many hours that night, leafing through his books of lore in the hope that he could learn just what might have happened to Prince Ivan. They told him nothing other than what was already far too plain.

It became somewhat more than nothing when thunder from a clear sky rang out over Prince Mikhail's kremlin, and of a sudden his brother Vasiliy was sitting in a chair at the far side of the book-heaped table. Perhaps it was typical of Prince Vasiliy, and perhaps it was typical only of his youth, but the Eagle's feet were already crossed at the ankles and propped up on the table.

'These books,' said Mikhail the Raven reprovingly, rescuing them from beneath the heels of Vasiliy's boots, 'are far older than you.'

'And most probably more boring,' said Vasiliy Orlov. He folded his arms with a movement that suggested a small, slight fluttering of wings, and glanced without much interest at the leather-bound volumes stacked across the wide library desk. Then he held up a blackened fork which had once been polished silver. 'Brother Ivan is in trouble,' he stated.

'Brother Ivan is dead,' said Prince Mikhail. 'And Koshchey the Undying has been loosed once more upon the white world.'

Prince Vasiliy raised his fur-brimmed hat a little and signed himself with the cross. 'Poor young fool,' he said, even though Ivan had been no more than four years his junior. 'I didn't know that things had come to that. Although from the way you say it, I can guess at something else. He was the one who released Koshchey from wherever he was being held.'

'Vanya was never one for remembering what anybody told him.' Mikhail opened one of his books of magic and thumbed through it . 'But bad memory isn't punished by death in any realm that *I* know. So I intend, with your and Fenik's help, to set matters to rights.'

'And just where is our sharp-eyed brother on this fine, clear night?'

'Using those sharp eyes of his, at my request.'

'Looking for. . . ?'

'Ivan.' Mikhail Voronov's dark eyes glittered in the golden lamplight, so that it was impossible to read what thoughts swam in their depths; but his voice was edged with faint disgust. 'Or whatever Koshchey *Bessemertnyy* has left of him.'

Vasiliy flinched at what was implied in those few simple words. '*Postav' tochku*, Mikhail Charodeyevich!' he said hurriedly. 'I don't want to hear anything more about it!'

'All right, Vasya,' said the Raven, smiling slightly at his burly brother's squeamishness. 'But once Fenik has found Vanya's body, you may have to carry him. You're by far the strongest of the three of us – except, perhaps, where your stomach is concerned . . . .'

'Very funny, dear brother Misha. Very funny indeed. Can you see how much it doesn't make me laugh?' Prince Vasiliy looked at one particular book amongst the many littering the table-top, raising his eyebrows slightly as he tapped its covers with a cautious finger. 'And what about the words in here?' he asked dubiously. 'Is reading them to be your part in all this?'

Mikhail glanced at the book and nodded. 'It will be the best and only part that I can play,' he replied 'And as you well know, that part is one that only I *can* play. Though I confess I relish it as little as you do.'

'I expected as much. *Boga radi!* Misha, necromancy is a chancy business.'

'I know that well enough. I do this for our brother Ivan's sake, and for our wives, his sisters. But I have no wish to make a habit of it. Some habits are impossible to break.'

'If the old stories tell it truly, that was how Koshchey began as well. Trying to do good, perhaps.'

'Perhaps. I cannot see what good can be done if you forfeit your soul in the process.'

'And what do we do now?'

Prince Mikhail Voronov stared hard at the book of necromancy, and at spells which told how even death could be turned back on itself and set at nothing. Despite his skill at bright magic, he shuddered slightly at the thought of such dark sorcery and signed himself with the life-giving cross. 'Now,' he said in a low voice, 'we wait until we hear from Fenik.'

*

It was not a long time, and it was not a short time before the ceiling of the kremlin split apart and Prince Fenist the Falcon stood before them. There was weariness in his face and sea-salt in his hair, but his bright eyes were as keen as ever. He reached into his belt, pulled out a silver eating-knife that now was black and laid it on the desk among the books of magic. 'I have flown many *vyorsty*, over land and over sea,' he said, 'and at last I think I have found the thing we seek.' Then he sat down and drank good wine as if to take a foul taste from his mouth.

The other Princes waited until their brother set his cup aside and was prepared to speak again, then Vasiliy the Eagle leaned forward and asked, 'What did you find?'

'There was a barrel floating in Azovskoe More. In bird's shape, I landed on it, but it was too heavy for me to drag onto the shore. It still floats there . . . . and it reeks of death.'

'Are you sure that Vanya's body is inside?' asked Mikhail the Raven.

Fenist Sokolov looked at his brother, and his face was grim. 'I am sure that what is inside was once Ivan Tsarevich,' he said softly, choosing his words with care, 'but from the size and shape of that barrel, I would be reluctant to call its contents a body any more. Koshchey the Undying is a savage enemy.'

'*Tak*,' said Prince Mikhail the Raven , pushing all his books aside except for one. 'It is as I had begun to suspect. Rest a while, Fenist Charodeyevich; you look as though you need it. And then lead Vasya to the barrel. Vasiliy, do what you can: lift it from the water, or pull it to a beach. But for your stomach's sake, don't open it. Leave that unpleasantness to me.'

'I have not the slightest wish to open it,' said Vasya, and his mouth quirked at the mere thought of what must be within that barrel after days on the open sea.

'Whatever is inside, it was once our brother Vanya,' said Fenist the Falcon sharply. 'Speak with a little more respect. You should do his memory that courtesy at least.' Prince Vasiliy had the grace to look abashed, but Fenist had already turned his attention to Mikhail the Raven. 'I am assuming, brother, from the way in which you give your orders, that you are not flying with us. So where are you going, and when will you return?'

Prince Mikhail lifted his book of necromancy and put it in the pocket of his belt. 'Find the barrel,' he said, 'and wait beside it. You will not wait long before I join you, even though I travel by a different route. There is a thing that I need, and I will only find it West of the Sun and East of the Moon.' He stood up from the table and spread out his arms – and a raven hung an instant on the air, beating great wings as black as midnight, and then was gone from sight.

*

No matter what Mikhail had told them, it was a long, cold wait on the beach with only the barrel for company. Just an ordinary barrel, stained slightly with salt from the bitter waters of the Azov Sea; yet it was company which neither Fenist nor Vasiliy wanted to share too closely. A scent hung about it as if something was leaking stealthily between the staves, and though it was faint in the still air it was more than enough to keep them both at a distance.

Vasiliy looked at it sidelong and then, for the third time since he had changed back from eagle to man, he went to the water's edge and washed his hands. Fenist the Falcon sat in the sand, chewing on a long spike of marram grass and watching his brother sardonically. 'You were in bird's shape, Vasya,' he said. 'You should really be washing your feet.'

Prince Vasiliy Orlov glared at him. '*Zamolchat'!*' he snapped. 'Shut up! You didn't have to carry it!' Then he scrubbed his hands with sand and water all over again.

Fenist gazed out across the sea with sharp eyes hooded behind their lashes, and said nothing. Vasya was not entirely correct in his accusation, for in the form of a bright falcon Fenist had settled on the barrel as it flopped ponderously through the waves, and had felt the ugly heaviness of it as it rolled sluggishly beneath him. No barrel so small should have weighed so much, except for those which sailors carried on board ship; and they, like this, were tightly packed with chopped, well-salted meat. . . .

Prince Fenist Sokolov stared at the barrel for a long time. Then he spat out his piece of grass as though it had suddenly begun to taste bad, and moved further down the beach.

There was a small, discreet muttering of thunder in the far distance, and a brief flicker of lightning nearer at hand, and Mikhail Voronov the Raven stepped out of the empty air with a stone bottle in each hand.

Fenist saluted with a small wave of his hand but Vasiliy, washing again, straightened up with a jerk – then bent again hastily to retrieve his hat, which had fallen off and into the sea. 'I wish,' he said irritably, 'that you would stop creeping about like that!'

Mikhail grinned crookedly at his big brother, who was wringing sea-water out of what had been a perfectly good furred hat and now looked like some kind of small drowned animal. He was looking baleful. 'Not everyone needs to travel on the wings of storm,' he said. 'And at least it took your mind off what was troubling it.'

Vasiliy glanced quickly, guiltily towards the sinister small barrel, and twisted his hat still harder. He took care to make no comment, about either the barrel or his feelings concerning it. Having been taken to task once on that account, he had no desire to repeat the experience, especially from Mikhail whose tongue and choice of words could cut like razors when he so desired. For all his size and strength, Vasya was a gentle soul. He clapped the mangled hat back on his head, where it first drooped and then slowly began to drip.

'West of the Sun and East of the Moon,' said Fenist the Falcon, standing up and flinging his latest blade of grass away. 'And what were you seeking there, Misha my brother?'

'These,' said Mikhail and held out the stone bottles. 'The Water of Death and the Water of Life.'

Fenist was astonished. 'How in the name of the good God did you get those?'

Mikhail looked at Vasiliy in his dripping hat and smiled a slow smile. 'Creeping about,' he replied.

Vasiliy used his finger to catch a drip running down his nose, and flickered it at his youngest brother. Though he said nothing aloud, his thoughts were plain in his face.

Fenist, however, laughed; then he too looked at Vasya and waved his hand in a general direction along the beach. 'Misha has things to do,' he said, 'and I doubt that you'd want to watch them. Certainly *I* don't.' He glanced pointedly towards Mikhail and the barrel, then began striding briskly off towards the farthest dunes, well out of sight of both.

Vasiliy looked at them: at Fenist, walking away; at the dreadful barrel, squatting in the place where he had dragged it with revulsion twisting at his features; and at Mikhail, prying off its lid with an expression of fascinated curiosity foremost on his face. He watched Misha longest of all, until the barrel's lid came free, and then made the mistake of looking inside. Vasya stared, eyes bulging from their sockets as he clapped one hand across his mouth, and then he sprinted for the safety of the dunes.

*

Mikhail Charodeyevich Voronov stood upright with a little grunt of effort and braced his hands into the small of a back outraged by the length of time he had been stooping. 'Aa-*arh!*' he barked as he straightened up and all the complex little bones went slotting back to where they should have been.

He looked down and thought that it had probably been easier for Vanya, since he could not have felt a thing in sinew, muscle or in bone. Ivan Aleksandrovich Khorlov, his sister's brother, lay more or less stark naked at Mikhail's feet, his body patterned criss-cross with livid lines where Koshchey the Undying had chopped it apart.

Rearranging all the pieces had taken Mikhail five hours on his knees in wet sand, and only then because he had given in to impatience at long last and used magic to bring all the smaller rags and fragments back to where they originally belonged. He had thanked the good God more than once that Koshchey had been so vindictive, so determined that no part of his foe should remain on the face of Mother Earth. Otherwise Prince Ivan might have lacked a finger, or a toe –or a kidney, lung or heart. Perhaps even his head, had Koshchey been in the habit of taking such trophies.

The stained shreds of Ivan's clothing were piled on his chest and the split halves of an iron collar had been restored to his neck. Mikhail had turned the pieces of the collar over and over in his hands before replacing it, shaking his head and wishing that this gallant young idiot had been less gallant, less idiotic, and had taken the time to ask questions of those who could have given him sound answers.

The husbands of his sisters, for a start. . . .

Misha dismissed those flickers of annoyance and sank to his knees, saying a small prayer that the good God would look favourably on a young man who tried to do good even though those good deeds had brought nothing more than evil. The prayers said, he opened the first of the two stone bottles, signed both Ivan and himself with the life-giving cross and sprinkled the clear and icy Water of Death across the sadly tattered corpse. From the feet to the head he sprinkled it, and then across the shoulders, side to side. '*Kreshchu tebya, sam kreshchus', day tebe Bog byt' tselym, vo slava Bogu!*' he said as the bottle gurgled empty. 'I sign you with the cross, I sign myself with the cross, God grant wholeness to you, glory be to God.'

As Mikhail Voronov held his breath, a faint silvery shimmering enveloped the body, like mist at twilight. Knowing he should look away and yet fascinated by the mysteries of his art, he watched as the ugly crimson tracks of cutting edges faded from Prince Ivan's skin to leave it whole and unmarred. Within a few seconds even that unbroken skin had faded from sight as his clothing, wool and linen, leather, silk and fur – all of them once-living things – flowed together in a blur of colour to leave Vanya's body as it had been in the instant before Koshchey the Undying struck off his head.

Mikhail released his held-in breath in a long sigh between his teeth. Thus far, at least, his hopes had become reality. There remained only the Water of Life and, presumptuous though the thought might be, there was no reason why that too should not work as he had hoped. The Raven held its stone bottle up to his eyes, as if he could see through the hollowed basalt to the liquid it contained and read there whether or not he was wasting his time. There was a film of cold sweat on Misha's forehead as he withdrew the stopper, a smooth plug of solid rock, but the scent that it released was at once a reassurance and a promise of success. Nothing that smelt like summer flowers and the green spring steppe after a shower of rain could do anything but good. He signed himself with the cross once more and, with a silent prayer, poured out the water.

It was black and icy cold, so cold indeed that it smoked like winter breath as each drop left the bottle. A little sprinkled on to Ivan's hands and a little on his feet, a little above his heart and a little between his brows, and after that the Water of Life was all gone.

And nothing happened.

Mikhail, *Knyzaz' tyomnogo lesa*, stared at the empty bottle like a man betrayed and drew his breath to curse, for all that he had was all that there was.

Then Prince Ivan opened his eyes and drew in a breath so sharp and sudden that it made him cough, and sat up quickly like a man too long asleep. One hand went to his throat and the other rubbed most carefully at the back of his head. '*Bozhe moy!*' he said. 'I have the devil's own ache in my neck, and it goes right from one side to the other!'

Mikhail had dropped to his knees beside his brother, ready to embrace him and to reassure him after all the horrors of his death – but when he heard Ivan say that, he collapsed forward in the sands of the bitter Azov Sea and laughed until he could laugh no more. . . .

CHAPTER EIGHT

How Prince Ivan went looking for a faster horse

'Dead?' said Ivan. 'What do you mean, dead?'

Ivan had been able to talk for only a few minutes – mostly to Misha until the others returned – and it was plain that he had no memory at all of how he came to be sitting on a beach with all of his brothers-in-law around him. The three sorcerer Princes sat on the sand and listened to what he had to say – which for the greater part was the same nonsense as a man woken suddenly from a deep and dreaming sleep. They watched him massage the muscles of his neck, and every now and then heard him complain about aches in that neck; and though for the most part they restrained their amusement to mannerly smiles, every once in a while he would say something that would cause one or all of them to burst out in hastily stifled laughter. His latest comment was perhaps the worst. Now that the ugly part of the business had been successfully accomplished, Fenist and Vasiliy were filled with the sort of idiotic good humour that normally comes with too much vodka.

Mikhail, for his part, sat cross-legged to one side and said very little, though he listened a great deal and it would have seemed – had anyone been watching him – that he was as amused by the foolishness of his two brothers as they were by the innocent ignorance of Prince Ivan. 'I mean dead, Vanya,' he said, 'as in having your head cut from your body by Koschchey the Undying.'

Ivan stared, round-eyed, his expression that of a man who *knows* he is the butt of some deeply-laid joke. His conviction of that was more certain still when Vasiliy and Fenist concealed smiles behind their hands, while Mikhail's expression did not change by so much as a single flicker. '*Eto polneyshaya yerunda!*' he said. 'That's full of nonsense! I was wearing an iron collar that no sword— '

'You still have that collar around your neck,' said Mikhail, sounding perhaps more impatient than he intended. 'Look at it before you make yourself more foolish than you have already.'

Perhaps it was the tone of Mikhail's voice, or perhaps the invitation to inspect something far more solid than mere voiced opinions, but Ivan fell silent and, despite the times he had already rubbed his neck and complained of aches and pains, for several seconds he became reluctant to move his hand towards it. When at last his fingers touched the collar and felt the burred edges where something had sliced it through, he became as white as the foam on the waves breaking behind him. With both hands he moved the sheared halves, rotating them in opposite directions until the neatly bisected iron catch met again beneath his ear. It was as if that was what was required to convince him, because his face – white though it had become when first he reached up – went as pale and bloodless as all his skin had been before Prince Mikhail sprinkled him with the Water of Life.

Ivan looked at the three Princes, seeing none of them, and struggled to his feet. He said nothing as he walked slowly away through the dunes and the rustling dry grass and, signalled to silence by Mikhail the Raven, nor did they. It was many minutes before he returned, and when he did the collar was no longer around his neck but held in one hand with the same caution as he might have used to hold a poisonous serpent. Its two halves chimed one against the other as he walked, marking each step with a faint clangour as of a church bell knelling for a funeral – except that in this funeral, the corpse had climbed out of his coffin and was leaving the graveyard behind.

'I still can't really believe it,' he said in a small voice, looking at the sheared collar. He shook it and its pieces rang together softly, balefully, a reminder of what had happened. 'Though this should be proof enough. I *was* dead. Koshchey killed me.'

'And we brought you back to life so that you could confound him,' said Vasiliy the Eagle, recovered from his earlier queasiness of stomach and growing quite pugnacious. 'And so that you could do to him what he has done to you.'

'Almost, Vasya,' said Fenist Sokolov, the Falcon, 'but not quite.' He looked at his brothers with a mingling of amusement and concern. 'We cannot allow Ivan to go charging back into the dark kremlin without some better protection than a restored life, or Koshchey will merely take it away again. You know he can. You know he *will*.'

Vasiliy shrugged. 'True,' he said. 'You could have spared yourself much misery, Ivan Aleksandrovich, had you come to us for help in the first place.'

'My thought exactly,' agreed Fenist.

'There was no first place,' said Ivan, and if his voice was somewhat sharp he thought it justified. 'Because there was no time. Koshchey himself told me that once Mar'ya Morevna was his prisoner past the dark of the moon, she would be his prisoner for always. And he still holds her. Did you expect me to leave her there without doing *something*?'

The sorcerer brothers looked at one another, then back at Ivan, and each of them had the good grace to look slightly embarrassed. Mikhail the Raven was drawing patterns in the sand with a small piece of driftwood; meaningless patterns, but of such a shape that the eye either flinched away from them at once or followed and was trapped. Ivan's gaze was one that flinched away and met Mikhail's calm stare instead. 'None of us said that, Ivan Aleksandrovich,' he said, 'so you can put your honour and your pride away until you need it. And after that, you can sit down and listen while we work out what to do. Last night the moon was just past full, so we have time enough to talk, at least.'

The discussion lasted for almost an hour, passing from one Prince to another. Each of them had questions for Ivan, interrogating him closely on whichever point gave most weight to their own argument of the moment. There was only one problem, and it seemed to Ivan that he had been the only one to see it: neither Fenist, nor Vasiliy, nor even Mikhail the Raven had said anything about how Koshchey the Undying might be killed. Escaped, yes; avoided, yes; imprisoned again, yes – although with reservations about how it might be done. But not how he might be done away with once and for all.

At first Prince Ivan had felt slightly uneasy about the ease with which his mind accepted that killing was the only solution to his problem, but when he brought the matter up his brother Princes laughed at such scruples.

'*D'yavol*, Vanya!' said Fenist the Falcon. 'The old bastard cut off your head! Doing the same to him is only right and proper.' Fenik hesitated, then produced a kind of helpless grin-and-shrug. 'Of course, first you have to find some way to do it so that he won't just get up again. . . .'

'*Spasibo, zyat'ushka,*' said Ivan, very dry and trying not to smile at the Falcon's expression. 'Thanks for reminding me of that small point – which leaves me as helpless as a man with one foot tied to his ear!'

They all laughed at Fenist's discomfiture, all except Prince Mikhail. 'I don't see anything amusing about your "small point", Vanya,' he said, stripping the length of driftwood down between his fingers until it was little more than a splayed brush of fibre. He shredded it still further until it came to pieces in his hands and fell to the sand of the beach, then raised his head and gazed into three pairs of worried eyes.

'Maybe I didn't tell you, all three of you, and maybe you just didn't realize – but those two bottles of the Waters, enough to complete my task, were all that I was allowed. Understand this: I may travel East of the Sun and West of the Moon again, but I may not go on Ivan's behalf. One visit to the Well and to the Fountain is all that any sorcerer is permitted. If Ivan Tsarevich is killed again, he stays dead!'

That pronouncement and the haunted look in Mikhail's eyes were enough to still all laughter. 'Then what can we do?' asked Vasiliy, closing his great hands into fists like hammers in his anger at being so helpless. 'What can we *do*?'

'Though we can do no more, we can advise,' said Mikhail, 'as we have done already, in a small way, through our discussion.'

'It sounded more like an argument to me,' commented

Vasiliy, who had not been getting the best of the exchanged opinions.

Fenist the Falcon slapped his hand against the sand. 'Discussion, argument, squabble, fight – it all means the same thing if something of use comes of it!' He glanced sidelong at Ivan and then looked long and hard at Mikhail. 'So what *did* come of it, Misha?'

'Less than I hoped,' replied Mikhail. 'But enough. And the most important thing of all is, that if Ivan can find a horse as good as Koshchey's then he can elude the necromancer's pursuit.'

'Is that all?' Prince Vasiliy the Eagle shook his head. 'If we can do no more for Ivan in an hour of'—he paused and looked scornfully at his brothers—'an hour of discussion, then we might as well have saved our breath. Can we tell him where to find this horse? Can we tell him what to do when he is able to outrun Koshchey the Undying, but not kill him?' Vasya pulled his sodden fur hat from his head, glared at it, admitted at last that it was ruined and flung it into the sea. 'Can we tell him anything, except that we can tell him nothing?'

'We can tell him to ask his wife.' Fenist Sokolov, the Falcon, spoke without raising his voice but his words carried as well as if he had shouted. Heads turned and the beginning of another acrimonious 'discussion' between Vasiliy and Fenist faded into silence. 'Koshchey was held a prisoner for many years in Mar'ya Morevna's kremlin. I think . . . . no, I believe that his capture of her is less an act of vengeance than an act of caution, out of fear of what she knows and what she can do to return him to his cell. *Tak*, if her knowledge is the weapon that he fears, then why not use it?'

'Koshchey always tried to catch us as quickly as he could,' said Ivan, speaking slowly as he arranged the patterns of his thoughts to match what he was saying. 'It happened twice; and both times when I saw his horse the poor beast was all but flayed alive. I thought that it was just another demonstration of his cruelty, but . . . .'

'But what if he was forcing the horse through fear, instead of cruelty?' asked Mikhail the Raven. 'Fear of what might happen if he *failed* to recapture Mar'ya Morevna? Think about that.'

'I thought about it long ago,' said Ivan. 'About my wife Mar'ya Morevna, and the powers written in her books of magic. And then,' he touched his throat and made a little, rueful cough, 'Koschey the Undying gave me something else to think about. But I agree with all of you, just as all of you agree with me. What I want to do is what I need to do.'

The Princes looked at one another, wondering whose opinion had proved most useful, and then back to Ivan as he rose from his seat on the beach and dusted sand out of his garments.

'And what I want to do,' he said, 'is see my wife again. . . .'

*

The dark kremlin had not changed since last he saw it, a lifetime ago. It was still as grim, still as dark and still as lifeless as those times before, but now – knowing more than ever what he had to lose if he was caught – Ivan slipped into the kremlin on soft feet and left Burka and his noisy hoofs far, far away. The Princes had restored not merely his life but also his horse, and Ivan had not taken time to wonder how they did it.

He paused briefly to press a hand to his aching temples, envying Misha and the others whatever early training permitted such lavish expenditure of power without apparent cost. Mar'ya Morevna had tried to explain it once, using phrases like 'controlled imbalance of forces' – which to Ivan's minimally tutored ear suggested that his brothers-in-law were gaining some kind of advantage from giving short measure. If magic was like reading, then they could understand monastic shorthand, his wife could read book-script – and he was still spelling out his words with great effort, one letter at a time.

Simple though it was, the charm that told him from a distance whether or not Koshchey was at home was taking its toll; hence his headache. At least – Ivan grinned crookedly – he had taken enough care over it to avoid another nosebleed. The feeling it gave him was like that delicate sense in the fingertips which can tell, without needing to touch, whether a coal fallen from the fire and now turned black, or a piece of metal left too near the forge, or even a dish fresh-washed in scalding water, was still painfully hotter than it seemed.

At least Koshchey's black kremlin was safely cold.

For all that Ivan had a sabre in his hand, a finely curved weapon with silvered mounts and grip, without a knuckle-guard, in the *shashka* style of the Cossacks. It had been given to him by Vasiliy the Eagle, handed over without a word but with a tight embrace about the shoulders which had driven all the breath from Ivan's lungs.

And then there had been a flickering of light, and he had refilled them with the cold air surrounding Koshchey's kremlin.

The sword's fine edge would be of little use against the master of the house, but Ivan – become more cautious and more devious in his dealings with Koshchey the Undying – was prepared for other things than Koshchey. Armed and armoured guards were foremost in his mind. He had broken into the necromancer's home not once but twice, proof enough that Koshchey's reputation was not quite the defence against thieves which he might have expected it to be. Even an ordinary *kulak* merchant would have taken steps by now to prevent the thief from gaining so easy an entrance on the third occasion he returned.

Yet the kremlin's gates had been left open wide, there had been neither sight nor sound of guards, and as he stood in the centre of the shadowed courtyard Ivan knew he was alone in all that sprawling heap of stone. It took him several minutes, time spent in creeping softly along the corridors that led to the high tower, before he realized just why Koshchey had not bothered to take any futher steps to defend his home. And when the realization struck Ivan's legs began to tremble until they refused to hold him up, so that he had to brace his back against the wall and slide down until he sat upon the floor.

There was a terrible need to laugh out loud bubbling within him, and he knew he dared not let it out, but still – his chest heaved in great racking, silent sobs of mirth – there could be very few intruders with the privilege of knowing that the ease of their intrusion this time is because last time they were caught.

And killed.

The laughter and the shaking receded as they had come, together, and Prince Ivan pushed himself back up the wall until his legs were once more braced under his weight. He took several deep breaths to make sure he was back in control of himself, then walked on towards the stairway leading in a spiral to the topmost chambers of the kremlin's tallest tower.

And Mar'ya Morevna was there.

At first she refused to move from her chair by the window, for in her heart there was only disbelief and certainty that this was a trick sent by Koshchey to torment her steadfast memory. She held that conviction right up to the moment when Ivan walked across the room and gathered her into his arms, and then all beliefs went quite away in the knowledge that her own dear husband was suddenly alive again. Then there was laughter, and there were tears, and there were long moments of silence.

And after that there was an explanation of what had transpired, told as fully as Ivan was able. Mar'ya Morevna listened, nodded wisely, cool and calm and controlled once more. 'So the Princes think that Koshchey fears me,' she said, and looked at Ivan with a glitter in her eyes like sunlight from a razor's edge. 'He is very right to fear me. Very right indeed. Before all this, I would have restored him to his cell and let him live. Now, I want from him what he has tried to take from you. His life – and his damnation to the hottest pit of Hell!'

'How?'

'My father's books contain many answers to that question, Vanya. I would not have used them before .... before Koshchey killed you. Now I will use as many as I need. But first,' she smiled thinly, wryly, knowing she was asking for the moon on a silver dish, 'I need to reach those books.'

Looking at the stillness of Mar'ya Morevna's beautiful face and listening to the music in her gentle voice, scared Ivan more than any roar of wrath from Koshchey the Undying had ever done. Prince Vasiliy the Eagle had spoken much as she had, choosing almost the same words; yet though he was a great, strong, square-shouldered man and she a slender, lovely woman, hers was the threat which rang more true. In that moment, Ivan knew that he would not exchange his own frail mortality for Koshchey's eternal life – no, not for all his happiness on Earth and all his hopes of Heaven.

'That was what Misha suspected,' said Ivan. 'So I need a horse as fast as Koshchey's. Faster. I need to learn where one might be found – and to learn that, *vozlyublenny moy*, I must leave you here.'

'I expected nothing else,' she said, 'so do not fret about it. If you had stolen me away, his horse would tell him as it has done on all the other times. We would get no further than you carried me the last time, before Koshchey overtook us. And Vanya, I could not live to lose you a second time.' Her voice had not the softness of one who speaks endearments but the firmness of one uttering a simple fact. The towers of Koshchey's kremlin were high and the courtyard was of hard, unyielding stone. Ivan knew exactly what she meant, and shivered as he had not shivered at the prospect of his own death. Mar'ya Morevna touched his cheek and smiled as he opened his eyes from that evil thought. 'I said, what would you have me do?'

Prince Ivan shook his head to clear away the darkness, and moved his mouth in what was a smile only because there was nothing else that could describe it. 'Be clever, be pretty, Mar'ya Morevna,' he said. 'Be wise, and be witty. And have drink close to hand for when Koshchey comes home. . . .'

*

Hoofs rang in the courtyard below the window of the high tower and Mar'ya Morevna leaned forward to look out of it. She watched Koshchey the Undying cross the cobblestones at a gallop, then haul back on his reins to wrench his black horse to a skidding, sparking standstill. Mar'ya Morevna watched him stable the horse, take off its saddle and give it hay and water; but she saw how he did not take the brutal bit from its soft mouth, for once out the horse would have died fighting against him before it allowed that bit to be put back in place.

She turned away, frowning – and then turned back, listening hard to the voices from the courtyard as they said things which made her raise her eyebrows and smile a secret smile. Koshchey, as he had done so many times before, was demanding of the horse that it tell how matters lay in his realm. Mar'ya Morevna could hear the animal's replies quite clearly, and just as clearly she could hear that its answers were far from complete. Though it made mention that she was still safely imprisoned, it said no word concerning the fact that Tsarevich Ivan, alive and well, was concealed in a linen-chest outside her rooms. Her smile grew wider and less cruel as she realized why. Ivan had been kind, Koshchey cruel. It was as complex, and as simple, as that.

Then Mar'ya Morevna, *krasivaya Tsarevna, prekrasney-shaya iz tsarits vseya Rusi,* lifted a flask of vodka, took out its stopper, turned it over in her fingers – and, as she waited for her Lord and captor to climb up the many stairs, she flung that stopper into the heart of the fire.

The door of her room flew open and rebounded with a crash from its stops, and Koshchey the Undying came in.

Mar'ya Morevna poured vodka for herself alone, then turned to glare at him. '*Muzhik-svoloch!* Is this the way you enter the rooms of a high-born widowed lady?' she asked, and threw the vodka at his face.

Koshchey blocked the spray of stinging liquor with an upflung hand and brushed the remnants of it from his beard. 'I smell a Russian smell,' he said, and glowered from beneath his eyebrows about the room.

Mar'ya Morevna laughed a nasty laugh and poured herself more vodka, spilling some of it across her hand and some across the floor. 'You smell,' she said, and drank it down, and poured herself another. 'And you still fear my husband, though you killed him. That is the Russian smell you think is here: no more than your own fear, born of the good and wholesome smells of Russia that caught on your clothing as you rode across Moist-Mother-Earth.' Mar'ya Morevna looked at the cup in her hand, and as she looked it shook so that most of the vodka splashed out. She changed hands to shake the last drops from her fingers, and then filled the cup again.

'How much have you drunk today?' asked Koshchey, looking for the stopper of the vodka flask and seeing not a trace of it.

'Not enough,' said Mar'ya Morevna, 'to compensate for a life spent with you!' She flung the contents of her refilled cup at Koshchey, but missed him when he ducked. Then she laughed – a wild, eerie laugh that would have raised the hackles of a mortal man. 'Sit down and drink with me, Koshchey the Undying, Koshchey the Old, and tell me how it was in the world before I knew only sorrow.' She waved the vodka flask at him, and crystal drops of spirit as clear as the Water of Life splashed across the rich rugs on the floor. 'And maybe after that I might tell you of how it was when I was happy, long ago.'

Koshchey was nothing loath, for though she was his enemy and his prisoner Mar'ya Morevna was a beautiful Tsarevna and the fairest Princess in all the Russias, and neither prison nor vodka could ever take that from her. Her hair was bright against the darkness of her widow's garments, for she had pushed back the black cowl from around her face. Though she could never have been called merry, yet in her resigned and bitter way she was a good companion for one who down the years had seen all of his friends die, or had been forced to slay them. It was as if something had happened at long last to make her realize that she was a widow, and that finally she had decided to make the best of things. So she talked, and she mocked, and she drank like a Russian, and because he was unwilling to be beaten by a woman Koshchey drank to match her cup for cup.

What he did not see was the amethyst set at the bottom of her cup, nor the amethyst ring on her hand – turned so that the stone was inward, out of sight – nor the great amethyst crystal hanging on a chain around her neck, beside the cross that she always wore. All the wise men from the beginnings of wisdom had written in their books that amethyst gave protection against strong drink, and Mar'ya Morevna had read their writings. But she also took care that when Koshchey was not watching she emptied her cup out of the window, or among the roots of the great plants set in tubs to make her cell look less a prison; and when there was no other way around it, and no way to divert his eye, she would spill some of her drink and then make sure to laugh so hard at her mistake that all the rest was spilled as well. Mar'ya Morevna knew all about the supposed powers of amethyst; but she believed in the practical approach as well.

They drank vodka and then they drank wine; and when the wine was done they drank *kvas*, and beer, and even some *kumys* that Koshchey found in its leather bottle hanging from a hook somewhere. And Koshchey the Undying, though proof against blades and proof against poison, became most monstrously drunk. He was content: his most annoying enemy was dead and hacked to pieces, floating somewhere on the Azov Sea as tantalizing food for fish; his next enemy was a despairing captive in his kremlin, so much resigned to her lot as prisoner and widow that she had talked and drunk with him and even made him laugh; and his name was once more held in the fear and respect which had been proper years ago. Koshchey closed his eyes and dozed – waking just enough to drink from the cup that Mar'ya Morevna kept filled for him but not enough to see that she no longer even made pretence to fill her own. When she spoke to him he laughed when it seemed proper, and for the rest answered in a drowsy voice close to the edge of sleep.

Until at last he slept.

Mar'ya Morevna looked at her cup, and at the amethyst within it, and grinned a crooked grin at the crystal as if it was a fellow conspirator – which in a way it was. Whether through the power of the stone, or by her own sleight of hand in spilling, losing or in other ways disposing of most of what she had poured in her cup, she felt no more ill-effects from the five hours of constant drinking than a slight, slow swirling behind her eyes and a tendency – hastily and carefully corrected – to put her feet on places where there was no floor beneath them.

She looked at Koshchey the Undying, sprawled back in his chair with bubbles dripping from his slack-lipped mouth at every grating snore, and felt her fingers itching for the hilt of a knife between them. If only the satisfaction of slitting his throat would do some permanent good. . . . Which it would not. Mar'ya Morevna dismissed the notion, and walked unsteadily from the room.

'The things I do for you,' she said very softly, breathing the words instead of whispering them so that the sibilance of a whisper would not carry.

Tsarevich Ivan, released from his place of concealment in a linen-chest, could smell the words as well as hear them and grinned in the dim light of the distant lamps. He needed no further explanation of what she had done, nor any assurance of its success. Mar'ya Morevna's presence was proof enough of that. 'What,' he said just as softly, after kissing her on the cheek, 'did he tell you – and is it of any use?'

'He told me enough, and more than enough.' Her voice was far more sober than her breath or her movements would have suggested. It was as if what she knew, and what she was saying in that hasty tumbling of words, burned all the good drunkenness away. As Ivan listened, he could well believe that was no more than the truth. 'First,' she said, 'you must take his riding-whip from the saddle in the stable, and then you must ride east. You will come to a river of fire—'

Ivan opened his mouth to say something, saw her expression change and closed it again with a snap of teeth.

'Have you come thus far and still want to ask questions?' Mar'ya Morevna said. 'Vanya, beloved, you and your world took leave of small, safe magics when Prince Fenist wed your sister. This is the world of tales, and dreams – and nightmares. So listen well! When you come to the river, wave the whip three times with your right hand and ride across the bridge. Then wave it again, but with your left hand, and ride on. When you reach your destination, you will know it as the place you seek. Do as you are instructed, nothing more, and as you love me do not linger when your time is done. The moon is waning. Twelve nights remain for me to leave this dreadful place. Only twelve nights – and that includes this one.'

Ivan said nothing until she had finished speaking, then held her hands as he looked into her eyes. For the first time he saw a flicker of despair swirl in their depths like a shark's fin cutting moonlit water. 'Places, times and knowing,' he said. 'Can you not tell me where I am supposed to go?'

Mar'ya Morevna released his hands from hers, put her arms around his neck and held him as tightly as though he was going to his death. There were tears standing in her eyes when at last she let him go. Then she said, 'Vanya, my love, my darling one, you must guard horses for three days to earn one as swift as that which Koshchey rides. And you must guard them in the land of Baba Yaga.'

Mar'ya Morevna kissed her husband on the forehead and the lids of his eyes; then on each cheek and at last, lightly, on the mouth. It was the way she would have kissed him had he been laid on silk in a fine coffin. 'Bring them back and give them back,' said Mar'ya Morevna. Then swiftly, before her tears began to fall, she turned and walked away.

*

Ivan crept towards the stable, waiting for the first sound that would say his presence here had been discovered. Though making Koshchey drunk had seemed a good idea at the time, now that the step was taken he had remembered things which should have been considered long before. Most important of all was Koschey's drunkenness. Though steel and venom could not harm him, it was quite plain that wine and ale could overpower him – but for how long? The effects of excess alcohol were nothing more than poisoning, after all, and too much would kill just as surely as a brew mixed for the purpose. Which meant that it should not affect Koshchey the Undying as severely as it would a mortal man. Prince Ivan found himself wondering how soon the necromancer would recover, and how soon after that he would discover that his whip was gone, and swallowed down a throat too recently recovered from the last time it was cut.

The stable was dark and Ivan was glad he had thought to bring a shuttered lantern with him from the kremlin. He opened it a crack to let a little light escape – then almost dropped the lantern when its flame reflected back from eyes that seemed as large as saucers. Koshchey's black horse stirred amidst its straw, watching Ivan with huge eyes which never blinked. He stared back at it, remembering that he had been warned it could speak with the speech of men – and could therefore cry a warning – and he thought that there was more intelligence in this animal's eyes than in those of many people that he knew in Khorlov. His pounding heart slipped back to where it belonged, within his chest, and though he knew that it could snap his fingers off as it might snap a bunch of carrots, he stroked the black horse's soft nose as he had done once before. 'Hush now,' he whispered, 'and go back to sleep.'

'I can sleep once you have gone, Prince Ivan,' said the horse, and though he was familiar enough with sorcery to have been expecting something of the sort Ivan still jumped at the sound. Being told that a horse can speak is little preparation for hearing one do so, especially in such a voice as this. Formed in so huge a chest and neck, it was far deeper than the deepest bass: inhumanly deep, which was entirely right and proper when the speaker was not human. The horse looked at Ivan, and though it had not the shape of mouth to smile it flared its nostrils and snickered with amusement. 'If you are here for what I think, you will find it over there.'

Ivan went to where the horse had indicated with a shake of its great head and found a saddle resting on a padded bar. He stared at its sleek, smooth leather and shuddered with a suspicion of that leather's origin; then he reached out, took Koshchey's riding-whip from where it rested on the pommel and for the look of things replaced it with another from the wall. The whip was ordinary-looking when compared with the sinister saddle, so ordinary that he took it back and showed it to the horse. The black horse put its ears flat back against its skull and showed its teeth. 'You need not doubt, Prince Ivan,' it said in that huge, soft voice. 'I know that whip. I know the sight and smell of it. And the weight and cut of it as well.'

'More than you or any other horse deserved,' said Ivan, made almost as angry by that as by all Koshchey the Undying's other crimes. He coiled the whip tightly and thrust it through his belt, turned to go and then looked back at the black horse. 'And if he needs to use the magic of the whip? What then?'

'Come back swiftly and he need never know,' answered the black horse. 'But there is no need to worry on that score. Not even Koshchey the Undying goes to Baba Yaga's country unless he has no choice, and now that he has me there is no need for him to go.' It showed its teeth at the expression on Prince Ivan's face. 'I could have told you things which would have seemed encouraging,' it said, 'but that might have made you careless. This way, at least, you will beware of everything you see and thus have a better chance of life.'

'Horse, black horse,' said Ivan with a crooked smile, 'the Tsars of the wide white world should all have such a counsellor as you, for then all of them would be too frightened to dare indulge in war.' Then he raised an eyebrow. 'But what will happen when I take something of Koshchey's from his kremlin?'

'You mean, will I tell him? Look at my back, Prince Ivan. Look at how my skin is split by that same whip. Now ask again – if you still need an answer.'

'Why?'

'Because yours is the first kind voice I have heard in my life.' The black horse saw disbelief in Prince Ivan's face, for it snorted angrily that it should be doubted. 'Hear me,' it said. 'Baba Yaga owned me when I was a colt running in her horse-herd; since then I have been the steed of Koshchey the Undying; and your wife Mar'ya Morevna sees me only as the means by which Koshchey recaptures her. Tell me, which of them would trouble to speak kindly – except you, when you pitied my whipped back and would not leave me for the wolves?'

Ivan said nothing. Instead he bowed low to the worthy animal, then walked out of the stable, and the kremlin, and returned to where Burka was tethered.

And then he rode out of the lands of men.

*

Ivan could not tell if he had ridden east for many hours or few. It seemed a little time and yet a long since he had left Koshchey's kremlin far behind, but in that long or little time the world had changed. The green steppes of Mother Russia had gone from under Burka's hoofs and now there was a rolling plain of ash and cinders, black and grey, dusty and dead. If ever there was somewhere in the world well-suited to a fiery river, this was it. Yet there was no sign of any river, filled with flame or filled with water – though the thought of water in this desert was an ugly joke.

East, always east, was the sole direction that he had been given, and east, always east, was the direction in which he rode, though there was no sun in the grey sky for him to follow. Sky and ground, horse and rider, all were the same colour. Burka had been grey before, but within ten minutes of their reaching the ash desert Ivan had turned grey to match. He stopped the horse and looked about him, even though there was nothing to see except the long, dense plume of dust that marked their passage through the ash, and wondered if – in this trackless waste – he had somehow been turned half about and had been riding north or south instead. Then he sniffed at the dry, unmoving air – and knew at once he was not lost after all.

It was not the smell of smoke but the smell of fire itself that hung before him, and far, far away on what might have been horizon had not grey run into grey without a boundary, he saw of shimmering of heat. Ivan did not gallop towards it: he had no desire to come upon the river of fire too suddenly to stop, and in this strange world where near was far and far was near that risk was all too real. Instead he swung down from the saddle and took Burka's bridle in his hand, and side by side they walked carefully towards the distant dance of shimmer on the air.

And without warning, as suddenly as he had feared, they stood on its brink.

The river of fire lay within the chasm it had eaten for itself out of the very living rock of Mother Earth – if this place was any part of the wide world at all – and in the featureless grey landscape it crouched invisible from sight until one was close enough to look straight down into the chasm . . . . and close enough to fall into the river.

Ognennaya reka did not look as Ivan had imagined it; if anything, it was far more ominous. In his mind the river of fire had been like an impossibly long hearth, all leaping flames and glowing embers. There were flames here indeed but few of them, small licking tongues of ghostly white, and no embers at all. But there was a glow like the maw of a furnace and an upward blast of heated air which stirred Ivan's hair around his face, rising from a broad and sluggish stream of molten rock that looked and moved like incandescent honey. Prince Ivan gazed down at it and listened to the vast eternal muttering of the earth-fires that kept it hot. He wiped his streaming eyes and shivered just a little bit, despite the heat. If anyone should chance to fall into that river there would be no swimming to shore, and no amount of the Waters of Life and Death could do a thing to help.

He backed away with beads of sweat glinting like diamonds on his face, and looked at Koshchey's whip. It was no more than a wooden handle bound in leather and a plaited bullhide lash. Vicious to be hit with, certainly – Ivan's face and Koshchey's horse both knew that much – but horribly ordinary for the task it was supposed to do. And yet he would have to try it, discover if it worked or not, or turn back now and admit defeat. At least waving a whip in the air cost little effort, and if nothing happened – so that he looked foolish – there was no one here to witness it save Burka. And that horse, at least, could not repeat what he had seen.

Right now he was flickering his ears to and fro in disapproval of the heat, the dust and most especially the low rumbling growl which drifted up and out of the fiery river. Prince Ivan patted his noble steed on the neck, raising a cloud of dust. Either there would be a bridge for them to cross, or there would be no crossing. The chasm was too wide for any horse to jump. He put his right hand through the wrist-strap of the whip, gripped it tightly with his fingers, wondered if there were some words he had to say . . . . then waved it anyway, once, twice and three times. And had he not used its wrist-strap, the whip would have dropped as sharply as his jaw a moment later.

The bridge was large and fine, high-walled to keep the heat away and paved with rough-hewn rock to afford a sound, safe footing. It arched out across the valley of the fiery river, a ghostly outline spanning side to side within the first wave of the whip, then taking form and solid substance in the remaining two. Prince Ivan cleared his throat, to take the place of all the other things that he might say, and finally decided to say nothing. Burka flicked his ears again, and in that tiny movement managed to say more than Ivan ever could. He looked at the animal and patted him once more, raising more dust. 'I agree with you entirely,' he said, and smiled.

It was an easily crossed bridge, wide and comfortable for both man and beast, but Ivan refused to ride across, choosing instead to walk at Burka's head. He had seen the walls were high to either side, but he had also seen that they were not so high that an unseated rider might not pitch over one or other of them and make that long fall from which there would be no returning. He walked, slowly and carefully, and despite the bridge's strength was glad to reach the other side.

It went away as swiftly as it came, vanishing like summer morning mist as he took Koshchey's whip in his left hand and waved it thrice. Ivan coiled the long lash around its stock as he prepared to put the whip away, back in its place thrust through his belt, but then he paused as a small frown furrowed his brow with thought. Changing hands again, he waved the whip just once and watched as the first faint outline of the bridge returned. He could see the fires through it and yet the structure looked deceptively solid. Ivan searched about for rocks or broken branches, then after some minutes without success – there was nothing on the ground save ash and finer ash – he opened one of his saddle-sacks and took out half a loaf of black rye bread, first making sure that there was enough other food in there that he could spare it. Then he threw the loaf out on to the bridge.

It landed almost in the middle of the span and, being somewhat stale, bounced twice. Then it simply lay where it had fallen. That was not what Ivan had expected. He looked suspiciously at Koshchey's whip, wondering what other little tricks it had in store, glanced back in annoyance at his half-loaf of bread – then gasped a small but heartfelt oath as it sank through the bridge like a hot rock through river ice and dropped into the fire. There was an insolently tiny puff of yellow flame, and it was gone as if it had never been there at all. Ivan wondered how big a puff of flame he or Burka would have warranted, and guessed that it would not have been much more. But he stored his discovery in his mind, and the whip in his belt, then mounted to his saddle and rode slowly onward – east and ever east.

*

The landscape changed again as Ivan rode away from the river of fire. Ash gave way to grass at last, and the world became green again. But this place was not a steppe and never had been: there were shrubs and bushes, growing ever closer together in the shadow of the trees. Such trees! Birch and pine, dark yew and bright maple, all growing in profusion, without regard for the way some trees were supposedly unable to live in the same soil as others. Ivan cared little for that aspect of it, though it puzzled him slightly. Instead he halted Burka more than once, just to sit still and enjoy the sight of something tall after an eternity of featureless steppe and ashen desert, to listen to the soft rustle of their leaves and needles, to smell the scent of pine and sticky sap. It was a wholesome place, refreshing to the spirit at any time and most especially to one who had seen Koshchey's kremlin, full of death, and the desert of ash which had not supported life in years.

Ivan breathed deeply in the cool, clean air and looked around him. There was enough dead wood to build a cooking-fire, and enough damp moss for him to build it safely. Thinking pleasant thoughts about the rich stew he could make with all the dried meat that he carried in his saddle-sack, Ivan kicked both feet from his stirrups and half-turned to slide down to the ground.

Instead, as Burka reared back with a squeal of fright, he fell. Cushioned by the moss and the great drifts of pine-needles accumulated over many winters, Ivan bounced as though he had fallen on to a thick mattress. And then he saw what had so frightened his noble steed, which had been unconcerned by Koshchey the Undying and by the river of fire. To a horse, the huge brown bear which had risen from its sleeping-place among the bushes was a far more deadly threat than either.

As the bear became sufficiently awake to realize that there was food nearby, Burka reared again, then galloped off with the bear lolloping in hot pursuit. Ivan scrambled to his feet and yelled, hoping to frighten the bear or to bring Burka back, but all to no avail. Hoof-beats and sounds of crashing undergrowth faded away into the distance, until only the small noises of the forest remained to keep him company. And the small noises of his stomach – awakened just as much as the brown bear had been – by the anticipation of some dinner. Except that with the horse gone, so were Ivan's bow, his arrows, his blanket – and of course, the saddle-sacks with all his food and water.

All that remained of his possessions were his sword and Koshchey the Undying's riding-whip, and they made neither especially good eating nor especially efficient tools with which to hunt. Ivan muttered something underneath his breath, then scrambled to his feet, brushed off the pine-needles and the shreds of moss, turned towards the east and began to walk.

Water he found easily enough, for there were many small streams running through the forest, but as the afternoon ran down to evening his need for food grew steadily more urgent. Given his lack of hunting weapons, he had determined to forage and to be content with a vegetarian diet for as long as was required. That decision had been the easiest part of the whole matter. With steadily increasing annoyance and even a certain sense of having been betrayed, Ivan was beginning to realize something which had happened to many would-be foragers and readers of old tales. While the *bogatyri* in the stories never had the slightest trouble in living off the land, almost everything he found was either out of season, not yet ripe or had been well enjoyed already by whatever bird or beast had got there first . . . . and that was when it had even been there in the first place.

As he travelled further into the woods and they grew thicker and darker and more tangled around him, it became plain that as the sombre pine and spruce and fir replaced oak and beech, so a dense layer of harsh brown needles replaced the soil in which things grew. This was the way in which forests usually were, and thus more natural than the confused variety of trees which he had seen that morning, but it was of little comfort to his empty belly. The occasional growths of fungus on soggy fallen tree-trunks became more frequent, but they were gross, liquescent things that looked like pallid maggots on a rotting corpse, and even if they had been safe to eat Ivan would still have been reluctant to go near them – much less touch or actually eat a single mouthful. Remembering the bear, as night fell he climbed high into a tree and wedged himself as best he could into a fork of branches too high up for anything so heavy as a bear to reach. It was tight and uncomfortable but it was secure – so much that he hoped he could get free again come morning. Then, with a prayer to the good God that the thought of shaking trees to find out what fell out of them should be kept from the minds of every bear and wolf in Russia, he pulled the fur of his collar up and the fur of his hat down, and between them fell into a shallow and uneasy sleep.

*

Prince Ivan awoke to a pair of equally unpleasant realizations: the first was that he had never been so hungry in his life, and the second was that from the feeling in his spine his hip-bones had worked their way up somewhere near the back of his neck. It took him three times longer to pry himself from the tree's embrace than it had taken to fit into it last night, and so far as swearing in discomfort was concerned he had grown bored with his own repetitions. On top of all else, he had barely slept at all.

Ivan drank water from a nearby stream, water so cold that it made this teeth ache, then rinsed his mouth, and face and hands in it until all thought of sleep was washed away. He no longer thought about the roots and nuts and berries mentioned in those lying tales; there would be other things to eat in so large a forest as this one, and he had a sword to kill and carve them with. Afterwards . . . . Well, the Tatars ate raw meat, though chopped up small and smaller yet, then well seasoned with spices, pickles and with – Ivan looked up sharply at the sound of wings in a tree above his head – *eggs*.

Those who claimed to know had begun to say that the eating of raw eggs was less than healthy, leaving the eater prone to illness from the poisonous uncooked food. Eggs, they said, should be boiled severely, or well fried, or treated in a dozen other ways which Ivan had neither the fire, utensils or the time to manage. Though he was a long way from starvation yet, his hunger was such that he was willing to put sense aside if that sense stood between him and something to eat. Taking off his sword-belt and his heavy outer coat, he began to climb the tree.

There was an explosion of feathers as the roosting bird shot from her nest, wings clattering and beak agape in a cry of alarm. Ivan closed his eyes and held on tight as twigs and leaf-mould showered down on his head, then climbed a little further. He could see the nest, snuggled as tightly as he had been into the fork of three branches last night, and he could almost see the eggs. As he reached for them, Prince Ivan hoped that they were not too far along, for though he knew the antique Romans ate equally peculiar things a chewy meal of whole but unborn chicks was not yet to his taste.

And then the mother bird came back. He flinched, expecting wings beating his head or a beak pecking at his eyes, then blinked and stared as instead she settled on his outstretched index finger. She was a little larger than a thrush, but with the bright black cheeky eyes that Ivan had only ever seen on robins, and her plumage was a simple, polished brown like the shell of a chestnut, except for a small tuft of golden yellow on her head which glinted as she bobbed up and down, flirting her tail and wings and gripping tight with tiny pointed claws.

Ivan looked into those glinting button eyes and saw there more than he might have expected from an ordinary bird. It was the same gleam of intelligence that he had noticed in the eyes of Koshchey's horse and he suspected, groaning inwardly, that it presaged the same ability.

He was right.

'Tsarevich Ivan, Tsarevich Ivan!' said the bird in the same tiny, scratchy voice as every other talking bird on earth. 'I beseech you, spare my unborn children!'

Prince Ivan leaned his face against the rough bark of the tree-trunk, holding on as best he could with both knees and one hand. No matter that the bird could fly considerably better than he could, it would have lacked manners to fling her from his finger as he went tumbling to the forest floor, as he most surely would have done had he not held on very tight. Despite anticipation of the event, it came as something of a shock to be addressed by a bird other than his brothers-in-law – who were somewhat special after all, and rather removed from the normal run of forest poultry. This one might well sound like all the other birds which might have been trained to talk, but it was more than plain that what she said was not something learned by rote.

'*Gospozha ptitsa*,' he said patiently, 'madam bird, I don't know where you learnt my name, and I don't care, but I haven't eaten in almost two days and I'm starving.'

The bird looked at him from one eye, than the other, and bobbed up and down some more. 'You could survive longer without eating, Prince Ivan,' she said, 'than my family could survive if you ate them!'

There was a crooked logic to that, Ivan was forced to admit; but logic did little to assuage his hunger and he looked speculatively towards the nest again. The mother bird bobbed low and flickered her wings as she would do if trying to distract a snake. Prince Ivan didn't know if that was some avian form of insult or not, but – though he would have eaten all the eggs without a second thought had she not been there – he was not yet so hungry that he would devour children with their mother shrieking in his ears at every mouthful. '*Nichevo!*' he said irritably, and slithered to the ground.

The bird fluttered round his ears all the way down, crying thanks and blessings on his head until Ivan was weary of her squeaky voice. Then at last she settled on his shoulder, bouncing, excited and tickling his ear. 'You ask how I know your name, Prince Ivan?' she said. 'It is a name well known! And for your kindness, I will help you when you least expect it!' There was a flurry of wings and she was gone, back to her nest where the eggs had been cool for long enough.

Ivan stared up, scratching his head for several more reasons than leaf-mould in his hair; then he picked up his coat and sword-belt and trudged off towards the east.

That was where he saw the wolf-cub, dozing underneath a bush. It was fat and milk-fed, plainly good to eat – at least if one had the taste for such a dish, and the Chinese beyond the White and Golden Hordes had eaten dog for ages past. Right now Prince Ivan was more than willing to sample wolf, and if he could light a fire so much the better; but even if he could not, then raw fresh meat would be more than welcome. Standing frozen to the spot, he watched as the wolf-cub rolled over with its plump little belly to the sky, whimpered twice, twitched once and sank into a deeper sleep. Then, as he had done so often when hunting in forests around Khorlov, he sank out of sight in the dense undergrowth and, lacking spear or bow, drew his sword.

'Prince Ivan, spare my child,' said a low, growly voice that came on a gust of warm breath to tickle Ivan's ear, while a huge paw came down on the flat of his sword and pressed it to the moss. Being a young man of rapidly increasing sense where his survival was concerned, Ivan released the sword and slithered well clear of it before he made another move, and that was merely to look up.

The grey wolves of Mother Russia are among the largest in the wide white world, and there must have been an elephant in this one's ancestry not so long ago. Tusks and all. Her lolling tongue was like a scarlet carpet, and her yellow-green eyes were deep and wide enough to drown in, if her fangs gave time enough. Prince Ivan blinked twice, very fast, and then remembered his manners. '*Dobryy den'*, *gospozha volchikha*,' he said, wishing the wolf a polite 'good evening' as he sat up very, very slowly.

'*Zdravstvuyte, Ivan Tsarevich*,' the mother wolf greeted him, in that same growling, thoughtful voice. '*Ty goloden?*'

'I am, *Volk-matushka* – though hunger does not adequately describe it. I am starving.'

'After no more than two days?' The wolf looked at him with those deep eyes, and grinned still wider so that all of her white teeth were showing. 'Go ten days in the deeps of winter and find nothing to eat save snow and ice, and then tell me you are starving. For now, Prince Ivan, your privileged, high-born and doubtless tender inner parts are nothing more than slightly empty.'

'Ah, I understand.'

'You do not. Pray you never will.' She turned her fanged head sideways to look at the sleeping cub, then glanced at the sword beneath her paw before gazing at Ivan once more. 'Will you spare my cub?'

'You give me little choice,' said Ivan, growing bold again now that the threat of long fangs in his throat had receded somewhat. The wolf twitched her ears and watched him narrowly as he picked up his sword again, only relaxing from her crouch once it was sheathed.

'You have every choice,' she said. 'To kill and eat us both – of course, before both of us eat you.'

'I seem to have lost my appetite,' said Ivan.

'But regained your sense.' The wolf flopped down beside him, for all the world like the great hunting dogs in Khorlov, and only her ability to speak, and the knowledge that she was one of the grim grey Russian wolves, kept Ivan from scratching her behind the ears.

The mother wolf looked sidelong at him and this time her ragged ivory grin stretched back and back until it threatened to meet at the nape of her neck. 'I believe that I can guess your thoughts, Prince Ivan,' she said, 'and if my guess is right, there is an itch just under my left ear. . . .'

Ivan grinned in his turn, weakly, with less teeth to show, then reached out to the deep grey fur and began to scratch. 'You should be in politics,' he said, 'or teaching cunning to the foxes.'

Volk-matushka wriggled luxuriously as his fingers rubbed the good places behind her ears. 'We have already taught the foxes,' she said. 'Where else do you think they learnt to be crafty? But they were so unsubtle about it, and made such a fuss of being clever, and made "cunning" such a thing that no wise beast would want to be, that we wolves despaired of them and taught them nothing more.'

'And politics?' asked Ivan. 'What of that? You have to be human to be in politics.'

'Innocent,' said Mother wolf. She turned her handsome head to stare at him, there was a flickering of light and dark and, for an instant and no more, a woman, tanned and naked, with black hair and wise green eyes, was lying at his side. Then the wolf was back and grinning more than ever. 'Men look so hard for men who turn to wolves,' she said, 'that they forget to look for wolves who turn to men. And I confess, it is such fun to herd the silly sheep instead of hunt them. Once in a while . . . .'

There was a nudging in his lap and Ivan looked down to see the wolf-club, more or less awake, rolling to have its tummy scratched. He smiled crookedly, then laughed a small laugh meant for no one but himself and began to pet the little four-legged pudding. Even with its mother in another Tsardom instead of breathing down his neck, there was no way that he could kill and eat this wolf-club now.

'Prince Ivan,' said the mother wolf, 'we do not take unless we give a fair exchange. Take this: for my cub's life, I give you aid unasked and help unlooked-for. Just be sure you take both when they come. *Do skorovo svidaniya!*'

She and her cub bounded away, and Ivan lay flat on his back and wondered whether to laugh, or be angry, or just to rub his empty stomach and wish that the next thing he chose to eat had not an advocate to speak in its defence.

Either he wished wrongly, or not hard enough, but the shock of the third occasion was set fair to end his troubles: hunger, life and all. Had she spoken earlier all would have been well; and had she spoken later, Ivan would have been very sorry but he would have had both feet on the ground and also something to eat.

As it was, when the queen bee spoke in his ear Prince Ivan jumped so hard and so fast that he lost his footing altogether and hung for several nasty, painful minutes by the arm he had thrust into a hollow tree in search of honey.

It was that she was a bee. Ivan Aleksandrovich had grown, if not familiar then at least accustomed to human words from creatures clad in fur and feathers. Insects were another matter. He was sitting cross-legged on the ground, cuddling the elbow joint which for three minutes had supported all his weight while bending the wrong way. He was cursing with a steady brilliance of invention and invective that would have gratified Guard-Captain Akimov, and the very last thing he wanted was a brown and golden honey-bee sitting on his knee. Especially when it was the same bee which had caused his slip in the first place.

'Thank you for not harming my children, Ivan Tsarevich,' she said, in that same high buzzing voice which had made him start so in the first place. As she spoke she danced; up and down, then side to side, then all the combinations of those movements. Ivan watched her as he had once watched the bees in Khorlov's honey-hives, and knew that she was talking bee-talk to him – although the dance, and the pain in his arm, and the shrill whining of her tiny voice served to make him dizzy rather than bring him any kind of understanding. He lay back at last, full length on the moss and pine-needles, and was not especially surprised when she settled on his nose.

'Prince Ivan,' came the tiny voice, 'for your kindness, some day I shall prove useful to you!'

The bee's constant dancing tickled Ivan's nose, and her choice of spot to rest and dance was making him cross-eyed. '*Pchela-matka*,' he said, squinting in an attempt to see her properly, 'I am famished. You could prove useful straight away if you could tell me where I could find some food.'

'Easily done,' said the bee, and sprang into the air. Ivan took that opportunity to rub his nose, since it would have seemed impolite to do so while the queen bee still sat there. He watched as she danced in the air, making little darting movements towards the east. 'Go this way for a little distance,' she said, 'and you will reach a clearing at the centre of the forest. Someone will feed you there. But be warned, Prince Ivan – as you value your soul and hope of Heaven, eat no meat!' The bee went twice around his head, buzzing loudly, and then flew back to her hive, leaving Ivan alone with his sore arm and his hunger.

*

It was almost a relief when at long last he found the clearing at the heart of the pine forest – almost, but not quite. He and his sisters had been told stories about the witch Baba Yaga, about her iron teeth and her hut with hen's feet, but all that Tsar Aleksandr's children had ever heard had been delightfully scary – that comfortable shudder best enjoyed when wrapped up warm by a great log fire, cuddling mugs of hot milk and cinnamon and listening wide-eyed to whichever storyteller their father the Tsar had paid to entertain the boyar-hall that evening. It was only now, confronted with a reality that he could see with his own eyes and, worse, smell with his own nose, that Ivan guessed just how much they had *not* been told.

Most of the truth.

At first glance all was plain and ordinary. The clearing was as round as a shield, and ringed by a fence, and there was a hut at the hub of the clearing. But at the second glance, and at all others after it, nothing was ordinary ever again.

The clearing had not been made by cutting away the trees and all the brush that grew between them; it seemed instead that it had come about because a great lid had been set down on the forest and left there until everything beneath it had withered away and died from lack of sunlight. What grass covered the sour bare soil was not green but a sickly yellow, and though its growth was short as any meadow Ivan could not imagine any animal wanting to crop at it – or even wanting to stay in the same area, because the stink that hung in the still, warm evening air was fit to make a goat vomit.

The stink came from the fence. What had seemed to be sun-bleached sticks lashed together with thin twine were indeed sun-bleached, but they were bones rather than sticks, and before they had been brought here to be a fence something had picked them almost clean of meat. But far from clean enough. The vile stink of corruption bore witness that the picking had been very far from thorough, despite the gouges visible in a thighbone here and a rib-cage there, gouges left in them by great jagged teeth. *Iron teeth ....* thought Ivan, gazing as steadily as he was able at the lengths of twine which a closer look had turned to what they always were: dried sinews and long strips of gut.

And then a crow cawed at him, and he looked up and saw the heads.

Some were simple skulls, domes and curves and angles scoured by the sun and rinsed by the rain until they were the colour of old ivory. Others were more recent. The flies and crows had been busy but, like whatever had been gnawing the bones of the fence, they had not been busy enough. These heads had yet to attain that state of cleanly grinning serenity, and their appearance made Prince Ivan wince and look away. The slender stakes on which they had been set reared up at intervals all around the horrid fence, and there were many – oh, so many of them.

Ivan thought of Mar'ya Morevna, a prisoner in Koshchey's kremlin until he came to free her on a horse which gave them the chance to get away. It counted for little against the way he now felt, for though he cherished her as he cherished hope of Heaven, yet he feared such a death as would await him here as no man who has not died could fear. Not even the sorceries of Prince Mikhail Charodeyevich could restore life to a corpse not merely hacked apart but cooked and eaten. Ivan shook his head and turned away from the clearing and its stink of death. He knew that honour required he earn his horse as Koshchey the Undying had done, with three days service guarding Baba Yaga's herds, but surely there could be small loss to any person's honour if they preferred instead to steal from such a monster as lived in this obscene place . . . .

'Many thought as you do now, Ivan Tsarevich,' said a voice at his back. 'And this one most recently of all.'

Ivan jumped in the air and almost out of his skin, and when his feet touched the ground again his sabre was already drawn and braced in a two-handed grip. The hut was no longer at the centre of the clearing but right next to the fence, rearing above him on the scaled, spurred legs of a monstrous chicken. When he was little and listened to the stories, he had always laughed at the thought of a house with its own feet selecting those feet from something so foolish as a common barnyard fowl. But there was nothing foolish about these, for they stood as high as the head of a mounted man and they had claws and spurs the size of scythe-blades. Ivan looked at them, thought of what a kick from them could do and felt sick.

As Baba Yaga stood in the doorway and stared down at him, she held someone's newly-severed head by the hair and ears. 'They come for horses,' she said. 'Sometimes they work, but not well enough. And sometimes they steal, but not well enough. But the place that they go is always the same. Up!'

The hut rose still higher, standing almost on tiptoe, and Baba Yaga shifted her grip on the head, tested the point of a stake with her thumb and then rammed the neck-stump of the head hard down on top of it. The sound was just the same as that produced by crushing a fresh juicy apple underfoot, and though he tried not to Prince Ivan winced.

'Down,' said Baba Yaga. The hut settled low, then lower, and became just a hut on the ground. Baba Yaga glanced up at the stake and said, 'Pretty,' then looked at Ivan's head and said, 'Prettier still.'

It was not a word he could have used about her. Baba Yaga dressed like a peasant *babushka*, and leaned on her fence like a gossipy grandmother, but she looked like a nightmare – and was.

Her straggly wisps of hair were snow-white; but it was the white of old snow that has lain for a week in a city's main street, and it was as busy with lice as that city would have been with people. She was warty and shrivelled and hunched, and even with his nose already clogged by the reek of the dreadful fence Prince Ivan still flinched from her smell. Her nose was hooked like a sickle, curved down to a mouth without lips that was only a slash in the seamed skin of her face; yet somehow that mouth contrived to shape a smile. 'Yes,' she said through that smile, 'perhaps the prettiest of all.' Baba Yaga reached out one bony hand and pinched his cheek. 'And the sweetest.' The smile became a grin and her teeth were grey except where they were rusty, for they were indeed of iron. Ivan did not want to think of how those teeth came by their rust, but the evidence was all about him. Salt causes rust on iron: and there is salt in the blood and meat of men. 'So what brings such a tender morsel to my humble home?'

'I have come,' said Ivan, as boldly as he could, 'to earn a horse.'

'Indeed?' said Baba Yaga. 'Then you can guard my horses from tomorrow, Ivan Tsarevich, since today is too well past already. And you can sleep in the stable, to get to know my herd a little better. But from the looks of you and from the sounds your guts are making'—Ivan blushed and rubbed his stomach —'you should eat before you sleep.'

She turned and went into the hut, and Ivan fought with his desire to run away, but when she came back there was a bowl and a platter in her hands. The bowl held steaming *kasha* gruel, and there was meat and black bread on the platter. 'Eat,' she said, 'and then sleep sound. Don't worry – you'll come to no harm, that I promise you. At least, not until you fail.'

Ivan looked at the food and then at Baba Yaga, and made his thanks as courteously as if she had offered him a royal feast, at which she laughed. 'Just a little something to make you fatter,' said Baba Yaga. 'I hate lean meat.' Then she went into her hut again and closed the door.

Ivan stared at the hut for several seconds, then walked across the awful clearing to the long, low stable in the shadow of the trees. It was full of handsome horses, all of them staring at him with as much amusement as a horse can ever show. Prince Ivan looked at them, already wondering which one would cause most trouble and which he would choose, and then sat down on the ground to eat his food.

The bread was good: coarse, black rye bread, such as he had seen before. Ivan ate it without a second thought, but when he turned his attention to the *kasha* he inspected bowl and gruel both before he dared to taste it. The pieces of meat smelt as savoury as good roast pork but Ivan, though he was still extremely hungry, had heard Baba Yaga and seen the freshly severed head she had seen setting on its spike. Even without the warning words of the queen bee buzzing in his mind, he would have left this meat well alone. Not caring whether Baba Yaga was watching him or not, he dug a little hole beside the stable wall and buried every piece of meat before he dared to sleep. Prince Ivan lay awake for a long time that night, with his eyes wide open, staring at the dark, and every time he thought of the next day he shivered.

CHAPTER NINE

Concerning Baba Yaga's country beyond the fiery river, and how Prince Ivan tried to guard her herd of mares

Koshchey the Undying wanted to die.

It was not a sincere wish, as such wishes sometimes went; but on the morning after he had so rashly tried to drink Mar'ya Morevna underneath the table he woke up with a pounding head which felt like the very wrath of God. He was sick in his stomach and giddy in his brain, and there was a taste and feeling in his mouth as though Tatars had been camping there. Death would have been far preferable: at least dead people were not hung over. Though he tried throughout the morning to go about his business, there was no point to it and at last he lay back groaning on his bed, the shutters and his eyes both closed tight to keep the sunlight from scorching hot holes through his skull.

Mar'ya Morevna had made matters worse, for instead of creeping about and groaning as he had done she had been bright and merry. For one thing, she had picked that day to sing. Koshchey had seen her and, what was far worse, heard her.

Mar'ya Morevna, *krasivaya Tsarevna, prekrasneyshaya iz tsarits vseya Rusi*, was indeed and without doubt the fairest Princess in all the Russias – but there had never been a rule that beauty of face meant beauty of voice. She had indeed the basis of a fine soprano voice, but no one had ever trained the ragged razor edges off it, and yelling orders to her armies above the roar of battle had done little to improve its sweetness. But her singing voice was good enough for Mar'ya Morevna, and what it lacked in quality she enhanced with volume.

She sang as she took her morning walk along the ramparts of the kremlin – and that was not so bad since much of the music was dispersed out on the open air to frighten passing birds. But she continued to sing as she clattered about the tiles and floorboards of the kremlin in a pair of red-heeled boots which struck the echoes back and forth from every wall, and whenever she came to a door she slammed it.

He could hear the slamming now, as she worked her way along the halls below his chamber, making sure that each door swung smoothly on its hinges and could close just as quick and hard as her strong right arm could push it.

Koshchey the Undying rolled moaning on to his queasy belly, and pulled the pillows and the bolster down around his ears.

*

That morning, Ivan was awake before Baba Yaga had even begun to stir. Despite her promise that he would be safe until he failed in whatever tasks she chose to set him, he had felt uncomfortable about being asleep while she was still creeping about. He had spent an uneasy, restless night with one hand on the hilt of his sword, and had learned yet another truth that the old stories didn't mention. All of the heroes who had ever slept thus had slept well and awakened refreshed; he had barely slept at all, and the only part of him that had gone right to sleep had been whichever muscles of his sword-arm had not developed cramps. He sat cross-legged in the straw of the stable, rubbing the pins and needles from his fingers, well aware that Baba Yaga's mares were staring at him with the nastily amused expression of people enjoying a malicious private joke at his expense.

He stared right back at them, thinking of Koshchey's riding-whip still through his belt and knowing from experience that for all its magic properties, it was still a perfectly good whip. The mares seemed to know what he was thinking, and several of them curled back their upper lips in what was either a kind of equine sneer or a deliberate display of teeth as big and yellow as those of any other horse – but far more sharply pointed than any horse's teeth should be.

Ivan looked at the teeth, and though they weren't the dreadful iron teeth which lined Baba Yaga's rat-trap mouth, he found himself wondering just what these horses ate besides grass and hay. Mares that ate men were not unknown in the old stories and he had seen – and suffered – enough already for his doubts about anything at all to be now completely set aside. Herding horses such as these might prove to be more difficult than he had at first suspected, and he was glad to have his sword as well as Koshchey's whip.

Baba Yaga rattled at the stable door. Whether this was simply to waken him, or an indication of annoyance that she hadn't managed to catch him sleeping after all, Ivan didn't know. What he did know was that he had seen more pleasant things than Baba Yaga first thing in the morning. She looked no more beautiful in the thin, sharp sunshine of dawn than in the warm light of evening, and as he got to his feet Ivan made sure that his sword was in plain sight.

Baba Yaga looked at the sword, and then at him, and smiled. Ivan managed not to wince at sight of those frightful teeth. 'Ah, Prince Ivan,' she said, 'you will not need your sword to herd my horses well. And you will not need your sword if you herd them badly. It will not help you either way – so why not leave it here, where it will be safe from harm?'

Ivan grinned an unpleasant little grin at Baba Yaga. He saw no more reason for politeness than did she, since every conversation that they had so far exchanged had been a kind of fencing match. Baba Yaga would kill and most probably eat him if she got the chance, and Ivan Tsarevich was determined that she would not get such a chance. That was why he grinned; and why he slapped the scabbard of his sabre so that the sharp-edged curve of metal within it clinked and rattled ominously. 'Thank you, Grandmother,' he said, 'but I prefer to keep it close to hand. This sword was a present from my brothers, and they would take it much amiss if I were not to carry it as they intended : *all the time.*'

Baba Yaga's smile faded as her strategem failed. 'Then carry it,' she said, 'But take care it does not weigh you down, for you may find that you will need to run a great deal when you herd my horses.'

'Perhaps, and then again perhaps not. Horse-herders ride, the better to keep up with their charges. So which one shall I take?' Ivan spoke boldly and with less courtesy than he would normally use towards an old lady, even one so repulsive as Baba Yaga. Mar'ya Morevna had been unable to learn how it was that Koshchey the Undying gained his horse, but Ivan was willing to wager money that it had not been through sweetness and asking nicely.

Baba Yaga glowered at him from under her bristly white eyebrows, her lipless mouth pressed so tightly shut that it all but disappeared and her hooked nose and wispy-bearded chin came close to meeting in the middle. 'Your manners are not what they might be, Prince Ivan,' she said at last. 'Beware your sharp tongue does not cut your own throat!'

'None of that, dear Granny Hag,' said Ivan, not much disturbed by yet another threat. It was fairly certain that he was showing Baba Yaga better manners than Koshchey the Undying would have done, when the old rattlebones was here on the self-same business. 'I merely act as present company dictates: *s volkami zhit' – po volki vyt'*! Live with the wolves, howl like the wolves.' He thought of the mother wolf he had encountered in the forest and realized that, grim and dangerous though a grey Russian wolf could be, he would as soon be in her company as in that of Baba Yaga. At least Mother wolf smelt clean.

Had he wanted to set fire to something, then the red glare in Baba Yaga's eyes would have been quite hot enough. There was an ugly promise in the way she looked at him, so that he would beg for the mercy of the pot and the carving-knife before she was done. 'If we are to bandy proverbs, little Prince, then you should have remembered this one: If you find yourself in a pack of dogs, bark or don't bark – but wag your tail.'

Ivan shook his head. 'Would any amount of tail-wagging like a subservient cur have changed your intentions for me, Baba Yaga? And would it help me at all if I started now? I doubt it. I shall howl and show my teeth for preference.'

'Oh, you will howl before your course is run, Ivan Tsarevich,' said Baba Yaga, grinding her iron teeth together. 'You will howl indeed.'

'*Budet!*' snapped Ivan, all pretence at courtesy gone now and his tone entirely that of a Tsar's son addressing a dirty peasant. 'I asked before: which horse do I ride when herding the rest?'

'Take your pick, Prince Ivan.' She indicated the horses, who had been watching their exchange of barely-veiled insults with every sign of amused interest. 'Just remember that my rules are very simple, so simple that even you should remember them. You need not serve the round year as my herder, but no more than three full days. And on each of those days, all my horses must be back in their stalls by sunset – all, including the one you ride – or your head goes on a spike and I dine well that night!'

Ivan had known more or less what she would say since he first saw the horrid fence and palisade around the clearing. With such familiarity, he had thought that when the words were spoken they would be no more than words. But he was wrong. His stomach gave a little flutter, and a shudder went crawling down his spine just as if what Baba Yaga said had come as a complete surprise. Perhaps it was the look on her face, or her hope and eagerness . . . . or perhaps it was no more than the way her mouth watered slightly as she spoke.

He selected a horse, one of the mares rather than the single stallion of the herd, even though as a Prince and a Tsar's son he might have been expected to ride the very best. But Prince Ivan had been taught horsemanship and weapon-craft by Guard-Captain Akimov – who was of the tribe beginning to call themselves Don Cossack on his father's side, and the other tribe of Kuban-Zaporozhiyy Cossack through his mother. Given how the Cossacks fought each other, never mind how they fought everyone else, that had surely been a marriage and a family alliance forged and hammered out on the hottest hearths of Hell.

It was most likely from his parents that Guard-Captain Petr Mikhailovich Akimov had learnt the arts of fighting and survival – by all accounts his home life had been an education in itself – but it had been from his other relatives on both sides, those not involved in the feuding, that he had learnt how to handle horses. The Cossacks could ride anything on four legs, and equally knew what sort of mount they should avoid. Solitary stallions, masters of a herd of mares, were one such. Ivan had been warned time and again that even ordinary stallions could be notoriously intractable and vicious. Baba Yaga's herd-leader, as intelligent as all the rest, was most likely actively malevolent. A quiet little mare would be good enough.

There were many saddles, bridles and whips on their racks along the wall. Ivan picked the sturdiest harness he could find, since even Baba Yaga's 'quiet little mare' was certain to prove more of a handful than the biggest, fiercest horse that he had ever ridden. But he did not take a whip; Koshchey's long-lashed *nagayka* was still pushed like a dagger through his belt, and nothing Baba Yaga's stable had to offer could match it.

To his surprise the chestnut mare accepted bit and bridle, then the saddle and his weight, without a trace of protest. Though he endeavoured not to show it, Ivan was pleased. This was where he had suspected his first trouble might occur – for it was certain that Baba Yaga was not about to let him herd her horses for three days, and then to choose the best of them and ride away, without making matters difficult.

Although there was always the whip. It probably smelt of Koshchey *Bessmertnyy's* brutal use of it on his own steed, the one he owned and supposedly took care of. How much more readily then had he lashed the horses that belonged to someone else, especially if controlling them with the whip might mean the difference between earning one of them as a mount and earning the sharp point of a tall stake stabbed up beneath the chin?

Ivan gripped the mare's well-fed barrel chest between his knees and uncoiled the whip's long braided lash, then looked down at Baba Yaga. 'Where do your horses graze, Grandmother?' he asked, feeling more at ease.

'Take them to pasture in the meadow,' said Baba Yaga, smiling. 'Follow yonder path until you reach another clearing, and there it lies.' She pulled back the stable door and the mares streamed out, tossing their manes and neighing loudly, glad to be in the open air once more. 'Only remember what I told you, Ivan Tsarevich. If you lose a single one of them, then I shall stake out your head to make my garden beautiful!'

Ivan did not reply, being already busy counting the number of horses he was supposed to guard. Despite the way they milled about between the stable and the fence, and sometimes galloped underneath the hen-legged hut for no reason other than high spirits, he could see no more than twenty. With the one he rode that made twenty-one, and with Koshchey's great whip to aid him the task was hard but not impossible.

'Here,' said Baba Yaga, giving him a parcel wrapped in a cloth. 'Good food for a good day's work.' Ivan took the parcel warily, not entirely certain what Baba Yaga would regard as proper rations and unwilling to find out. 'Bread,' she said scornfully, seeing the expressions chase one another across his face. 'Black bread, and mares'-milk cheese, and a horse-hide leather bottle of *kumys*. If you have ever met a Tatar, then you ought to know how those will taste. Food proper to a guardian of horses, Ivan Tsarevich, little Prince. But I shall not waste more meat on you, since you seem too squeamish to enjoy it, and once I have a fresh supply you will not be here to help me eat it!'

The point went to Baba Yaga, one well and wickedly scored, and Ivan scowled down at her from the horse's back, well aware – as was she – that the little mare was by no means big enough to give his glare its full effect. Such an expression needed a spired helmet with a nasal to stare past, brightly burnished rings of mail and all the height of a tall warhorse behind it. And perhaps a *bogatyr'*'s mace driven by all the righteous strength of his good right arm to drive the lesson home. . . .

Instead he closed his eyes for a moment, until all of his anger had cooled, and then looked long and hard at Baba Yaga. She met his gaze grinning, until he said, 'This between me and harm, and between us for always and always.' He made the sign of the life-giving cross over himself, devoutly, brow to belt-buckle, right shoulder to left, and bowed his head, and as he did so he heard Baba Yaga hiss like a scalded snake and grate her iron teeth together so that they sounded like shears being sharpened.

Ivan did not smile at his small victory, for that would have been improper. The cross of the White Christ was a sign of the triumph of light over dark, but for that it was no more Ivan's doing than any other sign he might have made. Half a hundred years ago, in the time of Lord Novgorod the Great, he would have made the spread-fingered sun-sign for bright Belebog and Svarog of the All-seeing Sky, for fiery Svarovich his son and for Dazhbog bringer of summer, and perhaps – had he felt bold enough – the spear-sign of mighty-armed Perun Stormbringer, god of the warrior nobility of Kiev. Three hundred years and more past that, among his long-fathers the Norsemen, he would have made the sign of the hammer to honour red-bearded Thorr the Thunderer, or covered one eye in respect to deep-minded Allfather Othinn, Lord of the Battle-slain, another Hanged God whose travail had lasted nine days and not three, dead, like Balder his son, for the good of men – and like the White Christ Himself.

Ivan shivered and shook his head as thoughts uncalled-for ran like ice-melt through his brain. *Where will I go when at last I truly die?* he wondered. *To Christ's Heaven, or beyond the sky, or to the halls of the old gods?* He was afraid as no man who has not already died can feel – but good or ill, heaven or hell, he knew that none of his eternity was of account unless he could go where Mar'ya Morevna was. It was too easy, far away from her and in peril of his life, for his mood to grow *toskliviyy*, that sadness which was the plague of the Rus and for which vodka and jollity was the only cure.

*

Mar'ya Morevna paused a moment to massage the pounding in her temples, and to drink down several beakers of cold water. She felt a deal less bright and merry than Koshchey suspected, but she would have died of shame and black affront before allowing him to know it. The amethysts which she had worn and concealed in her drinking-cup last night, and the small spells she had said over them, had done much to save her from the way Koshchey was feeling. But the quickness of her hand – in spilling much of what had been poured into her cup – had been good as well, and her wisdom in the way things worked had been the best of all.

After seeing Ivan safely on his way to the land of Baba Yaga beyond the river of fire, Mar'ya Morevna had been sure to drink a very large amount of water. In the little time it spent inside her before sending her in some haste to the privy, it worked swiftly through her body, helping to dilute and wash away the various mild poisons she had poured into it – for being mildly drugged and poisoned was what gave the blur and buzz of drinking and made it fun, and Mar'ya Morevna knew it. Then she had drunk still more fresh water, to make up for what she had just lost, and after that – though her stomach rebelled slightly at the prospect – she had eaten something. Mar'ya Morevna was a commander of armies and had learned a great deal during her campaigns about the simple art of keeping a clear head in the morning. Water was one part, food was another and sleep was a third. So she had gone to bed – dismissing her concern for Ivan Aleksandrovich as best she could, since it was out of her control – and slept as well as she was able.

And then she had got up next morning and set about distracting Koshchey the Undying, by indicating to him that though he had her as his prisoner he was not going to enjoy it. The longer he was concerned with his aching head, and with all the noises clanging through his kremlin, the less time he would have to wonder about what he might have said while drunk, in answer to some questions that no widowed prisoner should have had any need to ask. Because what would happen if he did begin to wonder, and remember, was something that Mar'ya Morevna preferred not to think about. . . .

*

Ivan found another cure for melancholy directly he and the horse-herd reached the meadow, for what was when all of the mares, and the stallion too, flipped up their tails and galloped off in as many directions as there were horses in the herd. The mare under him reared up, up on her hind legs until for just an instant he thought that she would topple back with him beneath. That was when he brought the long plaited lash of

Koshchey's whip up and around, and snapped it at the horse's rump. Without Koshchey's long, cruel practice in the use of the thing, it did not even break her glossy chestnut skin – but being bitten by the biggest horsefly in all the Russias persuaded her with the abruptness of a thunderclap that she should not complete that crushing backward fall.

The mare's forefeet slammed back against Moist-Mother-Earth with a solid impact that only Ivan found comforting, then her head swung around so that one eye could stare at her rider. There was a dull red glow within it, but to Prince Ivan – who had stared into the furnace eyes of Koshchey *Bessmertnyy's* great black steed – that glow was not enough to warm his hands. He reeled in the two-*arshin*-long whiplash, and doubled it in his two hands until the plaited strips of leather creaked one against the other, then met the mare's red eye stare for stare. Whether or not she could talk was of no concern to him right now; but from the look in her eye he felt certain that she could understand good Russian spoken clearly. 'Behave,' he said, like a schoolmaster, 'or you will smart all day.'

The mare snorted noisily, blowing out her lips and spattering Ivan's red-heeled boots with the green froth of a horse who has been sneaking mouthfuls of grass past her bit. He looked at the mess and decided, since he was not known as a fashionable young man, that he could live with the clash of colours. '*Tak*,' said Ivan to the mare, 'we understand one another. So understand this also: we are going to pursue your stablemates. And if I have cause to think that you are giving less than your best effort, then I shall cut that effort out of you with this.'

He let the long lash uncoil again, then snapped it just a little, down by the ground, cutting the tips from grass-blades and no worse. An ordinary horse might have started from the noise, but the mare just turned her head to study the whip, then back again to stare at Ivan. He did not like the way she showed her sharp, unhorselike teeth at him – it was a gesture too much like that which Baba Yaga used, and most likely for the self-same reason – but he had not warned the mare off threats. Not yet. 'One other thing,' said Ivan, tucking the whip-stock through his belt in its customary place. 'If you are thinking that you could bite off my knee'—he smiled thinly as guilt flickered through the mare's red eye,—'then bear in mind that I could have your head off first.'

Free of the whip's encumbrance, his right hand moved and drew his sabre from its scabbard somewhat too fast for the mare to follow. All that she could have seen was that his hand, one minute empty, was next minute filled with a long, sharp, curving blade. This time she did start, and whether from the movement or the spoken warning Ivan did not care. At least she had taken note of both.

*

The horses of Baba Yaga had run all across the wide meadow at the edge of the forest, and in every direction; but it was evident that they had not reckoned on Prince Ivan being astride one of their own kind when he came to guard the herd. Without need to strike the mare more times than he might have rapped an ordinary dumb horse like his own lost Burka, or indeed any harder than those few taps with the coiled-up whip, Ivan rode from north to south and east to west across the flat pasture-land, gathering the horse-herd together with all the skill of a Tatar or Cossack born to the work.

It was almost noon before he had rounded them up, and some of the loose horses needed more than just a tap from the rolled *nagayka* whip. One, the stallion – leader of the herd and determined to prove it – came at Ivan squealing, lips curled back from his great teeth so that their unsightly sharp points glistened like the fangs of a wolf. Prince Ivan let him make his charge and then, with heels and knees and one hand pulling tightly on the reins, made his own mount rear up and so sidestep as neatly as a dancer. The stallion, ears flat back and eyes half-closed, went barging past and gained his first lesson in manners when Ivan – well trained in the art of fighting from horseback and now more accustomed to handling the long whip -- laid such a stripe between his tail and withers as would take a week to fade.

'Enough?' he asked as the stallion danced back from the sting, and poised the whip behind his shoulder with his thumb extended out along its stock to the base of the long lash. Black and bright as broken coal and, from his flaming eyes, with a heart as dark and hard, the stallion of the herd skidded around on long torn tracks of soil to study Ivan with his head lowered like a bull. 'You are a fine creature,' said Prince Ivan, watching the black stallion as he might watch any other armed and deadly enemy, 'and I have no desire to hurt you – but you will recover from this lash sooner than I from being trampled underneath your hoofs. So the choice is yours.'

They stared at one another for many minutes, with no movement on the meadow since all the other mares were watching to see the outcome of the contest. Neither moved, neither willing to grant his adversary even that advantage . . . . until quite suddenly the stallion blew through his distended nostrils, then ducked his head still further down and began to crop the grass. Ivan did not relax for some seconds after that, and the too-quick pounding of his heart took many minutes more before it became slow and normal once more. He knew quite well that had he been on foot, either he would not have caught the horse-herd in the first place or the stallion would have bitten and pounded him into something like the chopped raw mutton which the Tatars ate – and *tsarevich po-tatarskiy* was not a fit state in which to meet Mar'ya Morevna again.

Ivan thought about what she would say to him if he dared appear in such a condition, and grinned a more wholesome grin than had dared to cross his face since first he came to Baba Yaga's country.

He was still grinning when the mare began to rear again, then changed half-way to a head-down back-arching buck which flung him and the saddle both together to the ground. His knees were still clamped tight around the saddle-flaps, his feet still through the stirrups – but there was no horse underneath him any more. He hit the soft ground of the meadow with a jarring thud, saw all the stars of a clear and frosty night in winter, and rolled up through those stars with Koshchey's whip in one hand and his sabre in the other, horribly mindful of far too many teeth and hoofs. There was no attack. Instead the horses stood around him, far enough away to be well out of reach, and gloated over his discomfiture. Ivan had been thrown by horses far too many times not to realize that there were some who took malicious pleasure in the act, but these. . . .

These were Baba Yaga's horses, with the wit of men at all times, and the speech of men to use when they saw fit; and though they did not speak, or even make a horse's noise, it was quite plain that they were laughing at him. Not because he had been thrown from his mount, but because of what that throwing meant: they would eat a richer mash tonight because of it.

Ivan's stomach clenched within him, as it had done when Koshchey the Undying dropped his sabre at his feet and dared him to bend and pick it up. At least Koshchey had not given him from noon till sunset to think about his fate: but Baba Yaga's horses were not men or even creatures in the shape of men, and expecting human feelings from them was like expecting warmth from frost.

Ivan's mare was standing closest, the imprint of the saddle still plain against her hide, and as he watched she grinned, grinned like a dog – then spat out the bit past her teeth and shook her head so that the bridle's buckles came undone and the whole thing fell away. Ivan looked at the bridle, at the girth-straps of the saddle still entangled round his feet and then at the mare. 'You could have done this at any time you pleased,' he said, too dazed and startled yet for anger.

'Of course,' agreed the mare, speaking for the first time. 'But this way gives more satisfaction, when you thought that you had caught us all. Poor Prince Ivan!' Though her words were sympathetic, the way in which she said them was most definitely not. 'You believed your task was easy. You thought wrongly, and your belief was false. And because of those mistakes, tonight you will die. Until we meet you again, chopped fine among the hay in our manger, we bid you farewell!'

Ivan tried to take a step, then stumbled and all but fell full-length to the ground. A single look told him the reason why. When he landed, still in the saddle, both his feet had pushed up through the stirrups until their iron loops now encircled his ankles like a pair of shackles and the saddle itself dragged behind like the weight of a ball and chain. Wrenching free the high red heels of his boots would take too many of the precious seconds he no longer had, and the horses knew it. An impulse to run after them regardless shot like a cramping spasm through all the muscles in Prince Ivan's body. Instead of pulling his feet out of the stirrups, he slashed twice with his sword and cut their leathers from the useless saddle. And then he stood still, head bowed, knowing it was useless. Even once he was free, a man on foot could never hope to catch them. . . . which was why they merrily raised their tails and pranced off at a high-stepping canter, not troubling even to gallop, and mocking him with neighing laughter the whole way across the meadow until they had gone too far for him to hear them any more. And there, just on the edge of sight, they stopped and insolently began again to graze. Every now and again, one would lift its head to watch him.

Ivan stared at them, then pulled the parcel of food from the wreckage of his saddle and unwrapped it. With the black loaf of Baba Yaga's bread held out as a hopeful enticement, he walked towards the mares with just the same slow pace as every rider from the very first who has ever tried to catch loose horses. The horses watched, unconcerned, until he was close but not quite close enough – and then in a flurry of manes and tails they scattered, laughing, to regroup and graze again just out of reach.

By the fifth, or tenth, or hundredth time it happened, Ivan was trembling all over with rage and hatred of the horses – and with a steadily increasing fear for what remained of the day, and his life. That time seemed now as short, and its end as certain, as any man who hears the scaffold being built outside his cell. Wild thoughts and wilder hopes went to and fro within his mind: perhaps if he moved into the woods and so skirted the meadow out of sight, he could stalk just one of the horses, catch it and, riding bareback, round the others up again; or perhaps he could reach the river of fire on foot and make the bridge again with Koshchey's whip, and having crossed so make his escape; or perhaps he could creep back to the hut in the clearing and kill Baba Yaga before she killed him.

And perhaps he could just hide on the far side of the moon, for that scheme was as likely as the others.

Closer than ever before, Ivan flung the useless loaf of bread aside and made a sudden dash at the small mare which had been his mount until she threw him. The mare reared back and sidestepped just as she had done with Ivan on her back, to avoid the charging stallion, and he fell full-length on the ground. She paused just long enough to eat some of the loaf and stamp its remnants into the soil, then snickered derisively and trotted daintily away.

Ivan lay where he had fallen, face-downward on the cropped grass, too weary even to feel anger any more. He was exhausted by his efforts, and still more by grief and fear and hunger. With the bread and *kasha* of last night, that loaf so casually destroyed by the mare had been the only food he had seen in near enough three days. The cheese and the bottle of *kumys* had been left somewhere on the wide meadow, but it was so great and they so small that by the time he found them Ivan knew he would have no more need of food or drink. All that remained to him was black depression, born of the knowledge that he had failed in all his hopes and his endeavours, and that he would never now see Mar'ya Morevna again. Not even the combined abilities of all three of his sorcerous brothers-in-law could restore life to a corpse that had been cooked and eaten. Tears of misery stung at Ivan's eyes, but he was too tired even to weep. He closed his eyes to blink away the tears and found it was more comfortable just to leave them shut, and to slip down into the darkness of a despairing sleep and pray to the good God that Baba Yaga would not take the trouble to awaken him when she came for his head. . . .

*

Tsar Aleksandr was working at one of the realm's great books of law, and hating every minute of it, when the door crashed open and Dmitriy Vasil'yevich ran in. The Tsar was so startled that he dropped his pen and made a blot over two hours' work, but that was as nothing to what he had seen.

The High Steward. *Running* . . . .

'Strel'tsin! Are you ill?' was all that Aleksandr could think
to say, knowing even as the words left his mouth that they
sounded foolish. The High Steward shook his head, so
breathless that even foolish words were beyond him. There
was a letter in Strel'tsin's hand; a crumpled, stained, dog-
eared sheet of parchment which normally the High Steward
would have been ashamed to bring into the Presence. That it
was here now meant something that the Tsar dared not guess
at. He filled a wine-cup and held it out, noticing with a little
thrill of horror that his hands had begun to shake.

'Someone,' said High Steward Strel'tsin, 'has tried to
assassinate the Tsarevich.'

Aleksandr blinked, hanging on to that one word *tried* as a
drowning man is said to clutch at a straw – except that in his
heart the Tsar feared his straw was already weighted down
with water. 'Does he live?' he asked at last. 'Is he hurt?' And
then, in a low, deadly voice: '*Who did it?*'

Strel'tsin set down the tattered letter, took up the proffered
wine-cup in both hands and drained it at a draught. 'Your son
lives, Majesty. He is unharmed. And I do not know who is
responsible, except to speculate: who most stands to gain
from the death of the heir to Khorlov?'

Tsar Aleksandr Andreyevich stared at his chief adviser
with horrified eyes; then he flung open the door and yelled for
Akimov and the other captains of the guard . . . .

*

Ivan awoke with a start in the cool evening, with dew soaking his
coat. The glow of sunset was fading from the sky, but his head
was still securely on his shoulders. He ran his hand from neck to
crown, just to be sure, and found more resting on his hair than
just his hat. Something small and solid tickled as it crawled over
the back of his hand, clambered over the wedding-ring given
him by Mar'ya Morevna and settled finally on the first knuckle
of his index finger. He had already half-guessed what he would
see, and the guess was right. A queen honey-bee was clutching
his finger with her six legs, staring at him from the dark eyes
which took up most of her head.

'Hail to you, Tsarevich Ivan,' she said, dancing the words as she spoke them in the same high buzz which had surprised him right out of a tree. 'Did I not tell you that one day I should prove useful?'

Ivan was barely awake and his mind was still half-asleep, or else he would not have started to say, 'How could you be of use to . . . .' And then the words dried up. He looked beyond the bee, who curled her antennae with an air of great satisfaction, and gazed out across the meadow.

He saw nothing but the green grass. All that expanse of open pasture-land was empty, and there was not a single horse in sight. Prince Ivan closed his eyes and his heart gave a great thump and began to beat far too loudly – like that of a man who, standing on the scaffold, sees a messenger bearing a reprieve. For some moments he was so busy with breathing that he could not speak, until at last the queen bee – eager and impatient – gave the hoped-for answer to the question that he dared not ask.

'Baba Yaga's stallion and her mares have been well stung by my people. They are running back towards their stable, each and every one of them!'

The tiny, buzzing voice had to say it three times before Ivan opened his eyes to look at her again. He made the sign of the life-giving cross over his heart and then, smiling, marked it on the air above the bee's small, striped golden body. It seemed only right and proper to bless one saviour with the sign made holy by Another. 'Thank you, little mother,' he said. 'This is the best help that any man could have, for you have given back my life and my tomorrow.'

'The service is served,' said the queen bee, and spoke more quietly than he had ever heard before; her dance on his fingertip was a model of propriety, and the small voice now held all the dignity that was proper when one monarch spoke to the son of another. 'And if I have given back your life, then it is only right and proper that I so repay you for the lives of my children and the food that feeds my people.' She spread her wings and droned into the air, then circled just above him, bobbing with her speech. 'It would be wise if you made haste back to Baba Yaga's hut, Prince Ivan, for it would look better if you arrived with the mares or close behind them, rather than coming late!' And then she flew away.

Wise to make haste or not, Ivan sat where he was on the dew-damp grass for several minutes after the bee had gone. His reason for doing so was simple enough: reaction to having his life saved – and never mind that it had been done by a talking insect – had left him shaking so hard that he could not stand up. He would have been sick if there had been anything in his fluttering stomach to make it worth the effort, but as the shaking and the flutters died away he began to laugh.

That laughter was as much a reaction as all the rest, and it progressed rapidly from chuckling to rolling on the ground and clutching his aching sides. Ivan had watched the same thing in Prince Mikhail Voronov only a matter of days before, when he had chanced to make some ill-timed comment about having a sore throat without knowing then just how very sore that throat had been – and a tiny, cool place right at the back of his mind was comparing the two and finding them very much alike. At long last he sat up again, wiping his face and feeling just a little foolish.

It was not simply shock that had sent him briefly into that near-hysterical burst of laughing, but the steadily mounting catalogue of unreality that he was being forced to accept as fact. That magic was real he had long since admitted to himself, with small choice in the matter given the evidence set in front of his own eyes. That birds and beasts and, yes, insects, could speak to him and he to them was equally beyond doubt.

But that good deeds should be rewarded by good deeds, all without further cost or question, was so far beyond belief that he still doubted it had happened. The world did not work so simply, and never had. Or did it? That was the question in the case, and Ivan was as wary of discarding one side as he was of trusting in the other. Were he to believe that good brought good, then he had no further fears for herding Baba Yaga's horses, since the other birds and beasts he had befriended on his journey would come to his assistance as the bee had done.

But if he was wrong, then he would have laid his neck across Baba Yaga's chopping-block without lifting one finger in his own defence. Ivan tore up blades of grass and ripped them to shreds between his fingers as he pondered, and at last decided to trust in whatever help God sent: starting with himself and as much strong rope as he could find. He stood up, dusted off the bits of grass and as much dew as had not already soaked into his coat, and set off back to Baba Yaga's hut.

It was just as he had been told: a great swarm of bees had driven the mares and their herd-leader stallion up and down the north end of the meadow – far enough away that the uproar did not disturb Ivan's sleep, which made him grin at such consideration – before finally letting them make their escape back to Baba Yaga, home and safety. Ivan could hear the old hag raving from a long way down the forest path. She was yelling at her horses, and so loudly that when he paused and leaned against a tree to listen he had no need to strain his ears. 'Bees?' she screeched. 'You were to stay away until after the sun had set, and yet you come running back here with your ears flat, babbling about bees! What do I care about bees?'

'Enough, if they were stinging you!' said one of the horses, and from the sharp flat sound that followed was soundly smacked for impudence. 'What else could we do but run home to the stable?'

'Mind your manners!' said Baba Yaga, lowering her voice as she regained some control of herself. 'Must I tell you how to do everything? Tomorrow, when I let you out to go to pasture, stay far from the meadow. Run instead to the deep lake at the edge of the forest and hide among the reeds along its edge. If any bees should chance to cause you trouble, then swim out and duck beneath the water as you do with biting flies.'

Knowing that he had heard all there was to hear, Prince Ivan walked on; but he took care to walk as softly as he could, and not do anything outrageous, since it was plain that he was the only person with a good temper in the entire clearing. It was impossible to say who glared at him more, Baba Yaga or her horses. Grandmother Hag was red in the face from all her shouting, and the horses were breathless and lathered; and when he glanced through the half-door of the stable, he could see from the lumps and bumps all over their sleek hides that the bees had stung them well indeed.

'Good evening to you, Baba Yaga,' he said politely. 'All your mares are safely in their stalls, and I have served for one day of the three.'

Baba Yaga stalked out of the stable, ignoring Ivan's courtesy as he held the door back for her. 'There are two more days, Prince Ivan,' she said, 'and I am not easily cheated.'

'I do not intend to cheat, *Babushka* Yaga. I do my service for a fair reward – as, I hope, do others.'

He hoped it indeed, as he ate black bread in the shadows of the stable and watched the horses watching him. There was a glitter in their eyes which was far more than just the wicked mischief of last night; it had become an active hatred, made sharper by the pain of all those stings, and Ivan knew that he would have to be extremely careful on the morrow if he was even to last long enough to provide a meal for Baba Yaga. When at last he curled up in the straw, his drawn sabre was beneath one hand and Koshchey the Undying's *nagayka* whip beneath the other. Ivan was not certain which the horses might respect more – but he suspected that it was the whip and not the sword.

*

A day passed, and a night, and still Koshchey the Undying did not stir from his bed. Had he been poisoned by an enemy, as Prince Ivan had once tried to do, then he would have regained his health and vigour within minutes. But he had poisoned *himself*, willingly and eagerly, pouring draughts of wine and beer and stranger things down his throat until they mingled in his stomach, and his blood and his buzzing brain were all overflowing with that evil mixture.

Mar'ya Morevna, pretty and clever – and crafty as a whole earth of foxes – became solicitous, bringing him bread and bowls of soup. And with them, great cups brimming with vodka as *opokhmelyat'sya*, 'a bite from the biter', to ease his head. That those over-large cupfuls also served to keep him drunk, and put him back to sleep, was just one more part of her plan. Certainly Koshchey was willing enough to have his beautiful prisoner bring him food and drink as he lay moaning softly with the shutters drawn, but less willing when once in an all-too-frequent while she chanced to drop the metal tray on which those things were carried.

On such occasions, her own head and headache quite recovered, Mar'ya Morevna would watch him with cold eyes and assess his reaction to the great shrill clangour as the tray bounced from the floor. When he merely groaned and seemed to suffer less anguish than before, then on her next visit she made sure to bring him quantities of liquor and to stand to one side with arms folded and foot tapping until he drank it down. She knew, as any general might, that such a transparent stratagem was too obvious to last; but while it lasted, it bought Prince Ivan so many little extra hours of time.

*

There was a long coil of heavy rope hung on a hook behind the stable door, and after he arose and worked the kinks and creaks out of his spine, Ivan cut it into lengths and knotted them into thick hobbles for each horse's legs. When he was done, the knots of the hobble-loops were each as big as his fist, with just enough slack rope between them for the horse to move at a walk. It was sufficient for an animal intending nothing more than grazing in the meadow, but most certainly not enough for one which planned to run away.

Putting the hobbles on was the most dangerous part of the business, for it meant that he had to go close either to the end which kicked or the end which bit with those fearsome teeth, but he managed it at last. Prince Ivan was no longer quite the blue-eyed innocent who had ridden from Khorlov in search of adventure; he had found adventure enough, and it had taught him that one way to survive such an adventure was to be more crafty than his enemies. That was why he tied the knots as he had done; large and clumsy though each seemed, they worked just as he had intended slip-knots to work – by closing and not letting go. One loop was all he had to fit around a given horse's leg, with movements not so far

239

removed from fishing. The other loop, spread wide, went on the stable floor, and when the horse set its other front or hind foot in the circle – which in the confined space of the stall happened sooner instead of later, try as the horse might to avoid it – Ivan caught up the slack with a rake and pulled all snug and tight.

It occupied him busily until all of the horses were secured, even the stallion, and even then he was well finished before Baba Yaga got out of her bed. She threw open the stable door and waited for her horse-herd to come pouring out, then stared in astonishment as they came instead with their legs tied together, treading carefully as dowagers.

'Your mares proved rather skittish yesterday,' said Ivan blandly, at some pains to keep a smile from his face, 'and difficult to keep together – so I thought that I should curb them somewhat.'

'Indeed,' said Baba Yaga, giving him another pack of bread and cheese. 'You are quite the clever one, Prince Ivan. Beware of that; they say that too much cleverness is unhealthy, and shortens the life.'

'Being stupid has the same effect, and far more often,' responded Ivan, recalling the several occasions when he had said and done things without thinking of the consequences until the consequences caught him by the throat. 'I should know.'

Baba Yaga sneered at him and smiled with all her teeth, but said nothing and instead returned to the hut on hen's legs, where she went back to bed beside the stove – there to snore until sunset or dinnertime, whichever should come first.

Prince Ivan watched her go, then turned away and began to drive the mares along the forest path that led to the pasture meadow. This time, not trusting even the littlest and quietest mare in Baba Yaga's herd, he walked. It was a slow business in the warm morning air, for the horses milled together, stumbling in their hobbles and complaining constantly with snorts and neighing. Ivan was relieved that they did not use human speech for more than the occasional curse, because he had no wish to hear what horses such as these might have to talk about. They would have seen, and eaten, far too many foul and horrid things for their conversation to be any different.

And then one of the horses on the far side of the herd broke into a gallop, charging down the path and out of sight.

Ivan's blood ran cold. He had not seen how that mare had slipped her hobbles, but slipped them she had, or she would have gone hock over postern at the first attempt to run. Now it was Ivan's turn to run, as he hurried round the herd in an attempt to find out what had happened. He all but tripped over the answer and for a moment had no idea what he was looking at. Then the picture slipped into place and he recognized what had begun the morning as a hobble made of rope with knots big as his fist. Now the knots were chewed away, and the rope itself so frayed that it was little more than a soggy lump of hempen fibre. And now Ivan remembered too late what apprehension had forced to the back of his mind: the great sharp teeth of Baba Yaga's horses.

A set of those teeth snapped at his face as the herd stallion warned him back from interfering. More of the mares – those which had been out of plain sight until he moved – were chewing at their ropes even as he watched. Those hobbled by the front legs freed themselves, then went to the aid of those whose hind legs were secured, and before more than a minute had gone by all the time that he had spent that morning was wasted and gone as the horse-herd ran free. This time they did not linger to laugh and mock but set off at a thundering gallop, spattering him with clods of earth thrown up by their frisking heels.

It was very quiet when they were gone, quiet enough for Prince Ivan to hear the blood rushing in his own ears. He listened through that whisper of sound, but could hear nothing else: no hoofs, no bird-song, no buzz of insects. He stood in the middle of the forest path and felt the oppressive stillness of the place sweep over him. It was a stillness that he might have enjoyed at another time, for the low sun of early morning slanted between the trees in bars of golden light, sparkling with tiny motes of dust. He had been in Khorlov's cathedral when it felt and looked like this, a time and place for introspection and quiet thought. Ivan's thoughts were introspective, but far from quiet; they assailed him with all the doubts that he had set aside, and all the questions for which the answer would be brutally simple. Either life. . . . or death.

And still there were no birds flitting across the sky; nor any distant howl of hunting wolves; nor even the heavy, soporific drone of bees blundering among the plants. Despite his earlier bravado, Ivan felt the first small tickle of returning fear. If he had reckoned wrongly, and placed too much reliance on the return of favours done, then he was in grave trouble.

Except that with what Baba Yaga had in mind, there wouldn't even be a grave.

*

Ivan sat moodily on a tree-stump at the edge of the pasture meadow, watching the sky flush pink with sunset as slowly, with obsessive care, he put a last and lethal edge to his sabre. He had tried to sleep during the warmth of the afternoon, but lacking yesterday's exhaustion and filled as he was with anticipated rescue from an unknown source, true restful sleep had eluded him.

Instead, as the sun dipped far enough behind the westernmost trees to send long fingers of shadow groping out towards him, he had returned with a jolt from a muttering, uneasy doze to find himself alone. No birds, no beasts, no bees – and certainly no mares to lead back to the stable in the clearing. That was when he had decided that if Baba Yaga wanted his head, she would buy it dearly. He had found a place along the edges of the meadow where the trees grew close, so that nothing could come at him from behind, and then he had taken his whetstone from the pocket of his belt and settled down to wait for the adventure that God sent.

Now he had been here for almost an hour, waiting, watching the sky change as the sun settled towards a horizon he could not see, and whetting at his sabre's edge. It had been sharp enough before he started; now the outer curve of the blade carried a silvery sheen that would reflect like a mirror if fined with a leather strop, and its point did not taper so much as fade away. Some swords were sharp enough to shave with;

this one could shave the north wind on Midwinter's Day and leave the snow it carried melting on the ground. Whether that would be sharp enough for Baba Yaga remained to be seen, but judging from the colour of the sky the time of testing would come soon.

Then small wings whirred in the cooling air and small claws closed on Ivan's wrist, prickling the skin, and the mother bird perched there – bright and brown, with that small golden tuft atop her head which looked like a Tsaritsa's crown. She tilted her head with one bright, black boot-button eye and then with the other.

'Prince Ivan!' she chirped, bobbing him a little bow that set her swaying on his wrist, 'I promised I would help you when you least expected it!'

Ivan released his pent-up breath in a long gasp that set the small bird swaying even more and indeed came close to blowing her back into the air. 'Best of birds,' he said, 'I had almost stopped expecting anything save Baba Yaga, hunting for my head. Since you were coming after all, could you not have come a little sooner in the day?'

'No,' said the bird, 'I could not. I owe you but one service for the lives of my children, Ivan Tsarevich. Had I and my people set about them with our beaks too early, they would have left the lake as they are doing even now, and run back to Baba Yaga's stable. But then she would have sent them out again for the rest of the day you are supposed to guard them, and though you are owed a third and final obligation which would have restored them once more to the stable, it would also have left you without aid for tomorrow's herding. . . . so that tomorrow's sunset would have seen your head set on a spike!'

'*Okh!*' said Ivan, slightly shocked to realize that this returning of favours was timed as tightly as the movement of troops in a battle. 'I understand, and I thank you for it.' He understood indeed, and tomorrow was suddenly free of doubts and fears now that he knew the protective paw of grim grey Mother wolf would be hanging over him.

The mother bird stared at him very hard for several seconds, as if she could see his deepest thoughts and disapproved of them. It was a look very like some Ivan had

243

received from his father, and from High Steward Strel'tsin long ago. Then she fluttered her wings in a gesture very like a tiny shrug, sprang into the air and hovered there a moment, holding station like a tiny kestrel-hawk.

'Do not assume too much from our aid, Prince Ivan,' she said sharply. 'You are not the first to think that Baba Yaga has been bested by the strength of your purpose and the goodness of your cause. You can see the others as you pass her fence. Now get back quickly to the hut with hens' legs and, as you love Mar'ya Morevna, keep your ears open and your head down!' The bird circled once, watching him, then flew away, and unless Ivan's ears deceived him she was laughing.

Baba Yaga was not laughing. Indeed he could hear her not laughing from even further down the path than before, and once again he paused to listen. The horses had followed Baba Yaga's instructions, and had gone to the lake which lay beyond the forest boundaries; but there they had been attacked – and not by bees, but by a great flock of birds which had followed them as they tried to take refuge in the deepest water. They had ducked below the surface and gained a little respite from the pecking, stabbing beaks, but those beaks had still been there when they came up to breathe. At last their choice had become threefold: swim and be blinded, duck and drown, or run for home. They had run. Ivan's grin grew wider still, then receded as he concealed it when he approached the stable door. Just out of sight he paused, listening to hear how Baba Yaga would instruct her mares for the next day. He was not disappointed.

'I can see where the bees stung you,' she said, 'and I can see where you were pecked. But what I cannot see is why you came back here on each occasion. When you were stung, you should have run straight to the lake, and when the birds pursued you, then you should have taken cover in the deep forest where they cannot follow in such numbers! So hear me well: tomorrow, go neither to the open meadow nor the lake but shelter among the trees – and do not return until the sun has set! I want Prince Ivan's head, to requite him for the times he has insulted me, and whether with your help or not I shall have it!' Her voice had risen with her passion until she screamed loudly enough to be heard back in the meadow.

Ivan had been smiling at her useless fury, knowing that the deep wood was just where the wolves would want the horses sent, but at her last words the smile went sour and crooked before fading altogether. He began to undertand just what the bird had meant when she said that Baba Yaga was not easily defeated: because she was prepared to *cheat*. Ivan took a deep breath so that he would sound calmer than he felt, and then looked in through the stable doorway.

The horses were the first things to meet his eye, and they no longer looked quite so magnificent as when first he saw them; not only were their skins still as bumpy as that of a fresh-plucked duck with the swellings from the bee-stings yesterday, but now their heads, and especially their noses, had the look of being curry-combed with a bramble bush. Baba Yaga looked no better; she was purple in the face with rage and frustration, and her stringy white hair was coming down. Ivan paid no heed to her appearance, but inclined his head in greeting as she swung round to glare at him with her red eyes.

'Good evening, Baba Yaga,' he said. 'All twenty-one of your horses are back in their stable, and I have but a single day to serve before I choose my prize.'

Baba Yaga did not trust herself to speak. Instead she ground her teeth together so hard that in the gloom of the stable Ivan could see them striking sparks from one another. Then she flung back the stable door with a jarring crash before he could move to hold it open for her, and stamped past him without so much as a curse or threat. Prince Ivan was relieved, for he had a feeling that once started she would not stop at merely cursing him. Tomorrow night would be the most hazardous of the three.

The horses were watching him as he took his platter of bread and cheese from where it had been set in the usual place, on an upturned bucket. As he sat down on the bucket and began to eat, he observed with some interest that they were no longer staring with the hatred of last night but instead with a wary, nervous respect. He had seen that look on a horse's face before, when Guard-Captain Akimov or one of his Cossacks was breaking a new mount to the saddle. It was a

245

look that came when the horse was growing tired of fighting the inevitable, and had started to consider that perhaps doing as its rider wished would be simpler in the long run. Baba Yaga's horses looked like that. He would not try any of them with a saddle, and most certainly he would not turn his back on any one of them – the stallion least of all; but if he had undertaken to herd them for four days instead of three, then it was possible that on the fourth day they would prove as docile as so many little lambs.

Or equally, of course, they would lose their tempers once and for all and trample him to a sticky wet spot in the centre of the meadow. No. Three days of this was long enough. Ivan finished his food, drank water and lay down to sleep. But no matter how the horses looked, he did not forget the way their mistress looked as well – and kept his sword close by.

*

Drawn up in their battle ranks by torchlight, the army of Khorlov looked grim, purposeful and impressive. Tsar Aleksandr hoped that the enemy would think as much – once Dmitriy Vasil'yevich had determined just *who* the enemy was. Kiev or Novgorod; Novgorod or Kiev. The names rolled like a litany through Aleksandr's head, questions without answers. Had he the strength of men, and sufficient confidence in those other Lords and Princes who claimed to be the allies of Khorlov, he would not have needed those answers at all: he would have marched out at the head of his hosts and crushed them both. Kiev or Novgorod; the answer would have been much more simple had the question been *whom do I crush first?* Simple indeed: whomever was encountered first.

And if for some reason neither Paval and Boris of Novgorod, nor even Yuriy of Kiev, had been responsible for the attack on his son, what then?

Then they would be crushed anyway, as a man might remove a thorn in his flesh which had been tolerated for far too long.

Dreams.

With neither the men, nor even the strength in sorcery, all he could do was watch his soldiers draw up in their ranks by torchlight and wait for Strel'tsin to tell him who the enemy really was.

*

'No cunning tricks this morning?' said Baba Yaga, watching all her horses running free. 'Why, Prince Ivan, you disappoint me.'

'And I hope to continue doing so, Grandmother. I like my head just where it is.'

Baba Yaga frowned, wondering at his new confidence, and Ivan closed his mouth in case he said too much. He had done so before, to his grief, and with success so close it would be nothing short of madness to throw it all away just on the chance of gaining some point or other in this constant war of words with Baba Yaga. Instead he took the familiar pack of bread and cheese – though by now he was growing thoroughly sick of the diet – then walked behind the horse-herd as it ambled out towards the meadow once again. He wondered if wolves liked cheese. Foxes did. . . .

Though he had been expecting it to happen on some part of the path before they reached the meadow, the suddenness with which the stallion and the mares went crashing into the deep forest took Ivan by surprise. Aware that Baba Yaga was still watching him from the door of her hen-legged hut, he played the part that she was expecting to see: running frantically up and down, waving his hands and shouting, before charging through the bracken in futile pursuit. In the far distance he could hear shrill, cackling laughter, and knew that Baba Yaga had been both amused and convinced by his performance; but he made certain that he had run well out of sight before he dared to slow his noisy, headlong pace. And then he perched on a stump, made himself comfortable and had a bite to eat.

The day went more slowly than he had expected, for without the impetus of fear to make him run about time hung heavy on Prince Ivan's hands. For all of that, there was still a certain degree of apprehension tickling at the back of his mind. It had to do with Baba Yaga, and the way she might react when he claimed the horse that she had promised him three nights ago.

If, as he suspected, she was prepared to go back on their arrangement and try to kill him just from spite – then would not his sword be just as effective now, while she snored beside the stove, as it might have to be this evening? Most probably. As it would have been yesterday, or the day before. And Ivan had rejected it on those days as he rejected it now, for the same reason – a reason which would have made both Baba Yaga and Koshchey the Undying laugh aloud, and had caused even Mar'ya Morevna to raise an eyebrow and smile her smallest, thinnest smile. To murder even a murderer in cold blood was not a victory, but a defeat. Self-defence was another matter altogether.

A cold nose pushed at his hand and a deep voice with a growl in it said, 'If you don't want that cheese, Prince Ivan, then give it to me.'

Ivan did not in fact jump half-way up a tree, he only felt as if he had. Once he had finished gasping, and saying all the things under his breath that nobody with sense says aloud to wolves who understand the speech of men, he opened the packet and gave the cheese to *volk-matushka*. Though she wolfed it down – as was entirely right and proper – nevertheless she did so with a deal more daintiness than he might have expected. 'I didn't know that wolves liked cheese,' he said with interest as she finished.

The mother wolf licked her lips thoughtfully before she replied. 'Some do. I don't. But it was food. We all like food.' And food, to a Russian wolf, was whatever could be eaten. Ivan took due and proper note. 'I told you, when last we met, that I would give you aid unasked. That aid is given, and thus I repay you for my cub.'

'Baba Yaga's horses?'

'Are running for their stable as though their lives depended on getting there. Which they do not – this time.'

'This time?'

The wolf looked at him with her green-yellow eyes and lolled her tongue, grinning with huge white teeth. 'Horse-meat is food, Prince Ivan. And very good food, too. But as I say, not this time,' She glanced up at what little sky was visible between the trees, then back at Ivan. 'There is the matter of another horse to deal with,' said Mother wolf. 'Your horse, earned from Baba Yaga by your own efforts . . . . and just a little help from those who owed you kindness. Get back to the clearing and the stable, and claim your prize – and if you will heed a word of warning at no extra price, sleep lightly tonight.'

And without a sound, the wolf was gone.

But Baba Yaga was not gone. Again Ivan could hear her screams and scolding as he walked slowly along the forest path to the clearing with its ghastly fence, but this time he did not pause to listen. There was nothing to hear that he had not heard already.

He was polite as always when he reached the stable, wishing Baba Yaga a good evening and asking after the health of the horses. They were well enough, though wide-eyed and sweating, and somewhat nibbled around the fetlocks. As Ivan stepped into the stable they stared, started and shied to the backs of their stalls, as if he was himself a wolf and not merely the one who seemed to command so many birds and beasts to do his bidding.

'You seem to have taught them manners,' said Baba Yaga, more mildly than Ivan had expected. 'Well, you can pick the best or worst of them come morning.'

She was putting as good a face on the matter as one so very ugly could, and Ivan would have thought that she was taking her defeat as well as she was able had he not sensed the tension jangling in the air, as plain as the sharp stench of boiling vinegar. It suggested that her good face and her good faith were both as little to be trusted as ice in springtime, and that Mother wolf was right to warn him. Far from sleeping lightly, which he had been doing all along, Ivan determined not to sleep at all; nor did he even relax his guard until Baba Yaga had gone from the stable.

His supper was beneath the bucket and Ivan wrinkled his nose when he saw it: bread and cheese again, and a leg of chicken. He stared at it for several minutes, then dropped the bucket back again. He had eaten enough bread and cheese in the past three days to last him for months to come, and he was not about to eat it on his last night under Baba Yaga's roof.

Rather than that, he preferred to go hungry. The chicken was more interesting, but just now his stomach was still fluttering sufficiently that putting anything in it would be a temporary pleasure at best.

As he sat awake with his chin propped on his sword, he could see from the lights and shadows moving about in Baba Yaga's hut that he was not the only one unwilling or unable to sleep. She, of course, had slept right through the day as usual, while he had taken no more than a cat-nap in the forest, but the gurgling sound of something boiling made him thoroughly suspicious. Prince Ivan had left his wide-eyed innocence behind a long time ago, and while he was still willing to accept the best from people without too many questions, when that best was plainly missing he could be as cynical as his own dear wife. And now was just such a time. It would be in keeping with Baba Yaga's character to let him win, and let him take away a horse, and then get it back because whatever she was brewing up there had left him with no further interest in owning anything. Shivering at the thought, Ivan resolved not to eat or drink a thing that Baba Yaga offered him, whether it be wine to celebrate his victory or merely more of the damned bread and cheese for him to eat on his journey home.

Bread and cheese. And chicken. . . .

Suddenly he was wide awake, and pulling the bucket aside once more. There was the strong smell of the cheese, and the sour smell of the black rye bread, and the savoury aroma of the roasted chicken – and under it was something else. *Eat no meat,* the queen bee had warned. All the time he had thought she meant man's-flesh, which was so obvious as to need no warning at all. But for no reason he had been given something that was safely, obviously, nothing more than a joint of temptingly roasted fowl. He sniffed warily at his untouched supper, and the hackles lifted on the back of his neck. He knew nothing about drugs or poisons, excepting only the one occasion when he had put poison on his swords in an attempt to kill Koshchey the Undying; but he knew that what he smelt right now was nothing to do with feeding him, and everything to do with putting him to sleep. . . .

A sleep from which he would never have awoken.

He looked out of the stable window at the hut on hens' legs, and wondered just exactly what was boiling. Some kind of witch's brew – or a simple stewpot, waiting to have meat put in it.

'Grandmother Hag is hungry,' said a soft, deep, growling voice from just beneath the windowsill, and then the wolf reared up to gaze at him from between her propped forepaws, a green-eyed shadow in the darkness outside. The horses stirred, but dared do nothing else. 'You had best make haste if you want to see the sunrise.'

'She tried to poison me!' whispered Ivan shrilly.

'Poison would have been the least of your problems,' said the wolf. 'Now are you going to discuss this, or are you going to get out?'

Ivan was through the stable door before the wolf had dropped her forepaws back onto the ground. 'She said that I should pick my horse come morning,' he hissed. 'So which one should I take?' He froze, listening, as a faint, familiar sound drifted through the still night air. Somewhere, some-one was sharpening a knife. Ivan's face went white, turning him ghostly in the starlight. 'Or should I even wait?' There was desperation in his voice, the beginnings of horror at not knowing what to do. Another few seconds, and he would have run headlong in any direction but the right one.

That was why Mother wolf sank her great teeth into the sleeve of his coat and held on tight. 'You wait,' she said, voice muffled and coming though her nose like someone with a cold. 'And you come with me.' Leading him by the sleeve, and by the arm inside it, she took him round to the back wall of the stable where he had never been before. This was hardly surprising, since the dung-heap was there, glowing with a faint rotting phosphoresence that seemed to grow brighter as Prince Ivan's eyes became accustomed to the dark. And then he swore as something moved in the sickly glow, and wrenched his sabre from its scabbard.

The wolf let go of his arm and sleeve and rumbled low in her chest. 'I knew I should have held your sword-arm!' she growled. 'Now put that thing away before someone gets hurt.'

Ivan had the good sense to sheathe the curved blade quietly, then he squinted through the gloom to see whatever else had frightened him tonight.

It was a colt.

Ivan had an impression of big eyes, a long mane and tail all sadly tangled and thick with dirt, and legs that went on for ever in all directions. Even allowing for the darkness and the dung, the colt looked both as unlikely a steed as he had ever seen – and one that was full of possibilities. 'What do you think of him?' asked *volk-matushka*. Ivan made some sort of noise which came out half-formed, before he meant it, and the colt's big eyes looked at him reproachfully. 'I know exactly what you mean,' said Mother wolf, not reproached in the slightest, 'but I have two messages which might help you to decide. One is that the nests of the swiftest hawks are never very clean, and the other that this creature may be grubby, but grubs can grow to butterflies.'

'Where do I find a saddle?' asked Ivan, without further ado.

Mother wolf looked at him and blinked her eyes in a patient manner. 'You were the one who slept three nights in a stable. Why do you ask me?'

Feeling foolish, Ivan fetched the saddle he had used when first he tried to herd the mares. It had been brought back from the meadow, and new stirrup leathers put in position to replace those he had cut through; with it he brought the matching bridle. The colt, unbroken though he seemed, allowed Ivan to put on both saddle and bridle, and to mount to his back; though when Ivan drew Koshchey's *nagayka* whip out of his belt, the colt laid back both ears flat against his head and showed his teeth. Despite the darkness, Ivan saw that they were ordinary horse's teeth and not the fangs of the man-eating mares. He patted the colt on the neck as he had been accustomed to pat lost Burka, and said softly, 'This whip is not for you, but Baba Yaga.'

'And do you wish to lay its lash across her now or later?' snapped the wolf, her patience at an end. 'For if you stay much longer, she will be down to find her supper – and I for one am not waiting for that. I have given aid unasked, Prince

Ivan, and help unlooked-for. What you do with it is your affair. Now get out! *Poshyol!'*

She took her own advice, for an instant later Ivan found himself alone but for the colt. He looked at it, and it looked at him, and then they both looked up towards the hut with hens' legs and the sounds of sharpening steel and boiling water that were coming from it.

'I think Mother wolf was right,' said Ivan, his voice just a little bit unsteady. He didn't know if this was yet another talking horse, and didn't really care. His sole concern right now was that it should gallop very fast in whichever direction took him furthest from Baba Yaga. 'I think we should get out. *Now.*' He lifted the reins and flicked them, jabbing with his heels.

And it was as if he had unleashed the whirlwind in a horse's shape. Ivan could do no more than crouch low as a jockey as the colt shot across the clearing like an arrow – if arrows moved as swiftly – and cleared the vile fence of dead men's bones without breaking his stride. After that, he galloped along the forest path that led away from Baba Yaga's hut and out across the ash desert to the river of fire, accelerating all the way. . . .

*

The army of Khorlov was on the march, with Tsar Aleksandr at its head. They had an enemy at last, but only the Tsar and his First Minister knew that enemy's name. It was not the Prince of Kiev, nor the two Princes of Novgorod. . . .

It was Koshchey the Undying.

When Strel'tsin brought the name at last, he was not running but walking like a man on his way to the block. Tsar Aleksandr had not known why until matters had been explained to him and then, to the Steward's horror, he had refused to be impressed.

'If what you say is true,' said the Tsar, 'this Koshchey has been defeated before, and by the very weapons we have here. An army'—he gestured at the ranks of armoured men leaning on their tall shields—'and a sorcerer.' The hand clapped against his shoulder felt to Dmitriy Vasil'yevich like the first practice swing of a headsman's blade. With his stomach twisting itself in knots, he tried to explain again about Koshchey *Bessmertnyy*, but the Tsar either could not or would not understand what he intended fighting.

Strel'tsin swallowed sourness and shivered inside the chilly armour that the Tsar had insisted he wear. He had hoped to die in bed, as was right and proper for a politician, but now it appeared he had a chance to do something much more original. And painful. Then he smiled a crooked little smile of relief. The army had to find Koshchey's kremlin before they could besiege it, and if they went in the wrong direction. . . . That was when he saw the birds, spiralling down to land right in front of the Tsar's horse.

Lightening flickered briefly, and then three sorcerer Princes came forward with offers of help and guidance. Dmitriy Vasil'yevich looked at them, considered once again the prospect of his own messy death and was promptly sick.

*

And at the same instant as Prince Ivan rode a stolen horse towards the borders of her country, Baba Yaga's hut stamped its hens' legs once, twice and three times, so hard that her great stewpot full of boiling water fell right off the stove and splashed her feet. She knew at once what had happened, and even if she did not the receding drumbeat of hoofs gave her a clue that something was amiss down by the stable. With a screech that was one-third pain at her scalded feet – clean for the first time in only the good God knew how long – and two-thirds rage and frustrated appetite, she limped and hopped across the floor as fast as ten parboiled toes allowed.

Although she owned a herd of horses and fed them on man's-flesh as often as it was available, Baba Yaga did not herself ride a horse. She was afraid of horses and deathly afraid of her own, having taught them evil appetites and then seen what they could do – and besides, no horse in its right mind, not even her own, could bear to carry her. Instead, she sprang into a great iron mortar and began to beat it with an iron pestle until the metals of both rang with that pounding like an unholy bell. Then a trembling passed through the mortar, and a shuddering and a shaking that stirred it where it sat, until within a minute it had begun to bound across the clearing in thunderous pursuit, with Baba Yaga crouched inside, flogging it to greater efforts with the pestle and sweeping away the tracks it left with her long kitchen broom.

Ivan reined in the colt as they drew close to the fiery river; he had not forgotten how the burning chasm could appear as if from nowhere right beneath his feet, and after all that he had suffered had no desire to fall into it at this late stage. He was still dazed with astonishment at the speed of the grubby colt, for it appeared that in every minute of its gallop it covered ground which had taken Burka an hour to cross. But dazed or not, and even with his ears still ringing from the hiss of wind and the beat of hoofs, he was not so deaf that he could not hear the commotion in their wake. What it was Ivan did not know, but he was wise enough to guess that it meant little good to either his steed or himself.

And then the glowing gorge that was the river of fire dropped sheer away before them, hidden until almost too late by the flat, monotonous grey of the desert to either side. The colt backed off hastily and Ivan did not stop him; he had never been convinced as to just how strong the chasm's edges were, and did not intend to put them to the test if it could be avoided. Instead – and with a nervous glance over his shoulder to where a fast-approaching cloud of dust was making noises like a gong in torment – he took Koshchey's whip in his right hand and waved it once, twice and three times as he had done before. As the great bridge shimmered into existence, looking at first like a phantom summoned from the haze of heat itself, the colt flicked his ears back once, then forward again with the greatest interest. 'Most impressive,' he said, so unexpectedly that for a second or so Ivan almost forgot the threat of Baba Yaga. Then the colt looked from the bridge to Ivan, and twitched those expressive ears again and said calmly, 'We should cross over, little master, while we can.'

After advice from every other animal he had encountered in the past few days, advice from his own horse was not so unusual as it might have been. Ivan nodded, dismounted and led the colt across the bridge; then he turned and stared down into the slow, muttering outflow from the earth's hearth-fires. He closed his eyes; but not from the glare or from the heat. Then, his decision made, Ivan raised Koshchey the Undying's riding-whip in his left hand and waved it once, and twice, and thrust it through his belt and drew his sword instead. Its sharp, sharp edge gleamed red in the dull light of the fiery river, and that reflection trembled just a little.

Baba Yaga came booming up, and beat the mortar to a standstill so that it stood rocking on the far side of the river gorge. She scowled at Prince Ivan, waiting quietly at the far end of the bridge with his sabre raised and resting on his shoulder, and looked as suspicious of deception as only a deceiver can. Far, far below the fiery river grumbled softly in its bed, like an old, hot-tempered man in fitful sleep. The fluttering of small white flames looked like the movement of his hair and beard.

And then Baba Yaga saw the grubby little colt which, caked in grey ash-dust like all else, had been invisible against the grey ash desert until it moved. She gave a screech of outrage at such a blatant display of theft and, pounding with the pestle, beat the mortar forward in a great bound that came down on the middle of the bridge's span . . . .

. . . . And went straight through without an instant's pause.

Baba Yaga screeched all the way down to the river of fire, and screeched no more thereafter. What words she had been crying Prince Ivan never knew, and did not want to know. He waved the whip one final time, so that the bridge faded away, then rolled its lash about the stock and tucked it through his belt. As he turned his back to the fiery river and his face towards the lands of men, he patted his new horse and knew that one thing was certain.

It was time that Koshchey the Undying learned the name of Ivan Tsarevich again.

CHAPTER TEN
How matters were concluded

Each morning Mar'ya Morevna went into the stable to look at Koshchey's saddle, and each morning saw the wrong whip looped from its pommel. Three mornings passed, then four, then five and still the whip was wrong. By her calculations, and by what Koshchey had said in his drunken stupor, Ivan's task of serving Baba Yaga with the herding of her horses should have taken no more than five days at the most. One day to go, three days to serve and one day to return. If he had been successful. Whereas if he had not . . . .

Mar'ya Morevna bit her knuckles. For all her magic, she was locked away from it in a far place and thus was not to know about the bear which had frightened Ivan's horse, so that he had been obliged to walk on his own feet for the best part of an extra day. And without that knowledge, valiant though she was, she could no longer suppress her fears.

She fretted all that day – even forgetting to make Koshchey's life a misery, so that he grew sober at long last – and slept badly when she went to her bed that night.

And awoke on the morning of the sixth day, when all was well again.

There was no sign of Prince Ivan, either in the kremlin or outside it, and if Koshchey's black horse knew something of the matter it stared at her from its bed among the straw, and held its own counsel, and said nothing. But the whip which hung from the saddle was not the same one that Mar'ya Morevna had seen so many times before, and when she put out one hand to touch it the tingle of the power concealed by its simple shape ran burning up her arm. She looked at the ugly, ordinary thing, smelling of cruelty and old blood.

And she cried for pure relief and joy.

*

It galled Ivan that for a second time he had walked unseen into the dark kremlin, and for a second time been forced to leave without his wife. It galled him more that this time he had not dared even to see her; but there had been an icy burning in his bones to tell him plain enough that the master of the fortress was at home, and he knew that neither he nor his horse was yet strong enough to meet Koshchey *Bessmertnyy* face to face and survive the encounter.

Instead, setting his back to Koshchey's kremlin and his face to the rising sun, he rode the leggy colt for many *vyorsty*, heading south by east at an astounding speed into the wide green grasslands along the quiet flow of the river Don. It was there, according to Guard-Captain Akimov, that the finest horses in all the Russias could be found – and this was an opinion shared by the Don, the Kuban and the Terek Cossacks, horse-breeders whose opinions were denied *smertel'naya opasnost'*, on the life of those who questioned them.

Ivan watched as the colt rolled on the grass and splashed in the river, and as he watched the muck of many weary days spent lying on the dung-heap was washed away. He knew that he was riding a finer steed than any which had cropped the Ukraine grass before, but he knew equally well that nobody would believe a word of it unless he was prepared to do a deal of work with water, brush and curry-comb. There was just one problem: while there was plenty of water, the last brush and curry-comb he had owned had been in one of Burka's saddle-sacks, last seen heading for Siberia with a bear in hot pursuit.

The next day a small band of Zaporozhiyy Cossacks passed them by, riding south in furtherance of some small feud or other with their Black Sea brethren. There had been a delicate few minutes' negotiation, while Ivan asked for the use of such tools as were needed to groom his horse and the Cossacks considered whether trying to steal that horse was worth the trouble. They decided not: there was a deadly look about Prince Ivan which suggested he was all too ready to make use of the *shashka* sabre hanging at his hip, a look which implied he had suffered more than enough in the way of nonsense from both man and beast.

The Cossacks eyed him for those few minutes and then decided that their feud was more a matter of sport than war, something from which both they and their enemies hoped to return with nothing more than a scar or two, and brag-stories to impress their womenfolk. There was something about the way this fair-haired young Rus looked at them, with his cool blue eyes like ice that dared a man to test it, that told one and all there would be no sport if he was forced to draw his sword. They gave him loan of grooming-brushes, without payment except to cook their food at his fire, and when he pressed them to take something more, asked only that he let his black colt run with their mares while they rested.

Ivan was willing enough for that, though had he been asked he would have said the colt was scarcely old enough to show an interest in anybody's mares. As it transpired, he was mistaken; and that was the first time he noticed just how fast that colt was growing.

The Cossacks made to ride on about their business, but spent an excessive time in exclaiming with amused envy about such horses as the colt being permitted to run free on the plain without someone of business acumen to make his fortune from stud-fees. That was when both Ivan and the colt grinned at them with far too many teeth, so that they made whatever excuses were appropriate and rode quickly to their feud along the shores of the Black Sea – a place which, though it might be alive with swords and arrows, was still far safer than where Prince Ivan was.

Once they were gone, Ivan sat down again on the bank of the river Don, flinging stones into its water and watching the colt run across the grass. Even now, leggy and gangly, it was the most handsome horse that Ivan had ever seen and looked well set to be one of the biggest. Washed and brushed and combed, the colt gleamed black as jewellery made from polished jet and looked to be blood-kin of Koshchey's steed; but it was finer-boned, less massive and so less brutal-looking, and he wondered more than once why it had been left to roll in the mire.

There was a way to find out, God knew, but despite all that he had seen and heard and lived through, Ivan Aleksandrovich still felt less than easy talking to his own horse. It was a thing done by men who drank too much vodka; and that the horse might speak to him again unsettled Ivan almost as much as the thought that it might not, and that he had imagined the few words it had said to him beside the bridge over the river of fire. Certainly it had not spoken since. But at last he asked, moved more by curiosity than the fear of looking foolish – for after all, there was nothing but a horse to see it if he was wrong, and if he was wrong the horse could not talk about it afterwards.

Except that this horse could, and from the tone of his deep voice, probably *would* as well. 'She left me in the muck because I would not eat the meat of men,' said the colt, and if he sounded annoyed with the memory Prince Ivan could not blame him. 'Because I had neither the teeth nor the taste for it.'

Ivan considered for a long moment that he was making conversation with a horse, and wondered vaguely what he might have said to any who had made the same suggestion a year ago. Then he shrugged; whatever that might have been, and to whomever it might have been said, it was all last autumn's leaves in the wind by now. 'Like the horse that Koshchey the Undying rides?' he asked.

'Yes,' said the colt. 'Like my eldest brother.' Then he lowered his head and began to crop the grass of the wide plain that ran along the river's edge. Ivan watched, chewing a straw, somewhat surprised that he owned a horse of the same blood as his dearest enemy, but pleased for all that with the delicious irony of the situation.

'And can you outrun him?'

The colt raised his head and blinked. 'Koshchey?' he asked, feigning astonishment and doing it quite well.

Ivan had encountered the dumb beasts who trod on his feet for fun, and the malicious mares of Baba Yaga, but a horse with a dry and wholesome sense of humour was a new experience and he liked it. 'No, your brother,' he said, and smiled thinly.

The colt snorted, laughing like a horse rather than a man. 'Of course I can, little master.' Then he looked down at his long legs, where knees had been fitted not so much as a joint but more as an afterthought. 'But I could do it better if I was fully grown.'

'*Chyort!*' snapped Ivan, and flung his well-chewed straw into the river Don. He was no longer smiling. 'And how long will my wife be a prisoner while we wait for *that*?'

The colt stared at him – and had a horse's face worn eyebrows, and had those eyebrows been visible through the silky fringe of mane that hung over its forehead, the colt would have raised them in surprise. 'Seven days,' he said. 'Why? Didn't you know?'

'Seven days,' echoed Ivan, feeling the blood go cold and thick within his veins. 'Know this, horse of mine. The moon is on the wane. If I .... we .... have not rescued Mar'ya Morevna by sunset of your seventh day, before the night of moon-dark, she will remain Koshchey's captive until *he* chooses to release her.'

The horse snorted expressively. 'As I said, little master. Seven days.' And then he fell to eating grass again, with more determination than before.

Ivan pulled himself another straw and ground his teeth down on it, feeling foolish. It was one thing not to ask too many questions, but it was another thing entirely not to ask a question just because you thought you knew the answer already.

Especially in a matter that involved a talking colt, where reality had already packed its bags and gone away. If a horse could speak good Russian and outrun the wind, then all the other reasons and excuses as to why it could not do such-and-such – as, for instance, come to full growth in seven days' time – were already set aside. Just as he had set aside his own disbelief a long time ago, for the sake of sanity.

He chewed on the straw, and watched the colt, and began to count the days.

Remembering lost Burka, whose name had come from an old story, Ivan took another of those names and called the black colt Sivka. Since his first bath in the quiet river Don Sivka was no longer a grubby creature, and as he grazed on the rich green grass his body expanded to fit those long, long legs, until by the time a week had gone by he was no longer leggy, nor indeed a colt, but a coal-black stallion eighteen palms high. Ivan looked at him and nodded. 'You should do,' he said.

He had spent a restless night and had been awake before dawn, early enough to see the last mocking sliver of the old moon climb up into the glow of the eastern horizon. In less than an hour its pallid arc was gone, washed from sight by the glare of the newly-risen sun. There would be no moon tonight. And no more time.

The old saddle which had come from Baba Yaga's stable still fitted Sivka's back, but only just; the buckles of its girth-strap would barely fasten after encircling that great cask of a chest. Prince Ivan looked at the great platters of hoofs at the ends of legs no longer gangly but corded with long muscles beneath the sleek black skin. 'I should have had shoes put on those,' he said.

Sivka raised a fore-hoof and pawed at the air, then scraped it across the ground so that a great gouge was carved into the soil. 'There has been no time to waste on such luxuries, little master,' he said in a huge voice, soft and deep and mellow as the bass register of a cathedral organ, 'and unless there is more money in your belt than I suspect, then I doubt you could pay for so much iron just yet.' He stamped, twice, so that Ivan felt the impacts shiver through the soles of his boots. Those hoofs were not platters at all; they were hammers such as the Polskiy horsemen carried and weapons just as lethal. 'Besides,' said Sivka, 'Moist-Mother-Earth is soft beneath my feet, and it is good to run unshod for a little while.'

'As you wish.' Ivan hopped for a few awkward seconds with the pointed toe of one boot through a stirrup and his knee up near his chin, then gave up the attempt. Sivka, grown into a huge courser such as armoured knights might ride in Frankland – and so almost half as big again as the small, quick horses of the Rus – was too tall to mount in the ordinary way. Too tall at least for Ivan, who stood two and one-half *arshiniy* in his red-heeled boots and thus could not even see over

Sivka's shoulders without standing on tip-toe. Instead he mounted as the Cossacks and the Tatars sometimes did – bracing one hand on the pommel, then bouncing once on his toes and vaulting up. 'Come on,' he said in Sivka's ear, 'let's go make mischief!'

Sivka reared back, lashing his great hoofs and bugling out a shrill challenge across the quiet waters of the river Don. High above the wide white world, astride a horse that was bigger, faster and more magnificent than any other he had ever seen, Ivan stood in his stirrups and ripped his sabre from its scabbard. He raised it high above his head, whirling the blade across the hot eye of the sun so that light splashed in diamond sparkles from its edge. His beloved lady awaited rescue, and there was an enemy to defeat. Ivan Tsarevich threw back his head and laughed, feeling for the first time as he had felt before only in his dreams.

Like a *bogatyr'* at last.

And a hero.

*

Mar'ya Morevna was walking along the parapets of Koshchey's kremlin, staring at the slow, inexorable slide of the sun down the sky, when she first heard the rumble of approaching hoofs long before there was anything to see across the steppe. It was a sound that rose and drummed in her ears until – even to one who had heard a Tatar horde at the charge – it seemed to cover all the world. And then she saw the horse.

At first she thought that Koshchey the Undying had returned early from whatever wickedness had taken him out across the world, but Koshchey's horse – poor, harried, beaten creature that it was – had never looked so fine as this. And Koshchey did not wear a red coat trimmed with sable fur, or have the pale blond hair of the Rus beneath his hat. The beautiful Tsarevna closed one hand on the cold stone of the kremlin rampart, and closed her eyes, and softly said a name that she no longer dared to voice aloud.

Say the name, and summon the named.

When she opened her eyes again Prince Ivan was in the

courtyard far below, mounted on the biggest, blackest horse that she had ever seen. There was a sabre like a slice of sharpened moonlight in his hands, and he was looking up at her and smiling. 'This time,' he cried in a voice that set the echoes booming between the eight walls of the dark kremlin, 'let Koshchey catch us if he can!'

Mar'ya Morevna picked up her skirts and ran down the many stairways as a plover runs across a meadow, then burst out through the great double doors of Koshchey's kremlin and leapt up breathless into the warmth of her husband's waiting arms. She was a commander of stern armies and a Tsarevna of wide realms, and such people would not cry; but she had seen the holder of her heart cut into pieces, and returned to her alive as she had never hoped to see – and then, for her sake, she had watched him ride away towards the threat of such a death as in his innocence he could not imagine. So Mar'ya Morevna held Prince Ivan close, as if she would never let him go, and buried her face in the deep fur of the coat above his shoulder, and sobbed and laughed for the happiness of their reunion.

'If I might express a personal opinion, dear little master,' said a vast bass voice that made her start, 'the sun is setting. Your love for your lady might be more easily expressed by leaving this foul place at once.'

Mar'ya Morevna stared about and realized at last that it was Ivan's black horse which had spoken. The huge beast met her stare with gentle eyes and snuffled at her ankles, then looked past her to Ivan. 'I begin to comprehend how you might not live without such a companion, master. But if Koshchey the Undying returns unlooked-for and finds you within the walls of his kremlin, or the sun sets and both of you still here, then this lady may have to live again without you. It would be as well, when he comes back, that we were all long gone.'

'Sivka, your wisdom goes beyond your days on earth,' said Ivan, helping Mar'ya Morevna to a better seat side-saddle. 'There is nothing more in this place that I want.' He released the reins, held his wife about the waist and let Sivka have his head. 'So act as you advise.'

The black courser snapped around in his own length and

galloped towards the kremlin gate just as the sun slipped stealthily beneath the horizon. In that same instant a great lurching shudder rippled through the ground and the dark kremlin trembled. Sivka whinnied as his hoofs briefly lost their grip on the skull-domed cobbles of the courtyard, then gathered himself and sprang through the gateway, crossing the bridge and causeway that ran across its moat with a single lofting bound. Earth and air shifted together, and a massive gust like the exhalation of a giant mingled with a single monstrous rolling boom. The horse squealed, pain and fright and stallion's outrage all mingling in that one high, shrill noise. Then, with Ivan and Mar'ya Morevna hanging on for dear life, he began to gain real speed.

With her hair whipping about her face, Mar'ya Morevna leaned back into Ivan's embrace and laughed as she watched the wide white world blur by, then said as best she could above the whistling wind of their passage, 'Koshchey will know now, as he did before.'

Prince Ivan's face was cold, and though he smiled there were too many teeth in it and the expression was not pleasant. 'As he may know the north wind blows,' he said. 'But let him catch it!'

Behind them, there was no longer anything that resembled a kremlin. Instead a mountain of bare black rock reared up into the darkening sky, and had any paused to look they might have seen – clamped in a crack that might once have been a gate – a fistful of strands, pulled from a horse's tail.

*

At that very moment, in a far Tsardom where Koshchey the Undying rode through the burning ruins of a village, his black horse stumbled beneath him. Koshchey caught at the flowing mane to save himself from falling, and wrenched it cruelly as he heaved back to his saddle; but he was too astonished yet to beat the black horse for its clumsiness.

Instead he sat stock-still and sniffed the air, and then said, 'No. I do not believe it.'

The black horse shook pain from the muscles of its neck, where all of Koshchey's stringy weight had hung from its mane and from the skin beneath. Then it winded the smoke-thick air with flaring nostrils that were as wide and red as pits full of blood. 'Believe it, Koshchey the Careless,' said the horse, 'as you believe no other thing beneath the bright sun. There is a Russian smell within the dark kremlin, where none should be. And because no other man across Moist-Mother-Earth could be so bold, it can only be Prince Ivan, come again to steal Mar'ya Morevna from your domain.'

'You lie!' snarled Koshchey the Undying, and this time he smote the horse with his riding-whip until its blood spattered his boots. 'I killed Prince Ivan! He is dead and gone!'

The black horse neither reared nor squealed beneath his rain of blows, suffering them as stoically as a cloud of midges on a summer's day; but it turned its head to stare at him as he cut its shoulders to red ribbons, and all the fires of the hearths of Hell were burning in its eyes. 'Koshchey the Undying,' it said, 'or Koshchey the Fool. Of course you killed him. And he killed you. But because he killed you, should I then just imagine the stripes that split my shoulders?'

'*Tak*,' said Koshchey, and withheld his further blows. 'That is so.' He coiled the long lash of his whip so that red blood dribbled from his fingers to stain the grass beneath his horse's feet. 'I did not kill him well enough. It is not a mistake I shall make twice.'

The black horse stirred beneath him and, frowning, Koshchey looked down at it. 'Why do you fret?' he asked. 'Surely it is possible to catch them?'

'It is possible,' said the black horse. 'Perhaps.'

Koshchey spoke an oath and struck the black horse between the ears with his clenched fist so that it staggered and all but fell. 'Perhaps? Why do you dare talk to me of perhaps, when at all other times you have caught the fugitives with ease?'

'Because at all other times they rode an ordinary horse. This time they ride my youngest brother!'

'So and indeed?' said Koshchey in a deadly voice. 'But you did not say that they are riding double, while you carry only me. I dislike deceitful servants almost as much as I hate those who aid my enemies. When all is done today, one way or another, I shall own a steed who knows what it means to cross me – and for the other, I shall feast on freshly roasted horsemeat. Now move!' He drove his wicked Turki spurs into the black horse's flanks. '*Skoreye!* Hurry!'

*

'Beware, Prince Ivan,' said black Sivka, 'we are not alone! Koshchey is near!'

Ivan exchanged a startled glance with Mar'ya Morevna, then looked over his own shoulder. Nothing could be seen, but he knew enough to trust what Sivka said. 'Why have you not outrun him?' he demanded. 'You are a horse as good or better than the one he rides.'

'But he rides alone,' Sivka replied, 'while I carry both you and your lady.'

'And besides, Koshchey knows when to beat his horse,' hissed Mar'ya Morevna in a low voice.

Ivan took the import of her words at once, putting a hand to her shoulder and swinging her around with a glare such as Mar'ya Morevna had never seen directed at her before. 'I am not Koshchey,' he said, softly enough that Sivka could not hear, 'and I do not beat my friend when he gives me the best that he can!'

'The best that he *thinks* he can!' responded Mar'ya Morevna. 'Call him your friend, or call him your brother – but riders do not wear whips and spurs just for cruelty's sake!'

Prince Ivan drew breath to say something – a thing that he might have regretted – then let out the breath in a great gasp of shock as Sivka wrenched sideways hard enough to almost unseat both his riders.

And in the same instant, the edge of a sword hissed past Ivan's neck.

Koshchey the Undying swayed in his saddle, thrown off-balance by the force of his own two-handed stroke which had missed only because Prince Ivan's horse had jerked to one side without command from rein or knee or heel. He raised his great cleaver to cut again – and was met by a fierce stop-thrust, as the point of Ivan's sabre slammed through his armpit and into his chest.

Koshchey *Bessmertnyy* reeled sideways, coughing as the steel blade ripped clear. Then he coughed twice more, clapping one hand to his body, and was whole and uninjured again. He leered into Prince Ivan's cold blue eyes, swinging his sword at the youthful face, hating it and despising it both for its lack of long years and for its innocence.

Ivan took the cut on his own braced sabre and was smashed back in his saddle by the impact. The sabre spat sparks and was notched, and the sound of the notching was like a church bell put to the torments of Hell. He had neither the strength nor the weight nor the thickness of sword to do other than glissade Koshchey's cuts, but with Mar'ya Morevna in front of him and Sivka beneath him, he dared do nothing but block. To do otherwise, even to duck or to dodge, would have been to let that awful ragged edge past him and into his wife or his horse. And if that happened, either way, all would be over.

Then there was a shrill crack, and a shriller squeal, and Sivka heaved beneath him. The drumbeat of hoofs increased in its tempo, and though Koshchey was riding at full gallop he fell back and back until he was no more than a vague shadow in the dust flung up by Sivka's hoofs. The crack and the squeal and the heave were repeated, and within seconds Koshchey was gone, lost in the haze of their passage. Prince Ivan glanced back, then looked forward – then grabbed his wife's wrist and twisted the tails of the reins from her fingers, and for an instant was on the point of using them on her as she had used them on Sivka.

'Do it,' said Mar'ya Morevna – not taunting, not daring, just looking him full in the face. 'The blow will prove something, besides what I just proved to you and your horse. It will prove that you're alive to do it.'

Had it not been for the sword-swinging shape somewhere in their wake, Ivan would have hauled Sivka to a standstill the better to have words with the pragmatic lady that he loved. But Koshchey was out there somewhere, still in pursuit, still carrying that dreadful cleaver that he called a sword. And anyway, Mar'ya Morevna was right. He let the reins drop, and instead put them to their proper use.

It was not enough. Sivka's pace had barely begun to slacken

before they heard the thudding of other hoofs drawing closer again. Ivan swore a bitter oath and drew his sabre once more. Its bright edge was sadly marred, and all to no avail; but it was the only weapon he possessed except for the thoughts that were running ever faster through his mind. 'I have to stop him, or slow him at the very least,' he said between his teeth, 'if I only knew how I might do it!'

Sivka, still galloping as fast as he thought he was able without the encouragement of a whip or the tails of the reins, turned his head in a flurry of black mane. 'I have borne you far from the dark kremlin, and far from the lands that Koshchey knows. When you fight, as fight you must, then pick a ground that favours you instead of him.'

'Leave that to me,' said Mar'ya Morevna. 'I was trained in such a skill by the best my father could afford – and that means the best in the wide white world!' She laid hand to the reins and Sivka slackened his headlong pace sufficiently for her to study how the land lay. They had passed beyond the steppes by now, leaving the flat plains behind, and had ridden out into rolling country where an ambuscade was possible amongst the wrinkled earth and the coarse shrubs that covered it.

'There,' said Mar'ya Morevna, pointing. What she had seen was no more than a gully cut by the run-off from a rainstorm, but it was fringed with scrubby plants that grew so thickly they might have been placed there for the purpose of concealment. 'Oh, that I had thought to bring a bow from Koshchey's kremlin,' she said, for the place was perfect for archery from deep cover.

Ivan shook his head. If a poisoned and enchanted sabre was of little use, than an ordinary arrow was of none at all. 'I thought of several things like that,' he said, helping Mar'ya Morevna slide down to the ground, 'but at last decided not to waste my time – either on arrows, poisoned blades or anything else.'

His wife stared at him with horror on her face. 'Then Koshchey will do again what he did before!' Her voice was tremulous, with fear and with anger at a needless waste. 'He will cut you to pieces and leave me a widow and, Vanyushka dearest, I will not bear that again!' Mar'ya Morevna hesitated as the wind brought a distant thundering of hoofs to her ears. 'Help me up again,' she said, 'and ride like the wind towards our own kremlin. If I can reach my books, then we might just have a chance!'

'I have a better chance right here, my beloved,' he said, drawing his sabre and resting it across his saddle. 'Koshchey is expecting us to run, and I have long grown tired of doing what he wants.'

Mar'ya Morevna looked up at her husband and the horror faded from her face, replaced by hope and even by the faintest hint of amusement. 'I begin to suspect,' she said, 'that you have done much more. What is in your mind, Prince Ivan Aleksandrovich?'

He leaned down from Sivka's saddle and kissed Mar'ya Morevna on the lips. 'That, for one. As for the rest, watch.' His sabre lifted, pointed to another gully further on and came back to rest again. 'But watch from safety. I don't want to lose you.'

She laughed hollowly. The approaching horse was drawing ever closer, and Mar'ya Morevna had seen enough fights between mounted men to know exactly what her husband meant. Beneath the wildly dancing hoofs of war-horses, a bystander was nothing more than something to be trampled into a secure footing. But before she went to the gully, she reached up to the back of his belt and pulled his small dagger from its sheath. Ivan looked from her hand to her face, and in his expression was appalled, perfect understanding. 'I said it before, my beloved,' she said, compounding the certainty. 'Either we will live together, or we die together. Koshchey cannot make me his prisoner again unless you are dead – and if you are dead, he will not make me a prisoner any more.'

A cloud of dust and grass-shreds became visible beyond a small rise in the ground; then the sounds of hoofbeats grew suddenly deafening as Koshchey the Undying came charging over it, and there was no more time to think of anything except action. Mar'ya Morevna had chosen her ground with a cunning eye, for there was only a single route by which Koshchey could approach – and that route took him straight past Ivan's front, into the perfect position for a charge from cover at his flank.

Neither Koshchey the Undying nor his horse had expected anything but a fleeing adversary; the charge, and the hulking size of the horse that charged, took both of them off guard. Ivan felt the thudding impact through his close-clamped knees as Sivka rammed his own eldest brother and then, just for a single instant as they went crashing past, nothing else existed in the world except for his sword-arm, his already-swinging sabre and a line that only he could see.

It ran across the top of Koshchey's head . . . .

The blade struck home with a heavy clank that jolted Ivan to the teeth, and as he twisted half around to wrench the sabre free he saw Koshchey *Bessmertnyy* spill out of his saddle like a burst bag of meat.

Koshchey hit the ground as limp as a corpse, skidding between the iron hammers of his own horse's feet, and then he lay still. Ivan wheeled Sivka and watched, his sword poised, carefully out of the necromancer's reach.

It was just as well. Koshchey twitched; then shuddered; then rose to his knees. He raised both hands to his head, horribly sliding the wet, shattered pieces of his own skull back together just as a man might adjust the sit of his hat. Then he bent down, lifted his sword and waved it at Ivan. 'Come down and fight,' growled the necromancer as he scrambled to his feet, Ivan's sabre-cut already no more than a livid stripe above his brows. 'Come down and show me what the courage of the Rus looks like!'

Staring at this old man who flung back the challenges which had been offered him for centuries past, Ivan shivered deep in the marrow of his bones. There were plans in his mind, and cunning stratagems; but they paled into nothing against the sight of an enemy who had just scooped his own brains back into place as anyone else might have tucked inconvenient loose strands of long hair behind his ears. 'You know what Rus courage looks like, old rattlebones,' he said at last. 'And a Rus heart, and eyes, and all the other things you cut from me when I fought on your terms. Now you will fight on mine.'

Koshchey muttered something in his beard, and tossed his ugly cleaver of a sword from one hand to the other as if it was a knife. 'You are a dead man, Ivan Tsarevich, unless you run while you are able.'

'I was alive, then dead, and now alive again. You have never been more than a corpse without a grave to lie in.' Ivan lowered his sabre's point and levelled it between old Koshchey's burning eyes. 'And if you think to make me run to save my life, and leave my wife with you. . . .' He paused and gave Koshchey a grin.

The necromancer was still waiting for Prince Ivan to complete his bold words when the Tsarevich slammed heels to his courser's flanks and Sivka lunged forward just far enough. Ivan leaned over, sword swinging around and then down with all of his hatred riding on its edge, and Koshchey's right arm came off at the shoulder.

'. . . . Then think again,' Ivan finished at last, sheathing the sabre. He twisted sideways, kicking one leg over his pommel to slide swiftly down and snatch up the severed arm before Koshchey could reach it. The necromancer, stunned but still living, closed his scrabbling fingers on emptiness.

Ivan all but dropped the arm again, because of its weight and the way that it felt, for it was like no limb that he had ever touched before. There was no warmth and no yield of flesh; instead it was as hard and cold and gnarled as a dead branch. But it had Koshchey's sword still gripped tightly in its hand, so that what he held looked like such a scythe as Death might carry.

Koshchey the Undying thought so too, for he began slowly to back away, glaring balefully at Ivan. *He cannot be slain by any man*, Mar'ya Morevna had once said. *Or by any weapon wielded by the hand of man.* Men died; Koshchey did not die; therefore Koshchey *Bessmertnyy Chernoknizhnik* was no man.

And what Prince Ivan held was a sword grasped by Koshchey's own unhuman hand.

'Ivan, no. . . !' cried Mar'ya Morevna, and there was horror in her voice. But then she saw how Koshchey was retreating and fell silent.

For many minutes that silence continued, save for quick, harsh breathing. And then the silence broke.

'Brother, why do you serve this monster? You owe him nothing!' Black Sivka gazed into the red eyes of Koshchey's horse, then stared at Koshchey the Undying while a red fire kindled deep within his own dark eyes. 'Leave him helpless here, while we find the spells to end his wicked life!'

Koshchey's horse glared at his master and reared back with his great shod fore-hoofs cutting arcs of polished iron across the air. Then he squealed and fell back as Koshchey the Undying struck out with his long *nagayka* whip, splitting the horse's soft muzzle in a diagonal scarlet slash. The necromancer laughed, and cracked the lash of his whip so that red blood spattered across the ground. 'Fool! He will not leave me!' snarled Koshchey. 'He serves me because he loves me! Because he fears me! Because he knows what would happen if he did not!'

Then he grunted, a thick, ugly noise, for Ivan had taken the opportunity that God gave him. Koshchey turned from beating his horse once too many times and stared down at the wide blade of his ugly sword. Most of that blade was between his ribs. Ivan's hands were crossed over the weapon's pommel to drive it home, but Koshchey's own cold fingers were still wrapped around its hilt, just as if he had stabbed himself.

'Not by the hand of man,' said Ivan quietly, and released the pommel. Koshchey looked at him, then at the sword, then at nowhere as the eyes rolled back in his head. Blood bubbled from his mouth and down his beard, and he fell backwards to the ground.

Ivan watched the body for a long time, eyes narrow and wary; then he turned away and helped Mar'ya Morevna up to Sivka's high saddle. This place stank of death and he was eager to leave it and go home. Koshchey he would leave as a gift to the scavengers who had been cheated of their rightful food for many centuries; there was neither a spade to dig the necromancer's grave, nor any inclination in his heart to take that trouble. 'You cried out,' he said. 'What was wrong?'

'I was frightened.'

Ivan raised his eyebrows, for that word was not one often heard from his wife. 'You? Frightened?'

'Of your great, original plan. Have you any idea of how *dangerous* that was?'

'No more dangerous than anything else. And it worked.'

'Because no one ever thought of that before. I'm sorry, Vanyushka. I thought of it, some years ago. But none of my books would confirm that it might work and,' she lowered her gaze and said in a small voice, 'I was too afraid of him to take the chance.'

Ivan smiled. 'No more of that,' he said, and turned towards Koshchey's horse. 'And no more beatings for you, I promise.'

Then he heard the tiny noise behind him where no such noise should be, and swung round with one hand dropping to the hilt of a sabre he already knew was useless. And Koshchey the Undying sat up, fitting his arm back into its socket as a man might put on a glove.

'You always hear, Ivan Tsarevich,' he said in a voice as cold as stone, edged with such eagerness as a headsman's axe might display when laid in readiness across the block, 'but you never listen. What matter that you kept my own hand closed around my sword: it was you who thrust it through my body and not I myself. You used sword and hand as your own weapon, and all of it was *yours* as surely as if you had used that foolish sabre . . . . with as much effect.' He stood up, lifting the cleaver, and pointed it at Ivan. 'I grow weary of this. Now you die.'

There was a quick thud of hoofs and Prince Ivan felt a sudden wrench of pressure that encompassed his fur collar and a good handful of his hair; then Mar'ya Morevna succeeded in dragging him far enough from the ground for him to be able to heave himself up behind her into Sivka's saddle. They were already pounding along the gully when they heard Koshchey's first screech of frustration and knew that he would soon be after them again.

'What now?' There was despair in Mar'ya Morevna's voice, something that Ivan had never heard before, and it frightened him as much as the sight of Koshchey the Undying recovering from what Ivan had been certain was a killing blow.

He shook his head, unable to think of anything except that dreadful scrawny shape putting itself back together after being butchered ten times over. 'That should have killed him,' he said. 'I was sure it would have killed him. I was so *sure*.'

Then he curled up the reins until they hung from his free hand like a double-thonged quirt, and patted Sivka's neck in apology for what the next few minutes might force him to do. 'And now,' he said firmly, trying not to betray how his voice wanted to tremble at the thought of his death following him again, 'we ride fast. Can we reach your kremlin ahead of Koshchey?'

Mar'ya Morevna shrugged helplessly and Ivan did not repeat the question; he did not want to ask anything of Sivka when steeling himself to beat such a willing and great-hearted horse. It would only have compounded the cruelty and made him no better than Koshchey.

Then a voice in his ear said, *'Idite syuda, Tsarevich,'* he heard Mar'ya Morevna scream a great oath and lash out with the dagger in her hand – and then something reached out with icy fingers and wrenched him from Sivka's back. Prince Ivan smashed into the yielding foliage of a small bush and rebounded to the ground, aware as he felt the impact run all the way from head to heels that at least his neck had not been broken.

Yet. . . .

He was being saved for something much more interesting.

Koshchey the Undying reined his horse to a sweating, eye-rolling standstill just as Ivan staggered to his feet with the whole wide white world spinning slowly around his head. He glanced at Ivan and then dismounted, plucking Mar'ya Morevna's dagger from where it was embedded in his neck but not troubling to draw his sword. 'You still do not listen, Ivan Tsarevich. I said *come here!*'

He reached out, seized Ivan with fingers so long that they went right around his head as a man might hold an apple, then flung him across the clearing. 'Not there. I want you to come *here!*' And he did it again.

And again.

And again.

He was watched in silent horror by the fairest Princess in all the Russias, and by two black horses standing to either side of the little clearing; horses that might have been stable-brothers, except that one was glossy and well treated and the other grievously torn by lash and whip. There were no other witnesses. Even the crows kept away from Koshchey *Bessmertnyy*, at least until he was finished with his victims.

'Draw your sword, pretty Prince Ivan.' Koshchey the Undying licked blood from his fingers and grinned. 'Cut off my head. Kill me. If you dare. If you can.'

Ivan pushed himself up on his fists and stared as best he could at his tormenter. There was blood trickling from his mouth, from his nose and from his ears, and one of his eyes was so bruised that he could barely see past the swelling.

'I can't,' he managed to say, and Koshchey laughed harshly. Then the laugh cut off as Ivan twisted his mouth into a horrible mockery of a grin. 'Because I can't quite reach you. Come closer.'

'Close enough,' said Koshchey. 'This no longer entertains me.' He drew his monstrous sword and stalked forward to jab its point briefly at Prince Ivan's mouth. 'This time there will be no return from death, Prince Ivan,' he said. 'Kiss the wide white world goodbye.' Ivan spat blood on Koshchey's feet. 'A fine, dramatic gesture,' said the necromancer. 'What a pity there is nobody to talk about it afterwards.'

His sword swung up, poised for the stroke, and then a voice which was neither Ivan's nor Mar'ya Morevna's said, 'My brother was right, Koshchey the Undying. I owe you nothing. Except this.'

And the two black horses reared up on either side. They were not men. They were not wielding weapons, for they had no hands with which to wield them. But each lashed out a single hoof which struck against the other like a hammer on an anvil, and Koshchey's head was in between: it exploded like a melon, so that only his beard remained.

The Undying necromancer stood upright for several seconds, while his body gaped and spurted with all the many years of wounds which had never done him harm before; and then, without any fuss or stink, he fell apart.

Prince Ivan Aleksandrovich climbed slowly to his feet and

looked down at the pieces, and for several seconds he could not believe the evidence of the only eye that was still working. It was too sudden, too neat and clean. Such a thing could not be final. His fingers gripped the silvered hilt of his own sabre as he watched and waited for the first twitch of renewed movement, and those fingers shook before they closed. Then Mar'ya Morevna put her hand on his and gently returned the half-drawn blade to its scabbard.

'It's all over, Vanyushechka,' she said, beginning to dab gently at the blood streaking his face. 'There's nothing left to do except go home.'

Ivan looked at her and nodded. 'Home would be good,' he said in a small voice. 'But not just yet. There is still one final thing to do.' Mar'ya Morevna was puzzled for a moment, until he hobbled off and began to hunt for sticks, for twigs, for anything that would catch fire without too much effort. And then she followed suit.

They burned the pieces of Koshchey the Undying on a great brushwood pyre and sat at a distance to watch them burn, piling more fuel on the flames whenever they began to fade – until when the fire went out at last for simple lack of anything else to burn, no trace remained of Koshchey except perhaps a finer ash among the rest. As evening drew on, a breeze began to whisper through the grass and among the little bushes, but as the sun set in a haze of rose and gold the breeze became a shrieking gale.

When it died away again, the ashes were gone.

Prince Ivan turned to Mar'ya Morevna and took her by the hands. Lightly, for it hurt his mouth to do even this, he kissed her on the forehead and the eyelids, on each cheek and finally, lovingly, he kissed her mouth. 'I brought them back,' he said, 'and I give them back. Now it's over. Let's go home.'

Then Ivan swore softly under his breath and his sabre whispered from its scabbard. Mar'ya Morevna looked at him in shock, then back over her shoulder to where Koshchey's body had been burnt. Nothing moved there except a drift of smoke and the faintest swirl of ash along the ground. But now she too could hear what had reached her husband's ears in the evening stillness.

The rhythmic tread of an army on the march.

Sword in hand, Ivan scrambled up the slope that edged the clearing, though what he might do in his present state was something yet to be decided. He stood on the crest of the little bank for several minutes, silhouetted by what remained of the sunset, staring out across the wide white world at whatever host was marching by.

And then he yelled, 'What kept you all? You're *late*!'

*

Guarded and escorted by the entire army of the Tsardom of Khorlov, Mar'ya Morevna rode on Koshchey's horse and Ivan on his own. They kept both animals reined back to a sensible speed so that the marching soldiers would not be left behind, and also so that they could enjoy their singing. 'There are few things more cheerful, Highness,' confided Captain Akimov, 'than an army which doesn't need to fight a battle after all.'

They reached Mar'ya Morevna's kremlin after an easy few days' march, and to Ivan's delight Burka was there, waiting for them in the stable where the servants had put him – sadly thin and somewhat scraped by bear's claws, but glad to see them both as any dumb beast could be. How he had crossed the river of fire from Baba Yaga's country, no one knew and no one cared to ask. But Prince Ivan held that it was done in just the same way he had escaped the bear: by swift legs, and by stoutness of heart, and by wanting to come home to those who loved him.

Once all was set in order and Mar'ya Morevna's wide domains were running smoothly, they rode out again, this time to visit Ivan's relatives, his sisters and their husbands, and at last came home to his dear parents, Tsar Aleksandr and Tsaritsa Ludmyla of Khorlov. In all the places that they went they were received with gladness, until at last – with all the visits over and all the feasting done – they rode back to Mar'ya Morevna's kremlin and there they prospered, keeping house as man and wife. They kept no more than wine in the cell that had once held Koshchey the Undying, and if they had visitors – whether Yekaterina and the Falcon, or Yelizaveta and the Eagle, or Yelena and the Raven – they drank as much of it as made them merry. And every now and then, they drank just a *little* more.

POSLESLOVI
(A final word)

But go out on a breezy day in summer and watch the dry sand on the shore. Go out in autumn and watch the fallen leaves. Go out in winter and watch the drifting snow. See, always, how they blow and swirl, apart and then together. It might be nothing but the wind. Or then again, it might be the ashes of old Koshchey the Undying, trying to become whole once more. But know this, for your comfort when the shadows grow dark and lengthen towards night: he has not succeeded.

Yet . . . .

Bibliography

Afanas'ev, A. N. (trans, Guterman, N.), *Russian Fairy Tales/ Narodnye russkiye skazki* (Pantheon Books 1945/Random House 1973).

Chamberlain, L., *The Food and Cooking of Russia* (Allen Lane 1982/Penguin Books 1983, 1988).

Fennel, J., *The Crisis of Medieval Russia 1200–1304* (Longman Group 1988).

Flegon, A., *Za predelami russikikh slovarey/Beyond the Russian Dictionary* (Flegon Press 1973).

Grimal, P. (ed.), *Larousse World Mythology* (Hamlyn 1965, 1989).

Gusarov, B. H. (ed.) and Kirillin, Yu. V. (art ed.), *Russkiye narodnye skazki v illyustratsiyakh palekhskovo kudozhnika Aleksandra Kurkina/Russian Fairy Tales, illustrations in the Palekh style by Aleksandr Kurkin* (Aurora Publishing 1975, 1986).

Golynets, S. V. (trans. Kochov, G. A.), *Ivan Bilibin* (Aurora Publishing/Pan Books 1981).

Riasanovsky, N. V., *A History of Russia* (Oxford University Press 1969).

Sykes, Egerton (comp.), *Everyman's Dictionary of Non-Classical Mythology* (J. M. Dent & Sons Ltd. 1952, 1968).

Wheeler, P., *Russian Wonder Tales* (The Century Co. 1912; P. Wheeler 1940/1946; Thomas Yoseleff 1957).

Zhukov, V. P. *Slovar' russikikh poslovits i pogovorok/A Dictionary of Russian Sayings and Proverbs* (Sovetskaya entsiklopediya 1966).

Zvorykin, B. V., (ed. Onassis, J.), *The Firebird and Other Russian Fairy Tales* (Viking Press 1978).